THE GOLDEN HARPY

To Julie
May all dream
be filled with
Happiness

THE GOLDEN HARPY

A NOVEL BY S.C. Klaus

iUniverse, Inc.

New York Lincoln Shanghai

The Golden Harpy

iUniverse, Inc.

For information address:
iUniverse, Inc.
2021 Pine Lake Road, Suite 100
Lincoln, NE 68512
www.iuniverse.com

ISBN: 0-595-31690-5 (pbk)
ISBN: 0-595-66372-9 (cloth)

Printed in the United States of America

For my son, Chris, whose love and support, has allowed me to fulfill my dreams.

For my daughter, Kari, whose determination and spirit keeps me inspired.

For my sister, Sharon, whose encouragement, kept me writing my fantasies.

C H A P T E R   1

▼

Kari stared out into the deep void of space through the ship's window. "Five more, just five more of these illusionary days before I am home," she said to herself. Her heart leaped a little at the thought of it. The stars twinkled in the distance as the giant gray spacecraft made a path through the black night. The petite young woman pressed her forehead against the cool plastic of the port window and could feel the vibrations of the engines as they made a low humming noise throughout this space vessel. She had become accustomed to the sound but had disdain for her small confining quarters. It was that dislike that had brought her to the dining area where she sat. The place was empty now for she came here while all the other passengers slept and the mealtime breakfast was still a few hours away. Every so often, she would hear the muffled voices of the cooks in the kitchen area as they prepared the bland food for the several hundred passengers that dwelled on board this floating log in space. She continued to press her blond head against the window while sitting at a small sterile table. This had become Kari's routine for five long months, to go to the dimly lit empty dining room and enjoy this large room in solitude, for solitude had become her way of life. Her journey through the dark would end when the ship reached the small obscure planet of Dora. It seemed like an eternity had passed, nearly half her lifetime, to return to this jungle planet.

Kari gazed out the window again and could barely see Earth's sun, as it twinkled among the thousands of other stars. Earth had been the ship's starting point and Kari turned away from its small star with a loathing as it reminded her of the misery she endured.

She eagerly looked out the window towards the bright little star of Duran. It was smaller than Earth's star but seemed huge in the black void as the ship came closer. Squinting her blue eyes, she tried to see Dora, the planet but could see nothing yet. "Perhaps it's on the other side of Duran," she thought, "or maybe we are still too far away."

The tiny planet of Dora had been her birthplace. It was a young planet. Its vegetation and animals were comparable to Earth, millions of years ago when large reptiles and colossal ferns reigned as kings of the forests. But with man colonizing it one hundred and fifty years ago, it was quickly and sadly yielding to the pressures of civilization. A dark green ocean covered half of it while the other side of the planet consisted of one large continent with numerous islands to the west. Dora, like its star, was smaller than Earth but what beauty it held. A thick multi-colored forest covered the landscape. Kari thought about Earth and how it too had once been covered with trees and life. But that had been hundreds of years ago, before man had destroyed it. Earth had gone from green to gray, its lands covered with buildings and machines. The machines ran everything even creating the oxygen, which made trees unnecessary. There no longer was any room or need for them.

Kari dwelled on her long ten years on Earth. At age eleven she had been sent to Earth by her father for an education. But to her, it was a prison sentence. Now at twenty-one, she could decide for herself where she wanted to live. The belief that she would some day return to her jungle paradise, had sustained her over the years. She reflected on her father and the bitterness would immediately rise in her. He had forced her to go, claiming it was for her own welfare but she distrusted his motives. Earth's schools were not the purpose of this painful lonely exile.

Her thoughts drifted back to the beginning of this banishment from her beloved little planet. It was a day that totally changed her and her life. It was the day, she lost her devotion and admiration for her father as it was replaced with resentment and oddly enough, it was a forest creature that won her admiration and devotion, a creature, which all humans resented.

Kari had taken a little secret path off a deserted shaded logging road through the dense jungle a distance from her home. After several miles, the trail ended at a small lake covered with thick water plants. The plants were in bloom with blue flowers and their sweet fragrance filled the air. On the far side of the lake was a hammock of trisom trees. Their bright yellow fruit was abundant at this time of the year. But it was not the fruit or the flowers that compelled her to make this long hot trek through the woods. It was the wild animals that came to eat the fruit that drew her on this quest. Kari crept beneath the giant blue and green ferns as she neared the shores of the dark murky lake. Her father would be furious if he knew, she had strayed so far from home to seek out these hazardous winged creatures of Dora. But she had dismissed his warnings as any child might when the reward was greater than the punishment. And so, every day for a month, when he worked at the wood mill, she would sneak off to this hidden spot. It was during her wandering in the woods that she had discovered this location and the harpy animal in one of the trisom trees. Harpies were the most mysterious, elusive creatures on the planet. They were highly prized by the human colonists as challenging and dangerous game animals thus they were hunted and killed for their large trophy feathered wings. Her father hated them intensely and the mere mention of a harpy would send him into a rage, cursing these winged vermin as his worst nemesis. As a small child, she had caught rare glimpses of them high in the sky and each time Kari was mystified and entranced by these flying beings. She could not see the evil in them. And now, since discovering this small lake, she could actually view these seemingly half mortal, half bird creatures up close. They were no longer a mere dot in the sky for she saw clearly their magnificent long brown feather wings and their tall slender torsos. They looked very human, if not for the wings on their backs. To her, they resembled handsome young men with long brown hair that swept around their tan shoulders. They wore no clothing except a sash that hung loosely draped around their hips. It was made of some woven material that appeared like webbing. Their beautiful flawless faces were chiseled like an ancient Greek statue, which lacked expression. Only their alert luring green eyes betrayed any emotion. To Kari, the harpies resembled silent graceful angels rather than the horrible demons, which her father professed they were.

Kari crept slowly and quietly through the underbrush to avoid being discovered. Since harpies feared humans she did not wish to frighten any away and she also was a little leery of them as she considered her father's warnings. Finally she reached the area camouflaged with thick underbrush near the lake's shore that revealed a clear view of the fruit trees on the opposite side of the lake. Gazing at the branches of the tall trees, they were devoid of any harpies. After a half an hour, nothing came to the fruit and she feared that this long hike had been in vain. It was at about that time, growing weary and impatient that she had decided to leave. Suddenly, a shadow flew over her head and settled down upon a large trisom tree branch. Kari's heart raced as she strained her eyes to see across the lake and through the limbs of the massive towering trees. Finally she saw him. His creamy yellow powder puff wings caught the morning light and seemed to glow as he hopped with little effort to another branch. The blond hair strands fell over his brow as he nibbled on the trisom fruit and relaxed his lean frame against the trunk of the tree. Kari could barely contain her excitement as she stared up at him. "It's a golden. A golden harpy" she thought to herself. These blond harpies were so rare and endangered now most hunter thought they no longer existed. The extreme hunting pressure had wiped out these fearless sleek goldens, who were known to protect and defend the flocks of the more timid browns. But yet, there one stood, tossing his shiny platinum yellow hair out of his eyes as he reached for another fruit. Kari watched the wild handsome creature but she noticed he seemed younger than the others she had seen. He was still tall but his frame appeared more like a teenager. He leaned away from the tree trunk and now moved to another branch out of her view. So intrigued and thrilled, Kari stepped from her hiding spot and threw all caution to the wind as she moved close to the edge of the lake.

It was in that instant, a mogel propelled itself from the dark waters and latched its slimy mouth around her leg. The giant ten-foot black eel thrashed in the deep water as it knocked Kari off her feet and began to drag her back to its watery domain. Kari let out a scream but she was too far from home to be heard. She struggled and kicked at the mogel's head with her other foot but it would not release its grasp. Its silvery eyes gleamed as it clamped down with its large fangs. The pain and a feeling of doom crept over her. Soon she would become the mogel's next dinner. Her leg went numb as the water monster released its poison into her wound thus disabling its victim more quickly as the slimy beast slowly and steadily dragged her deeper into the water. As a last effort, Kari grabbed hold of a large boulder that lay half submerged in the water and clung to it with her remaining strength. But her hands slid over the wet moss-covered rock as she became weaker. The mogel's long strong body coiled below pulled her beyond the boulder. She tossed and thrashed in the water briefly but it was hopeless and soon she could only shivered with despair. Numbed by the mogel's venom, she would soon drown. Suddenly, she saw a flash of gold wings glide past her. She stared down at the mogel and the young harpy had jumped on the creature's back. He wrapped his arms around the mogel's throat and the startled animal instantly released its hold on Kari's leg. The full body of the large monster came out of the water to dislodge the obstinate little harpy. The lake water erupted with this battle as the eel flared and swirled wildly for now it was the mogel that fought for its life. Its huge mouth snapped frantically at the slender harpy but the golden was out of reach as he clung to the slippery back and neck. The eel and the harpy then disappeared below and the lake surface became calm. Kari breathed hard with anxiety, fearing the brave little harpy had drowned. But after several minutes, both creatures floated to the top with the golden still holding its captive in a death hold grip. The mogel no longer bit at its predator and its mouth only gasped as the silver eyes closed. The eel was slowly being choked to death. The full length of the great ebony body went limp on the surface as the eel gave up its struggle to be free of the tenacious slight harpy. Sensing the water monster was nearly finished the golden gently released it while he stood in waist deep water. He gazed at the large eel that quietly floated next to him and strangely; he began to softly stroking its back. Slowly the eel began to revive. Ruffling his feathers, the harpy waded up towards Kari while she lay dazed in a few feet of water. He glanced back just the mogel created a giant swish and it disappeared below into the murky water. Kari was perplexed as she stared up at him, wondering why this harpy had spared this awful deadly animal. It was very apparent this tough lean harpy could have easily killed it.

The golden bent over Kari as he placed his arms under her and tenderly lifted her from the water. Carrying her safely from the lakeshore, he laid her down beneath the large ferns and knelt down beside her in the sand. Kari gazed up at him and was met by the most intense blue eyes she had ever seen. His bronze body shimmered from the dripping water as he flung the long blond wet hair out of his face. He leaned over her, panting slightly out of breath from his battle with the eel. He seemed to be equally spellbound as the same blue eyes as his own met him. He slowly touched the cheek of the eleven-year old girl. This spell was broken as Kari cringed from the pain in her leg. She glanced down and saw her leg covered with blood from the bite wound. Her eyes welled up with tears as she let out a slight moan. The harpy's face filled with concern as he examined her injury. He leaped to his feet and extended his wings. In one bound, he was in the air and disappeared into jungle as Kari called to him, fearing she had scared him off. She weakly struggled to rise but the poison was taking hold. Her heart began to race and she felt nauseous. She did not have the strength to make it back to her home. A few minutes had passed and she began to cry into her arms, as any child would under the circumstances.

In that moment, the young harpy sailed down beside her and folded his wings against his back. In his hand was a fine lime green moss. He quickly walked to the lake and doused it in the water and then returned to Kari's side. Kneeling down, he squeezed the moss and placed it deep in her wounds. Then he tore a small strip from his sash and tied the moss to her injured leg. Kari, at once, could feel the pain subside but tears still ran down her cheeks. "I must get home," she muttered. The harpy tilted his head and looked at her with curiosity as if her sound confused him. He brushed a tear lightly from her cheek, trying to sooth her. "Please take me home," she pleaded again. He must have understood her this time since he placed his arms under her and carefully lifted her up with little effort. Kari felt faint but she was able to wrap her arms around his neck. The handsome male nuzzled his nose affectionately against her cheek like a gentle palomino pony and Kari could not help but nod and smile at him.

Spreading his wings, he leaped into the air. Kari glanced down as she saw the lake disappear below her. He flew just above the tree line and Kari spotted the old logging road that lead to the back of her father's house. In less than five minutes, the harpy landed in a sprawling rolling meadow, a short distance from the front door of her home. Kari was surprised by how fast he flew since it had taken her an hour to reach the lake by foot. He laid her on the grass but still held her, not wanting to let go. But then the dogs began to bark and men yelled in the distance. They had spotted the dangerous harpy. Kari and the harpy could hear a laser blast as it soared just over his head. He stared one last time into her eyes and then looked up as two men came running towards him with weapons in their hands. He stood up and glared at them, sniffling slightly and tossing his long hair in defiance, while ruffling his feathers to challenge them. His bold nature did prove he was a true golden but it also showed he was indeed young and foolish to dare and threaten an armed man. This time a laser blast came closer and the harpy knew their next shot would not miss him. He darted into the sky as Kari in a panic struggled to her feet screaming, "Don't hurt him. Don't hurt him!" Then she collapsed on the ground into unconsciousness.

Her next memory was awakening in her bed the following morning. The housekeeper, Maria, was at her side. "You gave us quite a scare, Miss Kari," she said with a smile. She then called to the open doorway, "Mr. Turner, she's awake." Soon Kari's father came in and sat beside her on the bed.

"Thank God, you're alright," he said with concern.

"Dad, they didn't kill him, did they?" she stammered.

"No, he got away. Luke fired at him but of course he couldn't hit a barn but I'm surprised Charlie missed. He rarely misses his target," he smiled.

Kari also was smiling because she knew the old Indian had a soft spot for the harpies. He was the only person she knew that did not hate these undesirable creatures. She then became serious. "He saved me, Dad, that young golden harpy saved me from a lake mogel. He fought it as it was pulling me into the lake and then he brought me home. And Dad, he was so beautiful and gentle."

Her dad pulled away somewhat troubled but finally he said, "If he saved my little girl, then I'm glad that Charlie didn't kill him. Doc just left here and said that you'll be fine. He recognized that it was a mogel bite and got the poison in time but I need to get back to work now. We'll talk of this later." He got up and went to the door.

"Dad," she called and he turned to her. "Promise me, you won't let any one hurt my golden harpy." Her father just gave a weak smile as he left the room without answering.

Kari's thoughts returned to the space ship and the present. Within three weeks of that day, she had found herself on a space ship heading for Earth and the schools there. Her father avoided discussing the harpy or the whole terrifying experience. All though, she did remember talking Charlie's and Maria's ears off concerning the wonderful harpy with a child's enthusiasm. Charlie claimed that he had tripped as he ran towards her and the harpy and this was the reason he had missed killing the animal with his weapon.

"Lucky for that blond harpy of yours," he smiled.

And Kari smiled back, knowing this was untrue. But, her father became aggravated every time she mentioned the golden and the incident, creating a wall between them. He could no longer convince her that harpies were evil and should only be destroyed. Kari had seen and experienced the gentle harpy with her own eyes. It was because of this, he had banished her to Earth. All her pleading and crying would not deter him from sending her. His last words to her were, "You're growing up wild. You need proper training in a real school. I'm doing this for your own good." And she remembers the last words she spoke to him were, she hated him.

As she sat aboard the ship, it seemed like only yesterday that these events had taken place. Over a ten-year span, nothing had been resolved between them. He had sent her messages throughout the ten years but she had never answered him. She sent only one back six months ago saying, "I'm coming home. Kari."

Maybe if Earth had been a pleasant place for her, she would not be so bitter towards him. But, Earth had not been pleasant for a child born of the jungle. The huge buildings covering the planet lay beneath domes that blotted out the sky. Metal and concrete were everywhere. Her classmates were as cold as the steel buildings, for she had tried to make friends but they did not want to hear about jungles and harpies. They told her the planet Dora was barbaric and uncivilized. That only a fool would wish to dwell in such a dangerous wilderness. She tried to change and become like them but she had no interest in this modern sterile mechanical world. After several years, she gave up and became very quiet and shy as she sought solitude and fought off depression and homesickness.

Her only joy lay in a small park that she could visit once a week if she saved her credits. It was a small building that housed a few trees and grass and sometimes there were flowers. She befriended an old gardener, who took care of the place and she was able to talk to him for hours about the plants and animals on Dora. The old man enjoyed hearing about all the exotic life of her home and always ended their visit by saying, "If I were younger, I'd go there." Her eyes misted up as she thought about the old guy. He had been her only friend and he reminded her of Charlie, the Indian. Her last week on Earth, she had gone to say good-bye to him. The lady at the gate informed her that the old gardener had died in his sleep. Their ten years of friendship had ended and Earth held nothing for her now. She looked back on it and thought that perhaps he had needed her as much as she needed him for without their friendship, there was nothing.

The lights came on. Soon the dining room began to fill with passengers as they seated themselves at nearby tables. They were laughing and their voices were in a festive mood since their long journey through the stars would soon come to an end. "More colonists for Dora" she thought with contempt. "More people to tame the jungle and kill the harpies." Kari rose to leave and return to her small cabin when she heard a word that caused her to freeze.

"Harpies" said a robust man with a booming voice. Kari slung back down in her seat. "You don't have to worry about harpies, Miss. They just about have cleaned off the continent. And good riddance to those thieving, raping winged pests." He spoke to a woman at the table.

"Rape!" she exclaimed.

"Why yes, haven't you heard, those winged devils steal women. Even if a poor woman is rescued, her mind is gone after a harpy finishes with her. I guess stories like that don't make it to Earth, bad for Dora business and all. But you don't worry your pretty little head about harpies, like I said, they just about been cleaned out. The only ones left are locked up in the Hampton zoo," he laughed.

Kari closed her eyes and could feel her heart sinking. "Could this be true?" she thought.

The two things the man had said upset her terribly. Could the harpies be on the verge of extinction? And were they capable of kidnapping and rape? She thought about the beautiful golden male. He was living proof that harpies were gentle. He could have easily taken her under the circumstances. No, this must be lying. But the other part of this man's statements plagued her mind far worse. Could the harpies have been hunted so much in the last ten years, that only a few remained? Could her golden be dead? She reached in her purse and pulled out a small tin box. Opening the box, she held a tattered strip of woven material. Kari carefully twisted it through her fingers and brought it to her lips as she softly kissed it. His vague sweet scent still lingered slightly. It was the strip that had bound the moss to her leg so long ago. The thought of him consumed her and she was filled with his memory. This small strip had sustained her on many a lonely night as she fought off despair. She stared at the worn and thin material and could still see the pale blood stains on half of it, her blood from the mogel bite. "No," she decided. "He can't be dead." Putting the cloth to her cheek, she could still feel the gentle touch of his hand as he brushed away her tears.

The man continued to talk about the harpies since he had an interested audience with the party that sat at his table. He carried on that harpies were ugly filthy monsters and only a nuisance, which also destroyed crops. The more this man talked, the angrier, Kari became. She finally rose from the table and took a few steps toward his table until she was in front of him.

"I couldn't help but hear your conversation concerning harpies," she said politely. The man grinned wide as he stared up at the gorgeous young blond woman. Kari went on with a smile, "I just have one question."

"Sure little lady, what is it?" he answered, thinking he had impressed her.

"Have you ever seen a harpy?" she asked.

The man hesitated to answer. "Well, I, ah," he stammered.

"I didn't think so. You're lying to these people. I have seen the harpies and they're beautiful gentle creatures. If the truth be told, you resemble a monster more than any harpy." The man's wide grin quickly left his lips as he stared up at Kari with surprise. He had not expected this. Kari left the baffled group of people and heard some chuckles as she went back to her cabin feeling slightly vindicated. She nibbled on dry fruit in her bunk and fell asleep still clutching the woven strip.

The following evening, Kari found herself back in the deserted dining room. She had only been there a short time when a young man came in. He walked straight towards her table until he stood before her. "Hi," he said. "I don't mean to disturb you but I thought I could talk to you for a while. One of the stewards told me, you come here when the lights fade and the place is empty. Can I sit down?" he asked.

Kari nodded reluctantly. He smiled and sat across from her. "I just had to meet you. I was sitting at a table behind you last night and you're the first person on this ship that was able to shut up that old windbag. You gave all of us a good laugh, at his expense."

Kari mustered. "Well, it was not meant to be a joke" she said solemnly. "And I was wrong to embarrass that man in front of so many people."

"No," the young man grinned, "We needed a good laugh. But I can see now that you took it very seriously. Have you really seen them? I mean the harpies?"

Kari nodded slowly.

"So, you've been to Dora before?" he asked.

"I was born on Dora," she answered shyly.

"This is great," he said happily. "I've been looking all over this ship for someone who could tell me about the planet. And it turns out that she's the prettiest girl, I've ever seen."

Kari felt uncomfortable with the compliment, although, this by far, had not been her first. In school as she became a teenager, many a boy had flirted with her and had asked her out but years of solitude made her reserve and aloof. A few times she had tried to date boys but she hid her true passions for fear of being criticized and she had no interest in their world. After a while, she spared herself from this drudgery and declined their offers.

Kari could sense that this brown curly haired man, who was about her age and nice looking, was really more interested in her than the planet of Dora. A feeling of dread and anguish came over her for she knew what was to come. "What do you want to know about Dora?" she finally asked ignoring the compliment.

"Well, everything. Tell me about these harpies."

"The harpies have been portrayed as horrible beasts. They're not. They have handsome lean human bodies and pretty boy faces with long lovely wings attached to their backs," she explained slowly.

"I heard a pair of their mounted wings is worth at least twenty thousand credits. Is that right?" he asked eagerly.

Kari turned away from him in disgust and muttered, "I wouldn't know what their wings are worth. I have to go now," as she stood up.

"Hey, wait a minute. I thought since you know Hampton, that maybe you could show me around. I could buy you dinner or something," he said trying to salvage their conversation.

Kari turned to him and said in a sarcastic biting tone, "No thanks, but I'm sure you'll find plenty of girls in Hampton to give you a tour and tell you the price of a dead harpy's wings."

She left the dining area and walked down the long corridors leading to her room. Half way down the empty hall, she stopped and leaned against a railing. A tear rolled down her face. "What is wrong with me?" she stammered to herself. "I can't seem to carry a conversation on with anyone without either being hostile or uncomfortable." Kari could hear footsteps approaching towards her. She glanced up and it was the same young man. He saw her face and the tear as he slowly came up next to her.

"Look, I'm sorry if I upset you," he said softly. "I don't know anything about harpies and I get really nervous when I talk to someone who's as pretty as you. I end up putting my foot in my mouth. These harpies must mean a great deal to you."

Kari shed another tear and now she felt ridiculous to have been so curt with him. "No, I'm the one who should apologize. I also have trouble talking to people. But it's true, the harpies do mean a great deal to me. You see a male harpy saved my life when I was young and it upsets me that they are so unfairly persecuted. But, I should learn to control these emotions." she said quietly. The young man leaned against the railing.

"Oh, well that explains a lot. Guess the mounted wing thing was in pretty bad taste. Look, my name is Ted and I really would like to get to know you. Maybe we could help each other since we both have trouble dealing with people. Is there anyway we could start again and you could give me another chance? I'm pretty lonely since I left everyone I ever knew back on Earth. I'm planning on staying on Dora and making it my home. I really do want to learn about your planet and the harpies," he said with sincerity.

Kari brushed away the tears and smiled slightly as she looked up at him. "Okay," she said and they walked back to the dining room.

Kari's passion for Dora spilled out of her as she told Ted about the jungle and her life there and how the golden harpy had saved her. She could tell that these things definitely interested him as he asked more and more questions.

"Wow, I can't wait to get there. Dora sounds like one great adventure. I have all kinds of degrees in spacecraft repair and computers and have always lived in the modern cities but really I'd love to spend time in the wilderness. Maybe find out who I really am. But, there is one promise I will make to you, Miss Kari Turner. I will defend your harpies whenever I can, I give you my word." This pleased Kari and in a span of a few hours, she had grown to like Ted.

The next few days aboard ship, they spent together. He told her of a job he had waiting for him in the Hampton spaceport. "I only have enough credits to last me a few days after I get there, so I need to start work right away".

"Hey, you asked me to dinner when we first met. How were you going to swing that with only a few credits," she joked with him.

He shook his brown curly hair and he sighed. "If you had said yes to our dinner date, I would have been happy to go without food and shelter till my first paycheck."

Kari's eyes brightened. "That's pretty sweet of you. Maybe some day you can buy me that dinner in Hampton."

"It's a date then, friend?" he asked.

"Yes, I believe, we have become good friends," she answered.

On their last day they wandered up to the observatory and watched as the space ship circled the planet. Many people were there to see their new home. Kari noticed a woman with a little girl at her right. She listened to their conversation as the woman cheerfully explained to her daughter the wonderful life that lay ahead for them. The child asked many questions and the mother patiently answered them. Kari turned to Ted and spoke more to her self than to him. "I wish I had known my mother."

Ted stopped looking at the planet and now focused on Kari. He had heard about her father and how rocky their relationship stood but Kari had never mentioned her mother.

"Where is she?" he inquired with concern.

"She's dead," she answered blankly.

"I'm sorry."

"Oh, don't be sorry. She died when I was a baby. I never knew her. I'm not even sure how she died, some kind of accident. It's another one of those things that my father refused to discuss. It's just that sometimes, I wonder how different my life would have been if she had lived. Would she have allowed him to send me to Earth, I wonder? Would she have protected me? Just questions I have that I shall never know the answers."

Ted put his arm around Kari's shoulder and pulled her close for he could see the torment in this slender beautiful young woman. "We all have the same what if questions in our lives, Kari, but I will say this. Your father should never have sent you to the bleak confines of Earth I don't care what his reason were. A person with your passion and love of nature, Earth must have been a living hell for you." Kari put her arm around his waist and they stared out at Dora in silence.

The day finally came when the large craft landed inside the giant domed spaceport in Hampton. The station's enormous doors had opened as the ship went inside. Kari had gathered her belongings and met Ted for their departure. They walked off the ship together, past the huge crates of cargo that were being unloaded. The cargo contained everything from small hovercrafts to cattle fetuses. Kari was amazed at how much was on board their ship.

"Yes, I think our ship was more of a freighter than a passenger ship," Ted said. To the far side stood stacks of freshly cut timber that would make the return flight to Earth. The exotic woods were a multitude of different colors from blues, to reds, to yellows and whites. The forests of Dora had a greater variation of lumber than Earth, even when it was full of trees.

Kari walked toward an information counter as Ted followed her. She got in line behind numerous other people. "Ted, you don't have to wait with me if you have other things to do."

"It's okay. I'm not scheduled to report to work till tomorrow and I have plenty of time to find somewhere to sleep tonight. I'll just wait and make sure you are on your next shuttle." Kari smiled, happy not to be alone for the first time. The line moved slowly but eventually she found herself standing before a middle-aged woman at the counter.

"I need to purchase a ticket for your next hover to Terrance today," she asked.

"There are no more flights today. The earliest one leaves at noon tomorrow," the woman answered curtly.

"I'll take a one-way ticket on that one," Kari said, a little disappointed as she doled out her credits to pay for the flight.

"Well, we have one more night together. Maybe I can buy you that dinner after all and you can show me around Hampton, if you want?" Ted said happily.

"I don't even know my way around this city. I was only here once and that was long ago when I caught my flight to Earth and I couldn't ask you to pay for my dinner. I probably have more credits than you right now," she said as they walked towards the door leading to the outside.

"All right," he answered, "we'll do Dutch on the dinner tonight and we'll both explore Hampton unless you're tired of me."

"Not yet," she replied with a grin.

"Then, it's a date," he said and Kari nodded. "Wait a minute, let me ask some of these guys unloading cargo about a decent hotel for you. Hampton is known for being a rough place in some parts. I'm going to be working with these guys, might as well make their acquaintance," he said before jogging over to a group of men nearby. Kari waited and Ted returned in minutes. "There's one that's only a few blocks from here and it's reasonable and nice. Wow, prices are pretty cheap here compared to Earth. I might stay there myself."

"Thanks, Ted for looking out for me. I have to say, I'm not used to it." Ted grinned as they walked out the open door.

Kari stopped outside the door as a warm gentle breeze caught her long blond hair. She breathed deeply and could smell the wonderful flavors of plant life even though they stood in the largest city and capital of Dora. Her senses came alive after a decade of breathing stale filtered air. Ted gave her a moment as he watched her, knowing what this moment meant to her. She seemed frozen as she stared out at the tree filled street. The giant hardwoods towered over the three and four story wood buildings, shading the street beneath them. Insect eating brightly colored flowers seemed to be everywhere as they adorned the spaceport and surrounding buildings. After a while, Kari seemed to come out of this trance and muttered to Ted, "Look at the trees. Aren't they wonderful?"

"They are. They're the biggest trees I've ever seen." She glanced up at him and smiled.

"They're babies compared to the ones in the jungle."

Kari bounced down the steps like a child at a theme park with Ted behind her. On the sidewalk, he finally caught up with her. "Do you want me to get us a ride to the hotel if your bags are too heavy?" he asked.

"No, they're not too heavy and I'd rather walk," she mumbled as she reached the first tree. Dropping her bags, she put her arms around it as if she was hugging an old friend. Then she began stroking the trunk as it were sacred and sniffing the sweet fragrance resin in the bark. Ted smiled warmly.

"Kari, you're the most unusual girl, I believe I've ever met."

"Is that bad?" she said still focusing on the tree.

"No, it's not bad. It's actually delightful. You're just different than Earth girls, that's all." Kari pulled herself away from the tree and they began walking down the street. Every so often, she would stop and pick a flower or admire another plant or treasure of Dora. Eventually they found themselves at the hotel. They entered the small wooden hotel. Massive beams adorned the lobby as they checked in.

"Let's drop our luggage in our rooms and meet back down here. I just can't be indoors now," she said with enthusiasm. Ted agreed and soon they were back on the streets of Hampton.

As time passed, Kari felt a renewed sense of well being, as if this humid moist air held some magic potion that healed her tortured soul. They walked for miles, discovering this city built of wood. Eventually they came to the east coast and the mighty dark green ocean stretched out before them. From a cliff, they could see the Hampton seaport. It was filled with huge barges laden with timber.

"I wonder if some of those trees came from my home." Kari pondered as she stared at the barges.

"Tell me about your home, Kari. You never did say where you lived. Is it in Terrance?" Ted asked as they walked down the cliff on a small winding dirt road that lead to the shore.

"No, I live a long way from Terrance about five hundred miles west of Terrance on the western coast in a little village called Westend. Terrance is the last town with a station big enough to land a large hovercraft."

"How will you go the rest of the way then?"

"I could take a shuttle in a small hovercraft. That would be the fastest way but I'm hoping to rent a land vehicle and drive it. There is a narrow dirt highway through the jungle but it will take two days. Two days of heaven before I reach Westend and my father's estate."

"Kari, that sounds awfully dangerous. Maybe you should…" he stopped in mid sentence as she stopped walking and glared at him. "Hey, it's none of my business how you get home."

"Thank you," she said.

"Why in the world did your father decide to move so far away from civilization?" he asked changing the subject, since it was obvious this independent woman did not care to hear his advise.

"He didn't decide. It was my grandfather, who came from Earth and moved out there. He saw the fall of the last great forest on Earth. Guess he was so disgusted that when he and my grandmother, along with a young Indian named Charlie, landed on Dora, they moved as far away from buildings and people as possible. They truly hacked out a living in the jungle. My grandfather was a great man. He replanted a seedling for every tree he cut down. And he taught me everything about the jungle. I still remember our long trips into the wild with Charlie. When he died, Charlie took over and became my guide and best friend. I really have missed that old Indian. He's one of the few people that ever understood me," she said fondly.

They had walked the coast and came upon a small seafood shack that was built on the water. "I don't know about you but I'm getting hungry and it is dinner time. You want to try this place? It looks rustic enough for you." Ted laughed a little as he motioned to the run down building.

"Yes, this is perfect as long as we can eat outside on the deck," she answered. Ted ate a large bowl of seafood chowder, while Kari inhaled the rare fruits she had longed for. They finished the meal with white cakes covered in a berry sauce. Ted leaned back in the old wooden chair enjoying a gentle breeze from the ocean.

"I've eaten in some fancy places on Earth but who would have thought that a run down place like this would serve the best meal I've ever eaten and offer the most breath taking scenery."

Kari grinned. "Yes, Dora's fresh food is superior to Earth and the view of the water is so lovely here."

"I wasn't referring to the ocean view." He said while gazing into her eyes. Kari could only smiled shyly, feeling a little out of place with the compliment since she lacked experience in dating men.

Darkness began to creep into the sky and the twin moons of Dora appeared on the horizon. Ted and Kari made their way back down the quiet streets until at last they were in the hotel lobby. Ted took her hand and said, "I guess this is good-bye. I'm glad I met you, Kari. Maybe some day we'll meet again."

"I'd like that," she said and got up the nerve to kiss him gently on his cheek before leaving for her room.

Her room was small but comfortable. She took a quick shower and collapsed on the soft bed. She felt exhilarated. It had been one of the best days that she could remember and she really enjoyed being around Ted. She was too embarrassed to admit it to him but she really never had any friends her own age. Her years of isolation on Earth and being raised virtually in the jungle cause her to either be shy or confrontational. In either case, she dreaded dealing with people but her days spent with Ted had been easy and relaxing. With him, she could be her self. "Maybe there's hope for me yet. Now that I'm home, I must change," she thought with determination while snuggled under the sheets as she dwelled on him and the events of the day. Soon she was asleep.

Kari could feel his lightweight lean muscled frame over her in the dark as his soft warm breathe panted slightly against her neck. He nuzzled and licked her tenderly while his long flaxen hair tumbled across her face. The harpy's large cream wings fluttered nervously in the moonlight and Kari petted his silky hair to calm and sooth him, engulfed in his sweet animal scent. Immediately his wings relaxed and collapsed around her. Lifting his head slightly, his blank beautiful face gazed at her with his wild sparkling blue eyes. The golden harpy tossed his shoulder length locks aside and sniffled softly with anxiety as he rose to leave her. Kari's heart pounded and she shivered, inflamed by the seductive creature. In a puff, he was gone. Kari jolted forward, sitting up on the bed as she stared around the small empty dark room. She was drenched in sweat and still trembled badly.

"A dream, it was a dream," her shaky voice said. But it had been the most vivid dream she could remember. It was so real. She lay back down and breathed deeply and thought about the stunning golden harpy. She had dreamed of him many times over the years but none of her dreams had been like this. The passion and intensity of it shook her as she lay upon the bed. She glanced at the locked window and door, shaking her head. After several hours, she finally fell back to sleep.

Daylight approached as it filtered through the drawn window blinds. Kari rose quickly, even though it was still very early. She had plenty of time before her flight left at noon. She showered and dressed. Packing her bags, her mind was still focused on the dream of him. She closed her eyes and could still feel him. Her thoughts drifted to the harpies and she suddenly remembered something that terrible man aboard the ship had said concerning the harpies. There were harpies at the Hampton Zoo. Could this be true? Kari threw her things in the bag and rushed down to the lobby. She approached the hotel clerk and asked him how far, it was to the zoo. He told her it wasn't far but that it did not open for another hour. "Does it have Harpies?" she asked.

"Oh, I don't know, Miss, I've never been to it."

Kari thanked him and walked away a little disappointed not having the information on the harpies. She wandered into the hotel restaurant and decided to eat a light breakfast before the zoo opened. She had to go. Her mind was filled with the harpies and if they were there, she had to see them. The thought of these magnificent beings in a cage left her a little unsettled. This could be agonizing to see something so free and beautiful locked up. She envisioned the golden male as a captive and it repulsed her. Glancing around the dining area, she hoped to see Ted but he was not there. After eating some biscuits and juice, she caught the shuttle to the zoo.

In fifteen minutes, Kari found herself at the gates of the small zoo. The cashier had just opened the office when she approached her. "That will be two credits," the cashier said.

"Do you have harpies?"

The woman grinned. "We have two," she answered as Kari gave her the money. Kari entered the sprawling grounds of the nicely maintained enclosures. She hurried past the other exhibits, glancing briefly into some. Each animal she saw brought back a cherished past memory of her encounters with these animals in the wild. It would have been easy to spend days in this place but her time was short and there was only one creature she sought. Soon she came to an area that was labeled 'Dora's Creatures of the Sky.' She walked under the large sign and down the path. On each side were small aviaries containing flying reptiles, mammals and birds. All of these fell in to six-limb category. They had four legs for walking or grasping and two limbs that were wings for flight. Finally Kari came to a large cage. In front of it was a sign 'Harpy.' She was filled with excitement as she peered up at the trees into the branches. Then she saw them. In that moment her excitement diminished to sorrow. They were not the harpies that had dwelled in her memories. Instead of the strong noble wild beings that had fluttered from branch to branch, she now stared at two little pathetic fledglings. Their dingy and broken quilted tattered brown wings wrapped around them as they shivered in the morning dew. They slept curled up on a broad branch with their frail little arms hugging each other for warmth and security. The large iron bars of the cage seemed to break any spirit, which could have existed in them. Kari watched for some time and finally spoke softly, more to her self. "How could you poor little guys end up like this?" One of the little male fledglings heard her and opened his eyes. He glanced down at Kari and suddenly became interested in her. Spreading his tiny wings, he flew down and stood in front of her. He tilted his head side wards with curiosity as he studied her. Kari could see his full height and he appeared like a child of five years old. Suddenly the fledgling began to put his arm through the cage and reach for her. But a rope strung along the path kept her a short distance between them. Another group of people walked up the path and they also stood in front of the cage but this harpy fledgling seemed to be oblivious of them as he kept his focus on Kari. Soon the other fledging joined him and they both reached through the bars towards Kari. The other people laughed at their antics as Kari tried to appease them. "I don't have any food for you and I'm not allowed to touch you."

Soon an older stout man wearing a green uniform came up along side of Kari. In a stern voice, he said, "You're not allowed to feed the animals, Miss."

"I haven't fed them," Kari said defensively as the little harpies continued to reach for her. Another man from the group, hearing the conversation, spoke up on Kari's behalf.

"She didn't feed them anything. We've been watching."

The zookeeper observed for a long moment rubbing his chin. The harpies defiantly wanted something from this girl. He finally murmured, "Well, they certainly must like you. Never seen them take to a stranger like this."

"I like them too," Kari grinned as she stared at the fledglings.

The zookeeper laughed. "You must have just come off the ship from Earth."

Kari turned to him. "How did you know that?"

"The locals on Dora" he began, "don't care for them. They're about as popular as an Earth rat here," he chuckled.

Kari took a slight offense to this and could feel her resentment rising. "I was born on Dora and I have always liked harpies."

"Well, dear, you're an exception. Most natives would be glad to be rid of them."

"Why? What have they done?"

The man rubbed his chin again before he spoke. "Well, as far as I know, the harpies haven't done anything in some time. But that's only because there is so few of them left. But years ago when there were large flocks of them, men had to guard their wives and daughters since harpies would fly in at night and steal them."

"I don't believe that," Kari said flatly. "I flew with a harpy and he did not steal me in fact he saved my life after I was bitten by a mogel and brought me home." The old man had stopped looking at the harpies and was staring at Kari in amazement.

"Where and when did this happen?" he stammered.

"It happened in the outback near the western coast over ten years ago," she said as she reached down and pulled up her khaki pants. "Here's the scar from the eel bite."

The keeper seemed to become very excited. "Would you please talk to this new vet we have here? He arrived a few months ago to study the harpies and hasn't had much luck getting information on them. I know he would love to hear your story."

Kari glanced at her timepiece and said, "I have to catch a flight to Terrance at noon but I guess I have time to talk to him."

The old keeper led Kari to some buildings in the back. He escorted her into an office marked for employees. Kari waited as the man scurried off through another door. In a short time, he returned followed by a tall middle age man. "I'm Dr. Watkins," he said while extending his hand to Kari. They shook hands and Kari introduced herself. "Lester told me you had a harpy encounter. Would you mind telling me about it?" he said with skepticism, doubting this girl's story and her harpy flight.

"First I would like to know why you are studying the harpies?" she asked cautiously.

"I'm an expert in endangered species and a genetic scientist. The Dora government hired me to do this study. I'm hoping to prove that these harpies are a threatened species. With hard evidence there could be new laws imposed on limited hunting seasons or a complete ban until the species recovers. Right now they're being slaughtered and we're not even sure how many even exists. I'm hoping this study will give them some protection and perhaps save them from extinction."

"I see," Kari said slowly. "I'll tell you if it may help them but I don't see how it could. My encounter was over ten years ago when I was a child."

"Let me be the judge of that," he said.

Kari told her story as both men listened intently. When she finished neither man spoke. Dr. Watkins was no longer dubious of Kari as he said, "This is the first time I've heard of a person interacting with a harpy. I mean, I've heard plenty of hunter's tales which describe the nature and reaction of these wounded creatures but you actually told this golden harpy to take you home and he did as you asked?"

"Yes" Kari said, not knowing the significance of this act. "Is that so amazing?"

"Amazing, yes!" he answered. "It means that either the harpy understood the English language or he sensed what you wanted. I'm guessing, it sensed your desires. Kari, you must have a strong sixth sense and these animals can sense you like them. The sixth sense or instincts allows most animals to communicate with one another. It's unlikely a wild harpy knows our language."

"But, Doc, those fledglings understand me when I talk to them, especially when I mention food," the old keeper broke in.

"Yes, but they were taken from a nest and have been here for some time. They've been trained like any pet to respond to the meaning of certain words," Watkins answered, "Although there is no doubt these harpies are Dora's most advanced species. They at least fall in a category with Earth's apes."

"Have you ever tried to talk to a wild adult harpy?" Kari asked.

"Tried, yes." He shook his head with disgust. "Unfortunately, I can't keep them alive long enough to make any progress. The zoo managed to purchase a few adult males that were stunned and captured by hunters. The sad thing is they don't survive in captivity. They just curl up in a ball and suffer from shock. They won't eat or drink and have to be tube feed. The last one I had, I managed to save him from the shock and I was making real progress. Then I made the mistake of releasing him in to a large cage. Immediately he flew against the bars so hard he broke his neck before I could restrain him. But the question of their intelligence is the least of my problems. I can't find their nesting or breeding grounds and have yet to obtain a female. These zoo fledglings were taken from the western islands so I have to assume that some of those islands hold the harpy community but this is all speculation. And then, there are these mysterious loca eagles that the zoo just acquired. The DNA of these animals is very similar to the harpies. They're related somehow."

"Loca eagles, I've never seen them," Kari said.

"Well, you wouldn't unless you visited the western islands. They used to range on the continent a hundred years ago but they have since been wiped out from over hunting. That's always the trouble with the endangered animals, by the time a study is done, it's almost too late."

"Too late for the harpies?" Kari asked with a sad softness to her voice.

"I hope not but it's hard to get information on them. I have done research on a lot of animals, on many planets but these harpies are the most elusive creatures, I have ever encountered."

"I must leave now or I'll miss my flight. If there's any way I can help you, I will. That golden harpy saved my life and I'll do all I can to save them," she said quietly.

"Your information has been a help. It's proves these creatures are not only intelligent but they have a gentle side to them which goes against the vicious rumors which are said about them. I may have to go to your western outback for my answers. My research is stalled here. I can't learn or get a count on this wild species at a zoo. And the eastern harpy flocks have been exterminated. If I come, perhaps you could show me this lake."

"I'll be happy to show you the lake or anything else if it will end the hunting," Kari said with a smile. She walked out the door and the old zookeeper went with her. They went back up the path toward the harpy cage. The fledglings were back on their branch, sound asleep and in the same position as before. Kari kept quiet not wanting to disturb them. The old man motioned to another path.

"Over there is where we keep the loca eagles." Kari looked at the time and figured she still had a few extra minutes before the shuttle came. She rushed down the path to huge aviaries. Towering on another tree were the two giant winged creatures. Kari was impressed with the six feet high locas but to her, they looked nothing like an eagle or any other bird. Their body and wings were covered with the brown feathers but they resembled an ape with wings. The old man came along side of her. "They're very odd looking but they do resemble a harpy slightly," she said to him.

"Yes, they're little elfish facial features are similar," he answered.

"Well, I must run or I'll miss my flight."

"Take care, Miss Turner," he yelled as she hurried down the path to the exit.

Kari made it to the street just as the shuttle pulled up. She hopped on board as it sped away towards the spaceport. Kari gathered her things and walked toward the large circular ship. As she reached the doors, she heard a familiar voice call out her name. Kari saw Ted as he waved to her from beneath another smaller space-ship. "I'll miss you," he yelled, not caring who heard him. Kari blew him a kiss and then disappeared inside the giant hovercraft.

Kari entered the large ship and was surprised to find so many empty seats. A stewardess approached her and confirmed her ticket. "You may sit anywhere you'd like, this flight is not booked," she said to Kari.

Kari took a window seat across from an older gentleman. She had barely remembered the flight from Terrance, ten years earlier, since she had spent most of that flight in tears. She looked out the window in anticipation of the trip ahead. The hovercraft rose straight up out of the port and began moving rapidly west. Within minutes, the city of Hampton disappeared from sight. Beneath the ship laid the vast jungle. The colors of the trees exploded on the landscape like a giant painting as every color known to man was displayed before her eyes. It was this feast of beauty that Kari had been starving for. The breathtaking view seemed to overwhelm her as she stared out the ship's window as the jungle drifted past below. After a while, she settled back down in her seat with her eyes glued to the scenery, not wanting to miss a single thing. Every so often, she would get a glimpse of the highway road below as it appeared beneath the thick underbrush. This road ran from the east coast to west coast across the continent as it made its way through the deep mass of trees. Periodically, Kari would see a store and a few dwellings along this road, remnants of civilization surrounded by the wilderness. Even a small town with farms around it would pop into view for a moment. But soon it would disappear, hidden by the endless trees. "That's my road," she thought to herself as she considered her journey ahead. This highway would turn into an ill-kept winding dirt road after the town of Terrance for very few settlements rest along this roadway from Terrance to the ocean. She would be traveling the true outback and the very thought of it, delighted her. In three more hours, this flight would end and her adventure into the jungle would begin. The antici-pation of it, made her heart soar like a caged bird that would finally be free at last. She twirled her long bond hair nervously as the thought of the jungle beckoned to her.

The man in the seat across from her was consumed in reading as she glanced at him. He noticed this and without even looking up, said, "This must be your first trip across the continent to the outback. It's very impressive when seen for the first time."

Kari was slightly embarrassed since her obvious enthusiasm must have been apparent. "No, I was actually born in the outback but I haven't seen it in a long time," she said as she turned back toward the window.

"So, you're going home to Terrance then?" he asked as he kept his eyes on his papers.

"No, my home is north of Westend near the west coast," she answered.

"Ah, yes," he mustered. "I'm familiar with Westend. I was there once. It's a quaint little town, mostly deals with rare timbers. You still have a long trip ahead of you, when we land. My name is Dan Roberts. I work for the Hampton Bank as an appraiser, so I travel a great deal even to little towns like Westend."

"Kari, Kari Turner," she said as she introduced herself.

The man glanced up from his reading machine for the first time as he looked at Kari. "Are you any relation to John Turner of the Turner Estate?" he said with new interest.

"He's my father," Kari answered softly.

"Well, he's one of our bank's best customers in the western continent. I believe he has the largest timber estate in the outback. He must be a worried man about now."

Kari was puzzled. "Worried? Worried over what?"

The man leaned back in his seat a little as he studied Kari. "Well, maybe he didn't want to upset you and that is why, he did not convey his troubles to you."

Now Kari was very interested in what this man had to say and she no longer even looked toward the window. "What troubles?" she asked intently.

"There's no hiding it, cause you'll soon see for yourself before we reach Terrance. These beetles blight that's sweeping the western continent. Massive swarms of beetles that are consuming the land. They destroy everything in their path, homes, farms, timber, they fly in and when they leave every bit of plant life or wood is gone. A lot of folks like your father are plenty worried because nothing seems to kill them. Every kind of insecticide known to man has been sprayed on them, to no avail. They've tried surrounding them with fire but the beetles simply fly away before they're burned. Before long, we'll be flying over a ten-mile area that has been completely destroyed from their attack and you'll see for yourself. And there's more, the further west this hover travels. I'm amazed that you have not heard of this."

"I only arrived yesterday from Earth but I heard nothing about it, there or in the city of Hampton." she said.

The man nodded his understanding. "I'm not surprised. People don't take an interest unless it concerns them. But, I guarantee, they'd soon take an interest on Earth when the timber stops coming and in Hampton, when these swarms start moving east. The main export of this planet is timber and the whole economy could be wiped out in a few more years if they don't get these pests under control.

I'm on my way to Terrance to appraise a few farms north of the city that were hit by a swarm. It's an easy appraisal for me since there's nothing left. No buildings, trees, crops. It'll be completely barren. Only some of the equipment may be worth salvaging. I used to enjoy this job but when you see the faces of these people who have lost everything and the bank is reclaiming their land, it's very sad. The return flight to Hampton on this hover, will be full of broken lives," he said with remorse.

Kari was deep in thought for sometime before she finally asked, "My father's estate, have the swarms struck there yet?"

"Let's take a look," he said as he pulled a thin narrow computer from under his seat. After a few minutes, he grinned at Kari. "No, he's been lucky so far, but some homes south of Westend were hit pretty hard only a month ago. Which brings me to another question. How do you plan on traveling from Terrance to Westend? If you don't mind my asking."

"I was hoping to rent a terrain vehicle and take the old road."

"By your self?" he questioned with dismay.

Kari just nodded.

"That's a two-day journey and that road is barely useable. It goes through the heart of the jungle with few places to stop if you have trouble. There's a lot of dangerous wild life on that road, plus these swarms. They can clog an engine and leave you stranded," he said as he stared at the slender pretty girl.

"That is the path I have chosen, if I can get a vehicle," Kari stated with conviction.

He raised his eyebrows. "You may have trouble renting a vehicle for that distance and to such a remote area. But, even a small hovercraft is dangerous now with these beetles. Several hunters lost their life recently in the northwest. Their hovercraft engine became clogged with beetles and they crashed. The large hover we're in now, flies too high for the swarms to be a threat. I can't imagine your father would let you take this dangerous trip alone," he said as he shook his head.

"He no longer dictates my life or decisions," Kari said with a sharp resolve.

"I see," said the man. "We're coming to one of those areas, which has been destroyed by a swarm. You may change your mind after you see the destruction."

Kari turned her attention back to the window and before long she could see the blackened dirt of the forest floor, nothing remained. The devastation was unbelievable as Kari realized how these insects were a true threat to the jungles of Dora. The parched land spread before them as if a great fire had annihilated everything standing. The speed of the giant hovercraft moved swiftly over the doomed land and once again the colorful jungle appeared. Kari turned back toward the older gentleman with a sullen expression on her face. "It's unbelievable," she said quietly. "How long has this been going on?"

"It started about two years ago when the first swarm struck the southwestern territory of the continent but now they're everywhere in the western half. And there's no consistency to their movement. They have yet to strike a town directly but it's been close. Just enough to make people worry."

Kari glanced back at the window. "Yes, her father would be worried," she thought to herself. Something this devastating that could destroy everything he and her grandfather had sought to protect all these years. She thought of her grandfather. He was a true lover of nature. She remembered as a small child following him through the areas that had been harvested with his bag of seedling trees. For every tree cut, he would plant a new one. Then they would travel to areas, which were to be harvested. He'd mark the truly ancient trees so they would be spared from cutting. "These old trees deserved our respect since they have stood the test of time and we can live without their wood," he would say as he put his mark on them. It was almost a religion to him. Her father had continued the practice after her grandfather died. So the Turner estate was different from other timberlands. The trees were harvested but the forest remained. Other timber companies practiced clear cutting and it left the land as barren as a beetle strike after the men had cut every tree down, young and old that stood in their path. Yes, her passion and love of the trees had been bred into her as she realized how similar she and her grandfather and father were. A tinge of sympathy rose in her for her father. She knew he was facing a battle to save what they both cherished from these destructive insects. It was in that moment Kari made a decision to put aside her bitterness and anger. Rather than be confrontational, she would give him the opportunity to rectify their relationship. It was apparent that he did not need any additional trouble from her at this time.

Kari glanced back out the window. In the distance, she could see the northern mountain range as it dipped south into the western outback. The sleek black rocks pierced the grayish green sky as they jetted out of the kaleidoscopic jungle. The large hovercraft had reached the middle of the continent. Mr. Roberts had gone back to his reading as Kari kept her vigilant watch of the ground below. She counted eight more barren places made by the swarms. Some were very vast, while others only encompassed a few city blocks of land. She could not understand, with all of man's advanced technology that they had not discovered a remedy to kill these beetles. "Man had beaten nature on Earth but at what cost?" she thought.

"We're almost at Terrance, Miss Turner. It was nice meeting you," Mr. Roberts said as he pulled Kari from her contemplations.

"Yes, likewise, and thank you for the information," she responded.

"Well, you just be careful in that jungle when you head home. You're too lovely of a girl to have anything happen to you," he said with a smile.

Kari blushed a little and smiled shyly as she glanced back out the ship window. Duran, the star of Dora, was setting in the west. The sky was now filled with pinks, oranges and golds as the wispy clouds settled on the horizon and rays flooded through them. In the distance, Kari could see the approach of a mighty river that snaked its way among the jungle camouflage. The hover had slowed as it passed the river and was descending downward toward the town of Terrance. Large barges loaded with timber floated upon this body of water as they journeyed southward toward the ocean and on to Hampton. Terrance rose up from the river's banks with a display of multicolored raw wood buildings that enhanced the small city. Kari could see the meadows and farmlands that lay beyond. But further out was a large black void of barren landscape and she knew it was from another swarm strike. The town had barely escaped its wrath.

The hover set down on a large paved lot. Nearby stood a building with assorted small hovercrafts parked in no particular order off to the side. Kari and Mr. Roberts gathered their belongings to depart as they heard the hover doors open. "It's not as fancy as the indoor port at Hampton," he commented to her as they made their way to the exit.

Kari smiled. "I think I like it better. This town seems to have a lot of charm."

He laughed a little. "It's not so charming during the rainy season, I can assure you."

Kari walked toward the building with the other passengers. Once inside, she was surprised to find it crowded with people as they waited in a long line to board the craft she had just exited. The people seemed dismal and cheerless as they quietly waited in the building. Mr. Roberts had been right. This return flight held many broken lives.

Kari made her way to the information desk to inquire about a rental. The man behind the desk barely looked up as he said "Westend? We don't rent terrain vehicles to go that far but there is a small hover going there at the end of the week. That's the best I can do for you."

"Thank you," Kari said disappointed.

"Sounds like you need a ride," said a familiar voice over her shoulder.

Kari whirled around and saw Charlie, the old Indian, standing behind her. She immediately dropped all her belongings and threw her arms around him. She could hardly contain herself as she embraced the elderly man. She whispered in his ear, "I'm so happy to see you."

The roughed old Indian held her tightly. "And I'm happy to see you, as well," he choked with emotion. After a long heart felt moment, they pulled apart.

"Why are you in Terrance?" Kari asked as she sniffled slightly.

He looked at her with a scowl. "Did you really think that your father or I would have you make this trip alone through the jungle? And have I not always been your guide? The jungle is still very dangerous or have you forgotten?"

Kari beamed and nodded to him. "I have not forgotten and I am happy that you'll be my guide. There is no other person on the planet I'd rather be with on this trip home."

Charlie reached down and picked up her bags. "My vehicle is this way," he said as he strolled to the doorway.

Kari was delighted and laughed a little. "Charlie was never one for much talk," she thought to herself. She followed the old man with long gray braids through the doorway and out into the parking lot until they came to a dark green terrain vehicle. Charlie stored her bags in the back and opened Kari's passenger door. Then he got in and asked, "The light will be gone soon. Do you wish to remain in this town and get a fresh start in the morning or we could travel the road tonight? There is a small inn a few hours away. It is not fancy but the food is good."

Kari glanced at the brightly colored lovely Victorian buildings in this enchanting little town. "I'm sure the hotels here are far superior than the inn on the road but I think, right now, I would prefer to be near the trees and the jungle. I have had my fill of civilization."

Charlie nodded as he pushed the button and the terrain vehicle rose a foot off the ground. The Indian's eyes brightened as he turned and smiled at the now young woman. "You have grown but you have not changed. This makes me very pleased." Kari was also pleased that her dearest of friends had not changed either.

Charlie navigated through the streets of Terrance and they left the quaint picturesque city. Soon, they were on the dirt highway as they passed the rolling hills of meadows and farmland. As the light faded, they entered the jungle on this westbound road. The trees rose up on each side of them as their branches connected overhead like a canopy. Darkness came and only the headlights shining on the road lit their path.

"I can drive if you're tired, Charlie," Kari asked.

"It is not far but I will let you know if I grow weary," he said. The terrain vehicle moved along slowly since this dirt highway was full of dips, fallen trees and boulders. If the road had been smooth, the vehicle could move at rapid speeds but they were in no hurry and did not mind the slow pace. Kari asked about the swarms and Charlie told her that her father was doing everything in his power to eliminate them.

"He has built a lab at the mill to experiment with chemicals to see if any will kill the beetles we captured. He does not trust Dora's government to solve his problems," Charlie said with pride as if John were his own son. Kari listened quietly. "When a swarm struck south of town, your father sent all the men from the mill to help the two families there. Your father gave them all the lumber and workers to rebuild their homes.

He is a good man with a good heart."

"Maybe to others." Kari said softly not being able to control her smoldering resentment.

Charlie breathed deeply sensing her hostility towards her father. He slowly said, "Earth was difficult for you," as he glanced at her.

She tried to answer him but could not. With those few words, all the misery and loneliness and pain came flooding back to her like a dam breaking. She put her hand to her mouth and began to sob. Charlie stopped the vehicle as he reached over to hold her as she trembled and wept in his arms. She could not stop the release of all this pent up emotion. "I would rather die than go through it again," she said between her gasps. The forest grew darker as they sat on the road for a long time. Kari finally pulled away as she tried to apologize.

"Shhh," he spoke softly as he shook his head. "I worried for you all these years. Our souls are similar, you and I. I am old but I still remember my life on the planet of Earth. It is not a place for the free of spirit. I tried to tell this to your father but he would not listen to even me when he sent you there. But it is over now. You are home. The jungle will heal your torment and in time, you will forget all you suffered."

"Yes, I am home and only the vision of returning, kept me from going insane," she mustered. Charlie started up the engines again as they slowly moved forward. They had traveled for some time before Kari finally spoke again. "Charlie, I don't want to ever talk about Earth again."

"I understand," he acknowledged. "The inn is near. We shall eat and sleep. And you will feel better. Tomorrow will be a good day," he said.

"Yes, it will. Just being here with you again, makes any day, good," she answered.

They reached the inn. The building was made of rough timbers and along side of it were small cabins of individual rooms. Charlie went inside to check in while Kari waited in the vehicle. He returned in a few minutes. "That cabin is yours," he said as he pointed to the cabin to their right. "I have the one next to you. They stop serving dinner soon. Do you want to freshen up before we eat?" he asked. Kari just nodded. She took her small bag into the cabin and went to the bathroom sink. Splashing water to her face, she felt better. It was a ritual she had practiced on Earth. She soon joined Charlie outside.

"Are you all right now?" he asked with concern.

She smiled at him. "Yes, I'm fine now. It will never happen again," she promised.

They went to the office and beyond it, sat at a small restaurant. The place was virtually empty. Only one other table was occupied as they sat down. Charlie ordered a reptilian steak with a spicy herb sauce while Kari had a large plate of grilled vegetables over rice, all native to the jungle. Charlie talked about the beetles and how he had seen small nests of them over the years but they had never multiplied to such vast numbers till now. Kari listened to the wise old man as she ate in silence. He told her of events she had missed over the years and of his last great hunt as he killed a large zel stag with ten point antlers.

"Charlie, I don't remember you talking his much," she said with a grin.

"Nor I," he answered. "I guess I just missed you."

"Oh, Charlie, I missed you and your stories, more than you'll ever know," she said sincerely.

They both ordered dessert of a cobbler with wild berries and Kari ate every bite of the delicious sustenance. "You were hungry," Charlie commented cheerfully.

"Yes, you never realize how wonderful the food is on Dora until you leave," she beamed.

"It is good, you are enjoying this food now, for tomorrow night, we must camp and eat only my cooking. The last inn is closed before Westend."

"That sounds wonderful to me. And if I remember right, I never went hungry with your cooking when we camped." She smiled.

The lights in the modest restaurant dimmed as a sign they wanted to close. Charlie paid the bill and they walked back to their individual cabins.

"Tomorrow, we start early," he said as they stood in front of Kari's cabin.

"I'll be ready. Good night, Charlie, and thank you for giving me a shoulder to cry on earlier."

"My shoulders are there for you whenever you need them," he related and left for his cabin.

Kari went in and took a quick shower. She lay down on the bed but sleep would not come. She could hear the sounds of the night as if the jungle was calling to her. Rising from the bed, she dressed and stepped outside. A strong moist breeze caught her long hair, sending it away from her shoulder while the wind made a musical sound through the tree branches. "A short walk may help sleep come," she thought to herself. Stepping onto the deserted road, she noticed only two other terrain vehicles parked out front besides Charlie's. Kari walked a short distance into the dark as the twin moons of Dora loomed overhead, lighting her path. The jungle mesmerized her and drew her further down the road, away from the inn. Her senses became aware as she breathed deeply. It was like being in a dream. A dream she had longed for, for some time.

Suddenly she heard the low growl of a grogin off in the deep jungle. Glancing back toward the inn, she realized that she had wandered a good distance from it. Slowly Kari started walking back toward the gleaming lights. Another growl came and it was closer. Kari knew about grogins and they were dangerous. If she ran, she could stimulate an attack, for she would appear like fleeting prey. Grogins were large sleek brown animals that resembled a cat and a weasel at the same time. One thing Kari did remember about them, they always hunted in packs. If one existed, there would be others. As she passed the outline of some thick bushes, she heard another low growl. This time, the sound came from only a few feet away and was on the other side of the road. Kari froze in her tracks and faced the creature hiding in the bushes. Any movement now, would be an invitation for the grogin to leap on her. The growl and the snapping of twigs continued as Kari's heart beat rapidly. Kari could hear another growl and the underbrush giving way to several other animals behind her. They had surrounded her as they lay in wait in the dense forest. Kari moved one of her feet from side to side on the dirt until she found what she had been seeking. Slowly, she bent over and picked up a baseball size rock as she held it tightly in her hand. The sound of the crackling leaves was close as they converged on her. Sweat ran down her body but she dare not move. Then she saw the outline of a large female as it stepped onto the road, in front of her, cutting off her escape back to the inn. Kari carefully raised her hand and aimed the rock towards the grogin. With all her strength, she threw the rock against the side of this creature. The grogin let out a loud roar as it jumped back into the bushes. Kari hastily searched for another rock, but could only grasp a handful of small pebbles. She sent them flying toward the growls behind her. There were more growls and the crashing of bushes but this had not scared off the pride. They were only a little more leery of their prey now. In minutes, the large female was back on the road, stalking her. With each step, the grogin paced closer. The twin moons lit up the glossy chocolate brown body as it showed its large fangs to intimidate its quarry. Kari strained her eyes in the dark for another make shift weapon. Charlie had always told her to carry a large stick. "It will avert an attack by many a wild animal," he had said to her as a child. She looked for a stick but could see none in the darkness. She thought of calling out but doubted if Charlie would hear her and this surely would insight the grogin to pounce on her. The female grogin took another step closer as it crouched down and prepared to jump. Kari shivered with fright as the animal sensed its prey would not oppose it.

Abruptly, a dark shadow floated between them as the grogin leaped backwards away from this menacing figure. The dark wings extended upwards and confronted the grogin as it took several steps toward the frustrated animal. The animal growled fiercely at this new intruder but backed away from the shadow on the road. The harpy gave a low hiss and took another step towards the large grogin. Immediately the cattish creature fled into the underbrush in fear. He raised his wings to the other grogins behind Kari as they sprang back into the jungle. Their cries and frustrated growls rang out as they vanished.

Kari was so in shock that she just stood there trembling as she glanced up at the tall dark winged harpy. Folding his wings down, he walked to her. She shook as she looked upon his handsome face. The inn lights glittered on his bright green eyes while he stared at her with a questioning expression. Kari felt paralyzed and could not move or speak for several minutes. The terror soon left her and now it was replaced with fascination of this magnificent creature before her. His dark brown wings caught the light of the twin moons, as they almost appeared silver in color, as did the chocolate brown hair that floated beyond his shoulders behind his neck. Except for her golden harpy, he was the most attractive male she had ever seen. He nodded to her as sincerity and concern filled his luring eyes. "I'm not hurt," she finally said to him. He closed his eyes deliberately to acknowledge his understanding of her words. Immediately he jerked his head up away from Kari as she could see fear and apprehension fill his beautiful features. He stared beyond her towards the inn lights. Kari also looked towards the inn to see what was scaring this harpy. In a flash, he was gone. Kari was amazed at his speed as if he had almost disappeared. Kari could now see a figure approaching on the road from the direction of the inn.

"Kari, Kari!" came the voice of the old Indian as he jogged towards her with his laser gun in his hand.

"I'm here," she answered as she hurried to meet him.

"Are you all right? I heard grogins on the hunt and when I found your cabin door open and you had left, it scared me," Charlie said as they met.

"I'm okay, Charlie. You chased them off just in time," she related still shaken.

Charlie looked at her sternly. "I would scold you for forgetting the perils of the jungle but I can see that you have learned this lesson well tonight."

"Yes, I have. I'm sorry, I worried you."

"The worry, I can live with. I am just grateful that you are unharmed," he said as they reached her cabin. Kari nodded as she went inside and collapsed on the bed in relief and exhaustion. The near death experience still caused her to shudder but then she thought about the harpy and was calmed. This had been the second time in her life that she had come close to death and the second time a harpy had saved her. This could not be mere coincidence. Maybe she did have a strong sixth sense that drew them to her as Dr. Watkins at the zoo had suggested. Then she remembered that she had spoken to this harpy. She had told him she was unharmed. She tried to recall every bit of this encounter as she closed her eyes and lay on the bed. "He asked me if I was hurt," she said out loud to herself as she sat up on the bed. Kari realized that the harpy had indeed communicated with her. He had not uttered a sound but felt his question enter her mind as her own subconscious would. Kari got up from the bed and paced the room. "I really did hear him. Is it possible that I can understand them and they can understand me?" she murmured to herself. "Or have I finally lost my mind," she said as she plopped back down on the bed. She felt guilty about lying to Charlie about who had really saved her from the grogins. But her first harpy encounter had caused her enormous grief as a child. She was not about to confess that she had experienced another harpy encounter so soon after arriving on Dora. Only more grief and concern would come from exposing the truth. The truth, that for some reason or another, the harpies were drawn to her.

Kari curled up on the pillows in bewilderment, trying to rationalize why this was happening to her. She was confused but grateful that the harpy had protected her. Finally she closed her eyes and sleep finally came.

It did not seem long and she could feel his presence as he leaned over her. She reached towards him as she wrapped her arms around his neck and pulled him down close to her. His lips met hers as they lightly kissed. Slowly she ran her hand across his shoulder and along his ribs as she explored his body through touch. He quivered with excitement as this female handled him, tried to catch his breath and softly panted against her neck and face. Kari, too, now shuddered as he ran his hands across her body. The golden harpy affectionately rubbed his cheek against hers, nuzzling her with his nose. She could feel his strong lean body pressing and wiggling against her as he tossed his blond locks of hair from her face. She glanced up and could see his fluttering cream wings. The feathers ruffled with the sexual stimulation of holding a female so closely. Kari breathed hard and could feel the pit of stomach rise and fall, she was so aroused by this gorgeous creature. She was able to put her hand to his face pushing the golden hair aside as she stared into his deep blue longing eyes. He kissed and nuzzled her again, reluctantly pulled himself from her. "Don't go," she pleaded. "Soon." was the answer, he gave her, though he spoke no words or made no sound. Suddenly, as quickly as he had come, he was gone.

Kari jolted up from the bed and stared around the empty dark room. She was out of breath and wet with perspiration. Flinging her long blond hair out of her face, she jumped up and checked the locked windows and door. They were all securely bolted. "Another dream," she thought to herself, sitting back down on the bed. She tried to analyze the dream while it was fresh in her mind. Perhaps she could discover why it had reoccurred. Many nights on Earth, she had dreamed of this golden harpy. Of the flying with him and the rescue from the mogel but these dreams on Dora were very different. They were of total passion. The flying and rescue did not happen and there was something else that was different. He was different. He was no longer a mere animal, who had protected a young girl but had become her lover. And then Kari remembered something else about him. He was no longer the teenager of past dreams but was now a full-grown male harpy. "Why him?" she thought. A gorgeous brown winged harpy had just saved her. Wouldn't it be logical for her to dream of the brown harpy? It had been ten years since she encountered this golden. Kari lay back down and tossed and turned as the dream preoccupied her. Finally she went back to sleep. She woke to the sound of knocking on her cabin door. She glanced around and saw the bright morning light as it filtered through the drawn curtains. "Charlie," she murmured to herself as she stumbled out of bed, still in a daze. Opening the door, she found the Indian waiting patiently outside. "I'm sorry, Charlie, I overslept but it won't take me long to get ready," she said with a drowsy voice.

"You had a rough night so I let you sleep. I will meet you at the restaurant," he said as he turned toward the main building. Kari showered and dressed as her mind was filled with harpies. After she packed her small bag, she met Charlie as he sat in the empty dining room.

"This place does not have many customers. I think it may close soon," he said as he made small talk. Kari agreed. Charlie ate eggs and biscuits with coffee while Kari had fruit and a jellyroll. She told him in detail about the grogins that had nearly taken her life but she again did not reveal her encounter with the brown harpy to him. When they had finished, Charlie noticed that Kari had eaten mostly fruits and vegetables at dinner and breakfast.

She smiled bashfully, "I just can't seem to get enough of Dora's vegetation. I have missed it for so long." He grinned and ordered a large bag to take with them on the trip ahead. Soon they were back on the narrow dirt highway again. Charlie drove slowly through the rough terrain stopping at times to point out things of interest to Kari. They soon came upon a large herd of zels grazing in a clearing. Their dark green bodies with yellow stripes glistened in the morning light as they darted into the thick jungle at the approach of the vehicle. Among the trees, they popped their rust colored deer like heads up to see this thing that traveled the road.

An hour later, Charlie was forced to come to a full stop as a giant twelve-foot red lizard lay across the road as it sunned itself. Its high finned back arched upward as Charlie got out and prodded it with a long branch. The lizard sluggishly moved off into the jungle as it flipped its tail in annoyance. Charlie chuckled as he climbed back into the vehicle and they moved on. "Most men would have killed that lizard," Kari said to him.

"Yes, you are probably right. But then they would have to drag its dead body off the road to get around its high fins."

"That is not the reason you did not kill it," she said solemnly.

"You are right. I would not have killed the lizard unless it was its meat I sought. It is the Indian way. To only kill for need, not pleasure. I find there is no need simply because an animal exists."

"Why do they kill the harpies?" she asked thoughtfully. "Because they just exist?"

"You have asked me this question before and I have trouble answering you now as I did when you were a child."

"I'm no longer a child and I want to know the truth from you," she said quietly.

He glanced at her and could see the seriousness in her face. "Why do men kill the harpies?" he began. "I have never killed one, though I have hunted many animals on this planet. I, like you, believe they are more than just an animal and deserve our respect. But, you ask why others kill them. It is for many reasons. Harpies are very swift and smart. To kill one, is very difficult. Some men see the sport in this. To bring down something that is close to their equal. Other men are for the profit since harpy wings are very valuable. Then there are others, who simply hate the harpies and see them as a threat that should be destroyed."

"Like my father?" she said with disgust.

"Yes, when you were a child, his hate of them was strong."

"Does it have to do with stories of women being taken and raped by the harpies?" she asked.

Charlie raised his eyebrows slightly. "So, you have heard these tales."

"Does it?" she asked again.

The Indian took a slow deep breath. "This is a question that should be only answered by him. It is not my place to say. He must tell you of his hatred for the harpies."

"Well, I doubt if that will ever happen. He has always refused to speak to me when it concerned the harpies."

"Perhaps now may be different. You are no longer a child and he may find it easier to relate to you. I will tell you one thing that may ease your bitterness towards him. After you were attacked by the mogel and sent to Earth, your father did make peace with the harpies or maybe it was a peace with him self. He was so grateful to that little golden male for saving your life that he ban harpy hunting on the entire estate. For ten years now, the harpies have found sanctuary there and have flourished in peace."

This information did brighten Kari's mood. "Then perhaps my golden harpy still lives."

"Yes, he is alive for I saw him a few years ago and if he had been killed since, it would have been big news around Westend," Charlie related.

"You saw him? Where?" Kari asked excitedly.

"On one of my hunts deep in the jungle. He is still very brave and cocky just as he was when he brought you home from the lake. He stepped out on the path I was following and stood before me. I had my laser gun in my hand and could have killed him easily. He looked at me for a long moment and then flew away. I have never known of a harpy with such nerve. I am amazed that he has survived all these years. I'm sure your father's ban did spare him. Perhaps all golden harpies were like him and that is why there are so few. Their fearless bold nature may have been their downfall," he remarked.

Kari leaned back in her seat and she could barely contain herself. "I knew he was alive. I just knew it," she said excitedly. "Charlie, you have no idea how pleased I am with this news."

"I have never told anyone of this encounter with the golden, even your father. He has protected the harpies from the hunting more for your sake but he still is far from fond of them. It remains a sore subject so I would not mention this to him," Charlie said.

"Oh, I won't say anything to him about the golden harpy. I remember, just mentioning a harpy would send him into a rage. Right now I want to try and heal my relationship with him. I'm tired of being so bitter and angry."

"I am glad to hear this and I think, your father will do every thing he can to make things right between you as well. It may be wise to also not mention the brown harpy that came to you last night and saved you from the grogins," he said with a smile.

"You saw him?" she said with surprise.

Charlie chuckled a little. "I am old but my eyesight is still very good. I had my laser gun fixed on that large female grogin and almost fired when he landed between you and the animal. He saved you as well as that grogin."

"Maybe it was the harpy's intention to protect us both. He surely must have known you were there. The golden harpy did the same thing. He could have very easily finished killing the lake mogel instead he allowed the eel to live. Apparently harpies are not killers."

"Yes, it is well known, they do not eat meat and are not a predator animal."

Kari suddenly remembering that she had deceived the Indian last night. "Oh, Charlie, I'm sorry I didn't tell you the whole story about the brown harpy. I was just afraid…afraid that if it was known that another harpy came to me…" she stammered.

"I understand your reasons. You do not have to explain them to me. You were unfairly punished when the golden saved you. I can see why you would be hesitant to tell of a second meeting of these creatures. Many people would not understand and your father is one of them."

"Why do you think they have come to me and have saved me twice now?" Kari asked.

"You have always cared a great deal for the harpies, even as a young child. Maybe they sense this about you. Their animal senses must be very strong. I believe, that is why that young brave golden came to me. He could sense, I wouldn't hurt him." Charlie reflected. "Most animals can sense danger, fear and acceptance."

"But Charlie, you said, you thought they were more than just animals," she questioned.

"They have the instinct of an animal for without it, they would be annihilated by now. They are the most sought after game animals in this galaxy. Hunters consider them the ultimate trophy. And with all of men's modern technology and weapons, their animal instinct and intelligence is what has spared them. Even human intelligence could not survive this kind of hunting pressure. So, do I think they are animals? Yes, in part they have to be," Charlie stated.

Kari reflected on this for a while. "I met a vet at the Hampton zoo, who was doing a study on harpies. I told him about my golden harpy encountered. He believes as you, that the harpies can sense I care about them. He called it the sixth sense and thought it was strong in me as well. This is why the harpies were drawn to me," Kari said.

"He could be right about you. Senses and instincts can be strong in some people. My tribe spoke of it on Earth. Many years ago, when we were a free people, long before we merged with the white men. My people possessed the sixth sense and we were one with nature but that was hundreds of years ago and most have lost it. It is something to be cherished but this can be a curse if it continues to draw these harpies to you."

Kari looked at the old man with his last statement. It was apparent that despite his respect and fondness for harpies, he was displeased that these winged creatures were drawn to her. Why, she wondered. Maybe it went back to the tales of kidnapping and rape of women by the harpies. The obvious reasons that her father hated them. She wanted to talk about this further but changed her mind. It was a wonderful day. She was home at last in her jungle and the golden male still lived. Kari didn't want to discuss any thing negative about the harpies and ruin this day. Instead, she changed the subject from harpies and she began to discuss her past fond memories with this aging Indian. She and Charlie laughed and joked about their many adventures in the jungle when she was a child. "I remember you coming home holding a deadly poisonous lizard in your hands. You nearly gave your father and I a heart attack that day. Why that lizard didn't bit you, I'll never know," Charlie chuckled. The mood was merry as they continued their journey westward.

Evening approached and they pulled off the road into a small clearing with a stream running through it. Kari gathered wood for a fire, as she had done as a child, while Charlie set up camp and erected a small tent. Darkness came as the meager fire snapped and crackled as it burned brightly. The sounds of the night came alive under the star-filled night sky. Charlie prepared the food over this fire, even though the vehicle contained a heating element. He claimed that the food would taste better, although it was more work. The smell of the grilled meats and vegetables enhanced their appetites, along with the home made biscuits.

"You're an excellent cook, Charlie. These vegetables are grilled to perfection," Kari commented as they ate and watched the fire. Charlie only nodded the compliment. "Tell me, Charlie. What made you come to Dora with my grandfather?"

He looked up from the fire. "You wish to hear more from me? I have not talked this much in a period of a month." Kari laughed and knew it was probably true.

"No, I really would like to know and I enjoy listening to you," she smiled.

"I came here for the same reasons as your grandfather. To live my life among the trees and nature, which was intended for man but it was a hard decision to make as a young man. The last reservation of my tribe was nothing but desert, with no life in it. Even the snake and scorpion were gone from it. So, I left it and traveled to the cold north where I met your grandfather among the last remaining great forests. We worked together for a few years and had great adventures as young men. My tribe decided to sell the desert reservation to developers and all the members of the tribe received some credits for this. It was at this time, that your grandfather told me he was going to the planet of Dora that was covered with trees and life. He told me that he would pay my expenses for this trip, if I helped him build a new home there. The reservation was gone. It was the only home I had known. I did not want to live in the cities under the domes, so I agreed. But there was an Indian girl that I had to leave behind. I promised, I would send for her when I had made enough credits. When the time came for her to come, she told me she had found another and did not want to come to this wild planet. I never found someone to take her place. It is hard to find love again. But, I do not regret my decision. When your father was born, I loved him like a son, and you, like a granddaughter. I know, if I had stayed with the Indian girl, I would have loved her but I would have lived a life of misery in those cities and she would have grown tired of a husband that was so unhappy."

"Oh, Charlie, that's so sad," Kari said, feeling the old man's pain. "I agree that you made the right choice in coming here. I lived in those cities. It is no life for people like you and me."

Charlie rose and left the fire. "It grows late and we still have a ways to travel in the morning. I will take the tent and you, the vehicle."

"I can take the tent," Kari offered.

"The vehicle is safer, and I will sleep better knowing you are in it," he said sternly.

Kari knew not to argue with him when his mind was made up. "Well, good night then," she said as she crawled into the comfortable bed inside. She was exhausted from the lack of sleep on the previous night. And soon, she was asleep. Late into the night, the golden harpy came to her in her dreams. He nuzzled his nose and head gently against her. She smiled at him and stroked his silky head hair. "Do you have a name?" she asked him, this time using her mind, instead of her voice in this dream.

"I am Shail." came his answer in a soft male voice.

"Why do you come to me, Shail?" she asked.

He pulled away staring at her in confusion. "As I am yours, you are mine. As it was always meant to be," he related to her without speaking. He tenderly kissed her lips as he rose to a kneeling position.

"Don't go. There is so much I must know about you," she tried to convey.

He tilted his head slightly, still perplexed by her. "You know me. The light comes, it is time," he said as he stood up and extended the long cream wings for flight. With a one large flap, he was airborne. Fluttering for a second as he gazed down at her and then vanished.

Kari called to him. "Shail, come back. Please come back, Shail," she cried. She opened her eyes as she awoke and indeed, she could see the faint rays of dawn approaching through the trees. She shut her eyes again and tried to analyze this dream and soon was back to sleep.

Kari awoke to the noises of the jungle and the smell of the smoke from a freshly lit campfire. Looking out the window, she saw Charlie bending over it. His tent was down and neatly rolled up as he sipped from a cup of coffee. Climbing out of the vehicle, she walked to Charlie and the fire. "What's for breakfast?" she asked cheerfully.

He smiled at her. "There is coffee and biscuits and much of the fruit remains," he answered. Kari took one of the warm biscuits and perched herself on a rock as she nibbled on it. "Did you sleep well?" He asked with concern.

"Yes, just fine. I was very tired." Kari could see that something was bothering Charlie. "What is it?"

"This friend of yours, named Shail. You must miss him very much. You called that name several times and begged him to stay with you. You seemed very upset. I almost woke you to end this dream."

Kari laughed a little to hide her embarrassment. "I'm sorry I woke you, Charlie. I keep having this crazy dream since I came back to Dora. It's so real that I've found myself checking the locks on the doors and window to make sure I'm alone. It's very strange," she said.

"It is a nightmare then?" he asked.

"No, it's not a nightmare. It's kind of embarrassing but they're dreams of passion."

Charlie scratched his head a little. "I see, so this Shail was a lover. He is someone you met then?"

Kari smiled fondly as she thought of him. "Yes, I met him a long time ago on Dora."

Now, Charlie was totally puzzled for he was acquainted with all the people on Dora, who had entered Kari's life and none had this strange name. Then he suddenly realized, who it maybe. His face became serious as he walked to her. "Tell me, Kari, who is he? Is Shail the golden harpy?" he asked solemnly.

Kari took a deep breath and said, "Yes."

The Indian stood up straight, tossing the long gray braids back as he put his head back and looked at the sky. "We must go now," he uttered. "I do not want to stay another night in these woods." He began loaded the vehicle with the tent and other gear.

Kari could see the Indian, who was always calm, was terribly upset now as he tossed the gear in without packing it. Kari ran to his side. "Charlie, they're only silly dreams. They mean nothing," she said jokingly as she trying to reassure him. He just glanced at her and did not answer. Now Kari began to worry. It was apparent that Charlie knew something that she did not. She placed her hand on his arm. "Charlie, what do these dreams mean?" she asked him seriously. It had become no laughing matter now.

He looked at her and said, "It means, I must worry and fear for you now. It means your father sent you to Earth for no reason and you suffered needlessly."

"You're not making any sense. Tell me what all of this means?" she said more desperately.

He swallowed hard and said slowly, "You have been marked by this harpy. He has placed a spell on you and has merged with his mind with yours. Your father hoped that you and this harpy were both too young when you met and no spell could have been made that distance and time had spared you. But these dreams prove that he still searches and desires you and worse yet, you long for him. He will find you and try and take you now. This is what your father feared. I regret I did not kill him when I had the chance. He is very handsome and his courageous is to be admired. I would have found no joy in killing such a beautiful creature but to save you from this misery, I would have done it. Your father must be told of these dreams. There may still be time to end this danger before it is too late. You ask, why your father hates the harpies, this is the reason. They are a threat to you.

"Charlie, they're only dreams. My dreams. He is only guilty of saving my life. How can you say all this, when the harpies have rescued me twice," she said upset.

"The reason for the rescue is clear now. You have been rescued because he wants you. He seduces you in your dreams and clouds your judgment so you willingly go with him. Only his death can spare you and free you now. I must tell your father. It is the only way," he stated.

"Please, don't tell him, Charlie. I'll be strong. I won't go with him if he comes. Please don't give Dad an excuse to kill him. If he is killed on my account, I couldn't live with myself. And I would never forgive you or Dad if this happened. Never!" she screamed, trying to fight back the tears. "Charlie," she pleaded, "they're only dreams, my dreams. They could mean nothing. I have been so unhappy for so long and just the memory of him gave me hope while I was gone. Now you want to destroy the only thing that gave me comfort just because of a stupid dream," she said and she began to sob.

Charlie put his arms around her. "Hush, now" he said wearily. "I will not be the one to bring you more pain. Trust me, Kari, these are not only your dreams. When the golden comes, promise me, you will reject him. To be taken by a harpy, will bring only great grief and even death." he said quietly.

"What do you mean grief and death?" she asked as she pulled from him, wiping a tear from her cheek.

"This is something your father should answer. He knows well of this heartache and grief that these harpies bring. You must speak to him of it. Let us go now. We will speak of this no more," he said as he climbed into the vehicle. Kari followed and got in on her side. Soon they were traveling the road again in silence this time.

After traveling an hour, they came upon a vast barren patch of ground that went for three miles. "This is what a swarm does," Charlie said as he slowed the vehicle to a stop.

Kari stepped out to survey the damaged land. "This is terrible," she murmured as she stared out at the desolate and empty landscape. The black ground lay exposed as if a giant claw had reached out from the sky and ripped all life from it. Only a few sheared off stumps remained where the beetle had stopped eating at ground level. An eerie feeling crept over her. All the sounds of birds and living things were void of this place. Only the hollow sound of the wind could be heard as it swept through the vacant land. Even the wonderful smells of the jungle were absent as Kari breathed deeply. She could only detect the smell of sour musty soil. Kari climbed back into the vehicle as she took one last look around. "It's like a great storm came through here and blew everything away," she said quietly to Charlie.

"Yes, these beetles are like a storm, but worse, for they know no season and give no warning. And, unlike a storm, they destroy everything in their path," he said and started the engines to the terrain vehicle.

Soon they were back in the jungle. The sounds and smells of life filled the air with music and perfume. Kari glanced up at the magnificent trees that hung over the dirt highway making it cool with their shade. It was similar to traveling in a beautiful colorful cave of light and splendor.

Noon came and they stopped for lunch. Kari spotted some wild berries along the road and picked some to eat, as they journeyed west. The land became hilly as the northern mountain range dipped southward. They crossed two more barren areas that the swarms had devoured. "That is the last one. Unless they have struck again since I traveled to meet you," Charlie informed her.

The afternoon wore on and there were no other signs of a swarm attack. The little star of Duran began to set in the west between the brightly multicolored hills as the black mountains gleamed in the distant north. Charlie pressed the communication button and a small screen appeared between the two front seats. "Hello, Maria," he said to the screen.

An excited voice came back from it. "Charlie, where are you? Did you pick up Kari?"

"Yes, she is with me," he answered.

"Mr. Turner has called several times and is worried. He expected you here before now. Is everything alright?" she asked.

"We are fine and should be home by dark in time for dinner."

"You should have left the com on so we could reach you. Mr. Turner will be upset with you for making him worry," she scolded.

"He knows I do not like these communicators. They invade my privacy and if he is upset, it will not be the first time. Tell him we traveled slowly to enjoy the jungle but he will see his daughter soon enough." He grinned.

"Okay, I'll tell him. I'll call the mill right now. Tell Miss Kari that I have cooked all her favorites and I will be so happy to see her," she said cheerfully.

"She can hear you and you can tell her yourself when you see her in a couple of hours. Bye, bye," he said and quickly turning off the com. before Maria could respond. "That woman will talk your ear off, if you let her," Charlie said as he shook his head.

Kari smiled. "Some things haven't changed."

Charlie glanced at her. "If I had left this communicator on, she would have been calling me every hour," Charlie growled. "I think she likes to aggravate me."

Kari remembered that Charlie and Maria were fond of each other but they hid it with contention. Some things had remained the same in her absence and this pleased her.

Darkness once again covered the landscape but Kari began to recognize some old buildings along the road as they approached the turn off to Westend. The dirt highway became familiar the closer they came to her father's estate. The home was located at the very southern tip near the town and the small harbor but the large estate extended northward along the coast for over six hundred miles into the mountain ranges and was almost a hundred miles across from west to east. They passed the turn to Westend and went another ten miles until they reached the entrance. The jungle was gone as it was replaced with a large rolling meadow of pastureland and herds of cattle. After a mile, the drive forked. The road to the left went to the house, while to the right, it ended at the wood mill and the well maintained smaller homes of the employees who worked the estate. Kari felt a tinge of nervousness, as Charlie turned left at this fork. In a few minutes, she would be home at last. The thought of it, filled her heart with joy, but at the same time, she felt apprehensive, seeing her father again after a bitter ten years absence. Kari could see the lights of this imposing, grand white home as it sat on the largest hill with the jungle a short distance behind it. The vehicle rolled through the hills until it came to rest at the front doors. Two large Irish wolfhound dogs leaped to their feet as they greeted the familiar vehicle and the Indian they knew drove it. Their tails wagged as if he had been gone forever. Kari stepped from the vehicle and petted the dogs as the front doors flew open. The old plump Hispanic maid came running out as fast as her short legs would carry her. She threw her arms around Kari as tears of joy ran down her cheeks. "I'm so happy to see you!" she cried over and over again.

Kari embraced the older woman, who had been the closest thing to a mother that she had known as a child. "Maria, you haven't changed a bit," Kari declared with jubilation.

"Oh, my hair is grayer and I am fatter but you, you have blossomed like a beautiful flower. You have grown into an enchanting young woman," Maria said with admiration.

Kari gazed up beyond Maria and standing in the doorway was her father. He had not changed much as he looked out at her. His tall well-built body remained the same. Only his face seemed different, more weathered and rough from the years of work and worry. His thick blond hair hid any gray that may have existed. His blue eyes twinkled as he walked toward her and lightly embraced her. In a low voice he said, "It's good to have you home."

"It's good to be home," Kari said softly as she put her arms around his waist. Even with this hug, they both could sense the tension that lay between them.

"Maria has cooked a splendid meal in your honor. I hope you're hungry," he said as they pulled apart.

"Yes, I am," she said politely, "but I'd like to wash up first if that's alright. We camped last night."

"Of course," he said as he took one of her bags when Charlie unloaded them. And they walked into the foyer with Charlie following with the other bag. "Take your time, dinner can wait," her father said.

"I'll take that small bag now, Charlie," Kari said as she took the bag and ascended the stairs that led up to her old bedroom. As she reached her room, she could hear the low voices of Charlie and her father as they talked quietly. Kari froze at her door as she listened to the conversation below.

"How was the trip?" her father asked.

"It was fine," answered Charlie.

Her father looked at the old Indian. "I've known you too long, Charlie, you're holding something back from me. Something is troubling you."

There was a long moment of silence before Charlie finally spoke. Kari could feel her heart sink and prayed the Indian would keep his word and guard the secrets that could provoke her father's anger. She heard Charlie speak.

"The time has come for her to know the truth. She is very much like her mother and that is all I will say." There was a long silence. "I must unpack the vehicle now," Charlie muttered with fatigue in his voice.

"You are right. I promise, I will speak with her. Hopefully it will heal some of the hostility she feels towards me and understand my motives. It is the only way to mend our relationship. Thank you, Charlie," her father replied.

Kari heard the front doors open and close. She walked to her bedroom and went inside. All her old childhood things were there, just as she had left them. It was as if time had stood still in the room. Only a large vase of fresh flowers, that sat on the dresser was different. These were obviously the labors of Maria. She walked to the bed and picked up a toy stuffed animal that rested against one of the pillows and held it to her, remembering how this object had comforted her in the night. Then she walked to a dressing table and picked up a picture. It was of her mother, standing in a white gown, with the jungle behind her. Around her slender body, flowed her long blond hair as it rested upon her shoulders. She was radiant in this picture. And Kari could see the similarity between herself and her dead mother. "Is this what Charlie had meant?" she wondered. It was the first time she had heard Charlie refer to her mother. It was another one of those off limit subjects that she had learned to avoid as a child. No one would speak to her of this woman or her death and in time, she too, stopped asking all her childhood questions about her. But now, her mind was filled with questions again and this time she would insist on the answers. Kari returned the picture to its proper place as she went to the small bag and gathered the clean clothing from it. She was grateful that Charlie had kept his word and not told her father about the grogins and the brown harpy that had rescued her. And her mysterious dreams that consisted of the golden harpy as her lover. Perhaps her father's secrets were as complicated as her own. It did appear from the conversation below, that her father was finally willing to confide in her and give her the answers to the questions that had puzzled her all her life. She made up her mind to be patient and not pressure him. She had waited this long, a few more days made no difference now.

Kari quickly showered in the bathroom off her room and dressed. She went downstairs and could smell the aroma of the cooked food. "It smells wonderful," she said to Maria as she entered the dining room.

"I hope you still like my cooking and you did not get spoiled on Earth," Maria said as she placed a large bowl of steamed vegetables on the table.

"No, I didn't get spoiled. Earth food is pretty poor, compared to Dora," Kari said as she seated herself in her old seat along side of her father at the table. Charlie sat across from her.

"Did you enjoy your stay on Earth?" Maria asked happily as she served another bowl.

Kari glanced up at Charlie for he knew how painful this subject was to her. He looked back at her seriously. Her father also looked at her nervously as he set his drinking glass down on the table. Slowly she answered. "It was all right but I'm glad to be home." Kari took a sip of water as if this half-truth stuck in her throat and was hard to swallow. She quickly changed the subject because it was uncomfortable to all except the oblivious housekeeper.

"So, father, tell me of these swarms. Charlie and I passed three areas that had been destroyed on the road from Terrance and I saw quite a few in the large hover from Hampton. It's inconceivable, the damage from these beetles."

Her father seemed relieved from the change of subject. "Yes, it's very bad and going to get worse if we don't find a way to stop them. I'm expecting new chemicals any time now which the government assures me will work. I hope they're right since the whole continent is at risk." Her father continued this conversation about the beetles throughout dinner. Kari could see that he was obsessed with it and she could not blame him. She loved the trees and the jungle as much as he did.

After dinner, they went into the large spacious living room. Kari enjoyed gazing at all the past treasures this room held. Maria had cleared away the dishes and finished for the evening. She walked into the living room and asked if she could do anything else before she left for the night. "No, thanks. I'm fine, Maria. And thank you for the wonderful dinner and also the lovely flowers in my room," Kari said.

Maria smiled widely. "I will see you tomorrow. We have so much to talk about. Good night."

"Yes, good night, Maria and thank you," her father said.

"I will go with you and make sure you get home safely," Charlie told her. "I am tired from the long journey and you both should be alone now," he said and glanced at John. John only nodded to him.

Kari walked over and curled up in a large stuffed chair, while her father lit a small fire in the fireplace. "Was Earth really all right?" he asked somberly as he watched the flames.

Kari had known this question would come from him. When Charlie had questioned her about Earth, only the memory of the pain reared its ugly head. But, with her father, it was a memory of the bitterness and resentment she felt. For he had been the one who had caused her ten years of suffering. She squirmed in her chair as she tried to control these emotions of animosity towards him. "I don't want to lie to you. No, it was not all right. The fact is, I don't care to discuss it," she uttered.

Her father turned toward her and could see the anguish on her face and the betrayal she felt towards him in her eyes. He rubbed his forehead and looked back to the fire. "I want to tell you my reasons for sending you to Earth. You despise me and I don't blame you. But, we must talk and it must be soon. There are things about Dora that you must be made aware of, now that you're an adult," he said somberly.

Kari could feel her anger growing. Just being alone with him in the room, she was struggling to control her hostility. "I'm tired now, Dad. But I do want to talk about this. Perhaps in the morning, if that's all right with you. I do want to heal. I don't enjoy feeling this way towards you," she said with earnest.

He nodded his understanding and went to her, kissing her tenderly on the forehead. "Tomorrow morning we will have a long talk. I hope it will clear this barrier that lies between us. I'm so happy you're home."

"I am too. Good night then," she said and fled to her room.

CHAPTER 2

▼

Kari walked into her bedroom and opened the balcony doors. A cool breeze from the jungle infiltrated the room. The smell of trees and flowers floated in to mix with fragrance of the flowers that existed on the table. She took a few steps out on the terrace and stared off in the distance. Dora's full moons lit up the grounds below. Squawks and screeches of the jungle's creatures rang out in the still night.

She relished this moment, as she stared in the direction of the small lake that lay, hidden beyond the trees. Suddenly a terrible longing to go to it crept over her, to go to the lake and find him. Then she remembered Charlie's warnings and she backed away from the railing with anxiety until she was in the room. Closing the doors, she locked them and climbed in the soft bed. Wrapped her arms around the numerous pillows and coiled up and finally slumbered off in to a deep sleep.

The dream over took her as she wandered in the jungle. She was searching for the golden harpy as she pushed back the foliage. A dense fog seemed to cover this fantasy jungle and she could not see far ahead. Soon she called out his name. "Shail, where are you?" she cried while drifting through the trees. Finally in a small clearing and saw him as he lay on his side, curled up beneath a tree with his cream wings slightly extended and folded over him. She slowly walked to him but he did not move. She knelt down and pushed the blond hair from his sleeping face. He slowly opened his eyes as he looked up at her. His eyes were so sad and had lost all their fire and passion.

"You found me," he related softly.

"Yes, I must ask if you hold a spell over me," Kari asked in the dream.

He reached up and gently caressed the side of her face. "Fear not, our spell shall soon be broken. Only know this, my love has always been yours." he related silently and breathed deeply. He suddenly glanced beyond her and Kari could see the panic and pain in his eyes. She reached to hold him but the mist consumed him and he was gone.

She began to call for him again, this time with terror in her voice. She had felt his suffering and fear and she was petrified by it. She jumped up and began searching frantically for him. Screaming his name as she searched this dream forest frantically. The dream had become a nightmare. Her body trembled as she tossed from side to side.

"Kari, Kari!" she heard a voice in her dream. But it was not Shail's soft silky male voice. It was the voice of her father. She opened her eyes to the bright bedroom lights as the hand of her father shook her arm. "Kari, are you all right?" he expressed with great concern.

Kari tried to catch her breath and compose herself. "It was a dream. Another dream," she said wiping the perspiration from her forehead.

"It sounded more like a nightmare," he said with compassion.

Kari rubbed her eyes as she tried to focus and think. "I'm sorry, Dad. I woke you. I just had a terrible dream but I'm fine now."

"All right, if you're sure you're okay. I'll go back to bed," he said gently and rose from her bedside.

"Dad, is old Doc still in Westend?" she asked.

"He's still there but somewhat retired now. Why?"

"I just have had trouble sleeping lately. Maybe I'll go see him tomorrow and he can give me something that makes me sleep through the night."

"Well, I'm sure he could handle that. I'll see you in the morning. Good night" he said with a smile as he turned off the lights and shut the door.

Kari curled up around the pillows once again and stared off into the empty shadowy room. She, again, tried to analyze the dream, while it was fresh in her mind. The golden harpy had admitted that there was a spell but it would soon be broken. "What did this mean?" she wondered. Would it be broken when he finally came for her or was he releasing her from it? She dwelled on his words. He said he had always loved her. She smiled at this, for she had loved him since she had first laid eyes on him. Now, she became serious. It was the fear she felt coming from him that plagued her. What had scared this bold sleek harpy so badly? She agonized over it. The only emotions she had felt from him in previous dreams had been of passion and devotion to her. His fear had become hers as she thought of him. Kari shook her head. "They're only dreams. My imagination must be getting the better of me," she thought. She closed her eyes and eventually dozed off.

The morning light cast its bright illumination on the floor, as it spilled in from the balcony. She slowly opened her eyes and thought of Shail. Then she remembered the talk she must have with her father. The smell of baked bread seeped into the room and Kari realized that the household was awake and already at work. Throwing on a robe, she went down to the kitchen. Maria was there, slicing the bread.

"Hello, Maria." Kari said as she walked into the huge expansive kitchen.

"Good morning, Miss Kari. What would you like for breakfast? I can cook you anything," Maria beamed.

"Just a piece of that bread you're slicing and maybe some juice."

"That's not much of a breakfast. Your father waits for you in his den. He asks that you come when you're finished eating," Maria said as she poured Kari a glass of fruit juice.

Kari picked it up and sipped it. "I'll see him now. I don't want to make him wait," Kari said and took the juice and bread with her. She came to the den door and knocked.

"Come," was the answer behind the door. Kari went in and saw her father standing behind his desk looking at a screen. He pushed a button and the screen quickly dissolved back into the desk. "Sit down," he said with a smile and took the seat behind the desk. "I'm glad to see you. Did you sleep all right, the rest of the night?" he asked with concern.

"Yes, I think so, at least I don't remember any more dreams."

"Maybe old Doc can help you. He's still as cantankerous as ever," he said with a nervous laugh. He rose from his chair and started pacing the room as if he was trying to decide what to say next. He shook his head in frustration. "What I must say to you, is very hard for me. It brings back a lot of painful memories for me but it must be said," he spoke seriously. "It has to do with your mother. It is because of her, I sent you to Earth. Do you know anything about her?" he asked Kari in a low solemn voice.

"Not really, except that she was killed in some kind of accident. That is all that grandpa would say of her. At least, that's all I remember. It seems like she was a subject that I wasn't allowed to discuss," Kari said quietly.

John paced the room some more as he rubbed his forehead. Finally he stopped and looked out the window. "She's been gone for twenty years and I still haven't gotten over her loss," he said sadly. "You are very much like her. When you stepped from the vehicle yesterday, it was like seeing a ghost. She was beautiful and strong and she loved the jungle like you," he said, putting his hand to his mouth, fighting the emotions that had laid dormant in him. He cleared his voice and Kari could see the agony this brought to him. "We were very happy together. I want you to know that. And when you were born, I thought my life was complete. I had the two most beautiful girls on the planet under my roof," he smiled a little. He turned away from the window and looked down at Kari as he became very grave. "A golden harpy took that all away from me. He swooped down from the sky and grabbed her. I only had time to get off one laser blast, before he took her away." He walked to the chair besides Kari and sat in it. "I fired and the blast hit your mother. She died instantly," he said as he breathed deeply. "But the second blast, got him as he stood over her. I had never killed a harpy before. I was stupid and foolish back then. I always thought that they deserved to live on the land with us in peace." He shook his head with disgust. "After that day, I invited every hunter and poacher to come to the estate and exterminate them. Anyway, when I heard the dogs barking and I looked out this window, it was like a regression from the past. There you were in the arms of another golden harpy. I just wanted to put you some place safe. You were so crazy about the harpies and too young to know the danger. I knew, if one came to you, you would willingly leap into its arms and fly off with it, no matter what I said. You could be as stubborn as me at times."

Kari looked at him and knew he was right. "Oh, Dad, I wish you had told me all of this," she finally said.

He put his hand on her shoulder. "Kari, you were only a child. I just couldn't tell you that I was the one that killed your mother. I had planned on telling you when you were a teenager, but that incident with you and the gold harpy escalated things. I knew I couldn't protect you here. Do you think you will ever be able to forgive me for sending you away?" he asked.

She nodded, "Understanding your motives, I'm more apt to forgive you now. I was so miserable on Earth, but it was compounded by the fact that I thought were cruel and didn't love me."

"Oh, Kari, I love you very much. So much, I was willing to make both our lives miserable, so you would be safe," he said as he held her in his arms. They finally pulled apart. "I hope this will be a new beginning for both of us."

"Dad, there's one thing I don't understand. Charlie told me you ban all harpy hunting on the estate."

"Yes, I stopped the killing of male harpies after you left. You wanted me to protect that young golden harpy. It is a decision I still wrestle with but it was the least I could do for you and he did save your life. Every time I thought about that mogel pulling you into the water, it scared the hell out of me. I just thank God the young harpy was there. I owed him and these harpies have suffered enough for your mother's death. Hunters have spotted your golden male on the islands, so he has apparently made that his home. As long as he stays there and behaves himself, I'm happy with that. I'm sure that male has paired with a female by now and after ten years, has forgotten about you. But enough talk of harpies and the past. I have something for you, a coming home present of sorts. Come with me," he said as he got up from the chair and went to the foyer. Kari followed him. He opened the front doors of the house and a new hovering terrain vehicle stood in the drive. "It has everything in it that modern man can think of. Also, there's a new laser gun in the compartment. I want you to keep that with you at all times when you're away from the house.

"It's gorgeous, Dad, but I really don't think I need the laser unless I go off in the woods."

"Kari, keep it with you always. Your mother was attacked right here in the front lawn," he said sternly.

"All right, if it will make you feel better."

"It will. I must get to the mill. Some of the men seem to think it's a day off if I'm not there. I'll see you tonight for dinner. And listen, Kari, our discussion is a lot to digest at one time and I'm sure there may be more you want to know. Perhaps tonight we could discuss it further if you wish."

"Yes, there is more, I would like to know. And Dad, thanks for the vehicle. I think I'll get dressed now and try it out. I can take it to Westend when I see Doc. I'm anxious to end these dreams and sleep through the night," she conveyed.

He gave her a kiss lightly on the cheek. Then he walked toward his hovercraft that was parked along side the house. "I'll be home around five," he called to her as he hopped in the hover. In minutes, he was in the air and disappeared over the first hill.

Kari walked slowly back inside the house. She was deep in thought over the whole amazing story of her mother. The more she reflected the more questions came to her mind. "Were the harpies truly thieves and dangerous?" she thought to herself. She thought of Charlie's warnings and realized that this was the comparison he saw between her mother and herself. It had nothing to do with looks. It was the correlation that these golden harpies sought her mother and her self. Now she understood Charlie's and her father's fears. But, then she thought of Shail, her dream harpy and reflected on him. She could feel no evil in him. He was tender and sweet to her. And he loved her in these dreams. "Maybe Charlie is right. Maybe this male has not paired yet and he is enticing me to go with him," she thought to herself. "Maybe in real life, Shail truly was dangerous." Kari pondered the brown harpy she had recently encountered in the road. He had saved her from the grogins but for what purpose? Would he have taken her against her will, if Charlie had not appeared?

Doubt and frustration clouded her mind as she thought of her mother's kidnapping and death. "Is it possible, I've been wrong all this time? That I have been living with a false childhood illusion about these animals? Is everything I've believe in a lie?" she questioned herself. She began to realize that she was the only one who loved the harpies. "All the native Doreans hate the harpies. Can they all be wrong?" Even the horrible man on the ship, had described them as thieving, raping monsters. "Is this truly what they are?"

She felt sick and her stomach was in knots. She felt like she was experiencing the death of someone very close. Her love of the harpies had been replaced with fears and doubts.

"Are you alright, Miss Kari?" came a concerned voice of Maria from the dining room as Kari stood in the foyer, leaning against the stairs.

"Yes, Maria, I'm alright," she answered. The housekeeper started to leave. "Maria, did you know my mother?" Kari asked.

"Oh, is this what troubles you? I wish I could help you, but your father hired me to help raise you after her death. I never met her but have heard that she was a lovely woman," Maria said with melancholy.

"I have heard that too. Maria, you did a good job of raising me. I'm grateful to you," Kari said with a slight grin. "Did you see the new vehicle Dad bought me?" Kari asked trying to get her mind off these agonizing doubts.

"Yes, the whole town saw it when it was unloaded off a barge at the harbor a month ago. It is very fancy and a rich red color. Are you going to take it for a drive?" Maria asked.

"Yes, I'm going to get dressed and take it to Westend. See if the place has changed."

Maria laughed. "It is the same. A few more stores and houses, but it still a quiet little town that will bore you to tears."

Kari grinned, realizing she was more than ready for this boredom. She dressed quickly and went down to the awaiting terrain vehicle. She pushed the button and the shinny new red vehicle rose from the ground and began to hover. There was one thing her education on Earth had taught her, the knowledge to operate all types of transportation as well as an intricate education in all forms of technology. She learned about everything from weapons to communicators and was capable of using or fixing any of them. It had always seemed like a waste of learning since she planned on spending her life on Dora, which was limited to the advanced technology of Earth.

She maneuvered the vehicle down the drive as she stared out the window at the vast green meadows dotted with a bright array of flowers. The grass seeds of these meadows had been imported from Earth since Dora had no grasses before man inhabited it. Along with the grass came the cattle and other domestic animals of Earth. Even the large Irish wolfhound dogs that laid in the shade of the large front porch. They had originally been imported, before her father began to breed his own dogs. She reflected on the arrival of that first dog. She was very young but she could still remember that long trip to Terrance to get her first puppy. She smiled now, as she remembered her disappointment after such a long trip. Instead of a cute furry puppy, her father showed her a frozen fetus in a bag. He laughed at her unenthusiastic response and explained that if they had sent a puppy on the space ship, it would arrive as a large dog. "In a few months, you'll have your puppy," he had told her. She thought of this good old dog now as she glanced at the meadows. A tear rolled down her cheek. He had died the same year she had been sent to Earth. He was killed defending the cattle from a pride of grogins that had come in the night. She remembered how her father wept when he carried his large dead body from the same pasture she now traveled. It was the only time she had seen her father cry.

So many childhood memories flooded her mind as she traveled through the estate. The meadows ended, as did the last view of the house. Soon she was on the road again and surrounded by the trees of the jungle. She had passed the fork to the mill and decided to visit it on another day. Instead she continued for ten miles on the dirt highway road. She came to the turn in the road that led to Westend. A small run down sign displayed the entrance to the tiny village. Soon she was upon the small wooden homes that adorned its main street. Several other streets ran off the main one, as she passed them. In the heart of town, stood the modest grocery store, along with other meager shops. Maria was right. The quaint little town had not changed much in ten years. Soon Kari came upon a yellow cottage at the end of the street. Giant moss filled trees rose out of the front yard, each with a bed of flowers neatly planted at their base. An old weathered sign that read 'Dr. White' hung between the posts of the cottage. Kari brought the terrain vehicle to a stop as it settled down half on the street and half in the grass. She climbed out and made her way to the front door that lay on a well-shaded porch. Kari rang the old fashion bell several times, before a grisly silver-headed man appeared. "Hello, Doc," she said as he opened the door.

The old man frowned. "Who are you?" he asked gruffly.

"Kari Turner."

He eyed her closely, rubbing his beard in thought. "Turner, Turner" he said to himself. "Any relation to John?" he finally asked.

"I'm his daughter."

His eyes brightened. "Yes, I remember you now. I delivered you when you were a baby. I dare say, I should never forget that delivery," he mumbled to himself.

"What do you mean?" she questioned him.

"Nothing" he stammered. "Come in, come in, I don't plan on standing in this door way all day," he scowled and walked in the room. "I'm fixin fresh lemonade. Can't stand that garbage that comes out of those confounded machines. You want any?" he asked while making his way to the back of the cottage and now was in the kitchen.

"No, thank you," Kari said politely and followed him.

"Kari Turner," he mumbled to himself. "Yes, I do remember you as a kid. Never were sick much but didn't you get bit by a mogel? Yes, a gold harpy put licing moss on that wound to draw the poison out."

"Yes, he saved me from a lake mogel then he brought me home," she said.

The old man chuckled. "That harpy did more than save you from that mogel. That moss saved your life. If he had not put it on your wound, you would have been dead by the time I got to your home. That was quite a discovery in the field of medicine. We had no idea at that time, the properties of licing moss. Over the years, I imagine, that harpy has saved scores of lives with the discovery of that moss."

"My father never told me that," she uttered.

The old doctor chucked again, "I'm not surprised. Your father is not about to give a harpy any credit. He's not real fond of them."

"He has his reasons. He blames a harpy for my mother's death when it tried to take her," she said quietly.

"Yes, losing his wife made him a bitter man. And she was a real looker, prettiest thing I'd ever seen. Say, you look a lot like her. Yes, it was a real tragedy. How is your father? Haven't seen him in quite a while" he inquired.

"He's fine. Busy with this beetle thing," she remarked.

"Those beetles are everyone's problem. Well, what do you want? You don't look sick or hurt," he commented while pouring himself a glass of lemonade.

"I'm having trouble sleeping."

"Walking the floors at night, huh? You're too young to have to many problems."

"No, I fall asleep fine, it's just that I have these dreams. They're so real that they wake me up," she articulated.

The doctor looked at her with some seriousness for a moment. "Can't help you," he finally said.

"What do you mean, you can't help me? You must have something here that will help me sleep through the night."

"Of course I do, but you just said that you have no trouble going to sleep. Now you want me to stop you from dreaming, that's a different matter. You're a pretty bright girl and if I gave you the drugs to stop your dreams, well, let me assure you. You don't want or need that kind of drug. Everyone has bad dreams on occasion. Trust me, they'll pass naturally," he smiled.

"They're not really bad dreams, just very intense."

"Well, if they're not bad, you should learn to enjoy them. Wish I could dream more often," he mumbled. "It's been nice talking to you. Tell your father I'm still kicking. I have to get back to work on my garden. The rainy season will be here before you know it." And with that, he walked out the back door to the garden, carrying his glass of lemonade.

Kari was left standing in the empty kitchen. She slowly walked through the cottage. She noticed a small room to the left that was similar to a hospital room with old medical equipment, surrounding a single bed. After glancing around for a moment, she strolled outside to the front yard. She was rather disappointed and worried that this doctor had not helped her rid herself of these dreams. The dreams themselves, she could live with. And she actually enjoyed seeing this golden harpy. It was her father that worried her. If he discovered the nature of these dreams, as Charlie had done, then he may come to the same conclusions, that Shail was still interested in her. Her father would hunt the golden harpy down and kill him. Even she had become leery of the harpy but she definitely did not want Shail dead. Kari approached her vehicle just as a young skinny woman came sprinting up to her. "Kari, Kari!" the woman called as she neared the vehicle.

Kari recognized her as a past schoolmate. "Carol, it's nice to see you again," Kari fibbed. Carol had been one of those fickle children that chattered endlessly about nothing and had bored Kari to death. Kari remembered how she dreaded being around her.

"I'm so glad to see you," Carol exclaimed and threw her arms around Kari. "Now, you must tell me everything about Earth. I'm so jealous of you. I wish my parents had the credits to send me there. They could have at least sent me to school in Hampton but they want me to help them with the store, the clothing department, of course. You must come in and I'll show you what we have in stock. What am I talking about, you just came from Earth. I bet your closets are full of the latest fashions. Oh, you must let me come over so I can see them. It might help me with my orders." Kari listened politely, fighting the desire to flee as Carol rambled on and on. Kari could see that the people of Westend had remained the same. There was a slight pause in Carol's conversation, long enough for Kari to break in.

"Yes, we must discuss all of this sometime but I must be going now," Kari said quickly.

"You're not sick, are you? I saw you come from Doc's cottage. He's not altogether there, if you know what I mean and he's so rude and crabby. You should go to Terrance. That's where we all go unless it's an emergency. But I swear I wouldn't go to him if I were dying," Carol babbled on while fluffing her short bobbed hair do.

"I'm fine," Kari cut in.

"Let's get together tomorrow night," Carol said excitedly. "You'll love it. We're having a cookout on the beach. Some of the other girls from school will be there. Then you could tell us all about your trip to Earth. You'll be the life of the party. And I want you to meet my boyfriend, Jake. He and a bunch of his buddies went hunting and fishing on the islands. They usually cook what they bring back. It's so much fun. And I have just the guy for you. He's single and real cute. They'll be joining us on the beach as soon as they dock. Please say you'll come. You won't regret it, I promise."

Kari sighed a little. "I swore, I was going to change and learn to be more social able. This would be the real test. An evening with Carol," she thought. Kari smiled and turned towards Carol. "It sounds like fun. What time?" Kari asked.

"Around six. It's the last dock after the harbor. You can't miss it. It's right by the old shack. You remember, the shack?" she asked.

"Yes, I know where it is. Do you want me to bring something? Food? Or drink?"

"No, just yourself. We'll have everything there including the men."

"I can hardly wait," Kari said as she told another fib. "Good-bye," Kari said while slinking down into the seat of the vehicle and waved to Carol. She drove down the main street until out of the little town. The quiet of the vehicle consumed her. She was not look forward to tomorrow night but perhaps she might get along with others at this party, just as she had gotten along with Ted. She wondered if any of these girls had harpy encounters, as she had. They were the same age. Perhaps they had some of the answers she needed. She also had wanted to see the western coast and ocean since she came back. This would be the opportunity to do it.

Kari drove the dirt highway toward home and took the fork that would lead her to the estate. Slowly she brought the vehicle to a stop as she stared at an overgrown trail that led deep into the jungle. Kari stared at this old logging road for some time, while the vehicle hovered in place. It was the old road that led to the small lake. She swallowed hard as she recalled her last trip down this trail. It was where she had met him a decade ago. The road invoked her longing emotions. Of all the places on Dora, this place held her most cherished memory and now her worse fears. She closed her eyes and could still envision his deep blue eyes as he looked down on her as she lay beside the small lake. "I have to go and confront this spell, he and this place hold over me."

Despite all the warnings, she turned the vehicle on to the ancient logging road. It appeared that the road had not been used in years since huge ferns were now growing in the center of it. Kari adjusted the height of the terrain vehicle to its full capacity of four feet from the ground to clear the foliage and she proceeded slowly forward. The vehicle glided over fallen tree trunks that lay across this road. They were victims of great storms that came with the wet season. Large bushes and young trees encroached upon this narrow path the further she traveled. The jungle was reclaiming this man-made road and in a few more years, it would not exist. She had gone several miles when she came to a massive tree that lay across her path. Its tall limbs stretched upward as it rested on its side. Kari could see that there was no way over this obstacle. She set the hover down and killed the engines as she got out to survey if there was any way around the fallen tree. There was none. She looked beyond the tree and knew the lake had to be near. If she traveled on foot through the jungle heading east, she would come out on the opposite side of the lake from where she had visited as a child. She would be directly under the trisom trees instead of across the lake from them. Closing the door to the vehicle, she took a few steps into the trees. Suddenly she stopped and returned to the vehicle. Reaching inside, Kari took the laser gun from its compartment. Shaking her head with disdain. "It's for the wild animals" she tried to convince herself. But her heart was heavy because she knew, that she needed it to protect herself from the harpies. An anxiety flooded her emotions, hating this fear of them that had crept into her mind. Sticking the weapon into her belt, she started on this journey to the lake.

Kari crept deep into the forest, stepping quietly as she moved between the shadows of the jungle floor. Small flying lizards leaped from branch to branch in front of her as she roused the hiding insects they fed on. Pushing some blue ferns aside, she jumped back startled. She had nearly walked into some large purple vines. The vines looked harmless but she recognized them as carnivorous foliage that would grab her if she came too close. Sure enough, one of the vine-ends rose to sense its prey. Moving on, she stepped more cautiously. Colorful six limb birds floated on the white bark tree branches as they sang their merry little tunes. Then she noticed one of them, held a trisom fruit in its feathered arms. Finally, she came upon some young trisom saplings that grew in the wet low soil. The grove must be near. She went a little further and saw the towering trisoms that bordered the edge of the lake. It was late in the season but Kari could see a few trees still held the bright yellow fruit. Walking beneath them, the fallen scattered fruit rested on the ground. She looked to the branches overhead and could see they held no animals or harpies. A strong breeze blew across the lake making the trisom trees sway back and forth. Kari sat down on a large rock beneath the trees. She was hot and tired after the long trek through the woods. Wiping the sweat from her brow, she peered across the lake at the beach where the golden harpy had carried her to safety from the water as a child. "He just can't be dangerous. I just can't believe it," she said to herself. The breeze across the lake blew her blond hair away from her shoulder as it cooled her oppressed weary body. Time passed and this place seemed to renew her spirits. She felt alive and free here and leaving it, was hard. She glanced at her timepiece and knew she must leave soon if she would make it home before her father. Glancing at the scattered fruit on the ground, she decided to take some back with her. Maria could make a wonderful pie with them. She picked over the undamaged fruit and placed them in the front of her shirt. As she reached for the last one her shirt could possibly hold, she felt a presence behind her though she had heard no sound. Kari whirled around and jumped with fear as she saw a tall brown winged harpy standing only ten feet beyond her. She dropped all of the fruit, as one of them rolled towards his feet. She was so startled that she froze for a moment. She breathed rapidly and stared up at him. The harpy did not move but just looked at her calmly. Then, Kari recognized him. It was the same brown harpy that had come to her in the road outside of Terrance. Dread consumed her, as she jerked the laser gun from her belt and pointed it toward him. This could be no coincidental meeting, for a harpy to travel that far. He had to be following her. The harpy still stood quietly and did not move to flee or threaten her in any way. Kari was scared but she still could not help but admire him. His slender six-foot body and wings seemed to tower over her. He glanced with his deep green eyes toward the beach and then at Kari, as if he was trying to convey something to her. He flung the dark brown hair from his eyes as the wind blew it over them.

"Have you come to take me?" Kari asked with a frightened voice.

He shook his head slightly to mean "No," as he continued to watch her.

Then she heard a voice enter her mind. "You are his," the male voice said. "Go to him," it said again.

"I am not his," Kari said out loud to the harpy's silent voice.

The harpy breathed deeply and sadness seemed to fill his eyes. He reached down and picked up the fruit that had rolled to his feet. He stepped toward Kari unconcerned about the weapon she held in her hand. He soon was right in front of her and held out the fruit to her. Kari slowly lowered the weapon. This harpy knew she would not harm him. And for some reason, she sensed that he would not hurt her as well. She took the fruit from him as she looked up into his mournful piercing eyes. "He needs you," came the silent voice again. Kari looked at him with a questioning. The harpy lowered his head to her as he raised his wings. In a flash, he leaped into the air as his powerful wings fluttered for a moment over her and then he flew across the lake and disappeared into the trees.

Kari dropped the fruit and staggered over to the rock that she had sat on earlier. She eased herself down as she tried to catch her breath. Putting her hands in front of her, she could see them shaking. It was as if she had just stepped off a fast thrill ride. The experience had scared her but at the same time, filled her with joy. She sat for a long time dwelling on this harpy's words though they were few. They had filled her with more unanswered questions about her roll with the harpies. She wondered why this brown harpy had come to her twice and she still had not seen Shail. He had only come to her in dreams. She instinctively knew that the "he" this harpy spoke of, was the golden male. "If he needs me, why doesn't he come himself," she thought. She was suddenly filled with apprehension. If Shail had come to take her, could she have refused him or even protected her self? "I could never hurt a harpy," she muttered with the realization. Now Kari was even more leery and concerned. The harpies knew as well as she, that her affection for them had made her vulnerable. Charlie had said that her sixth sense could be a curse, if it drew the harpies to her. He had been right. It was drawing the harpies to her.

The afternoon was gone and evening approached as Duran was low in the red sky. Kari jumped up and perceived that she would be late getting home. She quickly gathered some of the fruit and darted into the woods as she moved rapidly towards her vehicle. Tired and frustrated, she finally reached the old road. After a half a mile on it, she came upon her vehicle. Kari opened the door and tossed the fruit on the empty passenger seat. She started to get in when she felt the laser gun in her belt. Placing it on the fruit, she mumbled with disgust, "A lot of good it did me," knowing it was useless against a harpy.

Kari pushed the button to start the hover vehicle. The vehicle reversed direction back down the overgrown trail. At last she reached the main road, as darkness would soon come. The miles went quickly now and before long, she found herself in front of the house. It was dark when Kari stepped from the vehicle. Charlie stood in the shadows as he walked to her. "We were beginning to worry about you. Your father has been here for some time," he said with concern.

"I'm sorry, I'm late. I was delayed in town," she answered him.

"You should have used the com. and let us know you would be late," he said.

Kari raised an eyebrow to him. "Perhaps, I'm like you and enjoy my privacy," she said jokingly to him. Charlie did not find this funny as he frowned at her. Kari went in and found her father in his den. "I'm sorry I'm late, Dad. I just lost track of time and I ran into Carol Baker and you know how she loves to talk. In fact, she's invited me to a beach party tomorrow night. Says she has some guy she wants me to meet," she said nonchalantly.

Her father grinned. "That sounds like fun. But could you could please let Maria know next time you're going to be late. It'll save me from worrying."

"I will. I'll just need a minute to clean up," she said and went back into the foyer to go upstairs. Charlie stood in the foyer. His face was grave as he held in his arms the trisom fruit.

"Should I take these to the kitchen?" he asked somberly.

Kari stopped short and stared back at him. "Yes, I picked them along the road to Westend," she said lowering her eyes.

"Trisom trees only grow near water and there are none along that road. I also see you had use of your laser gun, for it is out of its compartment." Kari knew there was no deceiving this wise old Indian.

"Yes, Charlie, I went to the lake. That's why I'm late, that's why I have the fruit and I took the gun with me. I had to go. I just had to see it again. He wasn't there," she said as she quickly ascended the stairs before he could lecture her. She glanced back down when she had reached the top. Charlie just gazed as her with sad eyes as he shook his head and wandered toward the kitchen. Kari walked into her room and threw herself down on the bed in confusion. She hated all this deceit, especially with Charlie. "All these years, I had a purpose. It was to save the harpies and come to know them, to see the golden harpy again. Now, nothing makes sense," she thought to herself. The harpies had become somewhat like an addicting drug. Despite all the warnings, she was drawn to them. They brought her fear and joy at the same time. She wanted to be free of them, like any drug user would confess when they lied and hurt their loved ones. But deep down, they longed for these drugs as Kari longed for this golden male. She knew the battle laid within her self. She was beginning to realize that she did not have the strength it would take to free herself from this hold, this spell he had over her. She shut her eyes and knew why Charlie had wished he had killed him when he had the chance. Only his death, would free her. And this brought her great sorrow. "Tonight, when he comes to me in my dreams, I must tell him to break the spell now or his life could be in danger," she thought. It would only be a matter of time before her father found out that she still longed and loved him. Charlie knew already.

Kari climbed off the bed and made her way to the bathroom to clean up. She ascended into the cool water of the shower. It refreshed her. She finally found herself coming to terms with the whole matter. "I just can't worry about my fate or his any longer. This anguish and these harpy encounters are driving me mad," she thought. Kari realized her own thoughts might hold some truth. Women lost their minds when taken by a harpy. Kari left the shower and dressed. She went down the stairs to dinner.

Charlie and her father were in the den. Kari glanced at Charlie and wondered if he had confided in her father yet. But her father smiled broadly at her approach, which told her, he had kept quiet. "I think it's wonderful that you're going to reacquaint yourself with your old classmates. I'm surprised, you never cared to be around them when you were a child," her father said.

"Well, people change and so must I," she said. Marie had come in the room and announced dinner. The table was set with assorted fruits and a large roast beef, surrounded by potatoes. They took the same seats as the night before. Kari's father sliced some of the meat and offered it to Kari."

"No thanks, Dad, I'll just stick with the fruit and some of the potatoes," she said. He glanced at Charlie and Charlie returned the glance with a critical look. Kari could not help but notice this exchange.

"So, have you become a vegetarian now?" he asked.

"I guess I have. I just don't care for meat any more. I really didn't enjoy it that much as a child," she answered.

Maria came in and noticed Kari's plate. "You don't like the roast?" she asked.

"I'm just not in the mood for it," Kari tried to explain.

"I can cook you some chicken."

"No, really. I'm fine. Just keep the fruit and vegetables around," Kari said with a smile, wondering why her eating habits had become such an issue.

"Tell me about your visit to town. Did you see Doc or was he off on one of his fishing trips?" her father asked, changing the subject.

"I saw him and he said to tell you that he's still kicking," she remarked.

Her father laughed. "That sounds like him."

"He did tell me something of interest. He said that the licing moss, the golden harpy put on my leg, actually saved my life by drawing out the poison. Said, I would have died without it."

"Yes, well, if they sent more scientists to this planet, they would have discovered the properties of that moss long ago. Just like these swarms. If they put some money in research on Dora, I'd have an insecticide that worked by now," her father said with disgust.

Kari could feel his anger. There was a long moment of silence before her father spoke again. "I'm sorry, dear. Doc did tell me about that moss. I'm a little on edge right now. Another swarm hit just east of here and barely missed the estate. They're getting closer and there's nothing I can do about it." He took Kari's hand. "I need to get a grip on my anger. I guess the mention of harpies still sets me off," he said in a low voice. "The swarms have me worried and I'm still worried about the harpies and you."

Kari smiled slightly. "We won't talk about them any more then."

"No, that's not what I want. That subject has been hush, hush in this house long enough. And it has brought too much heartache to both of us. We'll talk about it tonight after dinner and then we'll bury it." Kari just nodded and bit her lip.

They finished dinner and Charlie excused himself. The old Indian wanted no part of this coming conversation. He wondered just how truthful this discussion would be between the two of them. He shook his head sadly as he walked outside into the night air. He loved both of them dearly, but knew their hearts and differences. It had become apparent, that she still cared about the harpies and loved this golden male and this love could end her life. Her father still despised these male harpies. Once the truth was known to both of them, it would destroy their fragile relationship and possibly it could destroy both of them. They were headstrong in their beliefs and convictions. There was no middle ground in this impossible dilemma. He was an old man caught in the middle, unwilling to choose sides. There was nothing he could do to stop this. All his advice would fall on deaf ears. He walked into the meadow under a bright stars filled night. The two large wolfhounds walked along side of him, happy for the company.

John poured himself a glass of wine and offered some to Kari, but she declined. "You don't like meat or wine? Didn't they teach you about the finer things in life on Earth?" he asked.

Kari laughed a little. "I had access to all of that, but I guess I never developed a taste for them."

John now took a seat across from her. "So, what would you like to talk about your mother, the harpies? I want to clear the air tonight and get everything out in the open," he said.

Kari sighed. "Maybe a little of both," she answered softly. "Your hate of the harpies is understandable with my mother's death."

John leaned back in the chair. "The truth is, Kari, I blame myself as much as that harpy that came to her. I'm as guilty as he was. If it wasn't for my anger, I would have set that laser gun to stun and she would still be here now. I just wanted him dead and my wife paid for my anger with her life. And I'll take this guilt to my grave," he said quietly.

"Oh, Dad, it was just a terrible accident."

"It was no accident, that he came to take her. If he had succeeded, I would have never seen her again," he grumbled.

"Why do you think he wanted her?" Kari asked.

"He wanted take her back to his harpies and probable force her to become his mate," he said angrily as he rose to pour another glass of wine.

"Is that what other women have said?" she asked quietly.

"Other women?" He looked at her puzzled.

"Other women that have come back after being taken by a harpy?" she asked again.

"Kari, very few woman are found after a harpy takes them. The few that are rescued have no mind left. They're in shock. They can't even speak. They usually end up taking their own lives. Some have been known to wander in the jungle until they die. I have never heard of any woman surviving it and coming back normal. It's a fate worse than death," he said harshly.

Kari was deep in thought for some time. "Maybe it's possible that there are good harpies and bad harpies, just like men. It may have been a bad harpy that tried to take mother," she tried to reason.

He shook his head. "Kari, they're not like men. When are you going to realize this? They may have a human body, but they're minds are like an animal. It's just like saying there's good grogins and bad grogins. All wild animals are the same. It's in their nature to be what they are," he tried to explain.

"But the young golden who saved me, was he not good?" she argued.

He shook his head. "I knew that one would come up. Look, Kari, you were a child. As far as I know, no male harpy has ever taken a child, thank God. And he was a young male not a fully sexually mature yet. It was apparent, he was still very immature and cocky. He didn't even know about laser guns. He boldly postured and challenged those men even after two blasts nearly hit him. It's possible that he may have only saved you so he could claim you later when you were an adult. Believe me, I've considered this and it may be a mistake by allowing him to live."

"I went to the Hampton zoo and a vet there said that there hasn't been any reported cases of harpies taking women in some years," she said with almost a whisper.

"Yes, well that's Hampton. The east has been so over hunted, I doubt if any harpies remain there. But this is the outback and there are plenty of them still left. And, I suppose turning the estate into a harpy preserve has increased their numbers," he said as he looked at her with a questioning. "You're still looking for a reason to defend these creatures, aren't you?" he asked.

Kari sighed. "I'm just trying to understand. The golden harpy saved my life and it's difficult to distrust anything or anyone who has done that for you. I'm just having a hard time believing that he would harm me."

Her father stood up and poured another glass of wine as he looked down at her. He pushed the blond hair back from his fore head. "You still care about him. After all these years, you're still infatuated with that damn golden," he stated angrily as he paced. "I can't believe this," he chuckled with a sarcastic tone. "I sent you to Earth so you would forget about him. Forget about these lousy harpies. I hoped you would meet some nice guy on Earth and all this would be behind you. This craziness would be out of your mind. Seems my plan back-fired."

Kari could see that this had inflamed his rage against the harpy. "Dad, please. I don't know if I still care about him. I'm just very confused right now. I've been gone ten years now and I was not happy on Earth. When you're that unhappy, sometimes you cling to the only good memories you have. The harpy was one of those memories. It's difficult for me to turn against my beliefs that I had nurtured all these years. Just give me some time. I'm going to that beach party tomorrow night, mainly, so I can talk to others my own age about the harpies," she said.

He nodded his head. "Maybe it would be better if I eliminated this threat to you and end your confusion." he said, more to himself than to her.

Kari could feel a panic overtake her with her father's suggestion. She stood up. "No, Dad, you would not end my confusion. You would only end any future relationship that we could have. He would die. And I would be filled with the same guilt that you carry for my mother, if I was the cause of his death. I don't believe I could live with that kind of guilt. I'm no longer a child and I understand the danger of going with a harpy. I promise you, no harpy will take me," she said with conviction that left her a little shaken.

"All right, Kari, I won't hunt down this golden harpy as long as he stays away from you. But know this, I would sacrifice our relationship and your happiness if it came to your safety."

Kari could only nod her understanding. "I'm going to bed now," she said quietly.

Her father put his arms around her and gave her a kiss on the forehead. "Good night then," he said quietly.

Kari walked from the living room, leaving her father deep in thought as he swallowed the last of the wine in his glass. He was tormented and conflicted by the whole conversation with her. It was apparent that she still cared about the harpies. Ten long years on Earth had not extinguished her passion and fondness for these harpies or this young blond male. But was it admiration as anyone might feel toward certain pets that had befriended her or was it based on true love for this harpy that she had been with so long ago. Did this male have a hold on her or was it just her childhood commitment, she still clung to. He certainly did not want to destroy their relationship, which hung on a thread, as it was. John decided to give her a little more time. But if there was any clue that she was in love with this creature, then relationship or not, he and his men would relentlessly hunt down this golden whether it was innocent or not. "I'll not have two of these stinking golden harpies destroy both of the women I love," he thought to himself.

Kari crawled into the soft, fluffy bed. She was plagued by their conversation as much as her father. Had she sealed Shail's fate with her honesty, she wondered? She knew her father would have discovered she was still devoted to the harpies before long. And she was no good at this lying and deceit. She was raised that one's word is what made a person. It was better he knew of her confusion and indecision about the harpies. But, if he learned of these dreams or the recent brown harpy encounters, then this would send him over the edge and her father would go after Shail and kill him.

She closed her eyes and waited to fall asleep. When Shail came to her in her dreams, she would have to make it clear that the spell must be broken now. Although they may have been meant for each other, that it was not to be. That his life was in danger and no love was worth that. She thought long into the night about how to dissuade him from coming. Finally, she was in a deep slumber.

Kari woke as she squinted her eyes with the morning light. It was late morning. She lay wrapped in the sheets and pillows. As her mind cleared, she suddenly realized that she had no memory of dreaming. She concentrated, but could not remember anything. She breathed a sigh of disappointment and relief at the same time, while she climbed out of her bed to get dressed.

Downstairs in the kitchen, she found Maria and her father. "I hope I didn't wake you with my dreams," she said hesitantly to her father.

"No, I never heard you. I even went in, to make sure your balcony door was locked and you were sound asleep. Doc must have taken care of the problem."

"No, he didn't give me anything," she mustered.

"Well, good, the dreams took care of themselves. I have to run now. The barges will be at the harbor today and we're running at full capacity, trying to get the lumber out while we can. I'll see you tonight," he said as he kissed Kari good-bye.

"I'm going to that cookout tonight on the beach. I probably won't be home until late."

"I forgot. Well, if you're going to be real late, call, if you don't mind," he said as he headed for the side door of the kitchen.

"I will," she answered.

Kari hung around the kitchen, talking to Maria. After a while, she noticed Charlie working outside in the small vegetable garden along side of the house. Kari wandered out to him as he weeded a row of tomatoes. "Father and I had a long talk about mother and the harpies," she said to him quietly. He looked up at her, but said nothing. "I suggested that the harpy, which tried to take mother, was evil and possibly not all harpies were like this." The Indian still worked silently. "He said they were all the same even the young golden."

"He is right about that. They are all the same," Charlie finally responded as he stopped hoeing now. "Your father now knows you still care for the harpies?"

"He knows I'm confused right now. I don't know what the truth is anymore. It's like my heart and mind are working against each other."

"They will merge when all truths are revealed to you. Now you travel in a dense fog. You must wade through it even though it blinds you. When you reach the other side, all will be clear. No one can help you in this task. They can only give you their knowledge along the way and hope you take the right path that leads to happiness," he said as he returned to his weeding.

"Well, you should worry less. My golden harpy does not come in my dreams any longer. Perhaps the spell you spoke of is broken. I'm relieved of this," she commented sadly.

Charlie looked up again as he studied her face. "It is not broken. You are only relieved, since you fear for his safety. I can see he still holds your heart," he said wearily. "I will only give you my advice once more and then we are finished with this talk. The golden harpy will only bring you misery and even death, if you go with him. Once there is a bonding, there will be no second chance for you. Your life, as you know it, will be over." He uttered with remorse.

Kari nodded her understanding. She picked up a rake and began working quietly along side of Charlie. The serenity of the plants and soil consumed them. By late afternoon, the garden was free of weeds and the new seeds had been sown. Kari went inside to prepare for the cookout.

"You shouldn't have to work so hard," Maria stated as Kari washed her hands in the kitchen. "Your father bought an expensive weeding machine that would take care of that garden with the push of a button. But that old fool refused to use it and does it by hand."

Kari laughed. "I guess I'm a fool as well. I enjoy working with the dirt and vegetables."

Maria shook her head with disgust. "I think you spent too much time with that old Indian when you were a child. Digging in the dirt is not what a young lady should be doing," she commented. Kari just smiled at Maria's frustration. She went to her room to clean up and get ready for the beach party. Soon she was in her vehicle, traveling west.

It was only four o'clock but Kari wanted to spend some time at the harbor and do a little more sightseeing before she met Carol and the others on the beach. The dirt highway from Terrance came to an end at the harbor. It was on this road that people in the surrounding areas would travel to meet these barges destined for Hampton. The main export was the rare timber of her father's estate but the small farmers also brought their surplus vegetable and livestock to meet these barges. It was the cheapest form of transport to go around the continent rather than across it.

Soon the road ended and she was at the harbor. It had grown in the last ten years. There were more docks with barges floating along side of them. She passed several of the box shaped barges that held the freeze-dried foods as men worked the machinery to load them. Several piers away, she saw the flat barges that were loaded with the brightly colored sheets of lumber. She steered her vehicle towards them. The noisy machines were lifting large bundles off the giant transports and placing them on the waiting barges. Kari notice, they all carried the name of Turner displayed on their side. She pulled up along side of a man as he supervised this loading process. "Is Mr. Turner here?" she asked him.

"You just missed him. He went back to the mill," he yelled over the heavy equipment. "Can I help you?" he asked.

"No, thanks, I'm his daughter and I just stopped by to say hi. I'll see him later. Thanks," she said. The man smiled at the gorgeous girl and nodded as he watched her drive away.

Kari drove on past more piers and barges as her vehicle traveled the wide smooth shell-covered lot. She finally reached the end of it and came to a narrow coastal sand road. In the distance, she could see the little shack that sat off the beach. After a half a mile, she came upon the old weathered shack. Extending from it was a dilapidated wooden dock. Several ill kept boats were moored to the landing. Kari parked along side a few late model terrain vehicles. She assumed that these vehicles must belong to the men that were out fishing. Climbing out, she made her way to the shack in the loose sand. The shack was filled with rusted traps and other fishing equipment that had seen a better day. Alongside of this structure were a fish-cleaning table and a water hose. She turned the handle as a stream of cool water gushed from it. Kari took a sip and it tasted like water from a stream. Next to this table, a high pole extended from the ground with a chain and hook at the end of it. It was apparent that some of the fish that were caught here were of good size to require the use of this pole. In front of the shack, Kari noticed a large fire pit. The charred ashes and stumps were inside of it, surrounded by unburned logs for sitting. The wind blew strong off the water as she made her way down the long rickety dock. Duran was setting on the ocean. "It would be cool tonight," she thought and was glad she had brought a light jacket. She reached the end of the dock and placed the jacket beneath her as she sat down on it. The barges down the coast began to leave the large piers as she watched them motor out to the wide expanse. After they were clear, their hover engines would engage and they would rise above the waves. The engines would reach full throttle, moving them at great speed until they were out of sight.

Kari reveled in this peaceful setting. The colorful red and yellow sea birds began to land on the shore to prepare for the coming night. Only the wind and their occasional screams could be heard. She watched as they gracefully glided on wind currants before landing. She breathed deeply and her thoughts drifted to the harpies. "To be able to fly like that, must be wonderful," she envisioned. Kari was so submerged in the birds and tranquility that she failed to notice the footsteps on the dock behind her.

"It is beautiful here, isn't it?" came a soft woman's voice.

Kari glanced up and saw a young woman, close to her own age, standing along side of her. "Oh, I didn't even hear you come up," Kari said a little surprised.

The woman nodded and lowered her eyes. "I'm sorry if I startled you," she apologized.

Kari smiled. "It's alright. The wind is blowing so hard, it's difficult to hear anything."

"May I sit with you?"

Kari nodded as they both now sat at the end of the dock. "Are you here for Carol's cookout?" Kari asked her.

The she nodded shyly. "My name's Kari," Kari said as she extended her hand.

"I am Lea," she answered as they clasped hands.

"Yes, it is beautiful here." Kari commented, looking back at the water.

"You must have missed it," Lea said quietly. Kari gazed at her. "Carol told me of your travels to Earth," Lea said quickly. Kari now noticed how lovely this girl was. Her long brown hair drifted on the wind against the red sky.

"Lea, you're one of the few people that has said that to me, that I would miss Dora. Everyone else wants to hear how wonderful Earth was," Kari said. Lea only smiled at her. Kari instantly liked this strange, quiet girl. "So, you're a friend of Carol's?" Kari asked.

"I am acquainted with her. My mother and I make jams and jellies and sell them to Carol's father at his store."

Kari and Lea could hear the slam of a vehicle door as it came from the shack. Kari stood up and could see Carol and two other girls. She waved to them. And they waved at Kari to join them. "I guess we better go say, hello," Kari commented with a little dread. Lea rose and followed Kari off the dock. Carol's booming voice could be heard above the wind as it broke this tranquil setting.

"You're here already. And I thought we'd be early. You remember Beth and Cindy from school? And Lea, I see you showed up. That's a first," Carol said sarcastically. Kari said hello to the other girls as Carol took her arm.

"Can you help me, Kari?" I have a few more things back at the vehicle." Carol said as she dragged Kari away from the others. "I just want to tell you that inviting Lea was not my idea. It was my father's. He suggested she join us when she came into the store today. Personally, she kind of gives me the creeps. She is so quiet. I think she's missing a few marbles, if you know what I mean. Now don't get me wrong, I tried to be her friend when her mother and her first moved here a few years ago. I invited her several times to join my friends in activities, but she always refused. That's why I'm rather surprised to see her now," Carol said as she stared over the vehicle at Lea.

"I find her rather charming. Maybe she just needs time to get used to strangers," Kari said with sympathy as she recalled her own isolation on Earth.

"Well, if you enjoy a one-sided conversation, then she's perfect," Carol snapped.

Kari smiled. "How could a conversation be anything but one-sided, when it included Carol," Kari thought to herself.

They finished unloading the food and drinks and set them on a small table that Carol had brought. Kari and Lea strolled on the beach gathering firewood, happy with the soothing sound of the ocean and wind rather than the chatter of voices. Carol and the other girl set up the food and lights for the coming darkness. Soon they had a blazing fire burning in the large pit as night came.

"Kari, you must tell us of Earth now." Carol said as they sat and watched the fire.

Kari reluctantly talked about Earth and the schools there. She did not reveal her disdain or the depression it had caused her since she knew these girls would not have understood. After a while, Kari changed the subject. "Tell me, why does your boyfriend and his friends travel so far to fish and hunt? Isn't the first island over a hundred miles from here?" Kari asked.

"Well, that's partly your father's fault since he banned hunting on his estate. Jake has to travel that far for a harpy." Carol answered nonchalantly.

Kari could feel her heart race and her blood pressure rise as she slowly rose to her feet. "They're hunting harpies?" Kari exclaimed in shock and repulsion.

"Well, of course silly, nobody in their right mind would travel that far for any other animal."

Kari grabbed her jacket. "I can't stay here and see this," she said with contempt.

"Oh, come on, Kari. You've seen a dead harpy before. Your father holds the record on the planet for a pair of golden wings. He hung them over the doorway of his house for years," Carol mocked.

"How do you know this?" Kari asked angrily.

"Everyone in Westend knows this," Carol said in a huff.

"He doesn't hunt them anymore," Kari stated harshly.

"What, have you become a harpy lover?" Carol taunted her and giggled.

Lea leaned over to Kari, "Don't answer her. Some things are better left unsaid."

"Stay out of this, Lea. It's none of your business," Carol screeched with contempt.

Lea lowered her head. "You are right. It is best if I go," Lea said quietly as she got up and began walking toward the road.

Kari went along side of her. "Lea, I'll go with you," Kari said as she approached her.

"No, you should stay here. I wish to go alone," Lea said as she saw Carol walk swiftly towards them.

"Listen, Kari, I don't know why we're arguing over something so silly. Jake and his idiot friends have only gotten three this year and they go every weekend. They usually strip their wings over there. Very few harpies even survive the journey over the water. I've only seen one live one gutted and stripped on the pole here," Carol claimed.

Kari looked at her with horror. "You've watched this?" Kari exclaimed.

"Oh, Kari, it's not that big a deal. By hanging them alive, the blood flows out of the wings and doesn't get on their feathers. The thing only tossed and squirmed for a little while before it went into shock. Then it just hung docilely while the guys cut it up. But, like I said, I doubt if they even got one," Carol pleaded.

Kari turned to leave with Lea but she had disappeared into the darkness. Suddenly the sound of a motor could be heard coming from the dock. Kari could see the lights of the boat as it pulled into an empty slot.

"Come on, Kari. They're here. Maybe you can talk them out of the evils of harpy hunting." Carol said as she took Kari's arm and led her down the dock. Kari felt like she was in a bad dream but had to know its outcome as she reluctantly walked along side of Carol towards the boat. The boat lights lit up the dock and Kari could see a young man jogging towards them.

"Baby, you're not going to believe it," he yelled as he reached Carol and picked her up in his arms. "We are rich. I'm taking you to Hampton for a trip you won't forget," he said with excitement.

"What, Jake?" Carol asked.

"I got him. I finally got him. I've been after this one for years," Jake said as Kari listened. "The golden harpy I've been telling you about."

Kari couldn't breathe as she stumbled past them toward the boat. It was like her guts had been ripped out of her. She reached the large boat with a cabin. A small hovercraft was strapped to the top. One of the other men was securing a line when Kari looked down into the boat. He smiled at her. "You want to see the gold harpy?" he asked.

Kari could only nod to him as she climbed on board the boat. "Is he dead?" Kari muttered.

"Not yet, but we're fixing to string him up real soon. He's a real little fighter. Most don't last as long as him. Jake figured you girls would appreciate seeing the whole animal, rather than just his wings. Doubt if you'll get this chance again, these goldens are so rare. He's over here," the man said as he led Kari around some boxes in the middle of the deck. Kari swallowed hard as she followed the man. There on the deck, lay a mass of large cream and blood soaked wings attached to a slender limp body. He sat in a pool of his own blood as his wrists were bound and lashed to a boat cleat. His ankles were also tied together as he was forced to sit up against the side of the boat. One of his wings was twisted and broken from a laser gun blast. The golden harpy's head hung low, resting against his bound arms. Kari walked to him and knelt down. She slowly pushed back the blond hair, dripping with blood as she gazed into his face. It was him. It was Shail. Her eyes watered as a warm tear ran down her cheek. His eyes were shut and more blood trickled from his lips. She glanced down and saw another laser blast below his ribs in his side. She placed her hand to his chest and could feel his shallow breathing. Kari fathomed that this was the reason Shail had not come into her dreams last night. This was the fear and pain he suffered the night before as he spoke of the broken spell in their dreams. Now, Kari was living this nightmare.

"Miss, don't get too close. He may look dead but he could still hurt you," the man said kicking the harpy hard in his wounded side. Shail jumped with the searing pain and began breathing rapidly. He slowly opened his drained and mournful eyes.

"Don't," Kari screamed as this man moved to kick the harpy again. She put her hand to the side of the harpy's face. Shail's eyes began to focus on her as he turned his head toward her gentle hand and nuzzled her slightly. By now, Carol and Jake had come on board with the other two girls. Two more men appeared from the cabin below. One had his arm in a sling. Jake was cheerfully telling them of the hunt that lead to the golden harpy's capture. "We came across some fledglings in a tree. When they took off, I was able to wing one of them. We landed the hover and grabbed the little vermin before he could hide in the bushes. As soon as Hank snatched him up, bang, this golden harpy came sailing out of a tree. It was unbelievable. He kicked Hank's back and sent him crashing into a tree trunk and snatched up the fledgling."

"I think he broke my arm," said the man with the sling.

"Anyway I got a shot off and nailed him in his wing. He went down but then tried to flee on foot. I got him again in the side. We cornered him against a tree but he gave us a hell of fight. It took all of us to tie him down. Man, I've hunted enough harpies but this is the first time one has ever attacked us like that. Must be true what they say about goldens, they have more nerve and guts."

Kari half listened to this tale as her mind raced. Jake now noticed Kari as she had her hand against the side of the harpy's face. "Hey, you need to stay away from him. He'll take off one of your fingers," he told Kari.

"I don't think so," she answered quietly. They all noticed that the harpy was nuzzling Kari's caressing hand as he closed his eyes.

"This is Kari Turner, John Turner's daughter. She doesn't like harpy hunting," Carol mocked.

"What are you going to do with him?" Kari asked, not turning her attention from Shail.

"We're going to string him up on the pole and let him feel some real pain before we cut off his wings. I've been waiting for two days for this," Hank said with vengeance as he held his broken arm.

Kari brushed away the tear before she stood up and faced these people. Mustering her courage and hiding her feelings, she glared at Jake with cold hard stare. "I'll buy this animal off of you. How much do you want?" she asked with a strong and controlling tone.

Jake laughed slightly. "What are you going to do with him? Make him a pet? Even if he survives those wounds, harpies won't live in a cage. Believe me, I've tried it. I can barely keep them alive to make it back to the mainland even with minor injuries." he smirked.

"What I do with him is my business. Do you want to sell him or not?" Kari asked impatiently, trying to control her bitterness.

Jake eyed her. "You're just like your father, aren't you? Think your superior to every one else," he seethed. "Sure, I'll sell him to you. You, Turners got money. I want fifty thousand credits. That's the going price for a set of taxidermy gold wings in Terrance."

Kari realized she didn't have that kind of money on her. And even if she could get it, it wouldn't be until tomorrow. Shail would never live that long without treatment.

"A pair of wings in perfect shape, might be worth that but one of his is broken and there's a lot of feather loss." Kari stated. She purposely assumed her father's hard business attitude to deal with these hunters rather than being meek and pleading for Shail's life. "But I have an offer that may interest you. Parked by the shack, is a brand new terrain vehicle easily worth at least forty-five thousand. I'll trade it for this harpy even though if he not worth it and the temporary use of your old vehicle so I can move the animal."

Jake realized that this delicate gorgeous girl was a tough tenacious woman, who could not be manipulated or fooled. Jake breathed deeply in contemplation. "Let me go look at it," he said solemnly as he stepped from the boat.

"Jake," Kari said firmly, "this offer is only good for a live harpy. If it dies before I take possession then you're stuck with your bunch of broken feathers. So, I'd make it quick." He nodded to her as he jogged down the dock towards the shack. Kari knelt back down by the harpy. She noticed an old knife sticking in the slat of the boat. She took it out and cut the rope attached to the cleat. Shail immediately collapsed on the deck.

"Hey, he's not yours yet." Hank yelled at her.

She just glared up at him with repulsion in her eyes. She then rested Shail's head in her lap. The harpy slowly reached for her with his bound hands and she took them. "Just hold on Shail," she whispered to him. He nuzzled her leg as he closed his eyes feeling a little secure while Kari gently stroked his face with her other hand. No one spoke as they watched in bewilderment the harpy respond to this gentle treatment. The harpy no longer appeared like a wild animal as he clasped Kari's hand and curled his weak body around her as he lay on his side. Beth and Cindy moved closer to Kari and the harpy.

"I've never seen a live one, only their wings. He's really seems very sweet and he's so beautiful," Beth commented as she stared closely at his face. Kari only nodded. Soon the sound of running feet could be heard on the wooden planks of the dock. Jake appeared out of the darkness. He looked at Kari with the harpy wrapped around her as its head rested in her lap. The harpy licked and nuzzled its nose against her hand for affection.

"What did you do, tame that little devil?" he chuckled.

"What's your answer?" Kari said seriously, failing to see any humor.

"You can have him as long as you throw in that brand new laser gun."

Kari breathed a slight sigh of relief as she carefully removed herself from the harpy's grasp. Shail lay motionless on the deck and drifted to sleep, too drained and weak to stay awake further.

Hank jerked Jake's arm. "I can't believe you're letting her take it. I really want to see him hang," Hank said disgruntled. Jake chuckled a little bit. "Look at it, Hank. It's almost dead. If we strung it up, it wouldn't even respond to any kind of torture. The fight is gone and it would just hang there. Besides," he whispered, "she's right about that wing. I doubt if I'd get much for the pair in Terrance. And that vehicle is worth plenty."

Kari heard part of this conversation. "This deal is not over until the harpy is in a vehicle and still alive," she snapped.

Jake smiled. "Yes, Miss Turner," Jake said as he leaned over the comatose harpy. Jake placed one arm under the harpy's neck and the other under his legs and wings as he picked the harpy up and cradled him in his arms.

"Want some help?" Tom offered.

"Nay, he doesn't weigh much. I got him. As long as Miss Turner will open the vehicle door when we get there." Jake stepped off the boat and strolled down the dock carrying the lifeless body. When they reached an old blue vehicle, Kari opened the back of it as Jake rested the harpy on a worn blanket. He put his hand on Shail's chest. "Still breathing. Guess he's yours."

Kari ran to the driver seat and jumped in. "I don't know when I can get this transport back to you," she said in a hurry.

"Take your time," he said as he leaned in the window. "Let me ask you. Did your Daddy give you that brand new vehicle?"

Kari only nodded as she pushed the start button several times.

"Your father fired me from his mill for poaching on his land. When he finds out you traded that busted up harpy for your new vehicle," he laughed, "just tell him, it's pay back time."

Kari ignored him as the vehicle finally started to hover. She threw the old vehicle in reverse and pushed it to its top speed as it traveled down the coastal road. Soon she passed the harbor and was finally on the road to Westend. Kari decided to take Shail to old Doc. He was the only one she could think of right now. She glanced back at the motionless body and wondered if he still was alive. "Please don't die on me," she whispered more to herself. She had been strong and assertive throughout the whole deal but now that she was alone, the tears began to flow down her cheeks as her emotions came flooding out. Ten long years of waiting and dwelling on this single being and now he lay dying behind her. She pushed her wet golden hair out of her face as she tried to get a grip on her feelings. She stared at her hands and they were stained with his blood. "This can't be happening. It just can't end like this," she sobbed as the dark jungle flew past. The trip Westend seemed to be taking forever.

At last, she arriving in the little town as the vehicle sped through the quiet main street. She saw the yellow cottage and took the terrain vehicle close to the front door. Only a porch light was lit in the dark cottage. Kari leaped from the vehicle and ran to the front door. She rang the bell and beat on the door as she called for Doc. A light finally came on inside and in a minute the door opened. Doc was in his bedclothes as he peered out at her.

"Hurry, Doc. It's an emergency," she screamed as she led him to the vehicle.

"Okay, Okay. I'd be disappointed if it wasn't," he said calmly as he followed her.

Kari flung the back door open as a small light came on and shown on the still harpy. Doc looked in and then turned to Kari with a frown on his face. "You got me out of bed in the middle of the night for a harpy," he growled as he turned back toward the house.

Kari grabbed his arm. "Please, Doc. He's dying and I have no other place to take him," she cried. She dropped to her knees as she took hold of the old man's hand. "Please, I'm begging you," she moaned as she bent her head down and began sobbing out of control.

"Come now, dear. It's only a harpy," he said as he guided her to her feet.

"He's not just a harpy to me," she whimpered.

He took a close look at her as the porch light illuminated on her damp face. "Aren't you the Turner girl that was here yesterday?" he asked.

Kari could only nod. He looked back into the vehicle at the harpy. "Darn thing is a golden. Didn't even notice it with all the stained blood on his wings. Haven't seen his likes…." He paused in mid sentence and looked at Kari. She was leaning over the harpy gently pushing the hair from his face as she caressed him. Her hands were trembling as she touched the unconscious harpy and whimpered softly. Doc took a deep breath and sighed. It was very apparent how much she cared for this dying creature. "Is this the same golden, who put the moss on your mogel bite?" he asked.

Kari could only nod again.

Doc sighed. "Well, let me take a look at him. I'm awake now and I owe this little guy that much," he said with a tired voice. He leaned over the harpy and pulled back his wing to expose his body. He shook his head. "Oh, dear. That wound looks like it's at least two days old. I'm surprised he's still alive with the blood loss and all." He stood back from the vehicle and took Kari by the arms. "I know this harpy saved your life and you feel an obligation to try and save his. But this poor creature is suffering and he's beyond my help. Let me put him out of his misery. I have the drugs and he won't feel a thing. It's the kindest thing we can do for him now," he said gently.

Kari jerked free of the old doctors hold and stepped away from him. Her face was filled with horror and shock as she stared at the old man. "You want to kill him?" she stammered.

"This poor little fellow has suffered enough. It would be cruel keep him alive any longer," Doc said compassionately.

"No," she said as she shook her head. "He's not some injured animal. Not to me. He's been my whole life. I love him. You might as well give me your drugs too," she cried. Kari went back to the harpy and kissed Shail tenderly on his cheek. Wrapped her arms around his neck and buried her head against his wing and chest. She began to weep.

Doc watched her for a long moment as she frantically held and kissed the fragile limp body as if her love could possibly save his life. There was no doubt, how much she loved this winged male creature and it was the kind of love that could break one's soul. Doc calmly placed a hand on her shoulder. Kari stared up at him through her wet long blond hair. "I haven't done this kind of surgery in over twenty years. And our patient is very unstable. But, I guess I have nothing better to do. I can't turn you and your golden away without trying," he sighed.

She leaped up from the harpy and threw her arms around the old doctor. "Thank you, Doc. Thank you," she mustered between sniffles.

"Don't thank me. I want you to understand something," he said very seriously. "Your harpy is probably going to die. I want you to realize this and don't get any false hope."

She nodded as she wiped the tears from her face with her sleeve. "I understand," she finally said.

"All right, I'm going to get a floating stretcher so we can get him inside. I'll be right back," he said as he hastily walked back to the cottage. Soon he returned with the floating bed. Kari and the old man rolled Shail gently on it and carry his slumbering body into the cottage and the small room that contained the ancient medical equipment Kari had seen on the previous day.

"If word got out that I was now treating harpies, they'd think I really lost my mind for good," Doc commented as they put Shail on the operating table. Under the bright floodlights of the exam room, the full extent of Shail's injuries could be seen. Cuts and abrasions covered his sleek body, where the men had kicked and beaten him. His ankles and wrists were still bound with ropes that were so tight, Doc had to cut them from him. Deep gashes were revealed, as the ropes came off. Doc shook his head, as he looked at the severely battered body. "Who did this?" he stormed.

"Some guy named Jake," Kari answered.

"Jake O'Connell, I know him. I delivered him. He was a rotten kid and now he's a rotten man. If he did this to a dog, he'd be arrested for animal cruelty." Doc grumbled. "It's one thing to hunt and kill a wild game animal but this torture of these poor harpies goes too far with some of these hunters," he said as he placed an oxygen mask over the harpy's face.

"Why do they do it?" Kari asked softly as she wiped another tear from her face.

"I suppose it's come kind of twisted justification. I don't think these men see the harpies as another game animal. They see them as seductive males that steal and molest women, so these hunters show no mercy. This harpy hunting gives them the legal right to vent their cruel aggression. I've heard of some pretty unspeakable things that have been done to harpies. Your boy here, could have gotten worse," he talked as he scanned Shail's injuries with a tiny monitor and prepared the wound for surgery. Doc pushed back the blond hair from Shail's face and examined a cut under his left eye. He smiled as he gazed at the harpy. "And sometimes I think these hunters are just plain jealous of these pretty little harpies. Imagine looking like this and being able to fly as well. Male harpies are always incredibly good looking. Makes me wonder if harpies are really guilty of stealing our woman," he chuckled. Doc finished with the scanning. "Well, they busted a few of his ribs but they'll heal and so will that wing, in time. But right now, that blast to his intestines is the major concern. I don't dare operate without a blood transfusion," he said as he eyed Kari. "And you, my dear, are going to provide the blood."

Kari looked at him puzzled. "I'm no doctor, but doesn't blood types have to match? I mean we're not even the same species. Won't this kill him?" she exclaimed.

Doc looked at her doubting face. "Without blood, he will surely die. Most animals don't have blood types and he's animal enough. Now I don't have time to argue about it. Just let me be the doctor here and trust me. If not, you can take your harpy elsewhere," he said gruffly.

"I have no choice but to trust you," she answered in a low sad voice. Kari sat down in a chair in the front room as Doc drew her blood. When he had finished, he told her to stay there a while. "I took quite a bit and I'm too old to pick you up if you faint," he mumbled as he returned to the operating room and the harpy. Kari waited in the other room for a short time. But her anxiety and anguish over this blood transfusion got to her. She stood up and indeed did feel dizzy but managed to walk to the doorway. "Is he all right?" she asked with concern.

"Your blood and his are compatible. He is doing fine," Doc said not even looking up from his patient. Kari could hear the buzz of the machines, surrounding this room as Doc used the medical lasers on the harpy's wound. "I'm surprised these old lasers still work. Haven't used them in years," he rambled. Doc seemed to be enjoying himself as he began humming throughout the operation. Kari leaned against the doorway and watched, feeling a little weak.

"I'm going to have to cut out these damaged intestines but he's got plenty to spare," Doc murmured more to himself.

"Can I help?" she asked.

He glanced at her. "You better take it easy. You're pretty pale. Maybe in a little while," he said engrossing himself back in his work.

"Well, may I use your communicator? I need to call home," she asked.

"There's one on the desk in the front room."

Kari looked at it behind her. "Do you have a portable com?"

He smiled at her. "There's one on the kitchen counter that has a location shut off."

Kari made her way to the kitchen and called home. Maria answered. "I was just leaving for the night. Your father is in his den. Do you want to talk to him?" Maria asked.

"No, just tell him I'm spending the night with Carol and I won't be home tonight."

"Okay, Miss Kari. I'll tell him," Maria said.

She wandered back to the small hospital room. "I'm feeling better now."

"Sure you can stomach this?" he asked. Kari only nodded.

"You can't help me with this surgery, but you can start cleaning up the deep cuts with antiseptic, save me from doing it. I'll seal them and deal with that broken wing later. I put an antibiotic patch on him. Should help fight the infections," Doc said.

Kari began washing and cleaning Shail's wounds with the medical soap and then applied the antiseptic. First she treated the broken wing that hung down from the table and then his wrists and ankles. As she removed the dry blood that covered his body, a rage began smoldering in her as she saw how terribly Shail must have suffered. "I should have killed them for this," she muttered with animosity under her breath.

Doc glanced up at her briefly with surprise. "You really do care about this harpy, to feel that kind of anger."

She smiled a little. "Yes, I do care greatly for him and I can't even explain it. Since I came back from Earth, I've been fighting these feelings. But the moment I touched him tonight, the battle was lost. Charlie has warned me that it is a harpy spell."

Doc chuckled a little. "I don't know about harpy spells but I do know that true love is the worst of spells. Makes people do crazy things. Well, I'm finished," he said stretching his tired old back. "I sometimes surprise even myself." Kari looked at him with a questioning.

"I'd say this golden has a fifty-fifty shot of making it. Better than a few hours ago. This pretty harpy's looks are deceiving. He's a rough little character to have this much fight and resistance in him. His slight body is more resilient than a large human body. It's strange that these creatures lose the will to live so easily when they're captured."

"Thank you, Doc," she said.

"Hey, no thanks until the final results are in. Now, let's have a look at that wing," he said as he pulled the long cream wing up from the floor and rested it on a small table. "Looks like a clean break. He's lucky it's not in a million pieces or blown clean off. Yes, I can fix it with a good old fashion splint. But, it'll be sometime before he'll fly again. I don't have that expensive equipment they have in Terrance. They can mend a broken bone in less than a week there." Doc set the wing and wrapped it with a clear plastic splint. "That should hold it. He'll have a hard time getting that off of him." Doc chuckled. He then proceeded to seal all the open cuts that covered Shail's body. "If I had gotten him sooner, these cuts would be nonexistant but as it is, he may have a few little scars especially that one above the cheek. But, he'll still be a handsome creature, just give him a little character." Doc grinned as he finished with the cuts and abrasions.

"We need to move him to the spare bedroom. I don't have that many visitors or patients, but I don't think it would do any of us any good if they knew he was here," Doc said.

They moved the harpy with the floating stretchers down the hallway and placed him on a double bed in the extra room. Doc sat down in a chair as he looked at the sleeping harpy. "I'm beat," he said with a tire voice. "When you called home, did you inform your father that you were now the proud owner of a pet golden harpy?" he asked lightheartedly.

Kari became very serious. "My father would kill this harpy if he found out I had him," she uttered.

"Well, that creates a real problem but I figured as much since you used the portable communicator and didn't want your location known. What are you going to do with this harpy? He can't stay here. The whole town would know before long. And you can't take him home. If he survives the night, he's going to need a lot of quiet care. Turned loose too soon, he could die from those injuries. Also, harpies can't be caged or made into pets. They curl up and die quickly in captivity. I don't know how you're going to manage to keep him still when he starts feeling better. The problems you'll have are just beginning with keeping a wounded harpy."

"I haven't even thought about, what I'll do next. I've only been concerned with saving his life," Kari said realizing Doc made a strong point. The harpy stood a chance of surviving now but her father was Shail's greatest threat. Nothing would stop him from killing the harpy. And she had not fathomed, it may be difficult contain a wild harpy for a period of time. Her mind flooded with what she should do next to insure Shail safety and survival.

"Don't worry now. If he's still alive in the morning, then we can figure it out. Who knows you have him?" Doc asked.

"That Jake and his hunting buddies and then there's Carol" she was immediately interrupted.

"Carol from the store?" he asked loudly. Kari only nodded. "That blabber mouth. The whole town will know by tomorrow including your father. You better go move that vehicle you came in around back to the garage or they'll know exactly where you brought him. Tomorrow night you better plan on moving him if he makes it. I can see your father now, storming my door tomorrow," Doc said wearily. Kari rose to move the vehicle as Doc followed her out of the bedroom. "It's late. I'm going to bed now. You may want to wash up. There's some clean medical gowns in that closet also some blankets and pillows for the couch. Just make yourself at home."

"Thanks, Doc, for everything, regardless of the outcome," she said with sincerity. He smiled and ambled off to his own bedroom. She realized she had found a real friend in this gruff elderly man and so had her harpy. Kari moved the vehicle into the garage and shut the door to conceal it. She came in and used the bathroom to wash up, noticing her clothes were stained with the harpy's blood. Washing the clothing in the sink, she hung them to dry and then slipped into one of the clean medical gowns. Kari took a blanket and laid it on the couch and went to check on Shail one more time. The dim bedroom light illuminated the six-foot resting figure. The harpy breathed easier now. Touching his sleeping face, she comprehended that Shail may still die in the night. "If you die, you should not have to go alone," she said softly. Kari climbed onto the bed next to him. Taking his hand, she kissed it and held it to her face. A feeling of jubilation and contentment overwhelmed her as if this is where she belonged all along near his side. Shutting her eyes, she fell asleep.

CHAPTER 3

▼

Shail slowly opened his eyes. He gasped with the deep searing pain. The laceration to his side especially hurt him. He tried to rise but found he had no strength left and this slight effort made his suffering worse. Taking a deep breath to calm himself and clear his mind. He found himself in a giant enclosed cage that stank of men. Peering up at the ceiling, he realized he was in one of the human structures. He shivered with helplessness and desperation as a panic consumed him. These last few days had been the worst of his young life and it was apparent, it was not over yet. Suddenly he could smell fresh air flowing into this musty room. He raised his head and noticed an opening. The safety of the dark trees lay beyond. It was night and he could escape easily if he had the strength. The lure of the open window called to his animal survival instincts. Gritting his teeth, he tried to rise off this manmade cloth. Unbearable pain shot through his side as he sweated and cringed. He was breathing hard now with fright and anguish that made his body shake. Shail had acquired a new emotion in these last two lights while he was a captive of men. His cocky boldness had been replaced with tremendous fear. The excruciating pain and torture he had suffered, now filled him with anxiety, for these four hunters were known for far worse. Though he did not understand their sounds, he could sense their poisoned minds. Their only thoughts dwelled on this crucifying and maiming of his harpy body. Shail's heart beat faster now. If he remained a prisoner in this cage, this would be his fate. They would hang him by his wrists while they cut his maleness from him. His wings would be sliced off next. Then they would slowly gut him since they had found pleasure in feasting on a harpy's heart. Shail shivered and sweated, wiping his brow. Suddenly he realized his wrists were no longer bound and this per-plexed him. He was even amazed that he was still alive.

As his mind cleared further, he suddenly became aware of a figure by his side. He stared at her in the dim light. Her blond hair rested over her face. He sniffed her. The scent was unmistakable and unforgettable. Her mere presence made him relax slightly and breathe easier. She was the one he had been waiting for. Ten raining seasons had come and gone since their last meeting and at last, she lay beside him but how? He shook his head, forcing his memory to return. His mind was a fog from the trauma he had suffered. Now he remembered her holding him as he lay close to death but he had thought it only a dream. The same dreams he had shared with her since her return to his land. He nuzzled her slightly to make sure she was real. This was no dream that he experienced now.

Shail searched his memory for the events that lead up to this darkness. He had met Aron on an island after his long flight across the land when they heard the distressing distant sound of a human metal bird. It was approached the nesting grounds of many fledglings. They flew rapidly to this island to lure the hunters away but they arrived too late. Landing on a large limb, they gazed down and saw one of the hunters dangling an injured caught fledgling by his tiny wing. The huge human beast tormented and prodded the terrified youngster. Shail could hear the pathetic silent screeching of pain from this baby harpy's mind as it squirmed to be free. Shail relived the rage, which was a rare feeling for the gentle harpies but this emotion had been growing in him with the hunting cruelty. He had seen the maimed male harpy bodies after men had cut them up. As protector of his flock, he could not allow this to happen to the innocent fledgling. Moving to save the young one, Aron had grabbed his arm as the brown harpy sensed his intentions. "He is beyond our help. Be not reckless and the fool, your flock needs you," he had warned. Shail broke free of Aron's grasp and glared back at his friend. "This one needs me now." he related harshly to him.

Flying down from the treetop he fluttered over the man holding the young harpy. With both feet, he kicked him hard, slamming the cruel hunter's body into a nearby tree trunk. Shail quickly snatched up the fledgling as he hovered over him. Then he flapped hard to escape the laser blasts that zipped past him. Suddenly he felt a terrible burning in the middle of his wing as the wing went limp and he and the fledgling tumbled to the ground. "Flee." he told the baby and it scrambled into the dense underbrush. Shail went the opposite direction, knowing the men would pursue him. He leaped into the foliage but heard and felt a second blast hit him in his side, forcing him to drop to his knees. He gazed up and saw the hunters running towards him. Aron now swooped down and tried to entice them away as he fluttered and flopped his long brown wings on the ground like a wounded dove. "Look, a blast must have hit that large brown." one of them yelled when they saw Aron a short distance away. "Forget him, he's trying to draw us off the golden." another shouted. Shail gazed at Aron. "I am lost. Do not come for me. I order you to save yourself." Shail related silently to his faithful friend. Teary eyed, Aron leaped into the air and disappeared in the trees. Shail scrambled to the base of a large tree trunk as he held his wounded side and dragged the damaged wing. The men were swiftly upon him. He coiled low to the ground pulling in his limbs as he tried to shelter them with his wings while he hissed at the men. They tried to grab his legs and arms but he struck out at them with his fists as his uninjured wing beat them back. He snapped viciously with his teeth every time their hands approached him. They were startled and surprised by the aggressive golden since they had only hunted the docile browns, which never fought back. They began beating him with sticks to make him submit to their will. Shail tried to hide under his protective wings to deflect the blows. After some time, the affliction and abuse crushed his rebellious spirit and Shail finally coward and curled up. When he did this, the hunters saw their chance and leaped on him. Shail struggled with their weight as they tightly tethered his wrists and ankles and wings. Holding down his head by his hair to control his biting mouth. They laughed and poked at their new trophy as Shail timidly stared up through his long blond hair. He closed his eyes and gave up as his body went limp. He then submissively tilted his head back, exposing his throat to these predators. Demonstrating he would resist no more, if only, to be given an honorable harpy death by cutting his throat. This ritual was well known to both, hunter and harpy. It was a measure of honor between the species. A wounded harpy performed this act of surrender, would no longer hinder his enemy. And the hunter could prove his honor and decency by ending the suffering of the dying creature.

"You're not getting off that easy," one laughed. Their words confused him but Shail's instincts sensed their intentions. They lacked any honor and he would suffer a slow horrendous death. One man tossed Shail over his brawny shoulder and took him to their metal bird, roughly throwing him inside. The noisy bird rose and flew over several islands before it landed on their floating structure. Once there, his wrists were fastened to a metal stake above his head and the hellish journey across the water began. They kicked and prodded him unmercifully forcing him to thrash wildly against his rope bonds. By the second light the wounds, the fatigue and the blood loss had taken their toll on his slender body. He could only hiss softly at them as he trembled. Seeing he had become so weak, one stopped the abuse. Claiming their pleasure would be none, if he died, before the taking of his wings. This act of mercy was no mercy at all, for they wished greater pain and torture with his death. Shail remembers now, how he had tried to will his own death but the pain was so unbearable, he could not focus on it. Darkness came as they approached land again and soon Shail's death wish would be answered. It was at that time he saw her in a dream and she held him. She told him to hold on to this life. He knew now, it was no dream. She had come for him.

Shail gazed at her now as she breathed softly alongside of him. He mustered his will and slid closer placing his arm around her and extended his uninjured wing to cover both of them. She continued to sleep but unconsciously snuggled against him and hugged him with one of her arms. Closing his eyes, a peace settled over him. The panic was gone. He would not try and leave this cage, while this female remained in it.

Doc woke at daybreak. He was still very tired after only receiving four hours of sleep. But he forced his exhausted body from the comfortable bed. He was anxious to see if his harpy patient had survived the night. Dressing as fast as his weary old body would allow, he was soon walking through the familiar small cottage. He glanced at the couch and saw it empty. The girl had already gone to the harpy. He approached the bedroom door and slowly pushed it open. On the bed, sound a sleep, lay the girl and the harpy. Their arms clutching one another with the harpy's large cream wing draped over them. Their long blond hair mingled around their slender bodies as the harpy's boyish face rested against the lovely girl's head. Doc stared for a long time. They were breathtakingly beautiful as the morning light rested on them. He shook his head as this admiration turned to sorrow when he considered their futures. Even if the harpy survives his injuries, his life would be short since he was a much sought after golden. And the girl had no future with a harpy, except one of anguish. He questioned whether he had done the right thing by saving this creature that she loved.

The girl moved slightly and the harpy instinctively nuzzled his nose against her without waking. Even in sleep, their affection towards one another was very apparent. Doc sighed with sadness as he stared at the exquisite doomed pair. "Better they sleep now and enjoy what little peace they had in this cruel land," he thought. Closing the door, he went to the kitchen and made breakfast.

A few hours past and Doc knew that the harpy was overdue for another antibiotic patch. He had purposely given him a mild painkiller, in the hopes that the pain would force the harpy to lie still and allow the surgery wound to heal. He went back to the bedroom and opened the door. Both were still asleep. As he walked to the side of the bed, he noticed the harpy stir and breath deeply. Doc knew that a harpy's scent and hearing were acute, like any animal. In an instant, the harpy opened his eyes, as he smelled the man. Seeing the man, the harpy grasped the girl tightly in his arms as his protective wing swiftly covered her. His deep blue eyes glared with defiance as he made a seething sound through his slightly open mouth. His body trembled with the pain and he breathed hard with stress. Doc saw, he was still very weak but it was apparent, this bold little golden was ready to defend the girl.

"Easy, boy, I'm not going to hurt her or you. Just lay still so I can take a look at you." Doc said in a calm voice. Doc moved his small medical scanner toward the harpy to check his surgery wound. The harpy fist swiftly came out from under the wing and struck the scanner, sending it flying across the room. The harpy gave a loud threatening hiss through his teeth as a warning to stay away. Kari woke as the harpy gripped her firmly and moved his coiled slight body over her, preparing to leap and attack the man. "You're alive," she said happily as she smiled at Shail from under his wing.

"Yes, he is. And full of the devil," Doc said gruffly, picking his scanner up off the floor.

Kari gently pushed Shail's wing down, surprised to see Doc. "If he keeps moving, he'll damage all the work I did last night. Come away from him. I think this brassy little male is trying to protect you. He thinks I'm a threat." he said.

Kari unclasped Shail's arms and moved off the bed. Shail perplexed eyes watched her.

"Now, let's try this again," Doc said in a huff as he once again tried to approach the harpy. Instead of hissing and fighting the man, the spooked harpy scurried on his side away from Doc to the other side of the bed. "This is impossible. He's not going to let me touch him."

Kari leaned over Shail and began stroking the soft hair on the shivering frightened harpy. "He's so scared," she said sadly. "Shail, you must let this man touch you. He saved your life and wants to help you." She wondered if the harpy understood any of these words. Shail ignored her and glanced with desire at the open window, wondering if he had the strength to escape this man and cage. Kari spoke to him, but he would not let the man near.

Doc shook his head in disgust. "He's way too wild to treat. Even if I chase him into a corner, he's going to fight back out of fear but there may be one way to get my hands on him." he said as he left the bedroom. Kari stared at Shail. He looked so human but for the first time, she could see the animal that dwelled in him. His alert terrified eyes scanned the room like a trapped feral creature. No amount of her soothing words would tame him and allow him to be handled by a man. She took his hand and the harpy swallowed hard. Kari could sense the overwhelming distress and pain he was feeling. Doc returned and in his hand he held a large butcher knife. Kari was shocked as he came up along side of the bed. The old man raised the blade as if to strike Shail.

"What are you doing?" Kari screamed.

Doc glanced at the girl and smiled. "Just a little experiment. Trust me, I'm not going to hurt him." he said as he held the knife over the harpy's head. Shail looked at the knife and then at Kari. The terror and panic diminished from his eyes as he gazed at her with profound sadness and longing. Knowing his fate, he no longer fled from the man. Doc reached down and grasped his long blond hair and jerked his head back harshly. The harpy allowed this abuse and only trembled as he closed his eyes. Shail lay quietly in the man's hands as he tilted this exposed throat towards Doc. It was if the harpy had been given a powerful sedative. Only his body quivered with the fear as his feathers fluttered slightly. Doc put the blade down on the table. "Pretty good trick. Always wanted to see if it really worked. Just like putting an Earth gator to sleep when you rub the belly," Doc chuckled as he picked up his scanner.

"What's wrong with him?" Kari asked with concern.

Doc frowned at her. "For such a harpy lover, you sure don't know much about them. Now, come around here and grab his hair, the way I have it. He'll think it's me that still got a hold of him. If he moves or opens his eyes, give him a good hard jerk and keep that neck of his tilted back." Kari did as she was told. Shail moved slightly and she tugged hard on his hair and he immediately froze again. Doc put two patches on behind the harpy's wing where he couldn't remove them. He then scanned his wounds. Taking off the old bandage, he treated the injury with antibiotics before spraying it with another sealant bandage. "Watch what I'm doing. You may have to do this next time," he said.

The harpy remained motionless as Doc worked quickly on him. After a few minutes, he had finished. Doc took hold of the harpy's hair once again and motioned Kari away. The old doctor gently ran his hand down Shail's exposed throat as he released the hair. "Good boy, you're a brave little critter for a harpy," he said as he petted his head as if he were petting a dog. Shail slowly opened his eyes as he stared at the man in bewilderment. "I don't blame you for not trusting a human after the punishment you've been through. But, I'll not be the one to kill you," Doc said as he smiled at the baffled harpy. Once again, the harpy slid across the bed and coiled up to defend itself. Doc backed away, giving the wild nervous harpy some space so the animal could settle down.

"I don't understand. Why did he let you treat him?" Kari asked perplexed.

"Because he thought I was going to slit his throat and end his suffering. Any harpy hunter will tell you that a mortally wounded harpy will always give up and offer up his life. It's pretty strange but they're a strange bunch of creatures. No one knows why, they do it or how it got started. Some people think that they can't handle pain and it's cowardly. But this golden is no coward. I can tell he'd be a real handful, if he weren't injured. Even injured, that slight little guy was ready to defend you with his last breath."

Kari watch Shail. He kept his blue frightened eyes fixed on the doctor. Doc smiled.

"Yes, he's pretty confused. Can't quite figure me out, can you, boy? Never thought, I'd live to see the day, where I'd develop any respect for one of these creatures. He should go to sleep in about ten minutes. One of those patches is a tranquilizer. That patch will knock him out for some time. I'm going to have another cup of coffee and watch the news. You better stay with him and keep him calm. He was eyeing the window and with you out of the room, he'd probably attempt to smash the screen to get out. Can't believe he made such a fast recovery. Faster than a man." Doc said in amazement and picked up the knife and went back to the kitchen.

Shail watched as the man left the room. He relaxed slightly uncoiling his body as he looked into Kari's eyes. Kari bit her bottom lip as she placed her hand against his face and shook her head. "What am I going to do with you," she said in a quiet voice. "Not all men are bad, Shail." Kari lay back down beside him, stroking his wing and back. Shail took his hand and cupped the side of her face, running his thumb over her moist lips. He seemed fascinated by her. Kari smiled up at him as she quivered a little with his gentle touch. Shail realized there was no time for the traditional harpy courtship and he need desperately to make this female yield to him. He slid closer putting his arm around her and kissed her tenderly on her mouth. With his passionate kiss, she was mesmerized and became putty in his hands. Kari couldn't resist him as his soft full lips merged with hers. Now she could feel his hands exploring her breasts and body. She felt paralyzed and could not stop him as she breathed harder. Like the passion in their dreams, she had longed to hold him. Shail moved his hand up her legs until it was beneath the medical gown, tenderly rubbing her nude back and rear. He continued to kiss and nuzzle her, forcing her to submit as Kari felt his softly panting breath against her neck. Leaning over her, he allowed one of his legs to slip between hers as his body wiggled into the breeding position. She could feel his firm hard erection as it throbbed between her legs. He released some of himself to moisten and stimulate her further as it gently rubbed her with a pulsing up and down motion. Kari was so aroused, she was now gasping for breath between his kisses and every part of his being worked to caress and massage her sexually. She shook with excitement pulling his slender muscled body to her. With his over powering masculine effect, she willingly moved her legs to allow him in. When she did this, his breathing quickened as he hastily moved his other leg over her and prepared to mate her. She could feel the head begin to invade her. He gently pushed as it slid slightly inside. Shail fought the urge to drive deeper. Pulsing lightly in and out until she was totally gratified. He wanted her fully inflamed so there was no doubt this female completely accepted him. By accepting him as a mate, she would willingly care and cherish his offspring, rather than reject it. Kari closed her eyes and could feel a welling up and tremendous rush as thousands of stars danced in her head. She moaned softly. The male harpy could feel the warm release of her fluids as she climaxed, her mind only focused on consummating this bonding. She was ready to receive his sperm. Shail mustered all his strength from his battered weak body and shut out the searing pain from his mind. This breeding, for him, was not out of passion or lust or even love. It was a mating of hopelessness, despair and fear. The fear, he may not survive this captivity. Unlike a man, who mated for pleasure, the harpy was an animal, who bred for procreation and would endure any hardship and pain to complete a mating and insure its bloodline. This may be Shail's only opportunity to plant his seeds in this chosen female since he had come so close to death in these last few lights. Shail was the last of the golden males and without an heir, the line would end and so would the harpy's future rulers. He nuzzled her neck and then took a light hold of it with his teeth. Nipping hard, he forcing her to appease him and penetrated her completely, holding her down. Shail breathed rapidly from the stimulation and racking pain. His wings fluttered uncontrollably with the mating. Now he began copulating in a frenzy to release his seeds and impregnate his wiggling female that was now helpless to remove a fully aroused male.

Suddenly a sick dizzy feeling came over him. Shail shook his head frantically to get control of his own body as a frightening numbness took hold of him. Staring with panic into Kari's eyes, he laid his head down upon her as he panted. He had been one thrust away from the release and his own body had betrayed him. He managed to nuzzle her one last time before closing his eyes and falling into a deep sleep.

Kari pushed his beautiful slumbering body off of her, knowing it had been the tranquilizer that had stopped him. This spell, this control he had over her faded. She looked at him with apprehension and uneasiness now. In less than ten minutes, he had seduced her to his will with just one kiss. All her father's warnings came flooding back in to her mind. Was this the rape men spoke of? She realized any resistance had vanished against the seductive gorgeous blond harpy. Putting her hand to her mouth, the full gravity of it hit her. She had willingly let him invade her but was it love or a harpy spell that compelled her to have sex with him? Would she have lost her mind if the bonding had been completed? Perhaps, since her mind belonged to him under his spell. She wasn't even sure what Shail was. He appeared human but there was no doubt, he had a wild animal nature. She still loved him but the love was now tainted with distrust and anxiety. Even terribly wounded and weak, he had nearly taken her. What would she do when he recovered? Would he obey her wishes not to bond? It had come down to a choice. Would she choose her own safety or his? "I can't abandon him. I still love him too much. I have to take this risk rather than let him die," she said softly to herself. Kari leaned over and gave Shail a gentle kiss on his lips. Immediately her heart flutter and goose bumps covered her body. She could feel her desire rise and it was hard not to crawl between his arms. Even unconscious, his spell affected her. She rubbed her forehead wearily. "I must not kiss him again," she thought half heatedly. Kari rose from the bed and went to the bathroom to dress into her own clothes. There was so much she didn't know about Shail or the harpies. Maybe Doc had some of the answers. He had laughed off Charlie's notion of a harpy spell last night with the statement that love was also a terrible spell. Perhaps talking to him would ease some of her anxieties.

Doc sat at the kitchen table drinking a cup of coffee when she joined him. "Want some?" he offered and Kari nodded her head as she sat down at the table. Doc poured her a cup and sat down across from her. He looked into her eyes. "You look a little shook up," he said to her.

Kari nodded again. "I am shook up. I'm in love with a creature that I hardly know or understand," she muttered.

Doc nodded. "Very few people understand the harpies. They are Dora's greatest mystery. But, I think your little harpy is more like us than some are willing to admit. I want to show you something that may help you a little." He walked to an old desk in the kitchen and began rummaging through the drawers. "Here it is," he said as he produced a tattered ancient picture. "Look at this and tell me what you see," he said as he handed the picture to Kari.

She looked at it and could see three men standing under a great tree. Hanging from the tree by their wrists were two harpies. Their wings forced in the extended position as they waited for their deaths. It was obviously a trophy hunt as the men smiled with their catch. "It's awful," Kari said as she handed the picture back to Doc.

"No, look closer at those harpies," he said.

Kari examined the harpies and noticed they did not look likes Shail. More hair covered their naked bodies. Also, their faces were different. They had facial hair and were less attractive than present day harpies. "They're rather ugly for harpies," she said and gave the picture back to Doc.

"Exactly," he smiled. "They look nothing like your clean faced sleek skinned little golden. This picture is over a hundred and forty years old and was given to me by my grandfather. There are very few of these pictures around. Do you know why the first settlers named these creatures harpies?" Kari shook her head. "Harpy is a Greek word meaning "to snatch." Harpies were imaginary monsters from Earth's ancient Greek mythology like Pegasus, griffons and mermaids. Harpies were described as noisy, dirty female monsters with half bird, half human bodies that were thieves. Now take your harpy. He's a beautiful mute male. Only the wings and theft make him a harpy. I'm betting, the harpies in this picture were dirty noisy creatures. Now the interesting part, how did your handsome male change from his ancestors?" Kari only shrugged. "The blood transfusion I gave to your harpy last night. He has a lot of human blood in him. He's probably more related to humans than to these animals in this picture."

"Human." Kari said surprised. "But how?"

"You've heard of harpies kidnapping and assaulting women. They have mingled their race into ours. Why do you think your father and other men hate them?" he asked.

"But, if they're human, that means they're not animals and they shouldn't be hunted like game animals," she said.

Doc smiled. "Now you go into the politics and a hidden agenda. Do the men allow the harpies to live and continue to take our women, or wipe out this threat? If these new colonists from Earth knew, the harpies were another race of men, would they view harpy hunting as a sport or murder. It gets very messy. Then again, would they want to risk having their wives or daughters taken by these so called winged men. So far, it seems that the harpy extermination is the answer before this secret is out. More and more hunters are invading the islands. It's the last remaining wild sanctuary of the harpies. In five more years, the harpies will be completely extinct. I think your little golden male is the last of his kind. I haven't seen or heard of another blond in twenty years," he said as he shook his head sadly and poured another cup of coffee.

"What makes the golden harpies so special?" she said almost to herself as she reflected on their discussion.

"Well, they're the rulers of the browns. Royalty, if you could call it that. How they came to that position is anyone's guess. But, supposedly golden harpies have more courage and wit in their genes. I'm very surprised that idiot Jake managed to catch that golden." Doc said.

"Shail was defending a fledgling. He attacked one of Jake's friends who had a fledgling. Even broke the guy's arm in the process," she said quietly.

"Really?" Doc seemed pleasantly surprised. "Maybe what they say about the golden harpy line is true. Never heard of a harpy attacking hunters before. Then again, maybe he has too much of the human blood in him. Anger and aggression is a human emotion, generally not found in the submissive brown harpies," he said. "And how did you manage to get this prized golden from Jake?"

"I traded a brand new terrain vehicle for him," she answered.

Doc laughed. "If this golden is truly the last one then even dying, Jake is an idiot for making that trade. That golden harpy is very valuable and highly prized by the harpy hunters. Which leads me to another question. Have you decided on what you're going to do with him? He's going to need a good ten days to recover. And you're right about your father. John would kill that poor thing if he found you with it. He'll find out soon enough and he's not going to be very happy with me for treating it."

"Why did you save him?" she asked as she glanced up at the old man.

Doc sighed. "Maybe because he is the last of his kind, the last golden harpy and then maybe, because he saved your life with the licing moss and countless others. That harpy may hold a vast sum of medical knowledge and other secrets of Dora, that we know nothing about." Then Doc smiled at her. "And then again, maybe I did it for you. He will bring you only misery because that is the way of his life. He's recovering but his luck won't last. He's the most precious game animal in the galaxy. With so many hunters after him, he'll be killed before too long. But I can see, you love him and for some reason, that slender little fellow is committed to you. You both deserve a little happiness. Dora is a cruel planet for harpies and those that care for them," he said somberly.

Kari smiled at Doc. "Thank you, Doc," she said.

"Don't thank me. I may be responsible for bringing you a lot of pain when they kill him." Doc said, shaking his head.

Kari was deep in thought. "I need to take him somewhere safe, perhaps somewhere on my father's estate. He has banned all harpy hunting there."

"Yes, it's banned now but I can assure you when your father finds out you ran off with this harpy, he may lift that ban. Also with Carol running her mouth, every hunter on the continent will learn that's there one last golden harpy left. When that happens, the poachers and hunters will flood to the west coast in droves. They'll risk your father's ban for a chance of getting a golden harpy. Time is an issue too. It won't be long before your father and every other hunter finds out about your little broken winged pet."

"I'll leave tonight and hope that no one tells Dad before then," she said and took another sip of her coffee. "Doc, I have to tell you, I do love Shail. I don't know why. But this rape and taking of woman has me a little concerned. Do you really think it's true? I mean, don't the harpies have their own females?" she asked.

"Well, that's one of the mysteries, isn't it? Some people believe they have their females hidden in the northern mountains or the western islands. I personally think they're dead. Killed by some disease or something. I think, if the proper research was done, they'd find the mating of a harpy and a woman would permit only male winged offspring to be conceived. But, that is only one of my assumptions. The harpies are very meek creatures. They fear men and do everything to avoid them. For them to fly in among humans and take a woman seems more like an act of desperation. I don't believe they would do this unless they had no other choice."

"This taking of women baffles me. You know, I have encountered a brown harpy twice since I came back. He did not try to take me. In fact, he saved me from a pride of grogins. And he told me that my golden harpy needed me. I didn't know what he was talking about, until I found Shail with those hunters," she said.

"This harpy spoke to you?" Doc questioned with amazement.

"Well, he didn't speak or make any sound but I could, somehow, understand his thoughts."

Doc raised his eyebrows. "Never heard of anyone that could communicate with these creatures."

Kari smiled. "I was told that I have a strong sixth sense. But why do you think the brown harpy didn't take me? He had plenty of opportunity."

Doc glanced at her. "How long have you been committed to this golden male?"

"Probably since he took me from the lake when I was only eleven," she answered.

"Well, it's apparent that the golden marked you. Claimed you, so to speak. A brown harpy is not about to take a woman that has been claimed by a golden, especially if it's true that he rules them. I'm betting that the brown harpy was sent to protect you until this golden could come for you. Makes me wonder if I did the right thing by saving him," the old man said with a tired voice.

Kari put her hand on the elderly doctor's hand. "He won't hurt me. I can sense he loves me as much as I love him. And I'm willing to accept any risk to save him."

"In my retirement, I've been doing my own study on harpies. Keeps me busy. You're the first woman I've met that openly wants to be with a male harpy. I'd be interested to learn how you two make out," he said.

"Doc, I met a doctor at the Hampton Zoo that's also started a study on the harpies. He's trying to save them from extinction. He said the government was funding him."

"The government! That sounds fishy. It's the senators in our government that promote the harpy hunting. They just started some new legislation to add a bounty on harpy wings which would increase the hunting."

Kari was astonished at hearing this. "This vet seemed very sincere. I don't believe he was lying to me about wanting to help the harpies," she said slowly.

"Well, he's either being deceived or perhaps, there's a few in government that do want to help the harpies. His research could be used to hurt or help the harpies. Your own father had some nasty dealings with our senators. When he made it known that harpy hunting would be prohibited on his estate, they made life difficult for him. I heard he lost several big timber accounts. But, I know John, he was not about to have anyone tell him what he could or could not do on his own property. I think he kept the hunting ban on, just to prove his point, rather than to protect the harpies," the old man chuckled. "Maybe I should give this vet a call and pick his brain a little. If he's really here to save the harpies, he'd better learn what he's up against. I'd also like to know if his research is consistent with mine."

Kari beamed at him. "You're going to help the harpies?" she asked.

"Now, don't get me wrong, young lady. I'm not a great lover of these creatures but they deserve to exist and like I said, I think there's a lot we might learn from them. I'm seeking their knowledge and this vet in Hampton apparently wants to save an endangered species. Perhaps both our needs could be met, if we collaborate on this study. Besides, I enjoy solving a good mystery and there's nothing more mysterious than a harpy. Well, I'm tired now. Think I'll go to lie down for a while. You might do the same if you have a long night of travel. Does the communicator work in that old vehicle?"

"I don't know," she said.

"Well, take this portable on the counter just in case you have trouble. I can use the one on my desk. And don't forget his antibiotic patches. There are some in the cabinet. He'll need ten for ten days. Also, some of the tranquilizers, in case he doesn't behave or won't lay still." Kari nodded.

The doctor and Kari left the kitchen and walked in the harpy's room. "He certainly is a handsome devil. Looks like another golden I saw. It will be a sad day if these majestic creatures are all slaughtered before we even understand them." Doc said while caressing the shiny blond hair of the sleeping harpy. Then Doc headed for his own room.

Kari lay down beside Shail and curled up, careful not to touch him. He continued to sleep and soon, she too was asleep. Kari woke to the sound of the bell ringing on the front porch of the cottage. Soon someone was banging on the door and shouting to Doc. She froze with fear as she heard Doc answer their calls. "Had they come for her harpy?" she thought as she pictured her father racing into the bedroom in a rage. She crept to the bedroom door to listen. She heard Doc's calm reassuring voice speaking to the frantic man on the porch. Kari could not make out the conversation but soon the front door closed and Doc walked into the living room. The sound of a hovercraft taking off could be heard from the street. Kari stared out the window as several vehicles sped off at top speed. "What is it? What's happened?" she asked as she confronted Doc in the living room.

He looked so tired, as he walked to the medical room and began to gather some equipment. "A swarm. A swarm hit east of town and it sounds bad. This time, I think, there are fatalities," he said somberly. He glanced up at her as he worked feverishly throwing things in a case. "Most of the town people have gone to the site. This may be a good time for you to take your harpy and go. If there are survivors, they will be coming here so I can stabilize them before the trip to Terrance. Do you know how to work the portable stretcher?" he asked hastily.

Kari nodded. He handed her some liquid bandage. "Put this on that wound after you clean it daily. And don't forget the patches. I must leave now," he said as he rushed out the door to his old hovercraft. In minutes, he was in the air and gone.

Kari grabbed the medical supplies and the portable communicator and raced to the garage. Throwing open the door, she went in, placing them inside the old blue vehicle. She jumped in the driver's seat and pushed the start button. Amazingly, the engines fired right up. Soon the vehicle glided close to the back door of the cottage. Kari wasn't sure of how much time she had to get out of town but the old vehicle was slow and her harpy's life depended on this escape. She ran back into the house and brought the floating stretcher along side the harpy's bed. The drug that Doc had given to Shail for sleep must have been strong for he still slept with all the noise. Kari shook him hard as he slowly opened his eyes. "Shail!" she screamed at him. "We must go."

He seemed to understand her since he made a drowsy attempt to sit up but quickly collapsed as his eyes shut again. She screamed again and he shook his head, trying to rid himself of the drugs. "Climb on here," she motioned with her hand to the stretcher. He made a feeble attempt and with her help, he was on the stretcher. She pushed him through the cottage and out the back door. The warm fresh breeze seemed to revive him as he shook his head again and glanced around at the yard and trees. She opened the back of the vehicle and pushed the stretcher along side of it. "You must go in there," she motioned to him. Getting him to move out of the house had been easy since he was willing to get out of the enclosed large cage but now, she wanted him to go in a small closed trap. This had a whole different affect on him. Kari pushed his shoulder and wing towards the opening of this metal monster but he balked at it. He braced his hands and feet against the door and refused to move inside. He could tell she was frustrated with him as she tried to release his hold. Although he was weak, he still had the strength to resist her.

"If you don't get in, they will find you and kill you," she begged him. But her begging and pleading did not good. The harpy would not move. After ten minutes, Kari gave up, realizing he was too strong. She lowered her head sadly as she sat on the edge of the vehicle and tried to think of another way to get him in. Shail shook his head trying to clear his mind of the debilitating drugs that blocked his senses. He stared at the metal vehicle. He understood what she wanted him to do but it went against his better judgment to climb into a cage. He was devoted to this female but like her, they did not know each other well and he did not trust her yet. Shail relaxed his hold on the door and he stuck his head inside and sniffed the air. His body still racked with pain and this struggle with her had made things worse. She gazed up at him and spoke faintly. "Please, Shail, go in." Shail shuddered slightly. He realized she only wanted what was best for him and it was obvious, she wished to protect him from more harm. He would have to trust her. Reluctantly the harpy lifted him self inside the vehicle and breathed hard as he curled up in a ball. Kari stroked him gently. "Good boy, sleep now," she said as she shut the door and locked it. Kari leaped behind the driver seat and started the engines. The vehicle hovered down the deserted streets of the town and soon they were on the old highway, heading west towards the coast. She glanced behind her and could see that Shail's eyes were shut. The stress of the struggle with her had been too much for him and he had passed out with the pain. Kari breathed a sigh of relief, seeing him sleeping once again.

The vehicle approached the harbor and Kari turned on a smaller road to the north. She drove past several tiny cottages that sat on the ocean. They appeared vacant as weeds and debris littered the yards. After ten miles, the road became more like an ill kept path and there were no more buildings. She knew that she had reached her father's estate. The terrain grew rougher as mighty trees covered the cliffs overlooking the water. Over a hundred miles to the north, lay her grandfather's old hunting cabin. She was very small when she last visited it, a few years before he died. She hoped that her father and Charlie would think that she was too young to remember this place existed and would not search for her there. She reminisced about the dilapidated map that hung in her grandfather's bedroom. He had shown her many times the location of the cabin, since the map was of the west coast of the continent. The vehicle moved sluggishly as it barely cleared the large boulders and fallen trees. After an hour, she came to a stop. Shail had been awfully still and it made her worry. Opening the back doors, she found him sleeping peacefully. She caressed him as she whispered, "You poor thing. This will be over soon." Climbing back in the driver seat, she continued on this journey.

Duran was low in the sky as it began its decent into the ocean. Again the sky was a brilliant red with its setting. Kari pushed the vehicle faster, because she did not relish traveling this path at night. It would still be hours before she reached the cabin. And once there, she wondered what she would find. She had no time to bring food or water. Only Shail's medication and the communicator were in the vehicle along with a bloody old blanket that the harpy had been placed on the night before. She began to realize how ill equipped she was to defend herself from the wild animals or defend Shail from hunters without a gun. She had no clothing except what she wore and a thin blood stained jacket that she had used at the beach. It lay on the floorboards, next to her. She looked ahead and could see the black mountains in the distance. The path became steeper with each cliff. The engines struggled to maintain the vehicle's balance. Kari worried if this ancient transport would make it to her destination. Darkness came and she was forced to turn on the lights even though they would be seen for miles. She glanced frequently towards the sky in search of hovercraft lights but none were seen. All was still and silent except the noise of the terrain vehicle she drove.

She thought about her father and Charlie. They would be worried now. And this upset her but she dare not contact them. They would have discovered her fate by now, from the people at the beach. She imagined her father's distress when he learned that she had gone off with the golden harpy. All his warnings were in vain and it made her sick to think of the hurt and betrayal he would feel. She also thought of Charlie. He would be more apt to understand her. And her desire to save the golden harpy but he too, had warned her against him. They would have to realize, she had no choice but to save him. After all, had Shail not risked his life to save her ten years earlier? These thoughts flooded her mind and tormented her.

She began to think of Shail. And how she would handle him when he was no longer injured. She was astonished with his strength as he fought to not enter the vehicle. Even severely wounded and drugged, she still could not force him inside. She could see why it had taken four men and two laser blasts to subdue him. It had never occurred to her that the slender elegant harpy bodies could be so powerful and tough. She would be at his mercy when he recovered. If she made it clear, she did not want this bonding, would he obey? "Was Shail really capable of rape?" she wondered. Her instincts told her that he would never harm her and she put her faith in them. The night wore on as Kari dwelled on all these issues as she pushed the vehicle further north into the mountains.

CHAPTER 4

▼

John Turner had arrived at the wood mill early in the morning. He went to his makeshift lab that was in a room off his office. Another new batch of insecticide had arrived on a hover from Terrance and he was anxious to see if it worked. He poured the yellow liquid into a spray bottle and then removed one of the large black beetles from a holding tank. He had become accustomed to handling these insects over the last year and a half. Suddenly the beetle bit him. John jerked in pain and dropped the palm size vermin. It scurried across the floor and opened its wings. The beetle flew against a screened window and remained there. John looked at the bite as he swore a little. The beetle had not only bit him but had taken a sizable chunk out of his thumb. "That's a first" he said to himself. He had handled hundreds of these bugs and none had ever attacked him before. He walked to the window and stared at the beetle. There was nothing different about it. It looked like the rest of the beetles in the holding tank. He grabbed a net and caught the beetle. "Thought you guys only liked wood," he said to the insect as he placed it carefully in a separate tank, securing it with a see-through lid. He walked back to his office and out to the mill.

Charlie was talking to another employee as they stood next to some freshly cut lumber. He strolled over as Charlie told the other man, which logs should be cut next. "Look at this, Charlie," he said as he approached and held out his thumb. "One of those beetles just bit me."

Charlie examined the wound with concern in his eyes. "That is a bad bite. Do those beetles have food?"

"They have all kinds of leaves and wood chips in their tank," John answered.

"Maybe you antagonized it or hurt it." Charlie said.

John shook his head and smiled "I handled it like I've always done."

"It is very strange that one would bite human flesh, if it was not tormented."

"I'm telling you, Charlie, I didn't torment it, hurt it or squeeze it. It just bit me as it lay in the palm of my hand," John said somewhat annoyed.

"Then maybe your hand had the scent of wood on it and the beetle became confused."

"Maybe," John remarked. "Well, I'm going to try the new poison out and hope it works. Make sure the men get that stack of red wood done next. I got another order for ten bundles of the ruby red this morning," and he turned to leave.

"You should put something on that wound before an infection gets in," he called to John. John kept walking and nodded his head in agreement as he headed back to his office.

Once inside, he treated the bite with a lotion and sprayed a bandage over the wound. The wound stung and his skin became red around it. He was not too concerned, since the beetles were non-poisonous. But it did hurt. Walking back to the lab, he began to spray the single beetle with the new insecticide. The beetle scurried from the spray and lay in one corner. John watched for sometime but after ten minutes, the beetle began to walk around the small tank as if it had been sprayed with water. John shook his head in disgust. "With all the known chemicals, you'd think they would come up with something that worked," he said with disgust.

He went back to his office and pressed a button on his desk. A screen rose up and he spoke into it. "Maria, has Kari come home or called?" he asked.

"No, Mr. Turner, there has been no calls," she answered.

"She probably still sleeping at her friend's house after that beach party. But let me know if you hear from her."

Maria smiled into the screen. "I've heard those parties can last till dawn. She probably does sleep now. Do you want me to call in town and check on her?" she asked.

"No, I'm sure she's fine since she was with a group. I don't want to pry," he answered. He pushed the button and the screen disappeared from view. He sat down behind his desk as he glanced at a picture of Kari when she was a child. She was holding a caboo in her lap. The soft cuddly creature's six legs were curled around her little arm as she embraced it and smiled. How she had grown into an attractive stunning woman since this picture was taken. He still could not get over the fact that she looked so much like her mother. The past haunted him and he worried that they may be too much alike. Their last talk had told him that she still was interested in the harpies, the golden harpy. He was plagued with worry that he had allowed that young golden to live. It would have been easy back then to gather his men and hunt down this naive cocky young male but would it have been right to kill a creature that had just saved his daughter's life. He was so over-joyed Kari was alive that he had put away his bitterness and let the harpies and this golden live in peace. Now, he questioned himself and this resolution. Kari had come back to Dora, still drawn to the harpy and he was faced with a misera-ble dilemma. She was an adult now and no longer under his control. If she chose to seek out this golden or if the golden came to her, he would be forced to kill it in order to secure a safe future for her. But this cruel act of killing the golden male would cause more damage to their unstable relationship. Perhaps even end it. He sighed deeply. "Better she hate me than lose her to a harpy." he thought sadly. John realized it was a no win situation if Kari chose the wrong path. He would lose his daughter either way.

John picked up the picture and stared at it. Their relationship seemed to be healing and this pleased him. He wondered now how her evening had gone with the other young people of Westend. These young men, who hung out with Carol Baker were avid harpy hunters in their spare time. Perhaps they could convince her that the harpies were only wild animals despite their human looking bodies. To be taken by one, would be disastrous. Sometimes it was better to hear these things from her peers than from two old men. Placing the picture back on the desk, John went to go back outside to make sure the proper shipment was loaded. In a few days, he would have to leave to inspect the progress of timber cutting in the northeastern part of the estate.

The morning came and went as John and Charlie worked among the other men in the hot muggy weather. The large logs were run through the lasers by robotic machines until the rare timbers were cut into fine boards. The milky blue and bright red planks were stacked in a neat pile by the afternoon. John wiped his brow as he said to Charlie, "It's almost time to call it a day. I wonder why I have not heard from Kari?"

"Do you want me to call Maria?" Charlie asked.

"No, she knows to call me. I'll call the Bakers' store when I return to the house."

Charlie noticed one of the men running across the lot towards them. "Trou-ble" he pointed as the man dashed in the heat. He stopped in front of John, out of breath. "A swarm. Another swarm hit just east of town. And they say there's some deaths this time."

Not saying a word, John ran to his hovercraft as Charlie followed as fast as he could. They hopped inside. Charlie barely had the door shut when the craft lifted from the ground. In a few minutes, they had past Westend and continued east. It wasn't long before they saw the barren ground the swarm had left behind. In the distance, they could see other hovercrafts and terrain vehicles in a circle in the midst of all this vast dirt.

John set the hover down and leaped from craft before it had even touched the ground. He ran towards the small group of people and transports. The group of people had stopped talking as they saw him approach. John's only thoughts were of his daughter as he past them. One woman sat on her knees and cried hysterically. Suddenly John recognized her. It was Mrs. Baker from the store, Carol's mother. A lump formed in his throat and he swallowed hard, walking past her while her husband consoled her. Then he saw the red terrain vehicle as he stumbled forward like he was in a bad dream. A man caught him as he approached. "Mr. Turner, you don't want to see this," he said while holding John's shoulders. The whole town knew that the special vehicle had been shipped to Westend as a coming home gift for his daughter. John gently pushed the man aside and kept walking. He looked inside of the gutted vehicle. Even the leather seats were gone. Only the skeletal remains of three bodies lay on the floor. Two more remains were found outside of the open door. "No!" John cried with distress as his eyes watered. "No" he growled low with anger.

"I'm so sorry, Mr. Turner," said the man who had tried to stop him.

John stared in disbelief at the disaster. "Why didn't they just keep the doors shut?" John uttered pathetically.

"They did. The beetles came up through the engines and floor boards," the man answered quietly. Charlie walked up close to John and put his arm around his shoulder. John looked at him and could say no more as he broke down and began to cry. His whole world was gone and he felt like a broken man; first his wife and now Kari.

He didn't notice as another hovercraft set down near his. The old doctor climbed from his craft and one of the men met him. "There's nothing you can do, Doc. They're all dead," a man told him. Doc walked to the tragedy to see for himself.

"Who are they?" he asked, looking at the remains.

"One is Carol Baker and her boyfriend, Jake O'Connell also John Turner's daughter. This was her new vehicle. The others, we're not sure. It's hard to tell who they are. The beetles didn't leave much," the man said.

Doc noticed John with his faithful Indian, Charlie. His hands were to his face as he slumped over the vehicle's hood and cried. Doc walked up to him and spoke softly. "Come with me, John. There is something I must tell you."

"Leave me alone, Doc. I don't want to talk now," John stammered.

Doc took his arm. "This is something that you will want to hear."

John looked at him and could see the graveness in the old man's eyes. He walked with him a short distance away from the small crowd of people. Charlie watched as they strolled out to vast dirt and beyond earshot of the others.

"She's not dead," Doc said and John looked confused. "Your daughter is not dead," Doc repeated as if he was having a hard time convincing this man that he had know since he was a boy.

John shook his head in bewilderment, brushing away a tear from his cheek. "Doc, that's Kari's vehicle. She was with Carol Baker last night. You can't identify those bodies by looking at the remains," he proclaimed with distress.

"She was not with Carol Baker last night," Doc said.

"How do you know that?" John asked.

The doctor took a deep breath and sighed. "Because she was with me. She spent the night at my cottage."

"But her vehicle, I just gave her that vehicle," John sputtered.

"I know that" Doc said calmly. "She gave it to Jake."

"What? Why?" John questioned with a slight hysteria in his voice.

Doc rubbed his forehead wearily. "I did not want to be the one to tell you this but I can't let you believe that she is dead."

"What is it?" he screamed. "Is she alright? Is she hurt?"

Doc shook his head. "No, she's fine." He took another deep breath before he spoke. "She traded the vehicle for a wounded golden harpy. She is with him now."

"What?" John said harshly.

"She brought the dying little harpy to me last night and I treated its laser blast wounds." Doc stated.

John backed away from him as the fear and sadness in his eyes was replaced with rage. "You treated it? You let it live?" he exclaimed angrily. "Charlie, we're going!" he blared to the old Indian and turned to leave.

Doc caught his arm. "Where do you think you're going?"

"To your place so I can kill it. Something you should have done!" he yelled and glared at the old doctor. He began to walk away.

Doc called calmly to him. "They're not there."

John stopped short and turned back toward the doctor. "Where is she?" he raged.

"Aren't you at least glad she's not here?" Doc questioned him.

"Don't play these games with me old man. Being with that harpy is as dangerous as a swarm."

"Yes, that could be true with your frame of mind," Doc said with a cool serious tone. This statement caused John to freeze as Doc's words sent a chill through him. It was this same anger that had killed his wife. He was quiet for a moment.

Charlie had walked up to John. "She's not dead, Charlie. But she might as well be. She's with him, she's with that damn golden harpy."

The old Indian just nodded his head and he looked up at John. "I'm glad she's alive. And John, you knew this might happen. We were fooling ourselves, to think they could be separated. Their desire for one another is too strong." the Indian said quietly.

"The harpy is wounded and this old fool treated it. If he had just killed it…" John snickered, turning towards Doc.

"I have better things to do than listen to you call me names. We have a serious problem, far more serious than one little harpy. Your daughter is alive and well. Be happy with that. These swarms have evolved and are eating flesh now. Everyone and everything is in danger. Right now, I need to comfort the Bakers. They truly have lost a daughter," he sighed. "And I need to figure out who those other poor souls are."

Doc started to leave, when John stepped in front of him. "Where is she?" he demanded in a stern voice.

Doc glared at him. "I don't know where she is, and even if I did, I sure as hell wouldn't tell you. Take some good advice for a change and leave them alone. Let your daughter decide her own destiny. Only disaster will come, if you interfere with her life. You'd think you would have learned that by now," Doc grumbled as he walked around John and back towards the Bakers.

Charlie looked up at John. "Don't say anything," John growled at the Indian. He stomped off towards his hovercraft as Charlie followed quietly behind.

John climbed in the hover but did not start the engine. Charlie got in beside him. John just stared off in the distance and sat quietly. He watched the people milling around the devastated terrain vehicle like he was in a trance. Charlie was not about to disturb him.

"I can't let this go, Charlie," he finally said sadly. "I can't let her go with him. He'll ruin her life."

The Indian was silent for some time. "John, she has chosen. She has been warned of the risks and still, she has chosen to accept these risks to be with him. We both have under estimated her devotion to him. It is better to let her go now."

"Even if I stayed out of it, how long do you think that golden male has to live? It's amazing he has survived this long. More and more hunters are coming to this planet. The harpies are a doomed species and I don't want my daughter caught in the middle, trying to defend him," he said to Charlie.

"If Doc is right about the swarms, we are all doomed along with the harpies."

John looked down at his bandaged thumb and held it up to Charlie. "Perhaps that beetle was trying to tell me something," he said as he stared at the bite wound.

"Perhaps," Charlie said. John pushed the start button and the hover rose from the annihilated land. "Where will you go now?" Charlie asked as they reached a certain height in the sky.

"I'm going to Doc's house. I have to start somewhere," he answered. He flipped on the communicator. "Maria, has Kari called in?"

No, Mr. Turner," she answered with concern.

"Thank you," he said flipping the com. off.

They were soon at Westend and landing in front of the yellow cottage. John went to the porch and opened the unlocked door. He walked into the medical room and could see the operating table. A bloody plastic cover lay on it and around the floor. Charlie bent down and examined it. "A lot of blood. The harpy must have been gravely wounded," the Indian said.

"Yes, there's some on the porch leading in here," John stated as he walked to the kitchen and out the back door. He stood by the floating stretcher that sat beyond the door.

Charlie walked to the grass in the back yard. "A hover terrain vehicle was here. Look, the grass has been pushed down. Not a very big one. Doc's vehicle is over there," Charlie said and pointed to a vehicle along side the cottage.

"Yes, she must have put him in right here. So, she has a vehicle but whose and where would she go?" John mustered rubbing his chin. He turned and walked back into the cottage, followed by Charlie. He looked in Doc's bedroom and then in the bedroom off the hallway. The bed was unmade as if two people had slept in it. John reached down and picked up the medical gown off the floor. He sighed as he held it in this hand. "I don't believe this was on the harpy," he said and dropped it.

Charlie leaned over the bed and picked up a small broken cream feather. He held it up for John to see. John nodded and walked out of the room. They both had been hunters and knew that certain clues would tell a story about their prey. But the prey had now, become Kari and the harpy.

John stood in the living room. "I have to find someone from the beach party. They will know the vehicle that she's in and we can start looking for it."

"So, you intend to pursue them?" Charlie sighed.

John only nodded.

"And if you find them, what then? Will you kill her little male harpy?" Charlie questioned.

John glared at him. "If it will save my daughter from a miserable life, then, yes."

Charlie scoffed at the carpet as he watched John search the cottage for more clues. He didn't want to discuss Kari and the harpy when John was so agitated but he knew he had to. "If you kill her harpy, she will never forgive you," Charlie said softly.

"She'd get over it," John answered bitterly.

"No, she would not. Think John before you act. You will lose daughter over this. There must be another way."

John sighed and leaned against the couch, realizing Charlie was right. "Well, let's find them first. If he's badly injured, he can't force her to bond. Only if he hasn't touched her, will I spare him. And only after I neuter him and he's no longer a stud and a sexual threat. Hell, if she's so fond of him, she can keep that blond like a pet canary after that. I'll even build the cage for her," John said and walked out on the porch.

Charlie just shook his head, knowing this was no solution. To castrate or cage a wild adult harpy was a death sentence and John knew it. They left the cottage and meandered out on the deserted street. The little village was silent and vacant.

"Let's fly back to the accident and see if we can get more information. Someone there must know the kind of vehicle she was in," John said a little calmer.

The short flight took them back to the town's people and the destroyed red terrain vehicle. Some of the men had loaded the bodies in the vehicles with Doc's supervision. John walked up to the old man as he leaned over the last skeleton.

"This must be Tom Spencer. The red hair matches." Doc said with a tired voice to one of the men. He stood up and it was apparent that his knees and back ached. He noticed John behind him. "What do you want now?" he scowled impatiently at him.

"I'm still hoping to find my daughter."

"Go home, John, and let her have a little happiness," Doc stated.

"You call being with a harpy happiness?" he asked sarcastically.

Doc turned and confronted him. "With your daughter, yes. Don't you get it? That girl loves that harpy and for some reason that blond male is equally committed to her. Now, just go home and let them have a little peace for a while. Some hunter will get the poor thing's wings soon enough."

"I take it you're not going to help me by telling me what kind of vehicle she was in?" John asked. Doc only glared at the stubborn man. Shaking his head, he ignored John and began talking to someone else.

"He's no help," John said to Charlie.

"It may be too late for a search. The light will be gone soon," Charlie said.

John noticed two girls Kari's age, as they cried and hugged each other. He walked over to them. "I'm sorry to disturb you but I need help finding my daughter, Kari," he inquired.

One of the girls looked up at him. "I know your daughter, Mr. Turner. I was with her last night at the beach. I'm Cindy Williams. My father cuts timber for you" the girl said.

"Cindy, of course," he acknowledged. "I didn't recognize you. It's been a while."

The girl only nodded as she sniffled a little. "Didn't Kari come home last night?" she asked.

"No, she didn't."

"We were all wondering what she would do with that dying gold harpy after she left," Cindy said.

"How did she leave?" John asked.

"She took Jake's old blue vehicle. She and Jake swapped vehicles for the harpy. That harpy attacked Hank and broke his arm on the islands and they flew him to Terrance last night. They must have all just come back when they got into Kari's terrain vehicle and went joy riding when the swarm struck. I almost went with them," she sniffled again.

"Do you know if that vehicle had a communicator in it or even a radio receiver?"

"I think it might have but I doubt if it worked. Hardly anything worked in that piece of junk," she said.

"Well, thank you, Cindy. You've been a big helped." he remarked.

"Mr. Turner, I don't think you have to worry about that poor harpy hurting her. The animal was almost dead when she took it. Jake shot it twice. The guys said that even wounded, the golden had fought off all four of them when they downed it. Before they could tie it up, they had to beat the life out of that slight creature. The guys were betting, the harpy would die before she made it past the harbor."

John only nodded. "Thanks for the information," he said quietly and walked back towards his hover. Charlie was standing by it. "She's in an old blue terrain vehicle and the harpy is in pretty bad shape. Maybe with any luck it will die," he said to Charlie. They climbed in and flew over the highway out of town, late into the night, searching the main roads. Eventually they gave up and headed for home. "Tomorrow, I want the men pulled from the mill and put in every available hovercraft. We'll start our search in earnest at day break," he said as they flew to the estate.

The dark coastal road rose ever steeper, as Kari maneuvered the terrain vehicle slowly upwards. This journey was taking longer than she expected. Huge boulders ascended above and around this narrow path. The ocean breeze blew hard from the northwest and made the small hovering vehicle rock and rattle with each gust. She had stopped to check on Shail and put another tranquilizer patch on him to insure his continued sleep. Traveling this road made her nervous enough without having to contend with him. If he awoke and tried to get out of the vehicle, she would have a hard time restraining him. The dim lights lit the narrow path and frequently she would see the night animals before they would disappear into the jungle on the right side of the road. The further she went the more creatures were along this narrow path.

She had to stop at one point when a herd of raydons crossed the road. The giant six foot brown lizards had stopped when the lights shown upon them. They reared up on their strong back legs and had hissed and snapped at the vehicle before they slowly moved on. Kari was not about to get out and rush them since there were a good dozen of them. They were plant eaters but their large teeth could do some damage if harassed.

The night wore on and Kari was exhausted. It had been two nights ago that she had a full night of sleep. A pale light from the east began to glow through the trees as it descended upon the gray and pink sky. Morning was coming. The mammoth shadowy tree limbs began to take color as Duran ascended on the frontier. It was about this time that the narrow path snaked its way toward the jungle. After a short distance, the vehicle came to a small clearing surrounded by imposing enormous trees. Off to the left stood the small log cabin. Kari pulled the vehicle as close to the door as possible. She sighed with relief. The vehicle settled to the ground as the engines sputtered before becoming silent. Kari got out and stretched her limbs and smiled. They had arrived without being seen. Now, Shail stood a chance at recovery and freedom. She walked to the cabin door and tried to open it. But layers of roots and dirt had grown in front of it. After a few minutes of pulling and tugging, she had removed this rubble and was able to step inside. A pair of dell squirrel chattered at her from the rafters before they made their escape through a broken window. They had obviously made the cabin their home and didn't like this new intruder. The cabin was filthy. A thick layer of dirt rested on the floor. It was apparent that no one had stayed here since her grandfather. And that had been over fourteen years ago. Kari was relieved with this knowledge. It meant that few people would come here and discover her and the harpy. Walking back outside, Kari opened the back door of the vehicle. Shail stirred but did not wake. She gathered the disinfectant and liquid bandages and treated his wound. Afterwards, placing a new antibiotic patch on him. She left the door open and went back to the cabin. Hunger and thirst were on her mind since she had only eaten a little breakfast with Doc. In the cabinet doors she found some old packets of food but they were outdated and inedible. Even the water would not flow from the ancient faucets when opened. An empty jug lay by the sink. Kari picked it up and went back outside.

As a child, she remembered there was a meager mountain stream just beyond the trees. She ambled towards it pushing back the colossal ferns and vines aside, making her way through the old overgrown trail. A short walk later, the stream crossed her path. It was a little bit of heaven as she drank and washed in the cool, clear water. Wild berries grew in the rocks above a cliff and she feasted on them. After eating her fill, she returned to the cabin with the jug full of water. Shail surely had to be thirsty. She wondered just how long the poor thing had gone without food and water.

Back at the vehicle, she placed some water in the cup of her hand. Kari pressed it to Shail's lips. He swallowed several times before his eyes opened slowly. He glanced up at her and then stared at the inside of the vehicle. His eyes widened with fear as he struggled to sit up. The tranquilizer had worn off and he wanted out of this cage. "Easy, Shail. I'm going to help you out. But first, let me get something for you to lay on," she said softly to calm him. She moved from the vehicle to return to the cabin. Once Kari was out of his way, he uncurled his tall lean frame and scurried out of this cage as he made a feeble attempt to stand. The pain of his wounds and broken ribs caused him to double over and he collapsed on the ground. Kari rushed to his side as he curled back up and shivered with panic. Struggling against the pain, he tried to right himself again. Kari shoved him back down and yelled at him. "Lay still! You're safe here!" He panted a little hard as he glanced around nervously.

"You're safe now," Kari said more calmly. "Now stay. Stay put and lay still," she ordered as she wiped her brow with frustration, realizing he was going to be difficult to control. Shail sniffed the air and could detect no man odors in this place. He curled back up and relaxed a little. He gazed up at her with confusion, not understanding why she was obviously upset him. "Good boy. That's good. You must lay still so you'll heal," she said gently and stroked him. Kari slowly got up and walked quickly to the cabin. In minutes, she returned with a large quilt. She laid it next to him and urged him to get on it. Shail would have been happier on the dirt and leaves but for some reason, she wanted him on this filthy musty thing. He tossed his hair and sniffled with disobedience but he could sense her instant irritation. Not wishing her unhappy, he obliged her by crawling on the nasty material. Kari smiled and went to the cabin. She returned with a cup. Filling it with water, she put it to his lips. Shail hissed at it and backed away from the plastic object that smelled toxic. She drank from it and offered it to him again. He sniffed it and despite the smell, the tempting water lured him closer. Finally he eagerly sucked and lapped the water up in the middle of the cup, being careful not to touch the plastic with his parched lips. "You truly are a wild creature," she said softly noticing Shail didn't even drink like a human being. She petted his head to encourage him while he drank.

"I'm going to get you some food now," she said as she motioned to her mouth. She retrieved a small pail from the cabin and she hurried off into the jungle. Once she was gone, Shail forced himself to rise. He could not afford to be this helpless. Hoisting himself up, he cringed with the pain and sweated as he leaned on the vehicle for support. Shail swallowed the lump in his throat as he realized how terribly vulnerable he still was.

Kari walked from the woods and saw him standing. "Shail!" she screamed, rushing to his side. Wrapping her arms around him, she gently forcing him to lay back down as she looked at his distress filled eyes.

"Don't do this, my beautiful little frightened bird," she cooed to him. "There are no hunters here." Kari sat down and leaned against the vehicle as he wrapped his body around her, placing his head in her lap. She stroked his silky hair as he nuzzled her. "I guess this is the only way to keep you still. I hope, you won't force me to keep you drugged," she said quietly. They stayed motionless until they both had fallen to sleep.

Kari awoke to chatter of the squirrels as they leaped in the branches overhead. She jumped up, startled, and looked around for Shail. He was behind her, lying on his side as he leaned on one of his elbows. His deep blue eyes seemed to twinkle with confidence and contentment now. All his anxiety and stress was gone. Then she noticed the half eaten red fruit in his hand. At the corner of the quilt lay a large pile of assorted fruits and nuts. She stared at him perplexed. "Where did all this food come from?" she asked him not really expecting an answer. He tossed his hair out of his face and glanced upward. She knew that it was impossible for Shail to have gathered the fruit. She glanced up but could see nothing but the squirrels and tree limbs. Then she heard the answer. His answer "The harpies" he related to her mind.

"They were here?" she questioned him. He closed his eyes deliberately, confirming her question. With the debilitating drugs out of his system, Shail's mind was unblocked. He could use the harpy telepathy to enter her thoughts. He did not understand her sounds. But he could sense their meaning. Kari smiled wide with this first communication. She had heard Shail's silent communication in their dreams, just as the brown winged harpy had transmitted to her. Perhaps with only a few words of direct meaning, he could understand her better. It was a start.

Kari was happy the harpies had come. She could see Shail was tranquil and subdued with the knowledge his harpies had found him. Though she could not see them, they must be near. Kari began to prepare for the coming night. After rummaging around in the cabin, she found some old solar lights. She cleaned the plates and placed them towards the light, hoping they would recharge before dark. She found a few more quilts and placed them on some bushes to air. It would have been nice to sleep in the cabin tonight but moving Shail was almost impossible especially if he did not want to come in. The cabin was still very dirty and a night under the stars would have to do till tomorrow. Shail's curious eyes watched her with interest as she hurried around. He casually ate and began playing with the jug and the cup, learning to fill these objects over and over. She grinned at him thinking he was like a little boy. As darkness approached, Kari flipped on one of the solar lights. Shail put his hand carefully to it expecting it to be hot like fire but found it gave off no heat. He saw the switch and flipped it off and on and this human light became his new toy. Kari was surprised at how fast he learned. She explained, how the light operated but again she was unsure if he understood all her words. Night came as a cold breeze blew from the water. Kari grabbed the extra quilts and lay down beside him. She tried to cover Shail with a quilt but he would have no part of it as he flapped his unbroken wing and sent all the blankets flying. "I'm cold even if you're not," she scowled at him. He pulled himself close and put his arms around her and then placed his good wing over them. Kari became nervous and considered putting a tranquilizing patch on him. Shail gazed at her with his intelligent eyes and laid his head down submissively, showing her, he would attempt no breeding. Kari sighed and realized she would have to trust him. She snuggled under his wing and was surprised by its warmth. He nuzzled his nose up against the back of her neck and then lay quietly. The wind rustled the tree branches overhead and howled as it rose up from the cliffs near the ocean, which lay a short distance to the west. Kari lay deep in thought as this handsome male harpy held her. Never had she felt so alive and so complete. Gazing up at the stars through the tree limbs, it was like heaven as she ran her hand gently across the large soft creamy yellow feathers. When she did this, he clutched her tightly and affectionately faintly licked the side of her neck.

Her whole life had been of searching and longing and at last it was at an end. The object of her life-long quest, lay quietly sleeping beside her. As this exquisite male held her, all her misgivings of him floated away with the night wind. It just felt so right being with him. Perhaps it was the spell he cast on her or a form of hypnotism, she thought, but it didn't matter because for the first time in her life, she felt pure joy and love. She rubbed her cheek against his and drifted off to sleep.

The light slowly began to fill the morning sky as Shail opened his eyes. It was still very dark when he pulled himself away from her. Kari shivered a little when he lifted up his wing. Knelling over her, he glanced at the nasty quilts that lay in a heap by her feet. Shail picked one up and carefully covered her. She clung to this nasty rag, content with its warmth and continued to sleep. He stood up slowly as a sharp pain gripped his side causing him to wrap his arms close. Taking a few steps, he felt out of breath as the wound tormented him. Shail finally leaned against the terrain vehicle to ease his pain.

His eyes were fixed on the trees beyond as his instincts sensed the approach of another harpy. In seconds, Aron glided down and landed along side of him. Aron's green eyes were bright with elation as he gazed at his golden ruler. He bowed his head with respect towards Shail and there was no need to convey his happiness. Shail could sense it. Then Aron affectionately held him and they nuzzled each other's necks in greeting. Pulling apart, Aron glanced down at the sleeping female and then into Shail's eyes.

"At last she is yours." Aron's silent telepathic voice entered Shail's mind. Shail nodded to him. "The choice was a wise one, for she is very brave and her wit has spared you. I fear you would not be among us if not for her. Her journey far away made her strong for a female even if it brought you much loneliness." Shail nodded again in agreement.

"Yes, it made her strong but I fear it also made her strange. Her devotion to me is true but so are her doubts. She is confused and has made no choice of which world she shall dwell. And even worse, I harmed her trust by forcing a bonding too soon," Shail sadly told him as Aron walked a little closer to look at Kari.

"Time shall heal these doubts. It is wise to wait, she is worthy of you."

"Yes, but time, I do not have nor does my flock. And there are many who seek my pale wings, now that they know of them," Shail conveyed with worry.

"Things changed swiftly since your capture. The black beetles no longer only kill the trees. They lust for all living things. The hunters, who broke your wing, are dead. Killed by a swarm."

Shail looked up at him with surprise. "Their deaths, I celebrate but now this new threat comes to us." Shail breathed deeply and sighed. "Have all our male fly the helpless to the safety of the islands." Shail related to the tall brown winged harpy.

"It is no good. The islands are no refuge as you were nearly lost there. And more and more hunters go there and kill our kind since, this hiding place is known to them. We lost two more at last light," Aron related sternly.

Shail shook his head with aggravation as he ruffled his feathers. He sighed deeply. "And this recklessness in the fledgling's rescue has made me worthless as a ruler. This wound to my side heals but my wing, I do not know," he said bitterly.

Aron raised his eyebrow. "The western harpies follow me, for they know I speak for you. But the others of the river and east shall follow only a gold pair of wings. If you do not mend, all may be lost," Aron communicated with worry.

Shail nodded. "Secure your western flock on the islands for now. The time draws near to deal with these hunters. Take all males who guard me. We can spare them not in this task. Leave a fledgling only to gather my food. He shall give warning if trouble comes." Shail conveyed.

"As you wish." Aron said as he glanced at the pile of fruit on the quilt. "What of the ones protecting these lands?"

"Have them continue," Shail related silently.

"I shall leave you now, for you should take rest. I sense your suffering and it troubles me deeply." Aron said with sadness.

"Be not troubled, my brother. I shall try to heal quickly," Shail said as he wrapped his arms around the brown winged harpy and they hugged and nuzzled each other one last time before they pulled apart.

"May this long awaited female bring you the happiness, you deserve." And with that Aron raised his wings and flew through the trees towards the ocean.

Shail slid back down on the quilt and poured a cup of water from the jug. As he stretched out, the pain eased. He was troubled by Aron's news of the beetles and men. His entire race depended on him and he was of no use to them now. A short time later, a small fledgling fluttered down from the trees and shyly approached him. Once close, he bowed his head and waited timidly. Shail glanced up at him. "There is plenty of food for this light. Come at the dawn," he said to the young harpy. The fledgling nodded and flew away. Shail knew the fledgling was terribly intimidated by him but he also knew that the little guy was very proud to be given the honor of bringing food to the dominate male harpy ruler.

Shail picked up a few of the nuts and popped them in his mouth as he noticed Kari was stirring. She was so beautiful. He longed to clutch her in his arm and cuddle her but he had perceived her fear of him. Aron was right. She was worth the wait. Kari noticed the quilt that he placed on her. She sat up immediately slightly startled then she saw Shail behind her. "I was afraid you had crawled off into the woods," she said with relief.

Shail slid next to her and docilely rubbed his head against her side. Kari smiled and stroked him. "I'd love to lay here all day and do nothing but play you but I have work to do. Starting with treating that wound and giving you your medicine," she said as she stood up and went to the vehicle. After a few minutes, Kari had the antibiotics and other supplies to treat Shail's wound. Taking the old plastic bandage off of him, she reached for the disinfectant. Shail swiftly snatched her wrist as the bottle came near him. This startled her and she dropped it. Shail leaned over and smelled the contents immediately he jerked backwards as if it were poison and defiance filled his bright eyes.

"Shail, don't give me trouble. This will make you heal. You must trust me," she said calmly. He made a low seething sound through his teeth to conveying he was unhappy when she sprayed this stinky foreign stuff on his wound but Shail endured the treatment by holding still. After she had finished, he curled up on his side, pulling his arms and legs in. His body rested on his soft bottom feathers of one wing while the other wing covered him. Tucking his face deep into the feathers so only the blond hair lay exposed. Shail now appeared like a large nesting bird on the quilt, his human body completely hidden from sight. She smiled and knew he wished to sleep. She went to the woods for more water with the jug. "Here is more water for you," she said on her return.

Shail watched her go in to the man made structure. She was gone for some time and his inquisitiveness got to him. He could hear brushing sounds and banging from inside. After a while he struggled to his feet and slowly made his way to the doorway and peered in. Kari was scrubbing a wooden platform with some sort of object. He watched her with interest before she finally noticed him. "Shail you're supposed to lay still. Well, since you're here, you better come in and lay down on the bed," she said and pointed to a platform that rose from the floor slightly. It was similar to the one he had found himself on in the old man's home. Shail shook his hair and turned to leave but Kari quickly caught him by his arm and tugged at him to enter.

"Is everything I want you to do going to be a battle between us?" Kari asked him.

He stared at her and then the bed. Why did she not understand, he did not want to be near these human things. They made him uncomfortable and nervous. And to wish him to be in this cabin was worst of all since it was a human cage, which was deadly for a harpy. Kari could see he was scared but he fought it and sheepishly stepped inside, trying to please her. Shail stared up the ceiling and at the solid walls. His acute smell could only detect the vague essence of men. It had been some time since one had been in this place but harpies, by nature, were claustrophobic. Shail breathed a little hard and shuddered. He could bare no more and quickly stepped outside. Kari gently took his hand and coaxed him back to the threshold. "Come on, there's nothing in there that can hurt you," she tried to convey. He stared at her with pleading eyes. If only he could explain to her what he was feeling, she would not ask this of him. To compare it, would be to dangle a man from a shear cliff with a rope. Most men would be terrified even if the rope were strong. And this is the way harpies felt about being closed in even with an open door. The rope could break and the door could close.

Kari beckoned to him. "Just do this while you're hurt. After you're healed, you can sleep in the trees. I'm afraid that laying in the dirt may infect your wounds and it's cleaner in here," she tried to explain. Shail cringed and jumped slightly over the doorway. The bed had white material on it and it did look very clean. Kari had found the sheets sealed in plastic in an old trunk. Shail sniffed at the sheets before he leaned on the bed with one of his knees, abruptly the material collapsing with his weight. He jumped away startled as it were one of man's deadly nets that would tangle and snare him. This female giggled at his fear. He sniffled at her with annoyance and tried again. This time he realized, it was just soft like a nest of leaves. Shail was determined to overcome these fears that all harpies felt. He lay down on the bed and gazed up at Kari with a little pride. This seemed to delight her and she petted him with approval. This female continued to remove the dirt from this prison. Humans were strange creatures, he thought while he watched her. They tried to escape nature by closing themselves in and ridding themselves of dirt, leaves, and anything else that was natural. He could see that Kari and he had been raised worlds apart and he wondered in which they would live if they remained together. For now, he would dwell in her human world. It was the only way to gain her trust so she would accept him as his mate.

Kari smiled at her slender golden harpy curl up on the bed. She could tell he was trying hard to please her. All her initial fears of forcing a wild harpy to lay still and behave began to dissolve away. Shail would not need to be tranquilized. She busied herself with cleaning the rest of the cabin since it would be warmer at night inside and she may have to be here for some time. After the cabin was livable, she repaired the solar strips on the roof. Large tree limbs rested upon them, breaking the connection. She managed to remove the limbs and repair the damage. As Kari worked, she talked to Shail constantly explaining her efforts. He seemed interested in her words but did not respond to them so she had no way of knowing if he understood her. But, her talking seemed to keep him still and tranquil, so she rambled on about disinfectants and solar strips. Things, she thought for sure, would be of no interest to a harpy. Opening a small closet, she discovered some tools. Among them, an old rusted ax.

"I'm going to move the vehicle to the woods and cover it with tree limbs and ferns so no hover craft will see it," she said to him. Shail tilted his head a little with puzzlement. She went to the side of his bed. "Stay here. I will be back," she said firmly to him for she feared that if she left his presence and drove off in the vehicle, he would leave the cabin even to just follow her. "You stay here?" she tried to convey more clearly. He just stared at her and gave her no answer. He then signed deeply and rested his head on one of the pillows. "You understand me," she said a little sarcastically.

Kari hurried out to the vehicle and jumped behind the driver seat. Pushing the start button, the engines sputtered for a moment, before they finally ran smoothly and the terrain vehicle lifted a few feet from the ground. She drove as far into the jungle as the trees would allow and set it down under the thick blue ferns. Then, taking the old ax, she cut enough branches to cover the entire vehicle. Kari was hot and tired when she finished. Walking back to the clearing, she glanced at the cabin and did not see Shail. He had obviously stayed on the bed, as she had asked. It was late afternoon and Kari felt she had accomplished a lot in one day. Taking the path to the stream, she longed for a cool drink. The stream tumbled down a crest of rock further up and she climbed to this point. The cabin dirt clung to her sweaty body and she stripped her clothes off and stood beneath this little waterfall, wetting her hair and body. The cold water felt wonderful as it soothed her weary body. After a few minutes, she climbed out and dressed quickly not wanting to leave Shail too long. As she made her way back, the sound of an engine could be heard through the jungle. Her heart raced with fear, as she stumbled toward the sound.

Her mind flashed to her father. Shail would be trapped in the cabin and she knew her father would kill the harpy without hesitation. She puffed hard and she raced through the underbrush as the engine sound became louder. The sound came from the direction of the terrain vehicle, she had just hidden. Kari bolted through the ferns and stared at her vehicle. The engines were running as it hovered idly. "How could this be?" she questioned. Then she saw Shail as he hid behind a large tree a distance away from the transport. He started at it with wonder as he bent over and looked beneath it. It was obvious that he was trying to discover how this strange thing stayed above the ground with no wings. Kari casually walked up to the vehicle and shut it off. It settled back on the ground and the engines were silent. Shail slipped towards it cautiously while Kari watched him. He appeared to be in some pain but his scrutinizing of these human objects over shadowed the hurt. He came along side of the vehicle and tapped it triumphantly with his hand.

"Pretty brave aren't we today," she teased him. "First the cabin and now the vehicle." He ignored her as he looked inside through the open door at the many buttons and switches. "Shail, it's going to take longer for you to heal, if you don't lie quietly. The Doc said ten days," she said, as she held up her ten fingers. "It's only been three," as she held up three fingers in front of his face. He took her three fingers and put them down and he held her hand. He then touched her wet hair and this seemed to amuse him a little even though no smile came to his lips. Harpies seemed to lack the facial expressions of a smile or a frown as was true of most animals.

"You think it's funny that I bathed?" she smiled up at him. "Well, now that the cabin is clean, you could be next. Come back with me now. You've conquered this metal contraption," she said and walked slowly out of the woods to make sure Shail would come with her. Shail flung his hair and flapped his unbroken wing at the vehicle then marked it in several places with his urine so all other male harpies would smell his scent and know, it was his and he had defeated the metal beast. Then he proudly followed the female. Kari only shook her head at his wild animal antics.

Back at the cabin, Shail hesitated at the doorway. Then he once again leaped quickly over the threshold as if something would grab him. Once inside, he went back to the bed and lay down. Kari sat next to him as she took a piece of fruit from a bowl by the bed. "I'm glad you're at least housebroken," she mumbled and took another bite. Shail watched her eat it and he stretched his tall slender body out. Then he leaned over and licked the back of her neck while running his hand down her back. This simple act caused her body to be covered with goose bumps and she shook a little. Kari leaped away from him and stood staring at him. The desire to climb between his arms was overwhelming.

"You need to heal," she stammered to him. He could immediately feel her anxiety well up deep with in her. "And, I'm not sure we belong together," she expressed. She bit her lip as soon as the words left her mouth. It was her father and Charlie's warnings that had come back to terrify her. The fear, she lacked the will power to resist him. And it was the fear of him. Would he stop his advances when asked? This male was strong enough now he could easily overpower her. Shail lowered his head, the harpy way of showing submissiveness. He swallowed hard and slowly and meekly stared up at her. Kari could see he was sorry for scaring her.

Suddenly a soft male voice entered her subconscious. "The bond of you and I shall not be unless it is your desire. My fear of dying and leaving no fledgling urged the bonding too soon. My fears caused yours. This, I regret," he related.

Kari put her hand to her mouth and ran from the cabin. Now she understood Shail's motives and why he had tried to mate her. But did he understand that her unwillingness to be with him was not his fault? It was fear of the unknown, she dreaded. Would she lose her mind? Could this bonding kill her? It was these warnings and her mother's death that tormented her. She ran up the path towards the ocean, finally stopping at a high cliff overlooking the water. There she sat down and wept softly. Duran was on the horizon and it would be dark soon. Kari cursed herself as she wept. "What is wrong with me? I love him. I want to be with him always," she thought. Her own heart and body conveyed this to her. She could sense the honor in Shail. He was not capable of rape. She had sensed this about him all along. But it was the terrible question that kept her from him. Would her life be over if she gave in to him?

Kari stayed there until darkness came. She made her way back down the path until she reached the cabin. Walking inside the shadowy room, she could faintly see Shail's body as he had remained on the bed. She crept alongside of the bed until she rested upon it. He did not move as she lay there.

"I'm sorry, Shail. It's not your fault. You have done nothing wrong, it's me," she whispered to him. He listened to her. There were so many things that he wanted her to know but lacked the ability to convey them.

"Do not be this sorry," was the only thing that he could communicate to her. She petted him gently while he lay quietly. "Our time apart and her life among humans has filled her with the human fear of harpies and now we lay, side by side in the dark, just as a mated pair yet both fearing to touch the other," he thought. Shail had sensed Kari's love for him on their first meeting and her telepathic dreams confirmed her desires. Now he realized, these dreams did not hold her doubts. If he had known this, he would never have attempted this bonding despite his own desperation. "She loves me but she is afraid of this harpy world I offer. She needs more time."

He covered her once again with his wing as the cold wind blew through the broken window and out the door. He could feel the torment leave her body as she drifted off to sleep. She nuzzled him unconsciously and the urge to return this affection was hard. Instead he faintly kissed her cheek as she continued to doze. Cuddling against her would have to satisfy him. After a while, he too was asleep.

Charlie and John walked into the dining room and seated themselves at the table. Both were very fatigued. The last two days, they rose before dawn and flew over all the main roads from Westend to Terrance in search of the old blue vehicle. "Where could she have disappeared to?" John said as he stared up from his uneaten plate of food.

"She does not fear the jungle. Perhaps she has taken an old logging road and gone deep into it," Charlie commented. John only nodded.

"We will start with the ones off the main road tomorrow. I hope she did not go there. She has no food. No weapon. Even that harpy couldn't protect her if she got into trouble from what I was told of his injuries," John said with worry.

"Perhaps he is dead," Charlie mentioned.

John looked up from his plate. "He's not dead. If he were, she would have come home. I wish he had died. I'm kicking myself for not killing him years ago," John grumbled.

Charlie looked up from his food and stared at John. "Do not be too hard on yourself. If you had killed the young harpy and she discovered this, I fear she would never have come home or forgiven you."

John looked up at Charlie in anger. "Charlie, I don't want to hear that again. Maybe it's true but at least she would have a decent life. She wouldn't be out in the jungle with some animal. And I wouldn't be worried sick right now," he snapped at the old man.

Charlie was quiet and picked at the food in front of him. Finally, John said to him, "I'm sorry but I am just so worried. Not only about the harpy. You know how dangerous the jungle can be and now we have these man-eating beetles. What if a swarm attacks her vehicle? I hate to admit it but there is a part of me that wishes, that golden harpy could fly. At least he could protect her. Fly her to safety, if it came to that."

Charlie nodded. "Yes, I too have thought of this. But, I have also thought of the fact that he is a golden. I believe that the other harpies would protect them both from the perils of the jungle and the beetles."

"Do you really believe this?" John questioned him.

The Indian lowered his head. "I know this for a fact," he said quietly.

"Tell me what you know." John declared.

Charlie was silent for a long moment, for he knew that John would be upset with him. Slowly he began. "Your daughter has a guardian. He has protected her since she landed on the planet. I believe he was sent to her by the golden harpy."

"What? How do you know this?" John said a little hysterical.

"I saw him. Kari had wandered off into the night outside of Terrance. She was surrounded by a pride of grogins. Before I could get to her, a brown harpy flew down and scared them off."

John rose from the table and paced the room. "And neither one of you told me about this incident," he stammered.

Charlie lowered his eyes. "She begged me not to tell you for fear that you would go after the harpies, if they had come to her again. You would know that they were still interested in her."

"I can understand her reasons but what were yours? You should have told me. I know you aren't crazy about harpies," John stormed.

Charlie looked up at him. "If I had told you, it would have sent you into a rage. You would have gone after the harpies and you would have lost your daughter forever. I had hoped with time, Kari would have come around to your way. She came back still devoted to the harpies. It is unfortunate that she and the golden were thrown together with this hunt, although I never doubted that one day they would eventually meet again. But with time, she might have made the choice to walk away from him. With him injured and helpless, there was no way she could turn her back on him."

John returned to his seat and stared at the plate. He glanced up at Charlie. "You know her perhaps better than myself. You think she has made her choice to stay with him?"

The Indian sighed slightly. "I think she is full of doubt and confused but there is no question of her love for him. And I would have to agree with the old doctor, who witnessed them together. Their affection and devotion to one another is very apparent. John, if you kill that harpy, it will destroy her and her life will be meaningless. All her life, she has loved these creatures and I don't believe she will ever change. These words you do not want to hear but they must be said to you." Charlie said with weariness.

John walked around the table as he rubbed his chin. He picked up the glass of wine and finished it. "I hate that little golden male so much. I should have killed when I had the chance. These stinking nervy goldens have taken everyone I loved from me. I honestly don't know if I will be able to control this anger when I find them."

"Perhaps you should end your search and let Kari decide, if she will come home or stay with him." Charlie said in earnest.

"No. I can't live like this. I have to know if she is all right. When he recovers, he could hold her against her will. I will not stop the search for her."

Charlie rose from the table. "It is late and I am tired. I will see you at first light. I hope you will consider what I have told you. You know, I will help you all I can, even if I don't agree with you," he said as he went to leave.

"Charlie, what would you do if she were your daughter?" John asked staring blankly in space.

"She is like a granddaughter to me. But if she were my daughter, I would let her be. True love and happiness are hard to find as my own life has taught me. If this young male can give her this love and happiness then I would overlook the fact that he is not human. You should know this, since love has only come to you once. And you also know how it feels when it is taken away."

"Leave my wife out of this. Kari's situation is very different from mine," John remarked.

Charlie was now at the door. "John, I see no difference," he said before he left.

John sat at the table for a long time. He finally got up and poured another glass of wine as he walked through the empty silent house. He found himself in front of his desk in the den. Placing the half full glass of wine down, he sat slowly in the chair behind the desk. Glancing down at the bottom drawer, he pulled it open and took out an old picture. He put his hand to his mouth as he stared at the beautiful woman in the photograph. A tear ran down his cheek as he stared at his wife. The old Indian was right, he had only found love once and he could still feel the empty pit in his stomach when he lost her all those years ago.

At dawn Charlie came into the large house. He walked to the kitchen and found it empty. He wandered around looking for John, knowing he wanted an early start. When he reached the den, he saw the forty-year-old man as he slept with his head on the desk. Charlie approached and could see that the photo remained in his hand. It was apparent that he had slept here all night. "John," he whispered. "It is morning."

John stirred as his eyes opened. It took him a few minutes before he was fully awake. "Must have drank too much wine last night," he mumbled as he stood up. Charlie just nodded. "Is Maria here yet?" he asked Charlie.

"I did not see her."

John walked to the kitchen for some coffee. "Ah, I forgot. She told me she would not be in this morning. She's attending a memorial service for the Baker girl and the others that were killed," John said as he drank from the cup.

"You're not going?" Charlie asked.

"No, but I did have Maria send my regrets to each of the families. Some of the men from the mill are also going to it so there will be few hovers in the air for the search." John stated.

"What are you going to do about the swarms?" Charlie asked.

John just shook his head. "I've been so worried about Kari that I don't give a damn about the beetles but I guess, I'd better start dealing with them. I did order all the men cutting timber to return. No sense in risking their lives for a few sheets of lumber. In essence, I'd say we were shutting down. It's no longer safe out there. I guess the next thing would be to reinforce a building at the mill with every metal sheet we can lay our hands on. And then supply it with enough food and water to live on for a period of time. Why don't you organize this, Charlie? I know your heart's not in this search for Kari."

Charlie looked at him with surprise. "I worry for her, as you do but I want to see her happy for a change. I fear she did not tell you, how badly she suffered on Earth."

"It was that bad?" Charlie only nodded. John rubbed the back of his neck as he paced. "I did consider what you told me last night. And I hate to admit it but I'm somewhat relieved the harpies are protecting her." He shook his head. "Never thought I'd hear myself say that. But, I still can't get past the thought of that animal molesting my little girl. I can only hope that golden dies. So, I'm going. You'll stay here and work on the buildings then?"

Charlie nodded reluctantly.

"I'll have a few men check those logging roads with me. The rest can stay here and help you with the building," John mumbled as he finished his coffee and left. Charlie watched as John's hovercraft disappeared over the first hill. "I hope he doesn't find them," he thought. Climbing in his terrain vehicle, he headed for the mill.

CHAPTER 5

▼

Morning came to the small cabin as Shail woke from the sounds of a small bird chirping at the broken window. He stretched his streamlined body as Kari slept at his side. He sniffed the air and could smell the fledgling as he approached the doorway with some fruit in his hands. This was obviously his second trip there since several fruits already lay in the threshold of the cabin. Shail nodded to him with approval as he carefully set the fruit down and flew off for more. Shail climbed over Kari and stood up straight. His wound no longer hurt but his ribs still ached. Shail walked to the door and out into the clearing as the first rays of light filtered through the trees. Thirst was on his mind and no longer wished to drink the stale jug water. Wandered through the massive trees, he came to the same stream where Kari filled the jug. The clear water ran over the smooth rocks and tasted refreshing. His body felt sticky and stank of the medication. His pale cream feathers and hair were stained with the dried blood. Removing his sash, he climbed under the same small waterfall that Kari had used. It was the first time in a week that Shail began to feel like his old self. The pain was an annoyance but it no longer crippled him. He thought of the old man, who had treated him and was still puzzled by his kindness to a harpy. He wondered how many men existed on this land that did not wish to kill him. Shail closed his eyes as the cold water tumbled over him. When his wings and body were clean, he stepped from the waterfall and ruffled his feathers slightly so they would dry. He placed the blood-stained sash back on him and walked back to the cabin. The fledgling sat on a branch in a tree above the cabin. Shail motioned for him to come. In his excitement, the fledgling tumbled down barely landing on his feet. "Go to the makers and bring me new clothing." Shail told him. The fledgling nodded and leaped in the air. Shail knew it would be middle light before the eight-seasoned harpy would return.

Kari still slept when Shail entered the cabin. He raised his eyebrows and lightly stepped across the threshold, determining to rid himself of all these harpy fears. What more could these human things do to him which had not already been done. Facing his own death in the hands of those island hunters had indeed, given him more courage. "That which does not kill one, makes him stronger," he thought. Kneeling down by the sleeping lovely blond female, the irresistible desire rose as he reached out to stroke her. But suddenly, he pulled his hand quickly away remembering her torment from yesterday. Shail sighed realizing that he must also practice patience and must wait until she came unhindered to him. He no longer would coax or stimulate her into submitting to him. Kari slowly opened her eyes and saw him kneeling beside her. She touched his long wet hair and smiled. "You beat me to it," she said. He looked at her strangely, as she sat up. "I was going to wash that hair of yours today," she remarked while rising from the bed. Kari walked over to the pile of fruit that lay in the doorway and began picking it up and bringing it inside. "This is better than a store," she said as she took a bite out of one of the fruits. Shail stood up and began inspecting the many items in the cabin. "You feel better but you still need the medication."

Shail raised his head with insolence and began to move towards the door. Kari leaped in front of the doorway cutting off his escape.

"No, Shail. It's not going to kill you, to have the medication for a few more days," Kari said and led him to the cabinet. Shail endured the treatment once again. "And I need to wash this sash of yours." she said as she tugged on it. This was all the domestication Shail could tolerate for one day. He tugged back and shook his long blond hair and sniffled at her with annoyance. Then he retreated to the comfort of the outside. This female that he was destined to bond with, did not seem to understand that he was the king of the harpies and highly respected among his kind. Instead, this Kari treated him like a lame ignorant pet. "I want you to lay down," she called to him. He indignantly glanced back at her, flipped his long hair in rebellion and kept walking. Kari hurriedly ran after him. She could see his wounds no longer hinder him as he headed up the path lightly stepping erect and tall. They made their way to the beach cliffs as Shail gazed out at the ocean. Several winged lizards glided in the sky to his right, as they searched for insects among the dunes. He looked at the fly reptiles with a longing and Kari could sense, his desire to fly. "Your wing will heal and you'll fly again." she expressed to him. His face grew serious and she knew that this plagued his mind. She stoked his neck and shoulder to comfort her disabled little harpy. He tenderly nuzzled her to show his appreciation and then quickly withdrew so he won't spook or scare this wary female.

They stayed by the water for the rest of the morning and slowly walked the cliffs and seashore. Kari began to relax and grow more confident in this relationship. Shail had related to her, there would be no bond unless she desired it and she could tell by his standoffishness, he meant it. Her perception of him began to change. She was starting to see that he was not some beautiful injured animal only worthy of her care and defense but rather as another person with deep feelings and emotions to rival her own. His body language conveyed to her his devotion, annoyances and fears, as well as his joys and sadness. Shail was as complex as any human being. And with this knowledge, he was her equal she began to trust him and herself.

By late afternoon, they returned to the cabin to eat and drink. As Kari started to enter the door, the fledgling soared down between them. Kari was startled and jumped with fear to one side. Shail tilted his head back and gleamed at her. "He scared me," she exclaimed as she looked up at him. His blue eyes twinkle and he would have laughed at her if he had been a man. Shail took the sash from the hands of the young harpy and with a nod sent the fledgling back to the trees. He untied the old sash and dropped it to the ground, exposing his naked body. "I thought, you were just modest when you won't give me your sash. I now see you just preferred a new one." she said as he placed the small clean sash around his waist. Shail tossed his head and walked past her towards the cabin. It was obvious this female did not know the meaning of the sash. It was not worn to cloak his sex organs, which where already sheathed and covered in straight blond hair but it was a symbol, worn to demonstrate that harpies were more than just animals. And yet, like animals, harpies felt no embarrassment of their nude bodies unlike humans. He stepped with dignity across the cabin threshold since it no longer concerned him.

At night Kari washed her dirty clothes in the sink and wrapped herself in a torn sheet fashioned as a dress. Hanging them to dry, she joined Shail on the bed. They curled up around each other, as they had done on the previous night with his wing over them. As she snuggled up against him in the flimsy dress, she could feel him become aroused as he struggled to control his male urges, finally as a distraction, he pitifully buried his head in the pillows and lay quietly. The more Shail resisted, the more Kari admired and respected him and her faith grew for the handsome harpy.

The days began to blend into one another. They would rise with the morning light and eat the fruit in the cabin. Then set out for a day of exploring the beaches or jungle. They washed in the afternoon under the small waterfall. This is when Shail suffered the most as he fought his male lust and desires to caress her. He stared at her attractive slender nude body as the cool water flowed over her breasts beneath her long blond wet hair. He'd breathe hard and retreat from the water and her to seek the consoling jungle. Kari also was miserable as she craved to touch and stroke him but knew, this encouragement would only be torture for both of them. It was her mind and fears that created this invisible wall between them and it was a wall only she could tear down.

The days past quietly, Kari shed her clothing of heavy khaki pants and shirt to wear a short dress made from one of the sheets. It was cooler and lighter in the heat of the jungle. Soon her body was as tan as his. They drank from the stream and Kari never filled the jug again. Instead of her taming and domesticating him, it was she, who was changing and becoming more like him as she slowly slipped away from the human world. They were like two wild animals wandering in the wilderness. Kari never felt this much peace and happiness as she following this lanky blond harpy in the trees.

Shail no longer needed his wounds bandaged, as they were all healed. Only his broken wing remained, a weakness and an obvious distress for him. Kari continued to talk to him and she noticed how quickly he grasped the meaning of her words. She could vocally speak to him and now instead of only sensing his response, he answered her subconscious with the English language in sentences.

The process began of them learning from each other. Him quickly grasping the meaning of each word sound as Kari's sound and her mental thoughts would merge to convey the English language. And he was reluctantly learning about the human world while she began to fine-tune her sixth sense and communicate silently to him, while experiencing of a harpy's life in the deep woods.

Another week passed as they walked through the jungle. Kari's grandfather and Charlie had taught her the dangers of the jungle but it was this mute beautiful harpy, who taught her its mysteries. Every day had become an adventure for her, as Shail voice would enter her subconscious and telling her of the plants and animals. What amazed her was his relationship with the other animals. They showed no fear of a harpy, as these same animals would flee in terror from a man.

On this day, they traveled deep into the trees. Kari had stopped to rest on a log while Shail disappeared out of sight. She suddenly heard the low seething sound and crunching leaves of a large animal. She jumped to her feet as the large blue head of a carnivorous lizard appeared, awaken by her scent. Kari did not cry out but called silently to Shail. In seconds, he was at her side. The giant blue and red reptile came out of the underbrush and Shail just calmly stared at it while the animal came closer, flicking it's long tongue towards them. "It's going to attack us," she whispered.

"No, it has just fed. It is not hunting only curious of us. But the senses in its tongue, has smelled your fear as I have. You have made yourself a target and prey," he communicated to her. Shail extended his wings to make himself look bigger in the presence of the towering dragon then he fiercely leaped at it while he hissed loudly at the reptile. Immediately the startled giant lizard thought it had become the victim of the smaller winged creature. It darted into the woods with fright from the attack. "You must conquer these fears of the jungle, as I conquer mine of the human world," he related.

She glanced up at him. "You should be afraid of the humans, for they nearly killed you and would do it again."

"There is a difference between fear and caution, is there not?" he asked. Kari only nodded in agreement. "I shall keep the caution." Kari sat back down on the log and watched Shail pick a few mushrooms by the base of a tree. "These heal head pain but only a small one, should you eat." he related to her. She smiled at him, as she was deep in thought. She had initially admired Shail since he was so gorgeous and wild but now it was his intelligence, she revered.

"If only the people of Dora knew him as she did, they would realize that he possessed only the best of human traits. His gentle quiet nature and wisdom and honor, all made her love him more," she thought. "If only her father knew him, he would not hate him so."

Shail walked to her side and bent down to her. "You miss him?" he asked.

She looked up at him a little surprised. "I don't miss him but I know he's worried about me. If my father only knew you as I do, he would not wish your death."

This seemed to annoy Shail slightly as he stood up. "He knows me and the harpies as do other men. It does not stop the hunting or killing."

Kari rose up. "You don't understand, Shail, my mother was taken by a golden harpy and it resulted in her death. That is why my father does not like you," she explained.

"I do understand and I have seen this story in your mind. It is this story that scares you and separates us in the dark. But, I shall tell you this. Your father has told you this story, as seen through his human eyes. But I know this story from a harpy's eyes." he related. Kari stared at him incredulity.

"How would you know?" she asked him.

"It was my golden father he killed and your mother was not taken against her will, as your parent has told you, just as I have not taken you. Your mother died defending my father. She willingly stepped in front of the weapon to protect his life," he said as he turned away from her.

"Shail, I didn't know," she said and she could feel the rare anger burn within him.

"These humans say many lies about us. It is because of these lies, that we are hunted and killed. They say we are a threat and a danger but it is they, that are these things," he related as he took the path towards the cabin.

Kari followed behind him a short distance. "Was it true, her father knew that his wife was protecting a golden harpy just as Kari knew she would do the same for Shail," she thought. She watched the tall blond harpy as he walked ahead of her. It had come down to believing Shail's side of this story or her father. She knew she needed to choose. "Shail, wait for me," she called as he got further ahead. Shail stopped in his tracks and went back to her. He gently took her hands in his.

"I am sorry. This anger, I do not understand. It makes me say and do things that are not a harpy's way. I did not wish you to choose between your father and myself. You love us, both. And we both love you. You should not love him less, because of my father's death or his dislike of me. This man cares for you a great deal. Even now, he still searches, when most men would have stopped," he related.

"If Dad really killed your father, it is I that should say I'm sorry," she said sadly.

"These are sorry times for all harpies. But Kari, judge me with your own eyes and heart not with your father's. I think you know, that I would rather die, than see any harm come to you."

Kari could only look into his profound deep blue eyes and feel his compassion. She leaned up and kissed him on his lips. Something she had not allowed of herself since it had ignited an uncontrollable passion. He kissed her back as his arms wrapped around her. She ran her hand up the side of his legs and under his sash. He breathed heavy with excitement and she could feel him become firm as he pressed against her. Shail caught his breath and swallowed hard as he gently pushed her away by her shoulders. He shook his head with distress.

"No," he related, trying to compose himself. "Do not start something that I can not stop once I am fully aroused and committed to the mating. What you are feeling, is not what shall bind a pair. You feel guilt and remorse for me, and betrayal towards your father. I shall not bond and take you as my mate with these doubting feelings. It would be a bonding of regret for both of us. Come. It grows late and the darkness shall soon be upon us." He said and started once again down the path. She stood still for a moment and watched him leave. He knew her very soul and now, she was sure she wanted him. It was as if this handsome noble male was made to belong to her, regardless of any risks. Kari realized that Shail's quiet humble way was his way of gently courting her and it had worked.

They returned to the cabin in the dark. The fledgling seemed excited as he dove from a limb and rushed to Shail. Kari watch them converse silently with one another as Shail bent down and was now eye level with the fledgling. Shail took him by his tiny arms and Kari could see it was serious. The fledgling then darted off, towards the ocean.

"What is it?" she said to Shail as she walked closer.

"I must leave this place tonight. It is no longer safe. One of the human metal birds flew over the cabin. What is it you call these?" he asked.

"A hover craft," she said.

"Yes, a hover craft but it did not land, so I am not sure, if they know we are here or if they saw the vehicle you hide. Vehicle?" he questioned her language.

"Yes, the terrain vehicle," Kari said confirming his silent words.

"If you chose to come with me, you must make ready. I shall understand if chose to stay and return to the humans. A harpy's life may not be the best for you, for it can bring much fear and even death. I do not know the length of my life. There are many hunters who seek a golden harpy and they have learned of me and of my pale broken wing. They search hard now, on these lands near ocean, as does your father. If these hunters find me, it shall be dangerous for you. It is safer if you live among the humans than as the hunted," he said to her.

Kari put her arms around him. "Shail, I don't care about any of the risks or dangers any more. All I know is I want to be with you."

He held and nuzzled her. "It pleases me you wish to remain. A great sorrow would fill my heart if I lost you."

Kari turned on a light in the cabin and glanced around the room. There really was nothing for her to bring that the jungle couldn't provide.

"Where we go is cold, your human clothes may better suit you," he related.

She nodded and changed back into her pants and shirt. She grabbed a sheet for clothing and then thought of Shail's sash. The material was made by a large insect, which spun huge webs of the cloth. She dropped the sheet on the floor and decided against taking it. Then she saw Doc's old communicator as it lay on a table. She picked it up. "This is the only thing I will bring," she said finally.

Shail walked over and looked at it. "What is it?" he asked.

"It is called a communicator. It allows me to talk to other humans that are far away."

Shail examined it. "You wish to talk to others?"

"No, Shail, but it could be useful. Just like your wing, I don't know when to remove the splint. I could talk to the old doctor and he would tell me if enough time had healed it. I forgot to ask him when we left. Or, if I had trouble, I could call my father and he would come to me." Shail breathed deeply, for he did not trust this man made thing but he could see the value it could provide for her.

He finally nodded. "We shall eat as we walk. Let us leave this place now."

They put some of the fruit in an old cloth bag along with the communicator and went out into the dark jungle. "Where are we going?" Kari asked.

"Into the high northern mountains," he silently answered her.

They traveled through the night as Kari followed him on his trek north. The journey was slow since it took them deep into the thick brush and up over steep terrain. Kari had to use her hands to crawl up some of the high cliffs. "When do we rest?" she called to him.

"We stop and rest at first light," he answered.

This was not what she wanted to hear. "Won't it be better to rest now and continue on at day break? We're far from the cabin," she said, a little out of breath.

"Not far for a hover craft," his noiseless voice answered her mind.

"You certainly learn the human words quickly," she remarked. She could see him glance back at her in the shadows.

It had been a long night, when the first rays of light filtered between the trees. Shail had come to a mountain stream and leaned down to drink when Kari finally walked up to him. "I'm too tired to even drink," she complained as she dropped down beside him.

"We shall stay here and rest. With the dark, we start again," he told her.

"Won't it be easier and faster, if we slept at night and traveled during the day?" she whined.

"Yes, it would be easier but not safer. It is the harpy way," he related as he took another drink and then stretched out under some giant ferns. "You sleep and I shall find us some food in a little while. The fledgling has returned to the islands and tells my people where I go, so we must find our own food now," he related to her.

Kari was tired but managed to lean over the water and drink then she crawled next to Shail and put her arms around him and slept. She woke in the afternoon and found him gone but heaps of moss lay around her, where he had built a small nest to make her more comfortable. Stripping her cloths off, she waded into the stream to wash. Now that it was light, she could see the high cliffs that they had traveled over last night. The scenery was breathtaking as she stared across the valleys and mountains. The ocean could barely be seen from here. They had covered a lot of territory in one night. Lying back down on the soft moss nest, she saw Shail coming out of the jungle. He held two large fruits in his hands. He broke one open and handed half of it to her. "It is hard to get food, when you do not fly," he commented with annoyance.

She laughed a little at his frustration and his face formed a rare scowl. "You find this human humor funny, that I can not fly?" he asked silently in a displeased tone.

"Shail, sometimes you are a little too serious. Of course, I don't think it is funny that you have a broken wing and can't fly. But you're just so adorably cute when frustrated."

He shook his head again. "So it is my unhappiness that causes this humor?"

"Come here. I just think you're so sexy and appealing when you're a little vulnerable. I do love you so much," she said and pulled him closer and rapped her arms around his neck. Then she kissed him. Shail tried to pull away but she clamped her hands tightly and would not let him go. Giving in, he kissed her back, as she lay nude against the velvety moss under the giant ferns. Stirring his mating instincts, he quickly jerked away and trembled slightly. "This tempting causes much anguish in an unproven male," he pleaded and shook his blond hair to gain control.

"I do not want you to anguish any more," Kari said sheepishly and beckoned him to come.

He could sense her love and longing for him. "You wish me to become your mate?" he asked.

Kari only nodded and instinctively exposed her throat to him as a sign of submission. She was offering her life to him. He aggressively clutched her throat in a deadly hold with his hand as he knelt over her. "I accept this female life and vow to protect it as long as I breathe. You are mine now," he said and took off his sash.

Kari stared at his handsome nude body. Her insides ached with lust and love for him. He slowly leaned over her, lowering himself between her legs as his mouth frantically searched for the nipples on her breasts which lay hidden under her long blond hair. Now he began to feed on her as if he was a nursing fledgling. This aroused her maternal instincts creating a desire to bear his offspring. He continued to lick and suck like an infant until she was so inflamed, she craved him. He rubbed against her until they were united, all the while, distracting her with nipping and licking until he was completely penetrated. Now he began copulating slowly with his head lying over her shoulder but this female's wiggling body excited him terribly and he fought for self-control. Shail wanted this first mating to be tender and gentle with his new mate. But Kari had wanted him for so long, she wanted no part of this tame sex. Biting him hard on the neck, to encourage and stimulate him so he would lose this control. Shail's wings fluttered frantically with the breeding while he pumped hard, his animal instincts taking over. Closing her eyes, Kari ran her hands down the wet tense muscles of this sleek gorgeous creature that had become a part of her. Shail violently lunged against her until he was gratified with the release of his sperm. This mating completed, the bonding had started. As bonded pair, they belonged to each other until their deaths. Shail toppled on top of her out of breath. His body and hair was wringing wet with the nervous sweat of a virgin stud. Kari also breathed hard, as her head cleared of stars and dizziness. She never felt this good, this complete. She kissed him gently to show her approval and satisfaction. Slowly he slid to her side, still not wanting to release her. He kissed and nuzzled her softly, wrapped his limbs around his petite pretty bride.

They lay still for some time, as their breathing returned to normal. Kari rose to drink and wash in the stream as he watched her. Soon he joined her but thirst was not on his mind. Like a normal male animal, he sniffed her as she knelt by the stream. His keen nose and senses told him her egg was ripe. This excited him terribly as he danced around her, tossing his hair with his long cream wings slightly extended and ruffled. Shail was courting and pursuing her in true harpy fashion, like a breath-taking bird. Kari loved his flashy harpy performance. He truly was half bird and half man. She shook her hair and sniffled at him, copying his animal gestures when he wanted something, giving him consent to mount her again. Shail dropped to his knees behind her and firmly impregnated himself deep inside of this sensual female. Shail stroked rapidly to inseminate his seeds into her egg but she had just depleted him and he struggled to force a second release so soon. This distressed him as he lunged and nipped at the back of her neck to stimulate himself. Flapping and beating his wings against the hard ground with each thrust, he finally reached the pleasurable climax. Shail crawled, out of breath, into the stream and collapsed in cool water, washing the sweat from his weary body. Kari smiled happily at him and she joined him in the soothing water. They soaked for some time until Shail climbed out. Ruffling his wet feathers, he curled up on a stone in the light to dry them as he slept. Kari let him rest briefly as she ate some of the fruit and watched her drained little male. Now that she bonded with him, she couldn't get enough of his long slender beautiful body. She went over and lay down next to him. But soon, she caressed and licked him, forcing him to perform. Soon he was erect and breeding her again. Gone was the human kissing and harpy courtship as they mated more like the jungle animals. Once a female accepted the male, he would breed her until he dropped. This marathon of animal mating required him to mate her at least twenty times in a day. In between copulations, Shail would catch quick naps to regenerate himself. Now that the bonding had started, they would not be moving on as they mated through the night. By dawn the next day, Shail lay curled up alone in a ball, in the customary sleeping form of a bird with his head tucked under one wing. Kari slept next to him completely fulfilled and gratified in the nest. He slept for several hours but woke and nuzzled his nose against her neck to wake her. Shail's eyes filled with a questioning if she still wanted him. Upon seeing him, she smiled and pulled him to her. And once again, Shail ascended on her and the procreation began.

The bonding lasted for another day and night. During that time, Kari ate very little and Shail ate nothing at all. At the end of two days, their bodies could endure no more. Kari smiled strangely at him in the nest as he lay quietly watching her. His eyes light up and he pulled himself to her. "A fledgling grows in you now." he said elated as he kissed and licked her softly.

She looked at him curiously. "How do you know that?"

"A harpy can sense such things," he explained lying back down.

"Shail, are you telling me, you're animal senses are so good, you can tell when I'm pregnant?"

Now he sat up and looked at her. "No, I am the male and I would not know such things but you would. You would sense my seeds have merged with your egg."

"But you said a harpy would know." Kari questioned, still not understanding him.

Shail stared at her incredibly, swallowed hard as he tilted his head with confusion of his new mate. "I spoke of you. That a female harpy would sense if the bonding was fruitful,"

Kari laughed at him nervously. "I'm no more a harpy than my own father."

Now Shail eyes filled with panic as he stared at her with disbelief. He gently took her hands. "This is partly true. Your father is no harpy but your mother was. I thought you knew."

Kari jerked away from him in shock. She stared at her stunning blond husband and began to see, they did look very similar. It was not only looks that made them similar but also their behavior. She had always slept curled up and ate the same vegetarian diet as a harpy. Her love of the jungle and hatred of confinement was the same. This also explained why she was so drawn to the harpies and her undying love for Shail while at the same time, never seeking the company of men. Even her severe depression, she suffered on Earth was now understandable. Then she remembered old Doc's blood transfusion that saved Shail's life. Shail had received her harpy blood not human blood. And then there was her ability to communicate with the harpies. It had nothing to do with a sixth sense. She could speak to them because she was a harpy. All the mysteries began to fall into place. Kari stumbled away from Shail as the truth and realization sunk in. He meekly approached her as she sat in a daze by the stream. "Why didn't anyone tell me?" she mumbled.

"If your mother had lived, she would have told you. She would have told you I was marked as your mate. But the choice to accept me, still lies with the female."

"So I could have chosen a man. Do harpy males also bond with women?" she asked pathetically and confused.

Shail embrace her. "No, my love, our males are few from the hunting and only bond with one or two of our female harpies. There are more female harpies and some take men of honor as mates as did your mother. It is also known no woman can bear a harpy fledgling. And yet, we are accused of stealing and mating women but this is only a human lie."

"Then it's also untrue that a woman goes insane and dies when taken by a male harpy," she uttered.

"This is a half truth, since most humans think our harpy females are women since it is only the males that have wings. Our bonding is forever and to lose a mate, causes the despair. A female harpy, whose mate is killed and she forced back to the human world, shall often lose the will to live. If hopelessness and despair completely fills our minds and hearts, we suffer from shock and will our own deaths. Even us males suffer this fate when men cage us." he related gently.

"I know of this, despair and hopelessness. I fought it for ten years on Earth. I only wanted to die. I kept a small piece of your sash when I was sent away. I would smell your scent on it and the despair would fade. It saved me on many a lonely night and gave me the courage to go on till I found you," she murmured.

Shail clutched her tightly. "I too longed for you. I have flown the length of this land countless times over many seasons in search of you and every darkness, I sought you in my dreams." Shail also now understood his beautiful mate better. He sensed her love for him on their first meeting. Yet when she returned, she rejected him. He had feared her life in the stars and among too many humans caused her doubts. Now he understood, it was her true nature that had been hidden from her. Her doubts were not of him but of herself.

"My whole life has been a lie," she said with remorse as Shail held her.

"It is your father's lie, not yours. I shall tell you all of yourself, I know," he began. "It troubled the harpies greatly that their last golden female was being raised by her father, a man who had killed their ruler, my father. They started coming to you at the lake so you would know them. As your fear lessened, I went to see my future mate. Looking into your eyes for the first time as you lay injured, I wished for no other and your spell was upon me. But then you disappeared from the land. Your father knew the truth of us. And this is why he sent you to the stars. Since your birth, he has known, we were bred for one another. Your mother happily told him, you had been chosen to be the mate of the next golden harpy ruler. Your father rejected this harpy bonding, claiming you would be raised human and it would be a man that would become your mate. Your mother was face with a terrible decision. Should she leave her man mate, whom she loved or secure the golden line by taking you back to the jungle and the harpies? When my father and your mother met to decide your future, it was at this meeting they were killed. The harpy decision of your fate, died with them. This is the truth of your mother's death. And it is the truth of you. You and I are the last, Kari, the last of the golden harpies, the last rulers of our race. There are no others." he expressed.

Kari breathed deeply. "I understand. It all makes sense to me now."

"And to I. You are unhappy with this knowledge, you are harpy?" he asked nervously.

She pulled away and looked up at him. "I have always longed to be among harpies. The first time I looked into your eyes, I also wished for no other and your spell was also upon me. This knowledge has made me whole and all my doubts are gone. I know where I belong. It's with you," she softly stated. Shail kissed her and for the first time, he could sense true contentment in her.

The afternoon came and Kari helped Shail gather the fruit from the trees. They returned to their nest to eat them. Shail could feel the peace and security that dwelled in his lovely mate. She had traveled a long and hard journey of misery and doubts but at last, she truly was home. He watched her eat the fruit as she lay against him. Her thoughts were only of him and the arrival of their golden offspring. "We shall eat and rest for now. But, when the darkness comes, we must continue into the mountains. I have no regrets of our bonding in this place but I fear, we have lost valuable time in distancing ourselves from the cabin," Shail related.

Kari nodded, no longer questioning him. A complete roll reversal had taken place. In the beginning, she had ruled this relationship and made all the decisions as she treated Shail like wild animal. But now, she knew him. His intelligence and wisdom exceeded hers in his jungle. He was the dominant mate and ruled her fate. She trusted and loved him, and felt proud and worthy to belong to such a noble male. Shail placed a pealed piece of fruit in her mouth, feeding his little brave female, who now depended on him. Kari gazed up at him and tried to imagine, how she had once saw of him as only a wild innocent creature that needed her protection and care. Now, she could only see her mentor, her guardian her husband. Shail would willingly die to protect his female. She kissed and nuzzled his hand as he fed her another piece of the fruit. His royal blue eyes sparkled and he was feeling the same happiness and contentment that dwelled in her.

After eating their fill, they curled up in the nest as Shail covered her with his wing. Soon they were asleep. A few hours had passed, when Shail jerked his head up and sniffed the air nervously. He jumped up to his feet and sniffed the wind that rose from below. Kari woke and saw the terror in his alert eyes. "A danger draws near. We must flee quickly and quietly now." Walking to the stream, he beaconed to her. "We follow this water, for it leaves no trail."

"What is it?" she asked using her thoughts to communicate with him.

"The scent of men rides the wind to this place," he answered with worry. She now understood his terror. Only men could create this kind of fear in him. They quickly walked in the middle of the pebble-covered stream, careful to leave no prints behind. They were high on a cliff, when they finally came to a brief stop. Shail glanced back down to the valley they had left hours ago. The light was fading as Duran could be seen sinking into the ocean far beyond this peak. His youthful regal face was full of contempt, as he stared down at the trees. "There," he pointed. "There they are. They shall soon be at our bonding nest. We must travel the dark before they hunt us in a hovercraft."

Kari looked hard and could barely make out the human figures, as they stood in a small clearing on the side of the valley. She could feel his aversion towards these men that sought his wings as they moving forward up the valley walls. "Why do they not use a hover now?"

"I believe, they found our trail from the cabin and hoped to surprise us. It is this silent hidden way that these hunters succeed in killing our kind, for most harpies can evade a hunter if made aware of him. If the wind had not changed, I would not know of them. I would be their trophy now. As for you, I do not know of your fate. It is said, some hunters are gentle with a female harpy and allow their freedom, for it is you, who shall bear more males for them to hunt, just as a female zel is spared and only the males are killed for the trophy antlers. Other hunters are very cruel to our wild females and a female can suffers a fate worse than death. Come, we must continue on. We shall leave the stream and travel this hard ridge," Shail related, as he turned his back on the men below. "The moons shall be full tonight and you should see our path more easily."

Kari nodded to him, as she followed him on to a ledge. She hurried to keep stride with his long pace as all light faded. They had reached a summit and began their ascent down the other side. The wind picked up and it was colder as they traveled north deeper into the mountain range. Half way through the night, Shail stopped. "Do you tire?" he asked.

"I'm tired, but I want to keep going. I want to be as far away from them as possible."

Shail nodded and sensing she did not fear for herself. She feared for his safety. The full moons did light the path. As Kari traveled further, she became accustomed to the rocky trail. When they came to steep inclines, Shail would stop and help her descend them. Kari knew if Shail was alone, he could cover this ground more quickly, as he sprang from ledge to ledge with the grace of a bird. He caught her thoughts. "You do not hinder me but make this life worth living. Do not worry so. The danger has past. Men fear to travel the night winds into these mountains. We have escaped for now," he said. Kari smiled up at him, as the strong breeze whipped at his glossy long hair, sending it over his wings as his eyes shimmered in the light of the full moons.

"I'm glad to learn this," she related with her subconscious. She was slowly abandoning all human things and speech as she embracing her harpy side completely.

The golden harpy pair traveled till dawn and had ascended into a small valley on the other side of the mountain summit. Ahead lay the towering black mountain range higher and steeper than the ones they had left behind. The morning light shone on the giant black peaks that crested above all plant life as they greeted the dawn. The valley was thick with enormous trees and underbrush. Shail stopped next to some small water pools that had formed between the rocks. "We shall rest here for a while. There is much cover of tree and the hard rocks have left no trace of our coming." Kari went to one of the ponds and knelt down cupping the water in her hands and took a drink. "You rest and I shall bring back food for you," he related, seeing her fatigue.

She coiled up and watched him disappear into the trees. She was exhausted from the bonding and the foot travel. She didn't notice the fearless colorful birds that hopped from branch to branch right over her head. Shail returned soon with two large roots that dripped with a sticky substance. He walked past Kari, who had fallen asleep. Smashing one of the large long roots open against a flat rock, he began to eat the orange contents, as he watched her. "Better she sleep," he thought. When he had finished eating, he curled up next to her and she instinctively wrapped her arms around him and continued to sleep. He closed his eyes to rest but remained awake. He knew he could not afford to sleep yet. His enemies were a safe distance from him but they still searched with the light of day. They had been on his trail and had come close and they knew, he was probably still within this area, if they had knowledge of his broken wing. These thoughts kept him on edge despite the comforting words, he had told Kari. She did not need the worries of the hunted. It would only terrify her. This distress, he had faced all his life.

They rested for several hours and then Shail woke her as he nuzzled the side of her face. "We must go now and put this valley behind us on this light. There are few tree and cover on the top of the next mountain, this must be traveled under the cloak of darkness," he said to her. She got up sluggishly, as she dragged her limbs forward. "Eat this root as we walk, it shall give you the strength you need," he said and smashed the other sticky root against a rock. Kari took the root and chewed on it as she followed Shail through the deep forest. She was pleasantly surprised by its sweetness and enjoyed the bright orange pulp. When she had finished, she did feel a renewed stamina and energy as she glided along the forest floor behind this golden male.

As they crossed the valley, they came across a large herd of zels. The zels raised their heads and watched them but did not dart away. Suddenly, Shail froze. He raised his head and tilted it to one side as he listened. "Come quickly," he said to her. "We must move closer to these animals and lay on the ground as they would." Kari followed him into some very dense under brush along side of the herd of zels. She noticed that the zels too were no longer grazing on the foliage but had raised their heads while their ears twitched from side to side. They seemed unconcerned with the two harpies but had their attention focused toward the sky. Kari could now hear the sound of a hovercraft as it came closer. The zels scattered leaving the open forest floor. They darted into the thick bushes as well, curling their bodies to hide. The craft moved slowly overhead and stopped. It hovered for a while over the hidden zel herd and harpies before if finally moved on up the valley. Shail and Kari were motionless and watched it.

"These are good hunters, for they have guessed the direction we go," Shail said.

"Yes, they're good hunters. That is my father's hovercraft," she related seriously.

Eventually, the sound of the hovercraft could not be heard. They stayed among the zels for some time until evening approached. "It's lucky that herd was near since my father has a heat seeking device on his hovercraft," Kari told him.

Shail looked at her with interest. "Explain this heat seeking device," he asked.

"Your body gives off heat. This machine can see your heat through the trees."

Shail nodded, "I understand this now. We have always taught our young to hide among animals when it is too late to flee and a fledgling cannot out-fly these hovercrafts. It is known, these metal birds can see through the trees but other animals confuse their sight. I understand how this false sight is possible now," Shail said.

"Harpies learn quickly," she acknowledged.

"We all must learn or die," he commented.

Shail quietly coaxed the herd of zels to travel up the valley much like a collie herding sheep till they reached the next mountain. Darkness came and they left the animals. They began to climb in the black of night. Off in the distance, they could see the lights of the hover as it traveled to other valleys below. Kari breathed deeply and stopped for a moment to watch the distant lights. "I wish he would leave me alone. Can't he understand that I have chosen to be with you?"

Shail came up along side of her. "It is the worry and dislike of me, that urges him on," he said to her.

"Yes, you are right. To lose his only daughter to a harpy would be unforgivable in his eyes. If it was love that drove him, he would be pleased that I'm finally happy," she said sadly. They moved up the rocky cliffs and the lights of the hover eventually disappeared over the side of a mountain crest.

Shail was beginning to doubt his decision to send the cabin fledgling back to the islands and safety. Had he known that Kari's father was so determined to find them, he would have sent the young one to find Aron or one of the other adult harpies. They would have come and flown he and Kari to the mountains and out of her father's reach. But Aron and all the males were on the continent gathering the female harpies and fledglings and taking them to the safety of the islands away from the swarms. He doubted the young fledgling could have found Aron or the others anyway. And he did not realize, this hunt would last this long or go this far. These thoughts tortured him as he climbed in the dark. It had become apparent that this man would not rest until his daughter was found and he was dead. Even in the sanctuary of these high mountains, he was not safe from this man called Turner. This human was traveling the dangerous strong winds of the mountains at night. Shail knew most hunters would not take this risk, the risk of a powerful gust slamming the metal bird in to the sides of the dark mountains. "His love of her and his dislike of me must be very strong," Shail thought. He glanced up and could see the lights once again in the distance. Turner had killed Shail's father but as Shail watched the lights, an admiration for this man grew. "He is very brave, determined and devoted to her. He loves her more than his own life. But does he understand, I would do the same for her?" Shail wondered as he waited for Kari to catch up with him.

Shail heard her stumble behind him. He sprung down the crest and land beside her. "Are you hurt?" he asked as he took her arm and helped her to her feet.

"I just tripped. I'm fine," she answered.

"It is time to rest, you are becoming weak with this pursuit," he said to her.

Kari glanced around at the barren ground that held only small bushes. "Shail, this is no place to stop. There is no cover here and we need to keep moving. I know my father better than you. He's not the kind of man to give up, especially when he's so close," she said a little upset.

"Are you sure you wish to stay with me? I can make a fire and your father would come. You could go back to the comforts and safety of a human home. It is not certain yet that you carry my fledgling. It is only your happiness, I desire," he said somberly. Kari could feel his heart breaking with these words.

"No, Shail. No comfort could replace you. I would endure any hardship to be with you but I fear, I slow your escape and you're in danger because of me. If I left you, he would no longer hunt you. I would make sure of that," she whispered sadly.

Shail put his arms around her. "This danger I face has been with me all my life and shall continue, even if you leave with your father. And I, like you would endure any thing to have you as my mate," his mournful male voice entered her mind.

"So we will stay together?" she asked as she clung to him.

"Yes and love each other in the time we have."

The wind became colder as they made their way down the pinnacle of the mountain and gravitated to the northern side. Kari had only slept for three hours in two days and it was beginning to take its toll on her. She staggered slightly in the darkness but was determined to fight her fatigue until Shail was safe. She slipped on a wet rock and fell to her knees. As she struggled to get up, Shail ran beside her. "You must rest," he said profoundly.

"It's too dangerous here," she cried over the sound of the wind using her voice. It had become mentally too hard to communicate in silence with him in her weary state.

"The danger lies in you traveling these cliffs, when your body is weak. Stay here. You understand me?" he said, mocking one of their first communications in the cabin when she ordered him to stay. Kari smiled at him remember these same words and he affectionately nuzzled his nose against her cheek. "Do not worry. I shall find us a safe place," he said. In a bound, he leaped down the cliff as if his wings still functioned. Kari sat down on a smooth rock as the wind tugged at her. She was not only tired but also hungry, for she had only eaten the root early in the day. She shivered and felt sick and faint. Although she wanted to go on, she was somewhat relieved when Shail made the decision to stop. Her legs ached from the climbing up and down the steep slopes and she was cold. After a half an hour, he returned.

"I have found a place that shall do," he said. Kari stood up and felt a little dizzy. Shail reached for her and lifted her into his arms as his eyes filled with concern. "You are not well, this is my fault, I should have sensed your suffering" he said angry with himself.

"It's not your fault. It is my father, who chases us." Kari said with a muffled voice as Shail carried her down the mountain. She wrapped her arms tightly around his neck, just as she had done a decade ago when she was eleven years old. "Didn't our first encounter begin something like this?" she said with a weak smile.

"Yes," he answered and she could have sworn she saw a slight smile on his lips.

Shail leaped down the crest with speed as he held her in his arms. Soon he was walking towards a large formation of boulders that jetted out from the mountainside. Bending down, he went into a small cave. The sound of water trickling down the rocks could be heard from one side. He laid Kari down tenderly on the hard cave floor. "I shall find food and bedding for this place. I fear, we must remain here until you recover and the danger has past," he said. Kari only nodded and he disappeared out the crevice. He returned with his arms heaped with the large tangle moss. "Lay on this. It is not as good as your human bed but it is better than the hard rock." Kari precipitated, curling up on the soft moss. She was relieved just to be out of the cold night wind. Closing her eyes, she listened to the howling gusts, as they blew against the cave's entrance. She shivered and her whole body ached as she slumbered off to sleep.

Kari woke as Shail lifted the back of her head with his hands. "Eat this. It shall fight the sickness that has taken hold of you."

She recognized the bright purple fruit that grew deep on the forest floor. "You traveled too far for this. This does not grow in the mountains," she said weakly.

"Eat it, it shall help you," he said with great concern. Kari ate, what she could and shivered again. Shail crawled next to her and covered her with his large cream wing. The warmth came soon while he held her close.

"Did you eat, Shail?" she asked in a tired voice.

"Do not worry about me," he answered her. She knew he had not. She nodded off, once again as he nervously watched her and the outside of the cave.

As dawn broke, he could hear the faint sound of the hovercraft as it continued its search. He wondered if the heat device could see through the thick rock of the mountain. The hover flew over the mountain that they lay within but continued on to the valley below. Shail closed his eyes with relief and knew their heat was unseen through the rocks. Kari slept and never stirred from the sounds of the hovers engine. He nuzzled the back of her neck tenderly and closed his eyes for he had not slept in three days and nights. He rested quietly but remained conscious as he listened to the wind and smelled the air for signs of danger. He was hungry but decided to go without rather than remove his warm wing from her. He watched the afternoon clouds roll in as they covered the mountaintop in a dense fog. This made him feel more secure because it would hinder her father's search in this high place.

He nuzzled Kari to wake her in the afternoon and placed small pieces of the purple fruit in her mouth. Then Shail filled his mouth with water from the nearby rocks but did not swallow as he brought it to Kari's mouth and released it between her lips. She swallowed the water as their lips met. He did this several times until he was satisfied that she had her fill. Coiling his lean body around her in the soft moss, he once again covered her with his wing. She clung to him and shivered with fever as he worriedly watched his frail little female drift back to sleep.

The second night in the cave, he could finally feel her fever break as a warm sweat covered her body. He held her as her body temperature cooled. This eased his mind and with the cover of darkness, he finally shut his eyes and allowed the sleep to come to his fatigued drained body.

The morning of the second day, the wind had subsided as the mountain remained in a dense mist. Shail stretched his body and Kari stirred beside him. "I must find us some more food for this light," he said to her when she opened her eyes.

"But it's daytime and there are no trees. You may be seen," she said still drowsy.

"I shall go unseen. The clouds cover the mountain." Kari only nodded wrapping herself in the warm moss and drifted back to sleep. Shail walked out of the cave and sniffed the air. He listened carefully but could hear nothing unusual. After a moment, he leaped down the boulders as fast as he could travel until he reached the cover of trees. Once there, he took hold of a stout vine and climbing up the fruit bearing trees, dropping the fruit to the ground. Shail untied his sash from his hips and gathered the fruit, placing it in this makeshift bag. He started back and came across a small vine with bright pink flowers. Digging to their roots, he pulled a few more of the sticky roots from the dirt. Wrapping all in the sash, he made his way up the crest as he skittishly listened and looked around, like a frightened deer, before he stepped from the security of the trees. His animal senses could not detect any danger and with that reassurance, he sprang across the barren rocks, making his way back to the cave. He breathed a sigh of relief as he entered the cave. Kari was up and drinking some of the water when he walked in. The color had returned to her face as she smiled at him and his nude body.

"I love your seductive dress for gathering food," she joked.

Shail spilled the food on the cave floor and wrapped his sash back around him as he glanced smugly at her. "I see you feel well. Your humor has returned," he related. But his eyes twinkled with delight happy his mate was no longer ill. They lay down on the moss and ate heartily for they were famished.

"So, we move on tonight?" Kari asked him.

"No, we shall stay again this darkness. Though your fever leaves you, I would rather wait until you are completely well. This cave is safe for us right now."

She leaned close to him and kissed him on the mouth as her hand ran up his leg toward his sash. He pulled back from her and looked at her in the eyes. "You are well!" he related.

"Since we're stuck here, I thought we could finish this bonding thing," she smiled at him. She placed her hand back between his legs, until she had an uncompromising grip on him. He immediately became stiff as she massaged him. He shivered and became breathless with this stimulation. Kari slipped out of her clothes and continued to fondle him. She had him so worked up in frenzy that he could hardly contain himself. He leaped on her and immediately started to procreate hastily in her. She pulled at his posterior with each of her hands. This heightened stimulation causing Shail to instantly secret the fluids from his genitals, not being able to control them any longer. He weakly rested on her, out of breath. Kari allowed him to rest briefly before she encouraged him to rise again. The mating continued through the night and ended with the dim light of the following day. Shail slept soundly stretched out in the nest, too tired to curl up. Kari leaned over and tenderly bit his neck. He raised his head up with exhaustion, as she ran her hands over his naked body.

"Female, you take all my strength and make me very weak," he related with a dispirited gaze.

She kissed him on his cheek. "You're so strong and self assured that I some times enjoyed you when you're a little weak and helpless."

"It is apparent, you also enjoy this effort that makes me weak and helpless," he said, playfully rubbed his head against her side.

She smiled at him. "That cynicism sounds a little bit like harpy humor."

He nodded, flipping his long blond hair from his eyes and slowly got up. "I have not heard the hovercraft in some time," he said and looked out of the cave. "Perhaps your father has given up and returns to the south."

"Where are we going anyway?" Kari said, rising and taking a sip from the water stream.

"We go to the second highest mountain." He pointed and she came along side.

"And what is there?" she asked, staring at the huge black mountain in the distance.

"It is a sacred place of our people and very secure. When we reach it, I shall bond with you until you shall have me no more."

She flipped her head back a little and smirked. "More humor?"

"That is humor?" he questioned a little confused.

"It is to me, cause that day will never come," she replied.

He nodded his head. "Yes, I do see the humor of this since you lack to tire of me. I shall be the weakest of all male harpies. And happy to be so."

Shail stepped from the cave and sniffed the wind and listened once again. But only the mountain wind and jungle noises and smells came from the trees below. He stepped back inside. "Do you feel well enough to travel? We must go quickly down this mountain until we reach the cover of trees."

"I feel wonderful. I think your bonding cured me," she said with a smile.

"Are these untrue words, more humor?" Shail asked. Kari grinned and nodded. "I fear I must grow used to this human humor since you are very fond of it," he said drearily.

"It doesn't hurt," Kari said and walked in front of him. She reached up to wrap her arms around his neck and passionately kissed him. He kissed her back and began rubbing against her to seek arousal. His beautiful nude sexy mate was hard to resist. He jerked his head back, away from her, remembering they should move on.

"You make me not want to leave this place," he related with frustration. "If I was not wanted elsewhere, I would keep you in this cave and mate with you until the walls were covered with our fledglings and there was no more room."

Kari ignored his frustration as she quickly dressed. She grabbed the cloth bag, his sash, and a piece of fruit. She tossed his sash at him. It landed half on his head and shoulder, as she strolled past him out the cave door. "Are you coming?" she said to him with a raised eyebrow. "I'm in a hurry to get to that mountain to see if you're capable of making me want you no more," she smiled. Shail tied the sash back on him and joined her outside. He took her hand and they descended the mountain quickly in the light of day. Their pace slowed, once they reached the cover of trees.

All of Shail's playful banter left him as he once again became alert and serious. Again he took the role of a hunted animal, smelling the air frequently while his eyes shifted towards every little movement in the jungle. Every so often, he would stop to listen for any unusual sound. He had never been confined to foot travel and this made him even more leery and cautious. It was no longer only his life that depended on his instincts but his mate and the fledgling she may carry. This mating had changed him from a young reckless roaming single male, to a concerned husband and possible father. The broken wing also still lay heavy on his mind. If danger came, he would not be able to grab his mate and fly away with her. They made it to the bottom of the valley and stopped for water. They were surrounded by a large selection of fruit trees of different varieties. Kari sat down on a rock and Shail went to her, sensing something was wrong. "I just feel a little tired. Guess I'm not as recovered, as I thought," she said wearily.

Shail shook his head. "I should have fought this urge to bond with you and made you sleep," he related more mad at himself. "Some more of this purple fruit, you need. Some must not be far away since this valley is full of many foods. You rest here and I shall seek some." She nodded and lay down by the stream of water. Shail quickly disappeared into the trees.

Kari slipped out of her clothes once again since she felt hot and hoped the cool water would revive her. She splashed water on her face and body and this seemed to sooth her. Suddenly she heard the snap of twigs. She knew it was not Shail since he made little sound as he moved through the brush. She jerked her head around and saw a man standing several yards away. Kari scrambled backwards, out of the stream and retreated into the thick ferns as this hunter smiled and followed her. Immediately she felt two strong arms grab her from behind and lift her off her feet. "I got her," another man said as he held her. The other man walked through the stream and stood in front of her as she struggled to be free of the second man's hold. Kari was so terrified, she could not even scream.

The hunter placed Kari's long blond hair through a monitor. He smiled. "Sorry little baby, wrong D.N.A. She's a wild harpy all right. I told you this estate was full of them. And with all this fruit, it was bound to draw one," one man said to the other.

"Yeah, and this is the prettiest one yet. A little female golden," he said massaging her breasts under her long hair. "Where's your mate, baby? Is he as blond as you?" Kari fought the grip of this large crude man but he squeezed her firmly.

"Can't wait to jump on this spunky little female. She's got a hell of a lot of fight in her," he said as he rubbed his rough hands between her legs and he jammed his fingers up in her. Kari wiggled and panted hard with this abuse. Instinctively she began hissing loudly at the man as he examined his fingers. "She's got a mate. She was just bred recently. She's full of his sperm," the man said, standing in front of her. "You want some more, baby?" he asked as he jammed his fingers harshly back in her, enjoying seeing her helplessly squirm and thrash in the other man's hold.

"We don't have time for this," the other man barked at his partner, as he tried to restrain the terrified frantic female wrapped in his arms. "Her blond mate can't be too far off. We need to stun her quickly before she warns him. We'll string her up right here. She has to be paired with that broken wing male golden. After we bring him down, we can both enjoy his little female," he said as Kari continued to fight this hold.

"Can't wait. I'm going to enjoy taking the fight out of this one. Teach her how a man breeds instead of some gentle harpy buck. Bet she'll last longer. Too bad, these wild little females croak so quickly after their males bleed out." the man in front of Kari stated as he pulled a rope out from his back pocket.

Kari called silently to her mate in the forest. "Stay away, Shail! It's a trap! Do not come for me! Please, do not come for me."

The hunter grabbed Kari's wrists and tied them tightly together as he took the other end of the rope and tossed it over a tall tree limb. Jerking her up, he tied the rope off as Kari dangled quietly and watched him. "She's already played out and going into shock. Hope her male comes soon before she dies."

"Me too, besides hunting this estate makes me nervous. I've heard Turner take the law into his own hands when he catches poachers here." the man behind her stated as he massaged Kari's ribs and held her still. The other man calmly adjusted the setting on his laser gun to stun and pointed it towards Kari. Before he could fire it, Kari kicked the unsuspecting hunter hard in the groin, sending him to his knees. He dropped his laser gun and held himself.

"Bitch!" he cursed as his eyes watered with the pain. Kari twisted and flailed wildly on the rope, trying to kick at the man, who still held her. She could only think of Shail and his death. Suddenly she heard a thud behind her as the man's hands left her ribs and he tumbled to the ground unconscious. She saw the man in front of her scramble to his feet. His eyes were filled with fear as he tried to grab his weapon. Instantly, Shail sprung at him, striking him hard on the side of his head with a heavy piece of wood before he could get his hands on the gun. Shail unmercifully began to beat this man, who had assaulted his female, until his body was covered with blood and he lay still. Kari could see and feel Shail's rage as her wry lean muscled little mate stood over the huge immobile body.

He glanced up at her, slightly out of breath. Dropping the wooden tree limb, he rushed to her. "Are you hurt?" he asked as he released the rope and untied her wrists. He looked at her body to make sure she was unharmed. Kari could not answer him for a moment while she shuddered with fright. He wrapped his arms around her and held her. "I am here now. You are safe," he related softly. In that instant, Kari broke down and began to cry. Shail picked her up in his arms. As he still held her, he grabbed the cloth bag and her clothing and carried her off into the jungle. He walked for hours, as he would nuzzle her gently but neither of them communicated. Kari just shut her eyes and clung to his neck. She had finally experienced what it was like to be a harpy, to be treated like a wild animal. She'd shiver slightly every time she thought of the man groping her. When she did this, Shail would nuzzle and kiss her as he continued to walk. He left the valley and began to climb up the next ridge. Kari could tell it was growing difficult for him with her weight.

"Put me down, Shail. I'm all right now. I can walk," she said to him. But, he ignored her and continued to carry her. It was as if he was punishing himself. As it became very steep, Kari wiggled in his arms and ordered him to release her. He finally stopped on a slope and set her down on her feet. She looked in his large blue eyes and could see the great pain he was feeling. He dropped to his knees and wrapped his arms around her legs as he lowered his head against her.

"Forgive me. I failed to protect you," he communicated. His soft voice, that had always entered her mind, was now shaky.

"But you did not fail me. You did protect me," she said and lowered herself to be eye level with him. His eyes were teary and this encounter with these hunters, had affected him worse than it had her. He cursed this life that had given him no peace. And it had nearly destroyed what he loved most. They held each other for a long time. He finally pulled away from her.

"I promise you, this shall never happen to you again. Some day soon, I shall rid this land of these men," he said to her.

Kari sighed deeply. "Let's go to your sacred mountain and put this behind us." He nodded and rose to his feet. He took her hand and they traveled together over the next ridge in the dark of night. The following morning they ascended into another valley. As they rested briefly on some rocks, something made Shail rise to his feet and stare off in a certain direction.

"What is it?" Kari asked as she too stood up.

"A harpy comes." Soon a tall brown winged harpy could be seen flying low between the trees and brush. When he landed in front of Shail, he dropped to one knee and bowed with respect keeping his head down. Shail motioned to him and he stood up. Kari was surprised at how this harpy revered and honored her golden mate. She had never fully understood till now that Shail truly was the ruler of the harpies.

"What say you?" Shail asked him.

"Aron awaits your return. He sent many into the trees in search of you and your mate. There are many men among the trees now. He feared most, the metal bird of Turner as it followed your trail towards the mountain. He sent it away," the harpy communicated.

"How?" Shail asked.

"A distraction," the harpy answered.

Shail nodded. "The passage ahead, is it safe?" The harpy nodded.

"And the islands?" Shail asked.

"They too are now safe and all taken there."

"This pleases me. Tell Aron I continue this foot travel for two lights, since the danger has passed. I wish all males to gather others for this war. When I arrive, enough shall be there to start," Shail told the harpy. The harpy backed away with his head bowed and then took flight.

"War! What war?" Kari asked with alarm.

Shail stared at her. "These things are of no concern for you. We should go now. We can move quickly for your father is no longer in this area and no hunters lay ahead. We hide no more."

She pulled on his arm and forced him to face her. "Anything that concerns you also concerns me. Now what war are you talking about?" she said realizing that his earlier threat to rid the land of men was no idle talk.

"It is a war against the humans. If we do not rid them from the land soon, all harpies shall perish. As you have experienced, some hunters know of our females now. Before long, all hunters shall know and our females shall face the same danger as us males. The time to flee is over, we must stop them," he told her.

"But Shail, how will you fight them with no weapons? They will slaughter all your male harpies," she stated.

"They slaughter us now one by one. There is no difference." He told hold of her. "Kari, please ask me no more of this. It is something that only concerns the males. I shall not discuss this with you. Please, I beg you," he said with sincerity, gazing into her eyes.

"But Shail, how can it not concern me, when I could lose you."

"This loss, you have known about for some time. If this is not done I shall die by a hunter's weapon before long. We have no future and our son, you carry, also has no future. These butchers of harpies must be gone before his birth. I vow on my honor, he shall not suffer as I have. We talk of this no more," he said and turned from her and began walking on into the jungle. Kari chased after him, begging him to tell her of this war. But he ignored her. And she soon realized that he had meant it. He would not tell her when, where or how, this war was to take place.

They traveled the jungle and the mountains in the open, not fearing to be seen. Evening approached and they found themselves on a high ridge. The last rays of light were dimming, as Shail stopped along some jagged rocks. "We shall rest here through the dark. These rocks protect you from the cold wind." They were out in the open, devoid of plant life but a slight ledge, under a rock created a cover.

"I could go on," Kari said.

"No. To push your body, when there is no danger is needless. We rest this dark. Next light, we cover one more valley before we enter the sacred mountain."

They ate some of the fruits and nuts they had brought with them from the valley floor and then crawled under the covered ledge. Shail placed his good wing over her as she snuggled on the bottom wing for this had become their custom. Shail wrapped his arms around her and slept in security and peace, knowing he was not hunted this night.

Shail woke in the dim morning light and stretched his wing. Kari opened her eyes and kissed him before they both climbed out from under the ledge. A pile of fruit had been neatly assembled next to the ledge. Shail ate a piece while he scanned the distant land. Kari joined him.

"Where did all this food come from?" she asked.

"Aron has sent a provider and protector, to watch over us and bring us food."

"Who is this Aron you speak of?" she asked as she ate a small yellow trisom fruit.

"You know of him. When you entered my dreams, he watched over you as you traveled the land. He feared men may see my golden wings and convinced me, I should not take this risk now. It is he, who chased the grogins from you."

"Yes, and he also came to me at the lake, near my father's home. He told me 'you needed me.' I didn't understand what he meant, until I found you in the hands of those hunters."

Shail nodded. "Yes, he wanted to save me from those hunters. But I feared his death and many others would follow mine. I did not believe I could survive such wounds. He was very upset when he came to you at the lake. He felt your human knowledge and bravery was my only hope. I was not happy with him when I later learned of this. It is very dangerous for female harpy to reveal her devotion to a male. Those island hunters might have known about our females and guessed your nature. But Aron made the right choice in the end. You did save me."

"So, he is a leader like you, then?" she asked.

"He is a leader to many harpies who dwell in the west but not like I. He rules many but I rule all," he answered.

"It sounds like you trust and rely on him," Kari commented.

"Yes, he is more to me than a mere leader of my people. When my father was killed, it was his father that raised me. We are not of the same blood but he is like an older brother to me. And he is wise. I seek his advice often. Come, we must go now, for we travel one more light and dark."

"You are in a hurry to meet with him and talk about this war?" she asked.

Shail just looked at her, shaking his head in disapproval and did not answer, as he stepped down the path towards the last valley below. Kari followed. It was apparent that he had not changed his mind about letting her know the details of the war ahead.

They proceeded down to the trees once again. The air was colder, even in this last valley. Kari wished she had at least brought her blood stained jacket but they had left in a hurry. On the forest floor, they stopped along a small stream. Shail knelt down and sucked up the icy clear water between his lips while Kari still drank the human way by cupping the stream water with her hands and bring it to her mouth. Shail raised his head and sniffed the air. Shaking the droplets from the ends of his locks, he rose to his feet and stared off into the jungle. Kari tried to mimic him and was surprised, when she sensed another harpy in the area. Soon the graceful brown winged harpy landed beside them. In his hand was a cloth containing various fruits. Shail and this harpy only stared at each other, excluding her from their silent talk. She sighed and realized, they must be discussing this conflict that would come. This male harpy left and Shail and Kari continued their journey through the valley until they approached the base of the black sacred mountain. Shail stopped and stared up at the huge mountain.

"Do you tire?" he asked. Kari only shook her head no. "The light shall soon be gone. We can travel till then and sleep with the dark or travel the blackness and end this journey."

Kari gazed up at the ominous mountain. She shivered in this cold northern land. Even the trees were different up here, bearing little fruit or life on this ascending ridge. "I feel fine, Shail. I want to go on. I can rest tomorrow," she answered him. Her curiosity of Shail's sacred mountain outweighed her discomfort.

They began climbing the steep ridges as the light faded. Kari wrapped her arms around herself in an attempt to stay warm. She noticed the cold did not seem to affect Shail as he traversed the ridges ahead. As it became dark, the same harpy flew down to the path in front of Shail. He bowed with the same reverence and held out his arms. In them, lay a large cloth of the same woven material as Shail's sash. Shail took the cloth from him and walked to Kari, placing the warm blanket around her shoulders. "This shall keep you warm."

Kari glanced beyond Shail to thank the brown harpy but he was gone. The blanket of cloth was wonderful and she instantly felt the warmth. They walked on in the dark. Kari staying close behind Shail, for it was apparent that his night sight was better than hers. But she noticed her harpy instincts of hearing sight and smell had improved with this long journey. She told this to Shail while they climbed higher.

"You have the same animal senses as I. You have never used them, as a fleeing wild harpy must. If you remain in the wild, you shall see, hear and smell as I do," he told her.

They reached the top of a crest and wind blew fiercely. Even Shail was now cold and wrapped his unbroken wing partially around him. The other remained in the clear plastic splint, which he could not move. She could detect his frustration and desire to remove it. She threatened him that it must stay on his wing. If removed too soon, he would never fly again.

The climb became steeper and more difficult the higher they went. Soon only small patches of silver moss growing between the rocks could be seen in the starlight. This sacred mountain perplexed her. She understood why it was safe from hunters. The winds were so strong that even a large sturdy hovercraft would be out of control up here and would slam into the mountain crests. But, she wondered why, even the harpies would want to come here since they were a tree people and this place was void of trees and all other life on Dora. It was so cold and forbidding and dark. She thought of the little cave they had shared at their last bonding. It was far more pleasant with the trees close below it. It was also safe from the view of a hovercraft. What drew her mate to this terrible place?

The climb had become straight up and Shail flapped his wing to keep his balance while he scaled upward with his hands and feet. He reached a narrow ledge and stopped and waited for Kari to join him. "It is too risky for you to travel further. My harpies have come. They shall fly us the rest of the way," he said. Soon several harpies appeared out of the darkness, their wings flapped hard against the gusts to land. Kari recognized one of them as Aron. He greeted Shail with a fond embrace as the others bowed to their ruler. Shail and Aron gently wrapped their slender necks around one another as they nuzzled and licked each other affectionately. Kari was surprised by this male harpy tenderness to one another since it was unlike men. Aron pulled his face from the golden locks and shook his head.

"Brother, you take too many risks, with no thought of your valued life. I worried many lights as these threats hung over the land, in search of you and your mate. The cabin fledgling should have been sent in search of me when this danger first appeared in the sky. Instead, it is he you sent to the island safety and risked this hunt. Without your golden wings, we shall fail. And yet, you are reckless with them. This luck you live by, shall end your careless life," Aron ranted with distress.

"Aron, I am cold and hungry as is my mate. And too tired to challenge your disrespectful lecturing now," Shail told him. Aron nodded his head slightly.

Shail's eyes twinkled with mischievousness. He glanced at Kari. "He is very unhappy with me," Shail related and Kari only smiled. It was very apparent that Aron did treat Shail like a troublesome kid brother.

Aron walked to Kari and bowed his head. "May I have the honor of carrying you?"

"It would be my honor since I owe you my life on our first meeting," Kari related to Aron. He bowed again and carefully lifted her into his arms. Two of the other harpies took Shail as they leaped from the cliff and flew to a very high rim of the mountain. Once there, they put Shail down and disappeared through a small crevice. Aron followed with Kari, safe in his arms. Shail waited for them on the rim. It was so narrow that there was only room for three harpies. Kari joined Shail and he led her through a narrow passage of rock. Aron followed behind them. It was pitch dark at first as Kari held Shail's hand and followed him blindly. Soon the crevice entered a cave, which was even darker. But, eventually, a small glow of light could be seen in the distance as they walked towards it. The light became brighter, the deeper they went. Soon the journey through the cave came to an end. Shail led Kari out into an enormous space with high ceilings. Small stone pits were burning with fires on the floors and around each of these, were hundreds of harpies. When Shail stood before them, they all knelt in his presence. Kari was in awe of the place and all the harpies it held. Suddenly, she noticed the walls of this gigantic cave. They were not made of the mountain stone but of metal with beams and rivets. She looked at Shail, startled for she recognized this place. It was not a mountain cave but an ancient giant spaceship.

John Turner had searched a discouraging several weeks for Kari and the wounded golden harpy with no luck. His sources were limited since he only owned three other hovercrafts. All had been put in use to investigate every logging trail on the estate. But, this was an enormous job since these trails covered the property and consisted of thousands of miles. He was disheartened with the fact that he may never see her again. It was obvious by now that old Doc had done a good job and the harpy had survived, for Kari would have returned home if it died.

He had gone to Doc's house several more times to plead with him to reveal his daughter's whereabouts. But the stubborn old man would not help him for the girl's sake. Finally, Doc had convinced him that he really did not know where she and the harpy had gone. As time past, his hatred of the harpy increased, as he thought of the creature holding Kari in its arms. Time was against him because it was well known to him since her birth that she had been promised to bond with this young golden male. He was consumed with regret, for not killing this creature, even if it had saved Kari's life. The cocky teenage golden would have been easy to hunt down and kill back then for he was not yet wise in the ways of survival. Yet, this arrogant nervy male had managed to survive for ten years to John's surprise and disappointment. But it was apparent, he still was cocky and this had been his downfall when this male risked defending a fledgling. He was like his golden father, brave and careless. A brave harpy was a dead harpy, John thought. John had hoped Kari would return to Dora, drawn to her human side but this plan had backfired on him. She returned still infatuated with the harpies. He couldn't understand, why she could not see the future that lay before her if she bonded with the golden harpy. It was no future. Her mate would be killed soon enough and her life could be in danger, when this happened.

Word had spread from Westend all the way across the continent among the harpy hunters that one last rare golden male did existed and it was on the west coast. To make matters easier, the creature had been wounded and had a broken wing. They knew this precious game animal would be easy prey since he was defenseless to fly away. John decided it would be better if he kill this harpy, thus reducing the risk to Kari. She may never forgive him but at least, she would be safe from harm from all these hunters. Even if she and the harpy managed to remain free, what kind of life would she have? To be constantly fleeing in fear. And her golden fledgling males would face this same danger. They would be hunted relentlessly and killed for their yellow wings. He thought of the worry and sorrow this would bring her. If she married a man, she would most likely bear females. And she and her daughters would live a full happy life. "Could she not see this far ahead?" he thought.

Charlie had argued with him frequently on the subject and had sent John into numerous rages. The old Indian felt that Kari should have what little happiness and love she could get from the harpy. That too much time had past. The golden harpy had recovered enough to bond with her. "Once they have bonded, there is no separating them. It will destroy her," he had said trying to convince John. But John did not believe this.

"There are drugs that will make her forget him," he said. "And I don't care, if she is angry with me, when I kill him. At least she'll be alive and safe."

Charlie had finally given up. John was very stubborn, once his mind was made up. The old Indian pitied Kari and her poor male harpy because John would never give up his search for them. Even if Kari came home, John would still hunt down this golden thus ending this threat forever.

Charlie had finished the construction of the beetle-proof building and had rejoined John in the search. All hope seemed gone as the days turned to weeks that they would never find her.

John crawled from the hover and made his way into the house followed by Charlie. They walked in silence, for there was no more to say. Maria met him at the door with a questioning and a worry in her eyes but John only shook his head as he past her. She put her hand over her mouth as a tear streamed down her round cheek. She walked back to the kitchen to serve them a late dinner. The communicator began buzzing in the den and John walked to it. Pressing the button, the screen came on and a young man appeared.

"I'm trying to reach a Kari Turner," he said to John.

"She's not here. I'm her father and who are you?"

"My name is Ted. I'm a friend of Kari's. We met on the ship from Earth. I was just calling to see how she was," the young man said happily.

"She's gone. Gone with the harpies. I've been searching for her for weeks now. I suppose, you won't have any information that could help me find her?" John asked.

The screen was silent for a long moment. And John could see the distress on this young man's face. "Mr. Turner, I don't know where she is but Kari and I became very close friends in a short time. I knew she had planned to go back to the harpies and learn all she could about them. She was very determined to save them from this hunting extinction. She told me that a golden harpy had saved her life once."

"Yes, well, she's with that golden male now. And I feel her admiration for them is misdirected. That thing will only ruin her life," John said a little annoyed.

"Mr. Turner, I don't know you but I did get to know her. When she talked about him, her eyes would light up. She really cares for that creature. She convinced me that he would never hurt her. She must be very happy that he's alive. I was rather fond of Kari myself and I have to say, I'm rather glad that she found him. It seemed like the only thing she really cared about. Maybe it would be for the best, to let them be. She must know what she's doing" Ted expressed sincerely.

"You're right, you don't know me and you don't know what is best for my daughter. Good night." John snapped angrily as he pushed the button and all communication shut down.

He walked into the dining room and poured a glass of wine while Charlie stood in the doorway. John took one sip and threw the glass hard against the wall. "Some guy from Hampton telling me about how much my own daughter cared for that damn golden. Did everyone on the planet know about this but me? And then he tries to tell me how to run my life. He's preaching the same rubbish I've been hearing from you and that miserable old doctor. I'm sick of it," he stammered. Charlie just waited quietly.

Suddenly, the communicator started buzzing again. "If that's him again calling back, he's going to get a piece of my mind," John ranted and returned to the den. Pushing the button, he said "Hello," in a harsh tone, not waiting for the screen to appear.

"Is Mr. Turner in?" said a voice, as a middle aged man appeared.

"This is he," John responded, trying to collect him self and control his rage.

"Mr. Turner, My name is George McGill. I understand that you have offered a considerable reward for information on your missing daughter."

John now became very excited. "Yes, that true," he said trying to remain calm.

"Is that reward for just information or is it information leading to her return?"

"I'll give you the reward for just information, if it will tell me where she is."

"Well, sir, your memo on the monitor said that she was in a late model sky blue terrain vehicle and she had acquired an injured golden harpy with a broke wing," the man questioned.

"Yes, that's right." John said getting impatient.

"Well, I didn't see her or the harpy but I do believe I know the whereabouts of the vehicle. Does that entitle me to your reward?" he asked.

"If it's the vehicle she was in, you got the reward, Mr. McGill. Now where is it?"

"I saw it two days ago on your estate. I had mechanical problems with my hover and barely made it to Terrance before it quit on me. The solar strips were so worn; the darn thing won't hold a charge. This is the first opportunity I've had to use any kind of a communicator. Actually, I was hoping to take that harpy off her hands. Even injured, he's worth more than your reward but that darn hover put me out of business for a while. Figured it would be easier to call you and get something for my troubles. If you catch my drift."

"Yes, I understand, Mr. McGill." John knew he was talking to a seasoned harpy hunter and he disliked this breed of men who killed for profit. "You just admitted to me that you planned on poaching that golden male off my property. But, I'll forget it and send you the credits on line right now, if your information is valid. I'm a man of my word," John stated.

"Yes, I've heard that about you. Well, that vehicle is about a hundred miles north of Westend, along a narrow strip of coast road. It's parked in the middle of some blue ferns with bushes on top of it, next to an old cabin. Nearly didn't see it, till a little bit of glass caught the light and reflected it."

"Mr. McGill, that information is worth the reward. I'm sending you a ticket right now. You can collect the credits at the Terrance bank. Thank you," John said excitedly.

"And thank you, Mr. Turner. Easiest twenty thousand I ever made. Maybe we can do business again," the man said happily.

"I don't think so. And if I ever catch you poaching on my estate, I'll hunt you down like a harpy. And they'll never find your body. And remember, I am a man of my word." John threatened and with that, John disconnected the communicator.

John rushed back into the dining room. Charlie was helping Maria pick up the broken glass. "I'm sorry about that, Maria," he apologized.

"It's okay, Mr. Turner. I know you are upset about Kari," she said softly.

"Yes, but I have good news. The vehicle she was in has been spotted. Forget dinner, I'm leaving right now."

Maria smiled. "Let me put the chicken in something. You may eat it on the way and I'll throw in some fruit for Miss Kari," she said rushing from the room. Charlie looked at him somberly. This was not good news for him. He had hoped that Kari and the harpy would have gone on undiscovered.

Charlie had gone to visit old Doc while John was out searching the estate for her. He had finished with the beetle-proof building and thought, that maybe, Doc would tell him something that would help the search. It was apparent from John's rage that Doc wasn't going to give him the time of day. So, he had gone in his old green vehicle and figured one old man to another, that something good might come from this visit.

Doc was glad to see him and welcomed him into his cottage. They drank a few glasses of old scotch and talked about Kari and the golden harpy, she had saved and had also saved her.

"At first, I was skeptical," he had said, "but here was this poor girl on her knees begging me to save his life. I thought she was a fanatic. You know, one of those crazy animal rights people or something. But then I remembered the moss he had used. Maybe this little harpy had more medical tricks up his sleeve."

The more they drank, the more Doc talked. "Anyway," he went on, "I worked on him and was surprised he made it through the operation. The next morning, I went to check on him. They were asleep together. Charlie, if you could have seen them with their poor little arms wrapped around each other, it would have broken your heart. There's no doubt in my mind that those two really loved each other and belong together. Even when I tried to examine him later, he was so weak and full of pain but that feisty little devil mustered all his strength to defend that girl. He thought I was going to hurt her. Knocked my medical scanner right out of my hand. I knew, right then that I had done the right thing by saving him. Then I remembered something else that finally convinced me. It was the birth of that girl. I'll never forget it. You were gone with the old Mr. Turner up in the high country cutting timber and I doubt if John told you or his father. But anyway, Mrs. Turner had just given birth to the girl, and she was holding her, as John and I looked at the beautiful baby and low and behold, who walks in from the balcony door but a mature golden male. He walked right in, like he belonged there. He went to the Misses and the baby and then looked at them both. He even touched the little one on the cheek. John and I were so shocked we just stood there and couldn't move. And in the blink of an eye, he was gone, out the balcony and out of sight. Never heard of any harpy being that bold until Turner's girl brought me this wounded combative blond. John and I never discussed it again. And then, of course, you know about Mrs. Turner's death. That really never made much sense to me either. What the heck was she doing outside, right after having a child? Well, this made me think when I saw Kari and her harpy together. I think those two had to be promised to one another from the day they were born. There are just too many coincidences with that girl and golden harpies. And I believe, John knows the truth. But why he wants to jump in and ruin what little happiness they have in this upside down world, is beyond me," Doc had said.

Charlie had just sat and listened to Doc and never did get around to asking him, where he had thought they'd gone. Doc would have never told him anyway, even if he knew. Doc did ask Charlie if he would talk to John. Make him see the light. Charlie had tried but it did no good. John's hate of the harpy was unswayable. He didn't like anything taken away from him that was his. And he blamed these golden harpies for losing his wife and now his daughter. His hate was real. He was convinced that Kari would be better off, if her harpy was dead.

"Charlie, Charlie! Are you coming with me or not," John yelled forcing the Indian back to the present.

"Yes, I will come," he answered.

"Then, let's go," John said, as he hurried to the door with Charlie following. They hopped in the hover and were soon flying over the coastal road. "I can't believe she remembered this place," John said as they flew. "She was so young and I think, she was only there a few times."

"The place must have held fond memories for her to remember, after all this time," Charlie answered.

After an hour, they landed down the beach and had crept up silently to the cabin. John had his laser gun in his hand.

"I really wish you would reconsider killing that harpy. It is a mistake," Charlie said when they left the hover.

John gave him a dirty look. They reached the cabin but it was deserted. It was the middle of the night, and they decided to stay till morning. John walked into the cabin and was surprised that the lights worked. The place was clean with fresh sheets on the bed. A pile of fruit was in a bowl on the table. They discovered the used bandages in the trash and the old blue vehicle camouflaged in the blue ferns. There was no doubt that Kari had brought the harpy here. The discovery of the blood stained harpy sash that lay outside the door seemed to send John over the edge.

"I'll kill him! I'll just kill him, if he's touched her. I'll give him the kind of death that harpies fear most. He's going to suffer plenty when I'm through with him," he raged. He finally settled down and they slept till the first rays of light filtered in through the open door.

It took some time to pick up their trail since there were several foot prints leading to the stream and back. "These are harpy foot prints," Charlie commented as he studied the prints in the dirt. Charlie knew that a harpy's gait was very different than a man's. Harpies walked from toe to heal much like a flamingo, some times not even leaving a heel mark, thus they appeared to tiptoe, where as a strolling man walked from heel to toe. Eventually, John and Charlie found the freshest prints led north.

"We will follow on foot, it's the only way to sneak up on him," John said and start the trek north. They had traveled swiftly up the trail that led to the first mountain crest, following the two pairs of foot prints, one of a small shoe, the other the toes and ball of a bare foot.

Charlie stopped. "We should go around, to reach the crest and leave this trail. The wind has shifted, and it rides out back," he warned.

"No, we must stay on their trail." John said quietly.

"That harpy will catch our scent, if we continue this way. Better to go around and come in on the side," the Indian said again.

"Charlie, this trial is at least two days old. They're far ahead of us, and that harpy's nose is not that good."

Charlie shrugged and smugly grinned to him self, knowing, how good a harpy's nose was. They went on, until they came to a small stream. Next to it were many foot prints. John and Charlie checked all the signs. "They were here for some time, but why? There is no food or shelter." John looked under the large ferns and saw a nest had been made. The smashed moss lay under the ferns. He picked up several cream colored feathers that had been driven into the smooth surface of the moss. John fell to his knees and stared at the nest. Charlie walked along side of him. "It looks like a struggle took place under those ferns," he said quietly.

John glanced up at him. "You know, as well as I, what he did to her. He mated with her here." John uttered with deep remorse in his voice.

Charlie nodded his head in agreement. "They are a bonded pair now. To kill one, could kill the other. She is lost to us now."

John frowned. "I don't believe that. Kari is my daughter and she's strong! She'll survive his death," he said and rose to his feet and began looking around for more signs of where they may have gone.

"The tracks are gone. They either were flown away or they went with the stream. In either case, we have nothing to follow," Charlie said.

They pursued the stream for another hour then gave up. They went back down for the hovercraft. Two more days and nights seemed fruitless with the hover. It was, like trying to find a needle in a haystack. With only one hovercraft, and no men on the ground to flush a harpy out, it was almost impossible to bring down an adult harpy this way. Even with a crippled wing, a harpy's instincts could easily avoid a hunter as long as it was aware of one. But John would not give up. His rage spurred him on even flying the hover into the night despite the dangerous gusts of winds that could have sent him crashing into one of the mountainsides. But, he was determined to find his daughter and the harpy despite the odds. It was on the third day that one of the men from the mill called on the hover communicator.

"The swarms have hit again. This time, it's really bad. They took out the whole harbor. Nothing remains afloat. Even the barges are gone. Killed a whole bunch of hunters from Terrance that were loading on a boat to go to the islands. I'm afraid you also lost your whole shipment," the man said.

"I guess I need to go home and check the damage," John said sadly. Charlie looked at him and he appeared like a broken man. "She really is lost to me, isn't she? She's chosen him for a mate and a harpy's life."

"I think so," Charlie answered softly and rubbed John's shoulder to comfort him.

"Let's go home," he sighed and veered the hovercraft to the south.

Doc sat on his porch sipping his lemonade. A gentle breeze blew through the shade of his yard. He stared at the glass and knew it would be his last since he had squeezed the remainder of the lemons in the morning. There would be none till next year. He glanced up the deserted street of the little town. Most the folks had fled to Hampton and perhaps even beyond, into space after the last beetle swarm attack. Nobody felt safe anymore. But he had stayed, along with a few others, who were determined to ride out this plague to the end. He was too old to relocate and he had the same stubbornness as John Turner. He wasn't going to have a bunch of bugs, drive him from the home he had lived in all his adult life. There had been no more swarm attacks for some time and things had become very quiet. Except for the visit from Charlie, the Indian, and John Turner, he hadn't socialized with anyone. Not that he missed it but he was sorry to see the Bakers pack up and go. He had enjoyed his daily walk to their store and his chat with Mr. Baker on the news of the day. It was also sad, to see the loss of their daughter, Carol. Doc had always considered her an airhead but she was a nice girl. Now, he glanced down the street at the vacant store that had been boarded up. Those boards surely would not keep the beetles out if they came to this town but were a symbol, to keep other people honest. The Bakers had gone to Hampton and said they would return if the swarms could be destroyed some day.

Charlie had told Doc that he had reinforced a large room at the mill with metal, in case of an attack. And Doc was welcome to come there if a swarm was headed for Westend. Doc had thanked him and he had enjoyed the visit with the old Indian, despite waking up the following morning with a slight hangover from drinking too much scotch. Charlie didn't say much but Doc felt he knew more about Turner's daughter and the harpy, than he let on.

Doc now wondered how those two had made out. He was relieved at John's last visit, when he related that he still had not found them. Doc had tried his best to discourage John from this hunt but it had fallen on deaf ears.

Doc smiled to himself. He was pleased that he still had the skill to perform the intricate surgery and that his harpy, patient, had survived since John still could not find them. He thought about the harpy and the girl. Her blood had saved his life and it proved, that they were, somehow, related but how? He had told the girl that the harpy had human blood in him and that was why the transfusion worked but he wondered if she could have some harpy blood in her. He especially considered this, when she had told him the next day that she was capable of communicating with these creatures. He had never heard of this before from any human being. If she had harpy blood in her somehow, it was apparent that she was unaware of it, he thought. He then remembered something else that she had said that there was some researcher at the Hampton Zoo doing a study on harpies. He had promised the girl, to contact him about his theories on the harpies.

Doc rose from his comfortable porch chair, taking his last swallow of lemonade and wandered into the cottage. He had nothing else to do on this day. He went to the communicator and punched in the numbers to Hampton. Soon, he was talking to someone at the Hampton Zoo.

"You have some researcher or vet there, that's doing a study on harpies?" he asked.

"Oh, you mean Dr. Watkins, let me connect you," the woman said.

A middle-aged man soon appeared on the screen. "Can I help you?" he asked. "I'm Doctor Watkins."

"No, you can't help me but perhaps, I can help you. You're doing a study on harpies, I hear," Doc asked.

"Yes, that's correct."

"I'm just wondering, who this study will benefit, when it's done?"

"Well, I'm hoping it will benefit the harpies. Perhaps save them from extinction, which seems their predetermination at this time," Watkins answered.

"Who's funding this study?" Doc asked.

"The government is funding it."

Doc rubbed his snowy beard while studying the man on the other end of the communicator. "You realize that most of our senators are harpy hunters and they have made it clear, they want the harpies wiped out."

"Yes, I've already gotten a few visits by those senators. They politely voiced their disapproval of my research. The party that is sponsoring me has only the best intentions for the harpies. Now, may I ask, who you are? Before this conversation goes any further," Watkins asked a little suspiciously.

"My name is Doc White. I live in Westend. I believe we have a mutual friend in common, a Miss Turner."

Watkins thought for a moment. "Westend. Yes, I do remember her. She was a gorgeous girl who had some rather incredible experiences with a gold harpy," Watkins said.

"Yes, that would be the one. And she's still having them." Doc chuckled a little.

"Is she alright?" Watkins asked concerned.

"As far as I know, she's fine. She wanted me to call you. Thought I could shed some light on your research. I still find it a little hard to believe that there is any one in the Dora government willing to pay to help the harpies," Doc went on.

"Yes, I do agree with you. But let me assure you, this study is funded and sponsored by some one high up in government and I'm an expert in this field. There is no way I would risk my reputation, to aid anyone in the destruction of an endangered species. I do not plan to include harpy locations or any other information that would benefit a hunter. Let me be very clear about that. I also am suspicious with this study. When I asked the senators why they didn't want the harpies protected, they could not give me a straight answer and since then I have gotten a few ominous threats. I've never experienced this much resistance to save an animal before," Watkins said.

"That's too bad. I think there's more at risk than either of us realizes. Perhaps you should come out here to the west. We could possibly put our heads together and unravel the mystery of the harpies and also discover why there are people who want to threaten you. The information I have, I'm not willing to discuss over this contraption. Too many ears could be listening but I believe you will find it interesting about the girl and her golden harpy," Doc said.

Doctor Watkins stared at the bearded old man on the other end of the screen. His interest had definitely been aroused and he was making little progress at the zoo. "I think I will accept your offer. Are there any facilities that I can stay at and continue my work?" he asked.

"You can stay with me. I have an extra room and some equipment, even if it's outdated. But, there is a condition. You'll have to bring a few bottles of scotch. That's my drink of choice," Doc remarked.

Watkins laughed. "It just so happens, I'm a scotch man myself. I believe we may just get along fine. I have a few lab tests that I must conclude on some other animals but they should be finished soon. Then I'll make arrangements to come out with the equipment I need. I've been meaning to go to the outback, ever since I met Miss Turner. She's an intriguing young lady."

Doc nodded his head in agreement. "She certainly is, more than you know."

They concluded their conversation and each felt something had been gained by it.

CHAPTER 6

▼

Kari stared out at the enormous space as the harpies around the fire pits rose and gathered around Shail. They gazed at their noble blond ruler with great admiration. Shail stood slightly above them at the entrance of this wide expanse. "I sense how pleased you are to see me again," he related softly, "I survived the captivity of the hunters and return to you now in this time of need. Though my suffering was great, it did allow me to peer into the dark hearts of these men. There is no doubt these humans are the worst of all living animals. They do not kill us for need or from fear as other animals kill. It is a twisted cruel pleasure they seek. Our jungle must be rid of these destructive deadly creatures. We harpies have always valued all life but now we must change. We must abandon our gentle nature and fight back. To do not, all we love, shall be lost. We must destroy the humans or drive them from our lands. Only then, shall we know peace. The time is upon us and this war can wait no more. Much life shall be lost and this, I regret but our choices are none. When it is done, our offspring shall have a safe future with what we do now and our females shall live in security along side of their mates. So I sent you out to the extent of this land with a message to all our males. The gathering begins now, our weapons soon released. May we have the strength in the end to reclaim what is ours." Shail then turned and extended his unbroken wing and with his hand, he ripped out a large handful of feathers. Blood dripped from some of the large ones. He ripped a second handful out and tossed them in front of his feet. "Take these with you, so all shall know, these are my words. I shall see you at the river gathering." The harpies moved forward each picking up one of Shail's cream feathers, disappearing through the cave. They went to spread Shail's words across the continent. Aron moved closer to Shail as he watched the harpies depart. His bright green eyes glowed in the firelight. "So the death begins." he sighed. Shail glanced at him. He was serious and sad at the same time. "Yes." was Shail's only response. Kari could see the harpies did not want this war but as Shail had said, they had no more choices. To continue to only flee and hide would bring their extinction. She rubbed her head against Shail's arm to comfort him as he watched his harpies leave. She could feel the great stress and worry he was feeling. Though men could ignite his rage, he truly was gentle and peaceful at heart. Shail had refused to tell her of this war and she worried if he fully understood the tenacious nature of men. Did he understand that even if the harpies were victorious over the men of the planet that humans were not easily defeated. Millions more dwelled among the stars. They would keep coming to Dora until these winged creatures, which threatened men, were destroyed. She had learned from her Earth schooling that at one time there were other animals that defied man on that planet. The bear, lion, shark and rattlesnake had all shown bravery. Their courage and defiance lead to their annihilation. To kill men only ignited the human revenge and no animal could survive it. Only tame domesticated animals were allowed to live. Shail and his harpies could never be tamed. Perhaps this was the destiny of the harpies, to go down fighting like the fearless extinct grizzly bear. "Come," he said, tearing her away from these agonizing thoughts. "The dawn comes and you have had no sleep for a light and a dark. I shall take you to a place where you can rest and eat."

Kari followed Shail, as they walked through the large expanse. She kept her doubts to herself. They veered off on a long corridor, which lead to a large room. A small fire burned at the center surrounded by rocks. The smoke rose up to the vents in the ceiling and disappeared. A great mass of the tangled moss lay off to one side with various fruits next to it.

"You shall rest here," he said, taking her tenderly in his arms. "I sense your doubts, even if you do not reveal them to me and I understand the risk we face by defying the men and this threat that may come from the stars. Do not think me unaware," he related, taking a deep breath. "It shall be alright." He tried to reassure her.

Kari put her arms around him and squeezed him hard. "I love you so much. And I have waited so long to be with you," she said while clinging to him.

"Yes, the wait was long. I had nearly lost all hope. But I was told you would return to my jungle, so I waited." he related as he kissed her.

She looked up at him puzzled. "Who told you, I would come back?"

"The old human man with long gray hair and red skin, who dwells near your father's house."

"Charlie! He talked to you?" she asked with surprise.

"If that is his name, yes. He told me of you."

"When, how?"

"Let us lay on the moss and eat and I shall tell you all," Shail said as he led her to the moss and gave her a piece of fruit. "I saw this old man many times in the jungle. His senses are strong for a man. He greatly admires the animals and only kills for need of food. When I carried you home from the lake, he fired his weapon at me to frighten me, rather than cause me harm. I sensed his relief as I made my escape. Many raining seasons later; I worried if you still lived. I had to know since it was past time I take a female mate so I went to him in the jungle. I did not fear him. This man and his quiet gentle ways had surprised many harpies but he never harmed them. When I stepped before him, I could sense, he admired me then it was his fondness that came. I sniffled at him and pawed my foot to show I wanted some thing and with my longing eyes, he knew I sought you. He glanced up at the sky and said, "Kari is there but will return when older and free of her father." I nodded to him and flew back to the trees. There I waited for your return."

Kari shook her head with disgust. "That old Indian. I don't understand him. He warned me to stay away from you. Said I was marked and there was a spell on me. That my life would be over if I went with you."

"But Kari, all these things are they not true? Our harpy parents marked us to bond. This spell was on me, as it was on you, for I wished for no other female. And to choose a harpy's life over a human's may not be wise since we dwell in constant fear and danger. He is like your father. He wanted you happy and safe. He hoped when I came to you, you would reject me and seek a man for a mate."

Kari sat up and stared at him. "Shail, you like Charlie. I thought you hated all men."

"Hate? This word, I do not know."

"It is a feeling. It's the way you felt when you beat those men in the mountains that took me," she said.

"Yes," he nodded, "I come to know this feeling more and more. But it is a feeling that does not dwell in a wild harpy. Only the men's cruelty has made it come to me. No, I do not hate every man only the ones, who hunt and kill us. It is true I fear and distrust all men since they fear us. Their fear is dangerous. They fear and wish to destroy that which they do not understand. And then there are men like your Charlie and the old doctor, these hold the same honor and gentleness as us. I would wish all humans were like these," he related while eating a piece of fruit.

"You must hate my father. He has hunted you and killed your father," she said.

He looked at her perplexed. "No, I do not feel this hate for him. I understand his desire to kill me. He only seeks to protect you. He does not hunt other harpies. His mate was harpy and you are harpy. He loved both of you, like no other. We learned, he gave his lands as a sanctuary for us and protect my flock from the hunters for all the seasons you were gone. His protection most likely spared my young life. I could never hate such a man, who guarded my flock and is so devoted to my mate. Your father is only a protective parent."

"You are far more forgiving of him than I am. His idea of protection and devotion has only brought me misery all my life," Kari said sadly.

"Yes, but you look at the past and now the present. He only looks at your future. This is where the conflict lies. He knows a harpy life is dangerous and can bring an early death. But you are blind to this future. You only see the happiness and love we share now. If I fail with this war, I shall regret taking you as my mate. I am your guardian now and like your father, I must also worry for your safety and future," Shail said, stretching out on the moss.

Kari smiled at her handsome mate, "How is it you are so smart and have all this insight when most men only consider you an ignorant wild animal of the jungle?"

"As you once did? It is these ignorant animal instincts that allows me to peer into a man's heart and mind," he answered.

"With this war, Shail, what will happen to all these gentle men, who cause no harm?"

"I hope most shall flee this land as with the women and young. Any that remain shall perish," he related.

Kari sighed. "I don't think Doc and Charlie would leave the planet. I definitely know my father won't."

"If they do not leave, they shall die. This does not please me but I do not have the power to separate the good from the bad. I feel great conflict over this taking of life. But if the choice lies, to save the harpies or the humans, I must choose the harpies," he related, closing his eyes and curling up.

"Then I could lose everyone I love with this war," she said with worry.

"Sleep now, my beautiful mate. The dawn comes. I shall try and spare these humans you love but it is a promise, I can not make."

Kari curled up next to him. She could feel the great distress and tension in his tortured soul. She knew, this taking of life, any life, went against a gentle harpy's nature. She closed her eyes and put her arms around him and they finally went to sleep.

Kari woke and felt for Shail behind her but the moss nest was empty. She stared at the ceiling and the vents above with curiosity. "I must ask him about this old ship when he returns," she thought to herself. It was ancient indeed. A thin layer of white moss covered the walls but the gray metal could be seen beneath the plant growth. She thought it strange for harpies to dwell in this place since they were so afraid of being confined in a human structure. "Why did they think it was sacred?" she wondered. Suddenly, she could sense another harpy. Kari sat up startled and saw a girl leaning over the dim fire as she placed a small log on it. The girl jumped when she noticed Kari staring at her. She fell to her knees, with her head bowed. The long brown hair hid her face.

"Forgive me. I did not wish to wake you," the girl apologized with a human voice. Kari was caught off guard by the sound. It was the first time in weeks that she heard the sound of a voice.

"You didn't wake me and please rise. I'm not a ruler," Kari said.

The girl slowly rose to her feet. "You are a golden harpy and deserve our respect," the girl stated softly.

Kari had never realized that the harpies also revered her. "Come to me," Kari asked gently. The girl walked to her, keeping her head down. "Who are you?"

"I am Aron's sister but you also know me as Lea."

"Lea, the girl from the beach party. You're a harpy?" Kari said with surprise. Lea only nodded. "I knew there was a reason you were different and I liked you right away," Kari said.

Lea glanced up with a little smile and then the smile disappeared. "I failed you and our ruler on that beach," she uttered sadly.

"How could you fail me? You had nothing to do with what went on that night."

Leal lowered her head again. "I was sent by my brother to help you rescue our golden ruler. He had sensed your bravery and with your human knowledge, he thought you could save him. You fearlessly spoke against the harpy hunting and Carol taunted you. But I lack your courage and when her harsh words came at me, I fled and failed you. I watched from the dark bushes as you alone twisted the weak minds of those hunters and they willingly gave you our dying ruler. No female harpy has this bravery to confront four hunters and risk being exposed," Lea said.

"Lea, you mistake courage with ignorance. I didn't even know I was a harpy at that time, though I doubt it would have changed things. If they hadn't accepted my trade, my next plan would have been to retrieve my laser gun and rob those cruel men of their catch. I was pretty desperate to save Shail that night."

"Those men have paid for their cruelty. They are all dead, even Carol," Lea said.

"Dead, how?"

"A beetle swarm killed them as they rode in your vehicle," she answered.

"The beetles can kill?" Kari asked.

"Yes, it is of great concern for your mate and my brother. The beetles eat the flesh now and are a danger to all living things. All our females and young are fleeing to the safety of the islands. Aron brought me here instead so that I could serve you and give you comfort. I hope not to fail you again."

Kari smiled. "You didn't fail me. There was nothing you could have done. I am happy you're here. I hate to admit it but it's kind of nice just to hear another voice for a change. This mental talk is hard for me at times. I just feel like screaming once in a while." Lea giggled shyly. Suddenly her face froze as she lowered her head and backed away from Kari. Before Kari could ask her, what was wrong, Shail walked into the room. "You may go," he commanded. Lea quickly left the room.

"Why does she fear you so?" Kari asked.

Shail seemed perplexed. "Fear? She does not fear me. That is Lea, Aron's sister. I have seen her many times. You confuse fear with respect."

"It looked like fear to me," Kari stated.

"I am the dominant male of all harpy flocks and their golden ruler. It is the animal way that they show meekness to me. If they did not give me this respect, there would be much chaos and no one to lead or protect them. This would make the harpies more vulnerable to the hunters," Shail stated.

"And what makes you this ruler? Because you have blond hair and cream wings?" she asked.

He frowned at her. "Yes, this is the way it is and always has been and shall be, unless I lose my head with all these questions."

"How am I to understand all of this, unless I ask," Kari said to him.

"You are right. But my mind is elsewhere now," he related as he walked to her and gave her a kiss. "I came here to see if you are well. The answer is clear. You are fine. Taking a female mate, raised among only humans, can be trying," he said wearily.

"I make you unhappy then?"

Shail pulled away and stared at her. "I am happy with you. You are unlike any other female harpy. You are beautiful, smart, and brave but also very determined and you challenge me as if you were male. No other harpy would dare question me as you do. It is good. You force me to open my eyes and search for the truth. But, I shall admit, I do not know all. You ask why I rule, in truth, I do not know. The other harpies think, that because of my gold, I am smarter and fearless. I do not think that feathers or hair can make one more, in these ways, so I answer you, I do not know," he said a little rattled and Kari smiled at him.

Shail was normally so lofty and confident but Kari loved to see his humble tender side. The part he sought to hide. "I suppose, you don't feel like telling me, why we're in this old space ship?" she asked.

"Space ship? This word, I do not know or the answer you seek." he answered glumly.

Kari walked to one side of the room and tapped on the walls. "This, this is a space ship. This is a vehicle for traveling the stars, it was built by men, surely you knew this?" she asked in amazement.

Shail shook his head. "No. This is the creator's place. Where the harpies began. It has always dwelled under the mountain and never gone to the stars," he related with determination.

"Shail, I'm telling you, this is a ship. It doesn't look like its gone anywhere in a long time. In fact, I don't think I've ever seen one this old. But, I promise you this ship was in the stars at one time. How many harpies do you know that have traveled the stars?" she asked him.

He raised his head up a little indignantly. "Only you."

"Then trust me when I tell you this."

Shail walked to the ship walls and tapped them. He realized they were indeed different than the mountain stone. Taking a deep breath. "If you say this, it must be true. The harpies began here, is all I was told. Its story is long forgotten. But I do not believe this ship is a human thing. We ruled the jungle long before their coming. This story is very clear to me. These first men came from the sky and stole our females. When the males tried to reclaim them, they were killed. That is how it has gone till now."

Kari stared at him. "Maybe the harpies traveled the stars as men do now. If they did, they had the same machines as men at one time," she said, looking at the rivets in the walls.

"This could be true. Again, I do not have these answers." he said with a jaded silent voice.

She could sense he was feeling a little insecure by his lack of knowledge. Shail didn't know who this creator was or why this spaceship was sacred. He really couldn't even explain why he was chosen to lead. All these answers lay buried in the past. Right now his mind was occupied with this coming war and it was the lack of the human knowledge that most troubled him. The knowledge his mate had. She went to him and put her arms around his waist, feeling ashamed, she had made her proud little mate feel so inferior to herself. "I'm sorry. There is no way you could have learned as much as me. If you wish, I will teach you all I know," she said.

Shail sighed. "I do not desire this human knowledge but I fear I must learn it. With out it, my mind is as crippled as my wing against the humans. And time is fleeting. When my wing heals, I must fly from you and hope I have this wisdom to save the harpies," he said. Kari only nodded. Shail ate some of the fruit with Kari. Then he told her, he must go speak with Aron. He would send Lea back, to keep her company. It was apparent that Kari liked this sister of Aron's.

He left her and found Lea waiting a short distance down the corridor. "Go to her. Try to explain the harpy ways. Though she is very wise with the human world, she does not know us. You shall help me in this manner," he said. Lea nodded and went back to Kari's room.

Shail continued down the hall, glancing at the ceiling and walls. These things had now become of interest to him. "Was it true, this sacred place had once been among the stars?" he wondered. Shail went into a large room, where Aron and a few harpies waited. They bowed with devotion, as he entered the doorway. Shail walked past them and approached several of the large metal tables in this room. He stared at the tables, ignoring the harpies and then wandered to a small room with counters and a sink, like the one at the cabin. Turning the handles, as Kari had done, rust water trickled out. Shail ran his hand through it, realizing this functioned like a man thing. Aron came to his side. "Do you seek this counsel now?" Aron asked. He could see that Shail's thoughts were elsewhere and something troubled him.

Shail looked up. "Send the others away. I speak with you alone."

Aron motioned to the other harpies and they left, returning to the giant expansive room that held the fire pits. "What troubles your mind at this time?"

"Do you think it wise that no female harpy, who has dwelt among humans, was ever brought to this sacred place?" he asked Aron.

Aron looked at him strangely and tried to answer. "Those females live in peace, their true nature hidden from the humans. They did not need the sanctuary or refuge of the mountain. Why do you ask me of this" Aron questioned him.

"It is true, these females do not need to hide and did not need this mountain. But I wonder if we, males, have failed by not learning from these females who live with humans. They have knowledge of the human world. The human knowledge is powerful. Without it, we are as animals to men," Shail said.

"Yes, but as harpies, we prefer to be and live as a gentle bird than to become these cruel destructive humans. It is this wild gentle nature that makes us cherish the jungle rather than destroy it. To take the evil human knowledge, we would become like men. Soon we would kill the trees for dwellings and eat the animals for food. We would no longer be harpies. Why do you question this golden harpy rule not to seek this evil knowledge?" Aron asked.

Shail glanced at him. "Perhaps the evil is not in the knowledge but in those that use it. With the power of wisdom, we may have driven the humans from the jungle long ago."

Aron looked at him curiously. "You have changed a great deal, while in the hands of these hunters. You are no longer the Shail I grew with."

"Yes, these hunters changed me. They taught me well to fear and taught me of terrible pain. They found much pleasure in teaching these things to me. Strangely, they lusted for this evil pleasure as much as they lusted for my wings. I lost my golden courage and became like all frightened animals that are hurt and caught. And they changed me in other ways. As I once was only bewildered by hunters and only wished to flee, it is now, I long to attack and destroy them. Surviving their cruelty has brought an anger and a rage into me. But this human knowledge I question did not come from these men. It comes from my mate. She has made me open my eyes. In her effort to discover herself, she has forced me to accept many things. I have chosen to seek the human knowledge. And with this wisdom, I shall have better judgment and strength. Already, I have learned many things, yet I do not feel less of a harpy. And though I stayed in the man made structure, I still prefer the jungle as my home and have no desire to eat flesh."

Aron thought for a long time. "Yes, your time with the men and your mate has made you shrewder and stronger than any harpy. Perhaps it is wise you learn all from the enemy we must destroy."

Shail took a deep breath. "To destroy all, would be wise, if all were evil. But, Kari tells me, there are many good men that shall die. My own life was spared by one of these men. And there lies the conflict within me that this knowledge has brought."

"Shail, you know, the bad dwell among the innocent and the good. We cannot attack one, with out attacking the other. Even now, you protect a harpy killer and his land. One who should be destroyed for he only seeks to slaughter you. This is a mistake and I question your judgment."

Shail raised his head and flung his long blond hair while arching his wings. Posturing boldly while approaching Aron. "You challenge my rule?" he related harshly while his blue eyes flashed.

Aron backed away from him and lowered his head submissively. "This is no harpy challenge. You have proven long ago when we were young I was no match for you even though I was older and larger. Your aggressive unyielding nature is no even match for any male harpy. It is my love for you and your safety that causes me to question your decision to protect this Turner. He nearly hunted you down four lights ago and it is clear, he wishes to kill you just as he killed your father," Aron appealed to him.

Shail lowered his head and wings, ending the challenge. "Yes, he truly does desire my death. And I accept your concern," Shail said while leaned towards Aron and affectionately nuzzled his neck in friendship as any stud animal would when accepting a yielding male to his flock. "This man's desire to kill me comes from his devotion to his daughter and to protect her. He hunts me but is no threat to other harpies. My mate carries within her, the future leader of our people. We may fail, Aron. She shall need someone strong to defend her and my fledgling. If these swarms win the land, Turner shall send my family to the safety of the stars. He has proven his worth, as he risked the night winds in the mountains. He would gladly die to protect my family just as a harpy male sacrifices his life to lure a hunter away from his."

"Turner would protect your mate this is true but are you sure of the one she carries? It shall be a winged male fledgling. He may discard or even destroy it, for it may remind him of you," Aron related.

"This Turner only wishes to kill those that are a threat to his family just as my father was thought to be a threat. For ten seasons, he has protected us from hunters. He bonded with a harpy and his daughter is harpy. He loved them more than his own life. I have seen him over the seasons at the same lake where I meet Kari, grieving for his dead mate and lost daughter. He was not aware of me but I sensed his heart. It is not black, only confused. His confusion shall end with the love of my son. I shall protect this man and his land just as he shall fiercely protect my fledgling, which carries his blood."

Aron nodded. "As you wish."

Shail wandered to some steel metal doors. He opened one and found a bowl on a shelf. "This is for food," he said and held it out to Aron.

Aron looked at the object with suspicion. "It is unwise to disturb these things of the creator," he said cautiously while he stared at the bowl.

"Kari tells me, this place once traveled the stars," Shail said, returning the bowl back to the cupboard.

Aron shook his head, "She is mistaken. This place has always laid beneath the mountain."

Shail glanced at him and raised his eyebrows. "That is what I told her. But, she is the only harpy who has been among stars and knows these things. Our other females have always lived on the edge of the jungle and learned only the basic things of the human's world. Her knowledge and will exceeds all harpies. She has lived alone among the humans and survived it. Instead of her breaking down as most do, she has come out stronger. She fears nothing except my death. And she continues to teach me."

"Your love for her is very showing," Aron said fondly.

"Yes, I love her. She truly has the golden courage. If I should die, she shall be the last golden and your ruler, until my son is of age.

"Do not think of death for our victory draws near. The humans are fleeing swiftly since the beetles have killed."

"Yes, but how many and who shall die in the end? It was my decision to no longer hinder the beetles from multiplying. These swarms were only to drive the humans out of a barren land. Though this anger comes to me, I did not wish their deaths especially the deaths of women and children. But now, these swarms turn deadly. I fear in the end the blood of many innocent shall rest upon my hands. I even worry for our females harpies and young on the islands and hope these swarms shall not evolve to fly a great distance over the water," Shail spoke uneasily.

"So far, the swarms have remained in the jungle and it is at great risk we keep them there but this control grows more dangerous with each light, more and more queens are merging from these swarms," Aron said.

"Yes. I am aware of the danger. Have the harpies continue to defend these structures called towns where the innocent women and children dwell. Hopefully with more human deaths they shall flee in fear to the east and then to the stars. It is time to take our revenge on these hunters and start this war. These known hunting camps shall be the first to fall beneath these swarms now. This must be done swiftly before the hunters flee to the safe towns. When my wing is healed and all harpies gathered we herd the humans east across the land with the swarms at their back. When they reach the farthest human structures of the eastern ocean, they shall return to the sky and leave us in peace. Those who do not flee shall die. Then we shall proudly be, for which we were bred to be, protectors of the animals and trees as we destroy these deadly swarms. Bring the other harpies back, so they may tell me the locations of the beetles and these hunters. I begin to use this control now," Shail said. Aron nodded and left the room.

Kari smiled, as Lea returned to the room. "Your mate has asked me to teach you all I know of the harpies," Lea said.

Kari laughed a little. "I'm afraid, I drive him a little crazy with all my questions. He gets so aggravated when he doesn't know all the answers. And he's so sweet and adorable when he's frustrated. Do you have someone that you love, Lea?" Kari asked.

Lea nodded. "I chose to bond with a harpy. He is in the south now near Westend and your father's home. Most female harpies have male harpy mates Only a few seek human men and those men know it is a harpy female that has become their mate. They accept and protect their mates from discovery," Lea said.

"So this is how the female harpies exist?"

"Yes, it is done quietly. We are taught not to do or say anything that would reveal our true nature when we live among the humans," Lea said.

"I guess I broke all the rules, when I came back to Dora by telling many of my love for the harpies and ability to communicate with them."

Lea only nodded. "It was very dangerous for you to defend the harpies to so many humans," Lea said.

"Yes, I have learned of this danger. Two hunters took me in the jungle. They knew, what I was and they talked of what they were going to do to me. If Shail hadn't saved me…" Kari shuddered at the thought.

Lea went to her and put her arm around her. "Some of these hunters have discovered who we are. They found out by catching our males and females together in the jungle. To choose a life with your mate in the trees makes one as vulnerable as the males. It is safer to dwell with the unknowing humans but then there is the separation that is painful. This is the way my mate and I dwell. By day, I live as a woman, by night I live as a harpy. My mate comes for me at dusk and flies me to our nest in the jungle. It is the dark, I have learned to cherish," she said sadly.

"If all the humans knew we were related to them, they may not consider us animals and the hunting may end," Kari reflected.

"No! It would not end. This secret must be kept. We already know the outcome of this," Lea said nervously.

"How do you know?" Kari asked.

"Have you not heard of these first men, who came to our land?" Lea asked, somewhat surprised.

"I only know that the Dorial explorers came here about a hundred and seventy-five years ago. The settlers followed twenty-five years later. That's in the history books."

Lea's eyes were down cast. "Yes, the human history books. These Dorial explorers hide the truth from the settlers since it was too terrible to reveal," she said as she glanced up at Kari.

"Tell me of it," Kari asked.

"The story has passed from generation to generation about these first men, who came here. These Dorial explorers discovered the harpy community and the harpies, not fearing humans, welcomed them at first. But, these men saw that our females looked very human without wings. Soon the female harpies were caught and placed in chains and cages. Then they were beaten until domesticated so they could be easily raped. Many died from abuse and shock, others willed their own deaths, rather than living in cage. Our gentle males tried desperately to save them. The human weapons slaughtered the males, with each man saving the male's wings to boast of how many he had killed. It was a dark season for the harpies. But, then something happened that these men did not intend. The remaining surviving females became pregnant. When the winged males fledglings were born, it disgusted these men and they viciously cut the throats of these babies. This killing of innocent male fledglings began the ritual, which exists today. A wounded male harpy exposes his neck to the hunters, as a sign of submitting to honor the deaths of these past sacrificial fledglings. It is a death of honor among our kind, though many hunters think it a harpy weakness to end their pain." Lea said.

"And what of the female babies?" Kari asked.

"The female fledglings were spared perhaps because they looked so human. The females learned to hide their labor pains, if they bore a male offspring, giving birth only at night when the men slept. The surviving free adult males would come in the dark and take the male fledglings from the cages to rear as their own sons. When the settlers came, the daughters had matured and they passed as humans to these new people. So, the deception began and a wicked partnership was formed between the Dorial explorers and the harpies. Neither would reveal the true nature of these harpy daughters to the settlers. Our males continued to try and reclaim their females. But these explorers lied and said it was these winged male harpies, who were thieves and rapists. Thus began the lie that exists today. Most of these daughters longed for a harpy mate and went into trees to bond with the free male harpies. Many were found by the men and returned to the human world after their male harpy mates had been killed, defending them.

These females would suffer from depression and death since our bonding is permanent. It was then thought that a woman would lose her mind and die, if taken by a male harpy. And another lie was started to turn these settlers against the harpies. I know I would suffer this fate if my mate and I were ever discovered together by the humans and he was killed. I would not want to live without him, thus making their lie true. Do you understand all of this?" she asked Kari.

Kari was deep in thought for some time. "Yes, I understand it and know of this harpy depression you speak of, for I came close to it when I longed for Shail on Earth. I did not think I would survive it at times. But, Lea, if the truths were known to all humans and they knew that we carried the human blood, that our males were not rapists and the women that were taken, were really harpy females mourning the loss of their mates, if all this was revealed, I believe the hunting and killing would end. You know, that most humans from Earth know little of the harpies and do not hate us. If they had the proof of these lies, they would see us as another race, rather than as animals to be hunted and slaughtered."

"It is not these Earth humans that concern us, for what you say has merit. It is the descendants of these explorers that now rule this planet. They are the senators and they have known all along that we carry human blood but it makes no difference to them. These senators covet the secret, as we do and continue this wicked partnership of deceit. If the truth became known it would shame and disgrace them and they would lose their power, for they are just as guilty as their explorer ancestors for covering up the truth of us. Generation after generation of these senators have ruled Dora and have threatened the harpies, if the truth was revealed, they would summon a human army from the sky and kill all harpies, male, fledgling and even us hidden females. Right now, they are happy to let the hunters do their dirty work and only slaughter our males. Our brave males accept this fate to protect their female's secret. And us, females, have much to lose if all humans knew we were harpies. We would be hunted and killed like our males. We, females, are the guardians of our race. With out our deception, the harpies would have been lost long ago," she told Kari.

"The truth is slowly coming out and it is not the work of the harpies. Old Doc knows of it. He knows that Shail has human blood in him. And there is another researcher in Hampton that will soon discover it, if he has not already. The truth will soon be known and there is nothing that these senators will be able to do to stop it. The truth will come from men of science and all the people of Dora will believe it then."

"You may be right. But this proof takes time. And the time is gone. We will soon be at war with the humans and then it will not matter if they know we carry the human blood in our veins," Lea said sadly.

"But Shail could stop this war and give the research time," Kari said.

"The war cannot be stopped. It is years in the making. And, even if he could stop it, it is not certain that men would believe the truth and accept the harpies," Lea answered.

"How did things get so messed up," Kari said. "Shail will not talk about this war with me. But I sense that he really doesn't want it. It is the harpy blood and the human blood that conflict within him." Kari uttered quietly.

"In a short period of time, you have come to know him well. But he is not alone in his feelings. All harpies feel this way. They have always been peaceful. It is not their way to take life from any living thing. But those days are now over. We have no choice. We must defeat the humans, so we may live. There are more hunters now, than ever before. And there is no safe place from them. Soon all our males will be gone. Will you want to live upon this land, when this happens?" Lea asked.

Kari somberly stared at her. "No, I would not want to live. I have bonded with Shail. He is my life now. I don't think I could bear the loss of him."

Lea smiled at her and took Kari's hand. "You and he are the strongest and bravest of harpies. Both of you have survived hardships, which would have killed most harpies. The golden blood in you, allows this. Let us put aside these dark thoughts of death and loss. And take joy that both our mates are alive and free," Lea said. Kari smiled back at her and nodded.

Kari noticed that Lea no longer wore human clothing but a short robe made of the same material as Shail's sash. "You don't wear the store-bought clothes here," Kari asked.

"No, when I am among my people, I shed these human things," she answered.

Kari got up from the fire pit that they had been sitting around and went to the nest of moss. She picked up a large piece of cloth that the brown harpy had given her at the base of the mountain. "Can I make a robe like yours from this?" she asked.

Lea went to her. "I will make it for you."

Kari looked at the cloth. "I, too, want to shed these human clothes and learn the harpy ways. We will make it together, so I'll know how." Lea nodded with a grin. They sat down by the fire and Lea began to fashion the robe as Kari watched. They had become the best of friends.

Shail had finished gathering information from the harpies and sent them out to direct the swarms. The harpies had kept the swarms in the jungle and under control. But the swarms were growing so fast that he knew he only had a small amount of time to make his plan work and destroy the swarms before there were too many. If the humans did not flee swiftly to the sky, Shail would have to let them perish. There was not enough time to prevent this. Then he and his harpies would fly into the swarms and destroy them before their numbers were too great. If he did not, these swarms would rule the planet, consuming every living thing in their path.

The females and fledglings in the western half of the continent had been taken to the farthest islands and Shail hoped this was too far for a swarm to travel over water. Now, the male harpies had been sent to the east to gather the rest of the harpies and their females and offspring. It was too far to bring them to the islands in time. So, they were to go to certain places in the northern mountain range. There all the harpies would make a stand to protect them. The swarms did not like the cold weather of the mountains and Shail hoped this would protect them to some degree. But, his plan had been flawed when the beetles changed and began eating flesh. Two seasons ago, Shail decided to release the beetles, he had only hoped that they would drive the humans off their lands and back to the sky. He had not foreseen the beetles becoming flesh eaters. And this troubled him greatly. "By killing us, they have brought about their own destruction," he thought to himself. It had been the harpies that had protected Dora from the beetles swarms all these decades. As the harpy numbers became fewer, and Shail became an adult and ruler. He had ordered this protection stopped. "Let the beetles multiply and rid us of these murderers," he had said after seeing several slain harpies that he had been raised among. And so, it had begun. A silent war with no lasers guns or man made weapons. It was a war of nature against the human civilization.

He was weary now and longed to be in Kari's arms for this was the only thing that seemed to comfort him. He went back to the room. As he entered the doorway, he could hear Kari and Lea talking excitedly in the human voice. Shail entered the room and Lea immediately bowed to him and left the room, as Kari got to her feet. She stood before him in the robe of a female harpy. Her long blond hair flowed over her shoulders and covered some of the robe. She looked at him, as her blue eyes sparkled in fire light. He swallowed hard for her beauty was overwhelming for him. She stepped closer, as he just stood there watching her.

"What is wrong?" she asked him, using her mind instead of her voice.

"You are so stunning, I sometimes can not breathe," he said to her.

She smiled shyly. "I take your breath away, I believe is the term. You like the harpy robe?" she related to him again in silence.

"It is not the robe. It is what it holds, that takes my breath away," he answered, correcting the English language, he was learning.

Kari stood in front of him. She placed her arms around his neck and gently pulled him to her as their lips met. They kissed for a long moment before they finally pulled apart.

"You grow tired of this room. Shall we walk before we retire?" he asked her.

"Yes, I would like to do that," she smiled.

They walked the long corridor back to the large open expanse. The pit fires were not burning bright, as they had at their arrival and only a small glow came from them. There were no long any harpies in this great large room. Kari looked at him with a questioning in her eyes.

"All are gone but a few. They have flown to the east to make ready for what is to come. And I must join them soon," he told her.

"But your wing. You don't know if it is healed," she said.

"The moons form the human smile now as they gaze at the dawn but soon they shall be an open mouth. It is then I must fly, whether this wing is healed or not. I wait no more."

"But the full moons are in only seven days," she said with distress in her voice going back to the human voice. He only nodded.

They walked back through the crevice that they had entered upon their arrival to this place. When they reached the outside, it was dark and the moons were crested, as Kari stared up at them. The cold wind blew hard against the mountainside, causing her to shiver, even under the robe. Shail put his arms around her, as he stood behind her, warming her with his wings. They stared off at the stars and the mountains and valleys below them, knowing their time together, would soon be coming to an end, and wondered if they had a future together. The cold air caused them to push their bodies together for warmth. Shail nuzzled the back of Kari's neck and rubbed up against her. She took a deep breathe and knew he wanted her as she tossed her head back and snuggled against the side of his face, giving him permission to mate with her once again. Pulling the robe up to the back of her waist, he stroked, until he was within her. Soon they were bonding beneath Kari's robe while Shail held her tightly up against him. When he had finished, he turned her around to face him and kissed her softly on her warm, quivering lips. "I don't want to live without you," she whispered to him.

He smiled, ever so slightly and put her head against his chest as he held her. "I shall do my best to return to you when it is done. This much, I promise you," he related to her.

They clung to one another for several hours, not wanting to lose this moment in time. The cold fresh air heightened their senses and they felt alive and free on this mountain ledge. Soon the dark sky began to take color, as Duran rose in the east over the jungle beyond. They went back to the nest in the room and curled up around one another and slept.

Kari woke to discover that Shail had gone again and the room was empty. She got up and went to a small pool of water that had formed from dripping through the broken hull of the old ship. She washed and ate some of the fruit. Soon Shail had come in and kissed her lightly on the cheek, as she nibbled. "I have a decision I must make and it concerns your welfare. To do this, I must tell you all there is of this war, so you shall understand and help me decide what is best," he said.

Kari looked up at him with surprise. "I thought it was a big secret?"

"It was, but no longer. The nature of this war was not told to any females for some time. It is a ruling, I made long before you came to me. And I could not break it, even to you. Our females dwell too close to men and if any man knew our plans, they would have risen up and wiped us out not understanding it. If this had happened then all would die, harpy and human alike. You shall understand when I explain this war to you," he said, as he began to tell her how the harpies had allowed the beetles to multiply and the beginning of the swarms that now threatened all life. And, how these swarms would drive the humans from the planet. She listened intently as he explained everything to her, including his regrets that the beetles had become killers to all.

"They killed the hunters that wounded you," she said softly.

"Yes, Aron made that decision in my absences and brought a swarm down upon them, fearing they would find me and kill me in the doctor's structure."

"How did you create these swarms and how will you destroy them?" she asked.

"The loca eagles gave us this knowledge. They used to eat these beetles and destroy all new queens. When our loca cousins were killed and no longer on the land, we harpies took their place even though we do not eat beetles. We stopped the growth of new queens on the beetle mounds to protect our jungle. These swarms have always been. And after the humans flee, we shall destroy the swarms the same way, though it now comes at great risk to ourselves for we must fly into the heart of these killer swarms to retrieve the queens. I fear, some of us shall die in the end," he said sadly. "But now, you must help me decide for your safety.

You cannot remain here when I leave, for there is no way down off the ledge, if all should fail. I have sent all our females and young of the west to the islands and hope that the beetles cannot fly that far. But again, if we fail, and the land is consumed with swarms, even the islands may be at risk. Lea has told me that your father has built a great room that no beetle may enter. Maybe it is wise to send you back to dwell with him. You shall live in the disguise of a woman as other female harpies do. He shall protect you and our son. The harpies defend his home and lands. If they fail, there is his building and if it fails, he is capable of sending you to the safety of the stars as he did once before. It is for this reason, it would ease my mind if you were there but I cannot make you go," he said.

She looked at him startled. "Shail, I told you last night, that I don't want to live without you and I meant it," she said soberly.

"You must not think like a harpy now. You must gather from your human strength and be strong enough to survive my death. You carry the last golden ruler of the harpies. Our son is more important than either of our lives. He is the future of our race. I would gladly sacrifice my life and many others to ensure his survival and you also must learn to feel this way."

Kari stared blankly. "Who will he rule, if all are lost?"

Shail put his arm around her. "There shall be some survivors and he must be among them."

"Oh, Shail, this all scares me so much," she said and hugged him.

"It scares me also. It is my decisions that rule the fate of all living things on this land. It is an immense burden to carry and I pray I choose wisely.

"If it will help ease this burden some, I promise to return to my father, though I do not want to but you are right, he will protect me and you will not have to worry about me."

And so the last of Shail's plans had been completed. It was only a matter of time, before he would know the outcome. The next few days, Kari stayed at his side, not wanting to miss any time away from him. She taught him all she could about the human objects. How to open doors, how a hovercraft worked. She was amazed at what a good student he was and, how quickly he learned. She wasn't sure if he could use any of this knowledge, but he seemed to want it. Lea had gone back to the islands and only two other male harpies remained.

It was on this day, that she tried to tell him about a laser gun that he surprised her completely. "I have to talk in the human voice, to explain this to you," she said. "You know the language well enough now. And, it's easier to explain it this way, than for me to try and relate it to you through mental thought. Sometimes,

I wish you could just speak. I could teach you faster," she said, while drawing a picture in the dirt of the laser gun.

"What makes you think I can not," he related to her in silence.

Kari stopped drawing and looked up at him in astonishment. "You can talk?"

"Yes." he said with a soft silky voice that was almost a whisper.

She sat back in shock and stared at him. "But how? I thought that all male harpies lacked this ability to speak," she stammered.

"We choose not to speak. It is dangerous in the jungle, if heard. We stopped this sound when the first men took our females. Since we were able to relate in silence the animal way, this noisy talk was abandoned. Only our females kept it, only so they could mingle with the humans," he had gone back to communicating with his thoughts. "And," he went on, "before we met, I did not know all the human words as I do now. I only sensed some of their meaning."

"Let me hear you say something else," she said excitedly.

He frowned at her and pulled his head back a little puzzled. "You enjoy hearing this harsh sound from me?"

Her eyes twinkled and Kari smiled. "Your voice is not harsh but very soft and soothing. Yes, I'd love to hear it."

"What would you have me say?" he asked with his sensuous low male voice.

She leaped up and kissed him passionately on his lips.

"I should speak sooner," he said. Because it made Kari happy, Shail began to speak to her with the words of a human. The more he spoke, the easier it became for him, until he almost sounded like a soft-spoken man. He did not see the harm in it, for he did not feel less of a harpy. Because he loved Kari so much and wished to please her, Shail broke the ancient harpy rule of silence.

The days ahead were spent with Kari teaching him and the nights were filled with the passion of the bonding. In between Kari was determined to discover who had come in this space ship they lived in. They strolled through the old ship, discovering primitive artifacts from an earlier era. Each discovery delighted her and Shail went along, since it made her happy.

On this day, Kari rushed to a crushed doorway and tried to see under it. "I think this is the control room. The place where they guided the ship," she explained to him. Shail reached down and ripped at the dilapidated door, until he had created an opening large enough for them to crawl through. "Yes, this is it," she said excitedly and held a torch over the many panels of the guidance system. "Look, it's the captains log. We can now find out if humans or harpies brought this ship here. I can install Doc's communicator and get power to it."

Shail was less enthusiastic. He had too much on his mind to be concerned about where this ship came from or who had piloted it. But he was a little curious. They went back to their room and returned with the communicator. Kari worked for hours restoring and cleaning the log as Shail watched her with interest while she worked. "I think, it's ready now," she finally said. Kari connected a few more wires, as a gravely broken voice made a noise through the room. Shail jumped to his feet and spread his wings with alarm when he heard the man's voice. Kari grinned at her nervous wild little mate. He settled down, realizing the voice was harmless. After several more adjustments, a screen came on against the panel. It was a tall middle-aged blond man, who talked on the screen.

Kari glanced at Shail. "It's a man, not a harpy," she said and Shail nodded his head reluctantly, knowing that he stood in a man made structure. "Look at the date," she raveled as she read the bottom of the screen. "This ship is over three hundred years old."

"Is that amount important?" he asked.

"It means you were right. This ship was here before the first explorers and settlers came to Dora," she said and watched the screen.

"This, I already knew to be true," he whispered, happy he was right once in a while.

The man on the screen was talking about the cargo he was to pick up on another planet and the daily routine of running a ship. His voice was still gravelly and unclear. Kari made more adjustments and the man and his voice became clearer. "I'm going to fast forward this and see if we can find out, if anyone survived this crash." The man disappeared and there was a flashing motion on the screen. She stopped it periodically and listened to the screen, as the man's voice would come and go until she found what she was searching for.

"Star date twenty-eight hundred, forty-seven log of Princess, star freighter," said the voice on the screen. "The engines caught fire yesterday and are beyond our repair. We're just adrift in space with only boosters. Unfortunately, these are not enough to maintain our course. The closest system is a small star named Duran. We've decided to make for this star and hope that it has planets that are habitable, since it's never been explored. Even with this attempt, it will take at least five years. Morale is low among the fifty men under me. Captain James of the Princess, out."

Kari pushed in a sequence of numbers, adjusting the log to jump five years ahead.

"We are approaching the star, Duran. Food is low and the men fight amongst themselves. I don't care if they kill each other at this point. The calculations were off and it looks like it will be at least six more months before we reach the third planet. That's the only one, our sensor detect oxygen on. Captain James of the Princess, out."

Kari adjusted again. The captain seemed to be repeating the same messages over and over only changing the date and distance. She finally came close to the end.

"The planet is very close now and the men are excited. We just hope that the boosters work well enough to survive the landing. The planet is covered with water but there is one large continent. We hope to put down in the middle of it. God, it looks beautiful, very similar to Earth. I'll know in a few days if we're going to make it or not. The food has been gone for some time and we're all just hanging on. Doesn't seem to matter if we crash or not. It's better than starving to death. Captain James of the Princess, out."

"We made it to the surface. The boosters worked up till the end but quit, which threw us off course. We crashed on the side of a northwestern mountain, barely missing the ocean. When the ship hit the mountain, it caused an avalanche of rocks. Right now, the men are working in shifts to slice through the rock to get out. We lost four men in the crash and eight wounded. But, we're just happy to still be alive. Food is our main concern as I have been repeating for some time. It truly looks like we may make it. Captain James of the Princess."

Kari glanced up at Shail. His face was very serious as he watched the screen. Kari read his thoughts. He was wondering if this man was the one whom the harpies had named as the creator. It was unrealistic to him, that this Captain James could have held such a high honor among his people. The next log came on and Kari turned her attention back to it. She noticed that this tall blond man was gaunt and thin and his voice was very weary. She could sense the suffering he was going through.

"Star date twenty-eight-fifty-four of the freighter, Princess. Lost another man today. Joe Mahan was a good young man. Died of his crash injuries. The crew cut through the mountain rocks and with ropes, five of my strongest men have descended to the jungle below. I and other men have remained on board with the injured men. Our communication was destroyed in the fire but we're hoping to find the raw materials on this planet to restore it. The men in the jungle were sent to gather food and return to the ship. It seems like they should have no trouble, since our sensors tell us this planet is full of life. The weather is cold on this mountain but as I look out the crevice we made in the stone, the scenery will take your breath away. The trees are a vast array of colors. It is one of the most beautiful planets, I've ever seen. I can't wait till the men return and I can explore this new world myself. Captain James of the Princess, out."

"The men have returned to the ship with loads of food. Scanning the fruit, we find that it is edible. They even managed to bring back two large flying reptiles. They told me the hunting was easy, since the animals here have no fear of us. This seems like a paradise to all the men. The injured men are making progress and we are all thankful for our lives. Captain James of the Princess, out."

"I've decided to go off the mountain and out of the ship for an expedition into the jungle with twenty of the men. The rest will remain on the ship with the injured. There is ample food supplies aboard to sustain them until our return. I'm anxious to see the mineral content of the planet. Find out, if it will suit our needs to make repairs to communication. The ship is unsalvageable since a portion of the mountain rests on it. Captain James, out."

"Returned to the ship, after a week in the jungle. I lost one man, when we used our laser guns on a herd of giant lizards. As soon as one of the lizards fell, the rest attacked. We had to kill half the herd before they fled. We have learned the hard way to be more cautious on this new planet, which seems similar to Earth during the Jurassic period of dinosaurs. It has become more difficult to bring food back to the ship, so I am making plans to evacuate it. We found a place on the coast with ample food and water. I sent half the men, to build the shelters we'll need. The other half are packing and removing all the supplies that can be useful in the jungle. Since it is a difficult climb to come and go from this ship, I'm limiting my logs to every couple of weeks. Captain James of the Princess, out."

Kari skipped through the logs, pushing ahead in time. She wanted to find the outcome of these men.

"Returned to the ship. It's been one year since we landed here. Never did find any raw materials to repair the communications. Our only hope of returning to our world seems to wait until another ship discovers us. The men are in good health, except everyone misses their loved ones, especially the women. But we must face the fact we have been lost for six and a half years now and are probably assumed dead. But still, we hope. Captain James, out."

"Star date twenty-two-sixty. We've been here over six years now since our ship crashed on the planet. Lost three more men to animals in that time. The men are very lonely. But, our routine of gathering food and hunting remains the same. Sam Wise has found a root that we can make spirits from and this seems to please the men. A young man named Jack Harper made a pet of a creature we named loco eagle, since they're so crazy that they fly right to us. One was wounded when we shot her and he refused to let us finish the job and eat her for dinner. I think the boy is beginning to lose his mind somewhat. He nursed this creature back to health and it has become very fond of him. It's very friendly and seems to be the closest animal to resemble a human being. Their brown feathers cover their body, except the face, which is very smooth like our skin. They also have arms and legs with wings on their backs similar to a tall winged monkey but they have delicate facial features with large looming eyes. There is nothing else to report. Captain James, out."

"I had to return here and make this report. It has been one year since the last one. The female loca I mentioned in my last report gave birth a few months ago. The baby was a female and looks similar to a human being. The men are very excited about this and are organizing more hunts for female locas. It doesn't seem right but the men are desperate for companionship and I can't see the harm in it. Captain James, out."

Shail stood up and paced the room. "This is how the harpies were created?" he said in disbelief. "We were created by men? Show the rest," he said to Kari.

"Star date twenty-eight seventy-two. Tomorrow is my birthday and I'll be sixty-five years old. Don't know how many more times I can make it up this mountain to this old ship. The power pack for the ships log is running low. So this may be my last entry but we'll see. I had resisted taking a loca as a mate, like the rest of my crew but they captured a rare female with cream feathers and gave her to me. At first this creature was frightened of me but once I broke down and gave in to the temptation, she immediately became tame and treats me like her mate. She nuzzles and licks me constantly, begging for affection. She was so sweet I can't help but dote on her. She has won my heart. The loca flies freely during the day and feeds but every night she is faithfully in the nest I made for us. We have created a whole new race of beings by procreating with these beautiful loving animals. My two sons and four daughters are the most wonderful things in my life. They fill me with joy on a daily basis. The boys were born with wings and can fly and they taunt my girls a little but they are the gentlest of beings. There's not a mean bone in them. The other men have their own families and we have the most desirable of communities. The chatter of these children makes my heart soar. I'm particularly proud of my offspring because they are the only ones with my blond hair and the boys have the cream colored wings of their mother. The rest of the male harpy fledglings have brown wings. We've given them the name of harpy, since it was Jack Harper, who started this all. My oldest boy seems to take charge of the rest, when it comes to flying or games. He's very brave and smart and must take after his old man. If I sound like a proud father, I am.

They have given my life meaning and I no longer care if we are rescued. I can't think of any place in the galaxy, I'd rather be than in this Garden of Eden surrounded by these elegant gentlest of mortals." Captain James, out."

"There's one more log," Kari said. "Do you want to hear it?" she asked Shail, who was deep in thought. He nodded and Kari played it. An old man came on the screen.

"Today is my eighty-fifth birthday. It's hard to believe, twenty years has past since my last log. My son flew me here since there was no way this weary old body would make it. I just wanted to complete this final log before I died. I'm a grandfather with seventeen beautiful grandchildren. They're even more handsome than their parents. My son is the ruler of the harpies. They choose him since he is the most fearless and wise of the harpy males. He protects and defends his flock from other wild animals with his life. And his compassion is beyond approach. He's a far superior leader than I ever could be. I have brought him to this old spaceship, to tell him that this is where he was created. Most of my crew are dead now. Only three others remain beside myself. We talk about our offspring and what the future holds for them. If other men come to this planet some day, they surely will be impressed with the race of harpies. They're intelligent and lack malice toward all life. They refuse to hunt and kill the other animals, as we men have done but have taken the role of protecting the jungle and all the creatures in it. This humanity seems to bring them much pleasure. I'm grateful they have the gentle souls of the loca eagles."

Suddenly, another voice could be heard behind the old man. "Father, it grows very late and I fear it shall be too cold for you off the mountain." The elderly man smiled wide. "I'm almost finished, son," he said to the soft voice.

"Anyway, I want to leave this last log for a record for the harpies, as to how they began. Or, if any men find this, they will know that the harpies are their brothers and should be treated with equal respect. The harpies only have the best of qualities in them. They live by their honor and have a peaceful loving nature and they seem to lack the human emotions of hate and anger. I guess that's all I have to say. I'm ready to leave now, son. I want to be home before my great grandson is born. Do you think.........." and the voice trailed off. Captain James never even turned it off as he walked from the screen.

Shail bent over the blank screen and touched it with his hand lightly as he gazed at it. "I wish all men, who came here, were like this one," he said with his silky quiet voice. "He was kind and loved us."

"But Shail, do you know what this means?" Kari asked with a thrill in her voice.

He looked at her strangely. "It means, we carry this man's blood," he answered.

"Yes, but do you see, this is the proof we need. It's the proof that harpies are related to men. That they can't keep treating us like animals. They have to stop the harpy hunting. The old man said it himself. He left the log, so all harpies would be treated with respect by humans."

Shail shook his head. "It comes too late. In seven more lights, the swarms shall be out of control. The harpies have held them in the jungle long enough to allow the humans to return to the sky and escape. We can hold them no more and I shall not have my harpies die to save these foolish town humans, who refuse to flee. Enough of us shall die, when we attempt to destroy the swarms. Tomorrow the moons shall be round and I must join the other males at the river. The swarms are drawn to these towns and it is the human blood, they seek. By the next rise of the round moons, all shall be gone.'

Kari thought for a moment. "If I can get this log to the humans in time and you were convinced that they would end the harpy hunting, isn't it possible for you to start destroying the swarms, before they reach the cities? You have to destroy them anyway," she said anxiously.

Shail paced the room some more before he finally spoke. "I do not know if I could be convinced of this. We have lost so many in my lifetime and when I think of it, I can feel this emotion of hate growing in me. It is the human cruelty that feeds it. Now, you wish for me to save them? To give these humans life, when they gave us none. It is a lot to ask. And there is no trust. After the swarms are gone, it is more likely they shall continue to hunt us."

"Yes, this could happen, but if they know we have human blood and you save their lives, and they know, you can destroy the swarms, that without the harpies, the beetle swarms will rule this planet. If they know all of this, the hunting would end."

"Why do you wish to save them? You have been at the mercy of these deadly hunters. Their cruelty and dark hearts are worse than any living thing. They do not deserve to be saved."

"But Shail, I have been among many humans and these hunters are few. There are many more good ones that deserve to live and if they knew the truth, they would accept and cherish us like the old captain."

Shail paced again and took a deep breath, as he sighed. "You know it is our nature to protect not to kill. We do this with much regret and anguish. But there is too little time to grow such trust. Most humans shall survive. I have planned it this way. When the swarms strike the first city of the west, the rest of the humans shall flee back to the stars in fear."

"Most will die, Shail. There are not enough space ships or time to evacuate the whole planet. There are too many of them," she said quietly.

"Female, you make my head hurt. Take the log and do what you must. And I shall think on this. It is a decision that does not come easy. It shall be difficult to convince me of their honor and truth. But I shall try to be fair and wise in this and hope you succeed."

Kari leaped up and threw her arms around him, giving him a kiss on his cheek. She immediately dropped back down and started disconnecting the log. When she had this done, she began to reassemble Doc's communicator. "I'm going to call Doc. He'll know the best person to take this log to. And I can ask him about your wing at the same time. Though I doubt if you'd follow the doctor's orders anyway," she said happily. She pushed the communicator button and tried to make the call. "The satellite doesn't pick up in here. I have to go outside," she said and crawled quickly through the crushed doorway with Shail following her. When they reached the outside, the daylight was fading. She started to push the buttons, as Shail swiftly caught her wrist.

"It would be wise at this time, not to tell him we control the swarms," he said to her. Kari nodded in agreement.

"Doc," she said as the old man came on the screen. "It's Kari Turner, you know, the girl with the golden male harpy."

"Kari, I've been thinking about you. How are you and how's your handsome harpy?" Doc asked.

"We're fine, Doc, and thank you so much for saving him. But, I need to know when the splint can come off his wing," she yelled over the wind.

Doc rubbed his chin. "Let's see. Enough time has gone by and he's young. His bones should heal quickly. It could probably come off now but he shouldn't use it too much at first. It would be better in a few weeks. I imagine that high-strung little guy is getting pretty impatient. So, you still got him." he chuckled.

"Yes, we're still together and I have never been happier in my life. He's a real gentleman in truest sense of the word," she said and took Shail's hand.

"There's a friend of yours here staying with me. A Doctor Watkins. We've been discussing you and that blond harpy quite a bit," he said.

"Dr. Watkins is there? Can you put him on the screen," she asked continuing to shout over the wind.

Dr. Watkins appeared in front of the screen. "Hello, Miss Turner. I heard you say that you still owned the male golden harpy. Do you think, you could bring him here so I could get a blood sample for my research?" Watkins asked.

Kari laughed a little. "He's not tame enough to hold still for some thing like that. But, I may have something better. I have solid proof that the harpies are related to humans. And if you want a harpy blood sample, I'll bring you one. I'm picking up my vehicle in the morning and I'll see you both tomorrow night with the proof."

"Alright, Miss Turner, I'll be looking forward to seeing you again." Dr. Watkins said. And they were disconnected.

Shail and Kari walked back in the cover of the space ship. "You don't need to go to the cabin for the vehicle. I can fly you all the way to your father's home," he said.

"It's too risky for you to go on the estate. My father may see you. And you heard, Doc. You shouldn't use that wing any more than you have to. It's a short flight along the water to the cabin. The estate is too far for you to carry me. Besides, I want the independence of my own transportation." She could sense his doubts. "I'll be okay, Shail. The harpies are keeping the swarms away from my father's estate. And if I see any hunters, they'll think I'm a woman since wild harpies don't travel in vehicles."

Shail cast his eyes to the floor and just nodded. All she said made sense but he didn't like her alone and unprotected. "The last two adult males leave tonight for the gathering. I shall have one send a fledgling to meet us at the cabin. He shall be my eyes and ears. If danger comes to you, he can warn the adult harpies, who guard the estate borders."

"All right, if it will make you feel better," she smiled and kissed him lightly on the cheek for being so concerned.

They returned to their room and Kari carefully removed the splint from Shail's wing. Shail stretched it out and saw that new feathers had grown in to replace the damaged ones. He fluttered off the floor a little as he tested the wing. He could feel the weakness in it and realized that Kari was right. It would be better if he just flew a short distance to the cabin with her added weight. The last two brown winged harpies had left the old ship now, for none could be spared in the coming days. Kari and Shail were alone again. They curled up on the moss, as Shail put his arms around her and kissed her for a long time. They both knew this would be their last night to bond. Kari's body had told her that she was definitely pregnant and it was no longer just harpy intuition. This bonding was for their own pleasure and the possible loss they faced. Shail caressed her slender body, trying to remember every detail about it, as this memory would have to sustain him in the weeks ahead. She quivered and wiggled against him, her body stimulating his. He slowly made love to her, wanting this night to last forever. After some time, he could control himself no longer, and gave in to his urges. This desperation heightened their sex drive. He moved to kneel over her as she licked him and he was quickly aroused again. With each of his consummations, he only rested briefly as his lust for her body drove him to perform all night. By dawn, their bodies were wringing wet with sweat. He feverishly copulated within her, in a frenzy to release one last climax. Rapidly pumping, he consummated this final bonding and collapsed beside her. His heart pounded, as he gasped for air. His limbs so weak, he could barely move. Shail closed his eyes, as Kari moved to him. She panted hard, as her body throbbed with contentment and exhaustion, as she took him in her arms. She kissed and nuzzled him tenderly until Shail responded, placing his arms around her once again and they dosed off to sleep.

John Turner leaned over his desk, as the latest swarm report came in. "Where are they now?" Charlie asked as he sat across from him.

"It's another hit above Terrance but still in the jungle. That's the third one this week. Those town people must be getting pretty nervous by now. There were two hits to the south. Killed several hunters in a terrain vehicle and the other wiped out a hunting camp with five hunters in it," John answered.

Charlie got up and looked at the map. "These swarms seem to be hitting everywhere except on the estate," he mentioned.

"Yes, I've noticed that. Guess we've been lucky. I don't care if a swarm hits here, as long as they stay away from the northern mountain range and Kari," he said as he looked at Charlie. "You really think those harpies could protect her?"

Charlie nodded. "I think she's better off than we are. I've seen those harpies fly. They can easily out fly the beetles. There's no doubt about that."

"Well, the harbor is gone and most of the men have left for Hampton. I can't rebuild without the help and there's no sense in doing it, if a swarm hits it again. I plan on packing up one of the hovers and start searching for her again. I can't just sit here and do nothing."

The communicator buzzed on his desk and John punched it on. "Hello, Mr. Turner. This is Mr. Schmitt in the satellite communications. I have another correspondence on your property in the mountains. This one, I think, you'll be interested in. Doesn't sound like a bunch of hunters at all," the man said.

"Patch it through to me," John said to the man. "I was getting one or two of these a day. But these swarm attacks have sent the hunters running for cover.

Must be a few brave souls still out there, especially since I put the word out, if the swarms don't get them, I will," he told Charlie.

The man's voice came back on. "Do you want a two way hook up or just the person in the mountains?"

"Two way is good," John answered him. The screen suddenly had two pictures on it. John and Charlie froze, when they saw Kari on the screen. On the other side was old Doc. They listened intently, as the conversation took place between them. When it was over, the man's voice came back on.

"Is that a save or erase, Mr. Turner?"

"It's a save and I'll be taking good care of you for this."

Charlie looked up at John. "I thought that it was illegal to listen in?"

"It is. But some rules are meant to be bent, Charlie. Well, I have them now. I can get my daughter back and get rid of that harpy at the same time. Did you hear that? She is still with that winged vermin and soon he can fly. When that happens, God knows where he'll take her."

"I hear her say she was very happy and he has not harmed her. She is coming back on her own. Maybe we should just stay here and meet her at Doc's house tomorrow night," Charlie suggested.

"No, I want to end this and this is going to be the best shot I have of killing him. If I don't take care of this now, he'll just come back to haunt me. Let's pack, if you're going. We'll take two of the men that are still here and get there tonight. If we set it up right, we can surround him before he takes off. This time the wind will not be at our backs. We'll be facing the wind off the ocean," he said and walked out of the room. "Are you coming, or not?" Charlie only nodded sadly.

They took two hovers and parked them on the beach, a good distance away from the cabin. Then the four men quietly crept through the trees, till they reached the outskirts of the cabin. There they set up watch. The moons were almost full and the little cabin lit up from the moonlight. All was very still. The dawn finally came and their vision improved, as they searched the sky and woods for the girl and the harpy. The morning drew on until about ten o'clock. Finally, they spotted them. The search was nearly at an end.

Shail held Kari in his arms as they landed in front of the old familiar cabin. He set her down and stretched his one wing while she faced him. It was apparent that it still bothered him. She looked at the wing and smiled and gave him a short kiss. They were obviously communicating silently to one another, the animal way. They then walked to the hidden vehicle and began removing the branches from it. "Not yet," John whispered. "He is too close to the jungle."

After Shail had removed most of the stems, Kari jumped in the driver's seat and started up the old vehicle. She backed it to the front of the cabin and got out and turned it off. The golden harpy just leaned against the vehicle, while she stood in front of him. They seemed to be saying goodbye for they held each other's hand. Kari suddenly leaped into his arms and threw her arms around his neck. He held her close as they kissed. Kari ran her hands through his hair and it was apparent, she was upset. The harpy just nuzzled her neck and buried his face in her hair.

"This is as good a time as any. She has him pretty distracted," John whispered bitterly. The four men walked from the woods with the breeze in their face. Their laser guns pointed at Shail. Before they had taken three steps, Shail saw them. His face froze, as they hurried toward him. He saw the weapons in their hands and normally, he would have bolted but he thought of Kari. If they shot at him, they could miss and hit her. Kari saw Shail's face and knew something was wrong. She wheeled around and saw her father and the others. "Fly," she said to him.

He glanced at her. "Their weapons may hit you. I shall not risk it," he said in silence.

Now the men were on them as they surrounded the both of them. Kari and Shail still held each other while her father approached.

"Kari, I want you to step away from him and come over by me."

"What are you doing here?" she said with a plea in her voice.

"I've come to take you home."

"I was just coming home. Let him go and I'll come with you," she tried to reason.

Shail just stood calmly and quietly listened to their heated debate.

"No, he's going to ruin your life. It's better to end this here and now. I want you to come over here," he yelled with anger.

Tears ran down her cheeks. "Dad, please, he is my life. Can't you see that?" she cried.

"Yes, I can, and that's why you're better off without him," he yelled again.

Kari suddenly got a cold hard stare as she wiped away her tears and looked defiantly at her father. "Is this how it was Dad, is this how it was when you shot my mother, when she tried to protect a golden male? You will have to kill me as well," she said with ice in her voice.

John was startled by her cutting words. "That was an accident," he said defensively.

"And you can call my death an accident also," she retorted harshly.

Shail now realized that Kari was willing to take the laser blast for him just as her brave mother had. He pulled her to him and cupped her face in his hands. "I shall not have you risk your life for me," he said silently. "Now, go with him."

"No! I will not go with him. He's going to kill you. Don't you understand, Shail?" she asked out loud pleadingly and her tears began to flow again.

He kissed her tenderly on her wet shaky lips. He knew there was no way out of this. "You promised me you would go with him." Shail whispered, barely audible to the others.

"Not like this! I will never leave you!" she said and turned her head towards her father. "Dad, I know I'm a harpy. And Shail is my husband. Can't you just leave us in peace?" she was now crying very hard, as she put her head against Shail's chest and wrapped her arms around his waist.

Shail breathed deeply, realizing his mate would never willingly leave him and he did not want her harmed. He pulled her away from himself while he held her by the shoulders. Kari stared at him with terrified, puzzled eyes. He moved her gently to her father's reach.

John stepped close to Kari, grabbing hold of one of her arms and pulled her to him, keeping the laser gun pointed at Shail's head. He removed her from the harpy with a steady strong tug as she fought him, calling Shail's name. Shail did not move to stop this, while he watched Kari struggle with her father's strength.

"Let me go," she screamed as John gave her to Charlie. Charlie held her in silence while she pleaded with the old Indian. "Please, Charlie, stop him. You know, we love each other. Don't let Dad kill him. Please!" she begged.

"I can do nothing. He will not be satisfied till this harpy's blood is on his hands. I have tried," Charlie held her and tried to pull her away.

The other men stepped in and helped the old Indian restrain her. "Take her to my hover," John ordered. The men and Charlie dragged her clear of the harpy and John, away from the cabin. Kari was hysterical now and fought them frantically, while she continued to scream Shail's name to come rescue her. But, both men had each of her arms and were almost carrying her at this point. Shail tossed his long blond hair nervously as he watched her struggle with the men. He wrestled with his natural instinct and urges to leap to the defense of his mate though he knew she was in no danger. He finally turned his head away from her and looked down and shook a little, since he could not bear to watch this battle. He gazed back up into her father's eyes, while the man seemed to be studying him. Shail breathed a little hard but did not show any fear. John now walked closer to the harpy and placed his laser gun at his head. Shail could sense the man's hatred of him and knew he would kill him quickly.

"I do not wish her more pain by seeing my death. May we go in here?" Shail asked with a quiet velvety voice and motioned to the cabin.

"She taught you to speak?" John said with surprise.

"She taught me many things," Shail answered him.

"I bet she did," John said with disgust. "Get in there then." They stepped back into the cabin. Shail glanced past the man and could see that Kari was a distance away with the three other men. He now, turned his attention to John and took a deep breath to calm himself.

"I know you hold much honor. I would ask one thing of you before I die," Shail said with his quiet voice. John stared at the tall brave harpy. The creature didn't even quiver or shake like most harpies or men, for that matter, when facing their own death. He watched the harpy and was somewhat captivated by his calm elegant mannerism. "Do you have this honor, for what I ask?" Shail questioned him again.

"What is it? You want your throat cut so you can have a quick and painless harpy death?" John sneered.

Shail shook his head slightly, "It is not important, how I die or if the pain is long," the harpy spoke again, just above a whisper.

"What do you want then?" John snapped.

Shail sighed a little. The human words were hard for him to speak. John could see this cocky slender male's eyes were slightly teary now. "I have protected your lands and I have protected her. When I am dead, this protection shall end since she shall flee from you. Do not let her. Protect her and my unborn fledgling son she carries. I shall have peace with this death and I resist you not, if you honor my wishes," Shail said with a quiet dignity in his voice.

John stared into the harpy's deep royal blue eyes that were eye level with his. He knew this trim airy looking male could be dangerous, despite his delicate greyhound appearance. John had learned how the harpy had fought off four hunters even when gravely wounded and how a few weeks ago two hunters in the northern mountains had been attacked and beaten close to death by this young golden harpy. Kari's slight little golden male could definitely be threat if it didn't die instantly. The harpy obviously showed no fear of John or his weapon.

"You attack the two hunters in the mountains. Why?" John asked, curious of a creature that was normally known for being timid.

Shail tilted his head puzzled by the question that did not pertain to his request. He looked at John strangely. "They threatened my mate," the harpy answered.

John's rage seemed to subside a little. This brassy harpy would defend Kari despite any risk to itself. John gazed at Shail with new respect, realizing the winged male was just as devoted to his daughter as he was. And he proved it by his fearless actions and words. "I'll honor your wishes and vow to protect her as well as your son," John said in an almost normal tone.

Shail nodded, taking another deep breath for courage and sniffled slightly. He lightly stepped closer to the man. John nervously raised his weapon, putting his finger on the firing trigger but then Shail dropping to his knees right in front of him as the beautiful cream feathered wings cascaded out across the floor. Shail was performing the ritual custom of submission to a hunter. John realized this brave handsome male at least deserved the harpy death of honor. But, John had never heard of a strong healthy harpy performing this ritual, it was usually done by mortally wounded harpies. John pulled out a large hunting knife that hung on his belt and raised it above the kneeling harpy. Shail put his hands slightly behind him showing he would not oppose him as he tilted his head back to expose his throat. As he did this, he shut his large blue eyes and trembled a little. John grabbed the soft long blond hair from back of Shail's head and roughly jerked his head back even further, to give him more leverage and ensure a clean cut. Putting the blade to his exposed throat, he saw Shail swallow hard. John froze for a moment, as he stared at this exquisite noble creature that resembled his daughter and dead wife. John sighed deeply. "Ah, hell, I have to do this," he said as he dropped the knife and grabbed his laser gun. He pointed it at the harpy's chest and fired it. Shail crumbled to the floor face down with his cream wings extended unnaturally over him.

Kari heard the laser blast. With all her strength, she ripped free of the unsuspecting men's hold and raced across the clearing towards the cabin. Her father was just stepping through the doorway, when he caught her before she entered. He grabbed her arms as she struggled to get around him. Over his shoulder, she could see Shail laying still and quiet, face down. "It's over now, Kari. You don't want to go in there," he uttered.

Kari screamed Shail's name. She tried screaming to him mentally but she got no response from him. Even if he lay wounded, he would have answered her. He was dead. She felt very weak and began to collapse as her father caught her. He picked her up and began carrying her, while she sobbed softly. Saying Shail's name over and over again. Pleading with her dead husband to answer her calls. One of the men started to pass John going towards the cabin.

"Where are you going?" John barked at the man.

"Mr. Turner, you're not going to leave those gold harpy wings just lay there. They're worth a lot." the man said. This made Kari shake hard when she heard this.

"This is my land, my kill and my wings. Leave them as they lay," he ordered.

"Sure, Mr. Turner. Anything you say," the man said humbly.

"Go get your hover and return to the mill," John barked again. The man nodded and jogged ahead with the other man till they disappeared over the bluff. John looked at Charlie but the elderly Indian just shook his head at him with disgust.

"We'll be home soon. And then everything will be all right," he told Kari as he held her in his arms and walked towards his hover on the beach. He placed her in the back seat and she curled up in a tight ball and continued to weep softly. He glanced at her and she seemed like a wounded animal. He didn't even think she was coherent at this point. "She'll be okay." John said, more to himself than to Charlie. Charlie didn't answer him.

The ride home in the hovercraft was a quiet one. Only Kari's occasional sniffle could be heard over the hum of the engines. John was deep in thought, as doubts clouded his mind. Had he done the right thing? Some of words that the harpy spoke to him ran over and over through his mind. "How could this harpy claim to protect his land?" he wondered and then there was his concern of Kari. Did she, in fact carry the harpy's fledgling son? This troubled him greatly. If it were true, he wasn't sure, how he would handle it. Could he possibly convince Kari to rid herself of this unborn baby? He had promised the blond male, he would protect it. John glanced back at Kari. She looked so much like her mother, her limbs pulled up in the traditional way that all harpies slept on the hover seat. She truly looked like a female harpy now. He breathed deeply and sadly. He was a man of his word and he would honor the agreement he had made with the young golden male. He would raise and nurture this fledgling grandson and protect it at all cost.

They finally landed on the front lawn by the house doors. John got out and opened the back door of the hover and lifted Kari out into his arms. Her eyes were shut, but she still trembled. He carried her inside and was met by Maria. It was still the middle of the afternoon but dark clouds had gathered and blotted out the rays of Duran. It would soon rain. Maria followed John up the upstairs, as he held Kari but she did not say a word. She knew that Mr. Turner had probably killed Kari's pet golden harpy and Kari's pathetic condition suggested it. Maria glanced back down the stairs as Charlie came in. She bent her eyebrows with a questioning. And Charlie only shook his head wearily. She knew her assumptions were true.

John placed his daughter on her bed and she immediately curled back up into a ball. She no longer was crying but seemed to be more in a trance. Maria went to her and softly brushed her hair away from her forehead. "It will be alright, Miss Kari," she said softly. Kari did not respond but just stared blankly at the walls. Maria looked at Mr. Turner with worry in her eyes.

"Go call Doc and tell him to come over here. Maybe he can give her something," he said in a low voice. Maria left the room and John sat down on the edge of the bed. He stroked Kari's hair but she did not move, except to shiver. He spoke softly to her and still she did not seem to know he was even there. Time passed and he soon heard the sound of another hover landing along side of his. He got up and glanced out the balcony. And saw Doc below with another man. The other man was carrying a medical bag as they approached the front door and Maria let them in.

Doc walked into the bedroom and saw Kari curled up in a ball on the bed. He examined her eyes as she trembled. "Cover her up and keep her warm. She's in shock." He looked angrily up at John. "You killed her little golden male, didn't you?" he growled bitterly.

"It had to be done," John said defensively.

"You damn fool! You may have killed your daughter as well," he snapped. "Dr. Watkins, take some of her blood," he ordered as the other man got out some of the equipment and quickly drew some of Kari's blood.

"Why do you need her blood?" John asked.

"Cause I want to know if I'm dealing with a human or a harpy here. There is a big difference and you know the truth," he raised his voice.

John looked down at the floor and swallowed hard. "She's a harpy," John said quietly. Maria, who stood in the doorway, put her hand to her mouth and let out a gasp as she caught her breath at the surprise.

"John, you know the stories of women who are forced to come back to civilization after living with the harpies. They lose their minds and usually die. It's not what the harpies did to them that cause this, it's the men killing their harpy mates and forcing them to return, that's the culprit. It happens because they're not women, they're female harpies. A female harpy is just as vulnerable and fragile as a male that is caged. They both shut down under great stress. They're not as strong as us. And they have no fear of embracing death. Actually, I'm surprised that she survived all those years on Earth and didn't go into a deep depression and take her own life," Doc said, while he stared at Kari.

"How do you know all this?" John asked him, putting his hand on Kari's head.

"Because Dr. Watkins and I have been doing a lot of research on the subject lately. Every single case we studied of the supposed kidnapping and rape is the same. The male harpy is killed and the woman goes into a deep depression and dies sooner or later, as well. Your daughter bonded with that harpy. She has embraced the harpy within her and has cast out the human side. You will never get her back even if she survives this trauma, which doesn't usually happened. Once a harpy bonds, it's over. But I think you know that. I think, you know more, than you are willing to admit," Doc raged.

"I knew my wife was a harpy. My own father tried to talk me out of taking her as my wife. Said she would bring me nothing but sorrow. He was right. But, if I had to do it all over again, I would have still wanted her," John said with sadness.

"I don't know why you were so set on killing that poor male harpy. You have just destroyed her life as well. I told you this would happen if you interfered," Doc mumbled.

"I guess I had hoped they hadn't bonded or the bond could be broken somehow. The golden male told me, she carries his son. Do you thing that's true?" John asked.

"The harpy spoke to you?" Dr. Watkins asked with surprise speaking for the first time.

"Yes, he spoke fluid English. First time I've ever heard of one speaking or uttering a sound for that matter." John replied. "He also said he wanted Kari to stay with me and I should protect her and his baby."

Doc shook his head with more disgust. "Sounds pretty admirable coming from someone who is about to die" Doc said and reached in his medical bag, taking out a scanner. He ran it over Kari's limp body. "Well, congratulations, you're going to be a grandfather, if she lives," Doc said sarcastically.

"She's pregnant then?" John asked.

"Sure is," he answered.

Kari suddenly gasped for breath but her eyes were still fixed and glazed. Doc quickly scanned her again. "Oh, heavens, her heart rate is slowing rapidly and she trying to shut down her lungs. Give me a stimulant to keep them going," he yelled frantically to Dr. Watkins.

"She can do that?" John yelled hysterically.

"Yes," Dr. Watkins answered while he quickly worked on Kari with old Doc. "Harpies have enough concentration that they can create their own deaths. It happened to a few harpies obtained by the zoo. The autopsies revealed a complete organ shut down for no reason."

"Well, the stimulant seems to be working, thank God. Give me an anti depressant patch," Doc said, placing the patch on Kari's arm. "I'm going to load her with tranquilizers until the patch can kick in. Should keep her close to zombie state but at least she'll lose control of shutting down her organs. I read about this new treatment online from some of those sick harpy hunters when they want to prolong a caged harpy's life," Doc stated in disgust. Kari eventually closed her eyes and began breathing easier. "Seems to work but that was close. Your girl has her sights set on dying and it's going to take keeping her drugged up to prevent it. You'll never be able to leave her alone, not for a minute, probably as long as she lives," Doc said quietly as he glanced at John. "You got her back, John but at what price?" John looked at his daughter's frail clammy body as she still pathetically trembled in a slight coma state.

"I didn't do it," John finally said softly.

"What?" Doc asked harshly.

"Her harpy mate is not dead. I only stunned him with my laser gun. I hoped that if Kari thought he was dead, she would forget him or at least realize how dangerous it is to live as a harpy. Guess I was a fool to think I could separate them and she would be all right with it." Doc rose to his feet and just stared at him in disbelief. John just shrugged helplessly. "Look, I just couldn't kill him," John explained defensively. "It's just that after he started speaking to me, I saw him for what he truly was. I always thought the male harpies were wild raping animals totally different than the intelligent civilized female harpies. But when I spoke to her, Shail, I realized I have been wrong all these years. He was quiet and dignified and far from any animal. He loved my daughter as much as I did. Right up to the very end, that brave little golden didn't care about his life. He only cared about his family. He dropped to his knees and was willingly to die with out a struggle since I promised to protect her and his son. When I put the blade to his throat, I knew, it was a mistake and I would regret it. My life has had too many regrets. That heroic little blond deserved to live. I've never known any man with that much heart. Turns out, my own daughter is just as devoted to him. She'd rather die than live with out him." John said sadly.

Doc looked back at Kari. "Well, she sure does think he is dead. That stunning would have worn off hours ago. I believe he would have flown here by now since he's so protective. He'd have to know his mate might fall victim to this harpy depression especially if she thought he was dead. There's no way, he would let his mate come this close to death. Are you sure, your gun was set to stun or that stunning did give him a heart attack?" Doc asked.

"Yes, I'm sure. He was breathing peacefully when I left the cabin and I made certain all the men had their lasers set for a mild animal stunning. Do you think I was going to take that kind of chance again," he stammered. Suddenly his face froze and walked quickly out of the room. When he reached the balcony, he yelled down to Charlie. "Charlie! Charlie!" Charlie came to the foyer quickly and looked up at him. "Take my hover and go to the mill. See if those two men came back yet." he yelled with urgency. He glanced out the windows and it was getting late. Duran had set and darkness was falling swiftly.

They waited in Kari's room for Charlie to return. Soon they heard the hover landing again and Charlie rushed through the front doors as John leaned over the balcony.

"They did not return," Charlie told him.

John put his hand to his forehead. "God, he is dead then. Damn them," he cursed with anger as he bent over. "They killed him for some lousy damn feathers. I've made a mess of things," he uttered. Doc stood beside him and sadly shook his head.

"I wish you would have listened to me. Your daughter was coming back to Westend. She wanted to give something to Dr. Watkins that would help her harpies. Some kind of proof."

John walked back to Kari's bed. She wore the human clothing again. He felt her pockets and reached in and pulled out an old disc. "This must be, what she wanted you to have," John said quietly as he handed it to Dr. Watkins.

Watkins examined it. "Do you have anything we can play it on?"

"No, but I think I can rig something up that might work."

"Go ahead, I'll stay with her. She should sleep soundly for some time, before all these drugs wear off," Doc said while he stroked the beautiful sleeping female harpy.

John went downstairs and began to work on the equipment in the den. It took his mind off the harpy's death and Kari for the moment. Dr. Watkins joined him along with Charlie. After an hour, they had set up the equipment. Doc came down to report that Kari was still resting quietly. They all sat down to watch the log and the story of the Captain James and the freighter, Princess. When it was done, they stared around in astonishment at one another and did not speak.

"I need to take this to Hampton," Dr. Watkins finally said seriously, "and put it in the right hands."

John nodded to him. Doc stood up slowly.

"So, all our research and assumptions are correct. And now, we know why the harpies are related to humans and how it all happened," Doc said.

Charlie asked, "How is this possible that two different species could create the harpies?"

"Well, if given more time with my research, I'm sure I would have discovered that loca eagles have the same chromosomes as us, just like sheep. Sheep can conceive a fetus by a man but it never survives. Apparently, this fluke of nature between men and locas created a hybrid, which does survive and is not sterile. In which case you end up with the harpies," Watkins said.

"I wonder why the females have no wings?" John mustered while fooling with the disc.

"That's the genetics of these beings. Take for example domestic house cats. If you have a black female cat with black parents and it is bred to an orange male cat with orange parents, the litter would consist of orange kittens and black kittens. But, the interesting thing is, all of the male kittens would be black, like their mother and all of the females would be orange or possibly torte shell like the father. The female harpies pick up the genetic trait from their human fathers and the male harpies get their wings from the mother loca eagle. I'm betting, that if the harpies had ever chose to mate with the loca eagles then their females and males would have wings or if a woman conceived a baby by a male loca eagle then the females would have wings and the males wouldn't. But, none of this happened and as a result all female harpies are wingless. Which is lucky their ability to be a chameleon and mingle and hide among humans is probably the only reason, the harpies have survived. There is one thing that is interesting, if you ever look closely at a loca eagle, their features are very similar to men. They have very small noses and big beautiful piercing eyes with long lashes. Under all their softy body feathers, they have an extremely handsome tall slender body. It's just the right mix to make their harpy hybrids so attractive and good looking no matter what their human mates look like. The first harpies didn't look like this, since they had more soft feathering covering their bodies but with the human blood added over the years, the soft feathers are gone and now you have a being that exposes their sleek lean muscles and tall frame with a flawless face. No offense, Mr. Turner, but your daughter is gorgeous because of the loca eagle in her. It would be a crime if the harpies were exterminated. They're so magnificent," Watkins said.

Doc mustered, "We also did some research on our senators who promote this harpy hunting and seem to have a vendetta against the harpies. Turns out, most of our present day senators are the descendants of the Dorial explorers, who colonized this planet a hundred and fifty years ago after Captain James's freighter crashed here. We discovered the very first recorded kidnapping of a woman by a male harpy. The woman went insane and soon died. She was the daughter of one of the Dorial explorers. She had to be a female harpy. Knowing how docile and non-aggressive the male harpies are, it was our glorified founding fathers, the Dorials, who truly were the murderers and rapists. They probably caught and raped the female harpies when they landed on this planet. This is not only a theory but can be proved. We managed to find the passenger list of The Hampton, the Dorial's ship that landed here a hundred and seven-five years ago. Oddly enough, there were no women listed on board. Yet when the settlers began arriving twenty-five years later, these Dorial men had daughters. Now where did these daughters come from if not from the harpies? The Dorials created the lies that male harpies were dangerous thieving animals, guilty of the crimes they themselves, had committed. They had to lie since it's a felony to molest or harm intelligent alien life forms on other planets. By categorizing the harpies as ignorant hazardous game animals, there is no crime. And I believe our senators want to exterminate the harpies before all these facts come to light. If it came out that these poor harpies were only harmless intelligent mortals, only guilty of rescuing their own females, the scandal would destroy our senator's reputation and they would be booted out of office. Especially if the senators knew the true history of their famous Dorial ancestor's past crimes and knew the harpies carried the human D.N.A."

"Yes, and there's even more of a twist that would promote these senators to annihilate the species of harpies," Dr. Watkins added. "When I was researching the harpies at the Hampton zoo, I began to get death threats to stop this study. The fact is, it would be easy to compare the harpy's D.N.A. to the Dorial explorers' D.N.A. and prove they are related and these explorers truly were guilty of these past crimes against the harpies but here's the twist. It also would prove that your senators are related to the harpies and have this same genetic gene in them. I'd say that's enough of an incentive for the senators to eradicate the harpies and threaten me to stop my research. They want to avoid the mortification and embarrassment that they have some distant winged relatives."

John shook his head with disgust and said, "I've believed their damned lies all these years that the male harpies were dangerous, when I should have known better. I remember meeting my wife for the first time. My father and I were cutting trees on logging road behind the house. I discovered a lake off of it with trisom trees. When I went to it, I found a beautiful blond young woman in a long white robe. She was sitting beneath the trees, eating the trisom fruit. She rose and walked right up to me and told me that she had chosen me to be her mate. It was like a dream. I couldn't refuse her if I tried. I was instantly in love with her. She then confessed that she was a female harpy. It didn't matter to me, what she was. After we bonded, as the harpies call it, she became pregnant. By then, I knew the harpies weren't animals but another type of being. But, I still believed the lies that a male harpy would take her away from me some day. That day came and with it disaster. Kari met her male golden harpy near the same lake. I was afraid he'd force her to stay with him. When I spoke with him, I realize he had way too much honor for such a crime. Shail was a worthy husband. But I still was afraid of what the hunters would do to my daughter when they finally caught and killed her harpy mate. I wanted to separate them long enough to make her realize, how dangerous a harpy life can be. Maybe when he came for her, she would change her mind and stay in the human world."

Doc walked to John and patted him lightly on his back. "There's a lot of grief surrounding these poor harpies. Maybe this disc can give them a decent future. It's getting late and I'm tired. I'm going to check on Kari and give her another dose of tranquilizer before I go home. The last one should be wearing off." He headed for the stairs.

"I'll be right up," John called to him.

Doc reached the bedroom and opened the door as he peered in. He saw something that made him freeze when he stared at the bed that held Kari. A brown winged harpy was leaning over her, gently stroking her forehead. The harpy saw the man and quickly jerked his hand away, his eyes filled with panic as he started backing toward the balcony door. "Don't go. You may be the only one that can help her," Doc said softly to the harpy. The harpy stopped and looked at him a little hesitant. Doc now heard John coming up the stairs behind him. The old man whispered to him, "Stay back, John." John stopped on the stairs for a moment and then crept up quietly. By now, Doc had gone into the bedroom. He could hear him talking in a low gentle voice to someone. "Can you help her?" Doc asked. John realized that Doc was talking to someone other than Kari. He peeked in the room and saw the tall brown harpy standing skittishly by the open balcony. Its wings were slightly extended for flight as Doc was trying to coax it to stay. The harpy shivered with nervousness of the man and the room. His intense green eyes sparkled with indecision as he glanced at Kari. He swallowed hard and cautiously tip toed to the side of the bed. He bent over the sleeping female but his frightened eyes remained focused on the human. Gently the harpy began to stroke Kari's forehead and slowly she open her eyes. Doc knew the harpy was calling to her with their silent animal communication. The sedative had worn off in this late hour and she was trying to focus. Kari saw the harpy over her and she weakly put her arms up to it, calling it by name. "Aron?"

The harpy leaned closer, allowing her to wrap her arms tightly around his slender muscled frame. Kari buried her face in the glossy coffee brown hair and tan chest and began to cry openly. The harpy held her and tenderly nuzzled and licked the neck of the small weak female harpy, hoping to comfort and ease her stress.

"He's dead, Aron" she whimpered quietly and clung to him.

Aron faintly kissed her cheek and forced her head up from his chest. He could sense Kari had become a victim of the harpy depression and her will power to live was gone. He no longer concerned himself with the old man or this human cage of a room. Saving this last golden female was far more important than his safety. "Kari, we do not know if Shail is dead," he related silently.

"My father killed him," she said out loud.

"He did not. The fledgling arrived and saw two men drag Shail from the human structure. He followed them, hidden among the trees. These men tied Shail with ropes but before they finished, he came to life. He fought and defeated these two men. The fledgling then heard the sound of their weapon. Shail went limp and they placed him with in the metal bird and it flew away. The fledgling was not able to follow this fast flight. We do not know if Shail lives or is dead," Aron said silently.

Just then, Aron noticed Kari's father standing in the doorway. He jumped up with fright. This man was known to be dangerous unlike the kindly old doctor. Aron tossed and shook his dark locks at him, while hissing rapidly out of terror as he began backing towards the open balcony doors. His green eyes flashed with fear as he raised his wings, ruffling the brown feathers to ward off this threat. He hissed again, hoping this sound and his large extended wings would discourage an attack from the man before he could flee.

John immediately backed away. He could see the agitated frightened harpy was one step from leaping out the balcony. "Tell him, I won't hurt him," John said quickly with panic to Kari. Aron stopped in the balcony thresh hold, comprehending the man's meaning but still did not trust him.

Kari looked at her father and wiped away a tear on her cheek. "You didn't kill Shail?" she asked her father.

"No, I didn't. I only stunned him. Please ask this harpy to stay," John pleaded.

Kari glanced at Aron. "He understands the meaning of your words. He's not a stupid animal," she said with animosity. The drugs had worn off enough now that she could muster some of her own hostility. Aron anxiously stayed and shivered while keeping the open doorway to his back. His wings remained slightly spread for quick flight and he sniffled slightly with uneasiness and worry as he fought the desire to retreat.

"Does he know where your golden male is?" John asked Kari.

She shook her head. "He only knows that two men took him in a hover. The harpies don't know if they killed him," Kari said while rising from the bed. She was still dizzy and Aron caught her as she stumbled a little towards him.

"Is this the brown harpy who protects you?" John asked.

She looked at her father a little surprised. "He has."

John only nodded. "Tell him I want to save your mate, to save Shail. I have been wrong about the harpies all these years. I'll do every thing in my power to free him and make things right. I owe them and you an apology. If you wish to leave with this harpy, Kari, you may go. I won't stop you or him. I can see you're better off with them. But you must know, Shail did ask me to protect you and his son. He said you would want to flee but that I was to keep you here. Those were the words, he said to me."

Kari nodded. "It sounds like him," she sniffled. "Always concerned about me and not himself. He could have gotten away but he didn't even try. He was afraid your laser blasts might hit me, so he stayed," she put her hand to her mouth, realizing she was a little angry with Shail and he could be dead. Kari began to cry again and leaned against Aron, wrapping her frail arms around his waist. She put her head down against him as her long blond hair covered her face.

"Kari, I'm so sorry," John said and took a step towards her to comfort her. Immediately the brown winged harpy began to create a low seething sound and snapped its teeth at John's approach. This caused the man to stop short. Then it arched its wings and prepared to fly at him if John took another step closer. Aron defiantly stared at the two men, tossing his long hair to motion them away. He was boldly defending his golden harpy queen. Aron realized Kari was so unstable emotionally her life was at stake. If left alone with only humans, she could die. Right now, she needed a harpy's closeness and comfort to get her through this trauma. He would die fighting to remain next to this valued female who carried his future ruler. Aron would stay in the human cage and protect her, despite the risk of death.

John glanced at him and could see this frightened harpy had now become very fierce when holding a female. "Take good care of her," he asked in a mournful voice while he watched his daughter cling to the stunning male, who ruffled his brown feathers at him like a little bantam rooster poised for a cockfight. John lowered his head and walked out of the room. Doc sighed and followed John out and shut the bedroom door. Aron lowered his wings and breathed a sigh of relief as he and Kari looked out the balcony door. The rain had come and with it, the wind. It blew gusts and sheets of rain across the jungle and meadows.

"If Shail lives, we shall find him" Aron related to her and relaxed a little with the men gone. Kari nodded. She began to regain her strength with the new hope that filled her heart.

John descended the stairs deep in thought. "Do you think she'll be alright with him?" he asked Doc.

"I think that brown winged harpy can help her more than any drug I have. I just hope, for her sake, that her mate survives somehow. But he's a pretty tough character, beaten the odds before," Doc chuckled a little when he thought of the feisty young golden.

John glanced at the old man. "Sounds like you admire that harpy."

Doc smiled. "Well, I admit, I don't admire many but that one. What's not to admire? Even when the poor creature was half dead, that golden still had enough gumption to defend your daughter when I got too close. Men say these male harpies are cowards but they sure seem to get their courage and nerve up when defending a female. Even that skittish brown was ready to attack us if we tried to take your daughter from him. I think it safe to say, you've developing a health respect for these slender winged guys." Doc chuckled.

John grinned a little and nodded his head. "Yes, I'm man enough to admit when I've made a terrible mistake and have been wrong all these years. Kari's blond mate did show me his courage and devotion and proved he was far from the monsters, I once thought male harpies were. I just hope those men didn't kill him and I can get him back for her. I wish, I had taken your advice, Doc," he uttered. Doc just chuckled again.

Dr. Watkins took Doc's hover and flew to Terrance. He wanted to take the next available flight to Hampton. He was eager to expose this information to the person that had hired him. John had made several copies of the log. Telling him that it would be better than to risk losing the only copy in the wrong hands and Watkins agreed. Doc took a spare bedroom, since it was very late and he did not feel like driving in the rain with Charlie's terrain vehicle.

"Charlie can take me home in the morning," he had said.

Now the house was quiet as John finally made his way to his room. As he past Kari's bedroom, he stopped and wondered if she had remained or left with the harpy. He opened the door slightly and peered in. A small light glowed from the bathroom and filtered it into the room. He saw her coiled up in her bed asleep. On the floor by the open balcony, lay the curled up brown winged harpy. He lifted his head quickly and stared intensely at John. There was no doubt, this half human, half animal creature with the lean frame of teenage boy, was guarding his daughter with his life. The harpy flung his long brown locks out of his eyes as he hissed softly warning John to stay out of this room. John nodded to him, "Good boy. Stay with her," he said in a low reassuring tone. Aron closing his alert eyes slightly acknowledging, he understood the man. John closed the door and went to bed. It was the first time he was relieved to have a male harpy in his home.

The next morning, Maria went to Kari's room. She had left late at night while the doctors and John talked about Kari's condition. There was nothing else for her to do. Now, she was anxious to see how Kari was. She opened the door and let out a screech, as she saw a tall brown winged harpy standing by the balcony window. She raced as fast as her short stubby legs could carry her to Mr. Turner's room. John opened his bedroom door to the frightened housekeeper.

"Mr. Turner, Mr. Turner! There's giant brown harpy in with Kari!" she screamed frantically.

"Calm down, Maria, I know he's there. He won't hurt her, he may have even saved her."

"Then it's true? Miss Kari really is a harpy?" she asked.

"She's half harpy. Now go down to the kitchen and fix us all a big breakfast and make sure there's plenty of fruit. I have a feeling we'll need it with these harpies in the house. Doc stayed in one of the spare bedrooms, so don't let him surprise you," he said with a smile.

"He won't. Not like that harpy did," she shuddered as she scurried back to the stairs.

John went to Kari's room and knocked. "Come in," Kari answered.

John noticed that the harpy was gone. "Did Maria scare your friend away?" he asked her.

"No, he went back to the other harpies to see if any had found Shail. If he dies, I will never forgive you. You may not have killed him but you made him helpless and caused his capture. I'm only here now because I'm honoring Shail's wishes. He had more respect for you than I have. I don't trust you." Her voice had a bitter sharp tone to it and John knew she was restraining her malevolence.

John sat down on the bed beside her and lowered his eyes. "If he dies, I don't expect you to ever forgive me. I doubt if I'll forgive myself. But, I'm glad your here. I was so worried about you. The longer you were gone, the more I hated him. I just couldn't admit that you were lost to me. I'm sorry," he uttered.

Kari rose from the bed and distanced herself from him. "If you hated Shail, why didn't you kill him?"

John smiled a little. "That's the strange thing, I was determine to kill him for your safety and you, Charlie and Doc could not convince me otherwise. I ignored everyone. But your Shail convinced me not to kill him."

Kari glared at him angrily. "That's a lie. I know Shail. He has far too much dignity to beg for his life," she said incensed.

"No, he didn't beg, in fact he was very brave. His only concern was for you and his son. In those few minutes, I found myself respecting and admiring him. He was everything a man should be and maybe more," he said quietly lowering his head with shame.

"Then why, Dad? Why couldn't you just leave us in peace?" she asked with frustration.

"Because even though he deserved to be your husband, a harpy's life is so dangerous. I was afraid for you. If you thought, he was dead maybe you'd realize there is no future in his world. It could have easily been a real harpy hunter at that cabin instead of me. Then you and Shail would both be dead now. I just wanted you to realize that and maybe convince you to stay in the safe human world. I knew, when the stunning wore off, Shail would come for you. Maybe I just need some time to convince myself that you two truly belong together, no matter what the risks are. There's an old saying, 'better to have loved and lost, then never to have loved.' My life reflects that old saying. I don't regret for a minute bonding with your mother, despite the loss. I realized you felt the same way. And now I'm afraid, I may have caused your loss. I'm so sorry, Kari," he said soberly.

Kari looked at him and could see her father was truly sorry. "Maybe Shail was right about you. He called you a protective parent and graciously accepted your hatred of him. I'm glad you finally saw him for who he really is. He's the only one I will ever want. If he's dead, I just don't think I can go on. The emptiness is too much," she stated as she shed a tear. John went to her and put his arms around her.

"Kari, if he's alive, I'll get him back. Until then, just think of his son. Your fledgling will make you happy again, I promise. You gave me a purpose to keep going when your mother died. I'm so sorry, I am just so damned sorry," he mumbled. Eventually they pulled apart. "Why don't you clean up and come down for breakfast. Then, we'll take the hover back to the cabin and see if we can pick up any clues, on where those men took him. I need to report that hover as stolen. Maybe we can get the authorities working for us as well." She just nodded. Her father left the room and Kari got ready. She went down to the dining room as Doc, Charlie and her father were seated at the table. They stared at her differently now, for all knew what she was.

"Hello, Doc," she said softly with reserve.

Doc grinned, "I'm happy to see you are feeling better."

"Not better, just a little more in control of myself," she answered him soberly.

"I want you to put one of those anti depression patches on your arm daily. They'll help you through this," Doc said.

Kari nodded. "I'll do it as long as there's a chance Shail is still alive."

"Yes, well, what would you like to eat?" her father said quickly.

"Some of those berries," she answered and he handed her the bright blue berries.

Doc reached over and patted her hand across the table. "You'll find him. Your little male has a lot of fight in him and a strong will to live. He should have died on my operating table. I pity, those men who took him. They're in for rude awakening when they learn, he's nothing like a docile brown," Doc said to try and reassure her.

She looked at the kind old doctor. "Yes, Shail will fight his captors. I only hope, his defiance won't be his down fall. He would die before he'd yield."

Kari looked at Charlie but he lowered his head and eyes. She could feel, his remorse for not doing more to stop this tragedy. "Charlie, did you find an old disc that may have fallen out of my pocket in the hovercraft yesterday? It's very important," she asked.

John spoke before Charlie could answer her. "We found it last night and played it. Dr. Watkins left right away to take it to Hampton. It was quite an impressive ship log and if it came out, I think the harpy killing would come to an end. People would not tolerate the killing of another race of beings."

"You knew the harpies were more than just animals, yet you killed Shail's father and wanted to kill him. I thought the disc would change things but Shail didn't have much faith in it. Perhaps he was right. Even when men know we're part human, they still want us dead," she said blankly.

He looked at her. He could feel the animosity she still felt towards him. Despite his regret and explanation, she would never forgive him unless her mate was returned to her. John cleared his throat and slowly said, "don't compare me with the cruel harpy hunters who kill for profit or pleasure. The killing of Shail's father was very personal. I would have killed anyone, harpy or man, if I thought they were a danger to your mother or you," he said as he bit his lip. "It turns out, it's my own anger and stupidity that has been the biggest threat to everyone I've love."

"Well, nobody's perfect, John. Your intentions may have been noble, even if they were terribly misguided," Doc said.

"So, the disc goes to Hampton. The senators will want to destroy that disc," Kari said.

"We know this and so does Dr. Watkins. He'll protect it and I have also made copies of it in case it falls into the wrong hands," John stated. Kari only nodded. They finished breakfast and prepare to leave for the cabin.

Aron flew hard and carelessly towards the eastern dawn. Instead of gliding cautiously through the cover of trees, he flew in the open. He could not spare any time or be concerned with his own safety. Time was an issue with a captured harpy even one as brave as Shail. The cabin fledgling had told him that the hunters had used rope to tie Shail up. This gave him hope that his younger blond brother could still be alive. Men would not need to tie a dead harpy. Two hours into his flight, his carelessness almost became his demise when he heard many laser blasts coming from below him. The blasts sipped past him and Aron knew he had inadvertently flown over a nest of hunters. He began to stagger his flight to avoid being hit. One blast tore through his brown feathers but missed the muscles in his wings. He automatically faked an injury and went into a tumble until his lifeless body fell to the safety of the trees. There, he quickly righted himself and fluttered before colliding with the ground. He then navigated low to the ground around the trees, being more cautious until he was past this danger. These stupid hunters would now spend hours in the area where he had made his descent, searching for his maimed body.

Another hour and half had passed when he came to the mighty river, which flowed from north to south, dividing the continent. Flying south low over the riverbank he finally came to a vast marshland. Twenty miles across it, lay a densely treed island. It was here, far from where any human would come that the harpies gathered. There was a multitude of them when Aron fluttered over them. He recognized some from his own flock but there were many more he did not know. Landing with dignity and pose he walked to these strange males of the river and of the east.

"I am Aron. I rule the flocks of the western shores and islands. I bare ill news of our golden ruler. He has fallen into the hands of hunters and his fate, we do not know," Aron stated. This perplexed the massive group of harpies as the flock leaders communicated amongst them selves. Aron flapped his wings to get their attention and called to them. "We shall continue to keep the swarms at bay as the humans flee their structures. Only the known hunters and their dwelling are to be attacked by the swarms now. The swarms shall be kept west of the river until the innocent humans have fled. These are the golden's wishes. All spare harpies from all flocks across the land shall be sent in search of our ruler. We must learn his fate."

An older and larger male approached Aron, facing him eye to eye. "Unless my eyes deceive me, your wings are brown yet you order us as it they were gold. Why should we submit to a young brown winged male who barely has reached his full wing length?"

"You shall submit to me for I speak for the golden. His wishes were known to me since we dwelled together. If any of you challenge my words, it is a challenge you shall regret," Aron stated while he flung his long brown hair and arched his wings at the large male while he strutted around him in a circle. This male did not did not back down but raised his head meeting Aron's challenge. He sniffled at Aron and then flew at him to strike him with his feet. Aron flapped and dodged the kick. Instead of fleeing this large male, Aron flew back striking him hard with his foot in the shoulder. Both harpies landed and began to pace around the other as they arched their wings like rival dancing birds. This larger, strong male began to study his younger arrogant lean challenger. It was very apparent Aron would not relent to him or any others. These challenges were more for show for the sake of acceptance by a future female mate and the males were rarely injured but this harpy could sense Aron meant business. This rash young western leader was willing to risk sever injury to prove his point.

"You are very brave to challenge me and challenge so many others that are older and more experienced than you. Perhaps some of his gold did rub off on you. I am Seth and I dominate many flocks of the east. For your courage, I shall submit to you for one more light. We shall follow your words and search for him but by the fall of the next light, we desert these western swarms and let them go where they may. We shall not protect these fleeing humans who deserve to die when it is our families that need protection. By then we shall know our golden ruler is dead for even he can not survive a cage and hunters this long."

"This one can survive for he has already done so. I return now to west for I have been given the honor of defending his golden mate and unborn fledgling," Aron said to Seth, ending his defiant posturing. He walked towards his own flock of males. "Search well my brother harpies. Shail must be found. If not, we all may die under the swarms." Aron told his western harpies. They nodded to him and

Aron spread his wings to return to Kari. This gathering had gone as he expected for no harpy leader of a flock would follow the commands of another brown winged harpy. He was only happy his bold posturing and challenge had bought him a little more time to find Shail and keep the swarms in check. Only a golden winged harpy could order the flocks to destroy the swarms after the humans had fled the land. If Shail were not found, there would be total chaos with the lack of rule and in the end it is the swarms that would rule this land.

Aron flew at neck-breaking speed to return to the coast. By late afternoon the thunderstorms had moved in and the stinging rain hit his face and body. He lowered his head so his long brown mane of hair would protect his eyes. Though the rain was an annoyance, he now felt more secure with this flight since these feeble humans did not like this water from the sky. They usually sought shelter and rarely hunted harpies during a rainstorm. Beating his wings hard, he knew it would be dark before he returned to the Turner estate.

John, Charlie and Kari loaded up in the hovercraft along with Doc. They dropped Doc off at his home and flew on to the cabin. The day was overcast but Charlie was happy to see the ground, when they landed. "It did not rain here last night, so we still may see some signs to discover what happened."

John set the hover down close to the cabin. Kari ran into it and glanced at the empty floor with relief. She had to see for herself that Shail's body had been removed. Kari sniffled slightly while staring at the inside of the little cabin she and Shail had shared as their first home. Her father looked on sadly, seeing the misery he had caused.

"Come." Charlie said as he looked in from the door. "Here are the tracks where they dragged him." They followed the tracks to the beach and saw where a hovercraft had set down. "It is apparent that they had dropped him in the sand, while one of them went back for the hovercraft. And look, a great struggle took place here but there is no blood. They must have stunned him again with their laser guns," Charlie said.

John rubbed his chin as he looked at the scenario. "Yes, but did they mean to stun him or kill him, is the question. Remember, I had ordered all of our guns set for stun for Kari's welfare. Now did they forget that the guns were set to stun, when they fired? If that is the case, they would have reset their weapons and finished the job or did they want to take him alive but what for? And why drag his body when they could have easily hacked off his wings in the cabin and carried half the load to the hover. I'd say they wanted him alive for some reason but what could they want with a live harpy and especially one that had given them such a fight," John said as he rubbed his chin again.

Kari stared at the struggle marks in the sand. She walked over and picked up one of Shail's feathers and held it to her lips as she spoke, "Perhaps these men were cruel, like the ones that wounded Shail. They did not kill him immediately either. They wanted to string him up and torture him before they took his wings."

Her father glanced at her. "No, I don't think so, even if they were angry with him. I knew these men. They were greedy, not sadistic plus they were in a hurry to leave the estate before I missed them and my hover. If they wanted only his wings, they would have killed him right here. Shail had to be worth more alive than dead. This gives me hope that he's still alive somewhere. Let's go back and see if there's any word on the stolen hover craft."

They left the beach as it started to rain. It was the beginning of the wet season and soon it would rain every day. The gusts of wind blew the hover and it had become a rocky ride home. They eventually arrived at the house. It would pour the rest of the afternoon.

John went to the den with Kari close behind him. He placed a call to Terrance as the communicator rose from the desk.

"No, Mr. Turner" the officer said. "No word on the hover or a pair of gold harpy wings. Most of those stores that would have carried them are closed. In fact, the whole place is pretty shut down. The town people are fleeing to Hampton right now. They're afraid of a swarm. The flights are booked. Maybe they took your hover to Hampton? You might want to try there."

"Yes, I will, but it would be risky taking a small hover that far. It did not have the range."

"Well, people are pretty desperate right now. We had another strike this morning and it was only twenty miles to the south. Killed over thirty hunters in camp there. Even the major flights are shutting down. Tomorrow is the last day. They don't want to take the risk of setting down in a swarm," the officer said.

"Yes, I can understand that. There is one more thing. This blond harpy may still be alive. In any case, I want him back unharmed if you find him," John said.

The man looked at him curiously. "You had a live harpy? But you said it was just a pair of gold wings these men stole from you," the officer remarked.

"Well, the harpy belonged to my daughter. He was her pet. I had originally thought they had killed him and took his wings but I have learned, they may have kept him alive. That is what I'm hoping for." John smiled at the officer.

The officer frowned a little as he looked at John through the screen. "Never heard of a pet harpy. Didn't think they could be maintained in a cage for more than a few days but with your kind of money, I guess, you can make a pet out of anything."

"Yes, well he was unlike most harpies. Thank you, officer. I appreciate it if you keep me posted." John concluded the conversation. The officer nodded and transmission ended.

Kari sighed a little. "I'm going back to my room now and rest a while."

"Alright dear, I'll come get you, if there is any new information."

Kari went to her room and discovered the balcony doors had been closed by Maria to keep the rain out. She pushed them open and the rain blew in on the floor. Then she crawled into the soft bed and curled up with the feather she still held in her hand. She closed her eyes and hoped that Shail would come to her in her dreams as he had done when they were separated before. Soon, she was asleep.

She woke to the sound of the balcony doors being closed. She saw her father as he stared out the window. "No, I want them left open. Aron may return," she said quietly.

Her father nodded and opened the doors again. "I didn't mean to wake you. Go back to sleep now. I'll wake you for dinner," he smiled a little.

She nodded and shut her eyes again. She could feel the deep hopeless depression that plagued her mind. She was familiar with it since she had fought it on Earth. This time it was close to crippling. With the loss of Shail, she barely had the energy to breathe. Only the anti depressant patches were allowing her to maintain. Shail had not come into her dreams as before when they were apart. She trembled and thought of his death or the terrible suffering he faced in captivity. She reached over and replaced the patch with a new one. "I must stay well until I know if he's alive. I can't help him like this." she thought sadly.

Hours past and her father woke her for dinner. She went downstairs but did not stay. She took a few pieces of fruit back to her room. As she entered, Aron was waiting for her. His wings and body were soaking wet and he breathed hard as she went to him. She could tell he had been flying for some time, probably since he had left in the morning. He tossed his wet hair aside and looked at her, as hopelessness filled his bright green eyes. "He still is not found and the harpies are beginning to fear the worst," he related to her.

She put her arms around his powerful streamline body and he embraced her. "We can't give up hope. We must find him," she said to him. He nodded. Aron was grieving this loss, as much as she. They watched the rain, as it wailed across the meadows and the jungle beyond. Eventually they settled on the floor in front of the open window doors. Kari curled up and Aron coiled his body around her as he held her in his arms and covered them both with his large brown wing. Though he was not her mate, it felt good to have him hold her as Shail had done. Aron could feel the tension leave her body with his secure arms around her and his wing kept her dry from the rain that swept through this opening. John checked on Kari before going to bed. He found her a sleeping on the floor in the arms of the brown harpy. The harpy's wild green eyes stared at him but it no longer hissed. John closed the door quietly. There was no doubt Kari was lost to the harpies. They were her world now. Only her promise to Shail kept her in his human house.

Aron caressed Kari's cheek with his nose to wake her as first rays of dawn filtered through the balcony. She smiled, happy to see he still lay beside her. "I must go now and continue my search. It is not only Shail I grieve for. It is also the harpies and all life on this land. Without a golden ruler, the harpies follow none. They may not destroy the swarms when it is time. All may flee to their families and the safety of the islands or mountains and let the swarms consume the land. Already Shail's wishes are in question with his loss. Shail would have destroyed the swarms after the men were gone. These beetles must be stopped before their numbers grow too great. If this happens, then all harpies shall lose the power to stop them. Already the beetles have grown the harpies struggle to hold them in the jungle. The attack on the humans draws near," he related.

Kari stared at him. She had always thought that with or without Shail, the harpies would destroy the swarms in the end. Now, she realized, without him everyone and everything on the planet could be lost. Aron touched her face, bringing her attention back to him. "I must fly this light and try to convince these flocks to follow Shail's rule. I do not know when I shall return to you. Do you feel well enough for me to leave you?" he asked as he rose and ruffled his feathers.

Kari nodded. "Aron, do what you must to save Shail and the jungle. I'll be alright."

"Other harpies wait in the jungle if you have need of them. Stay in this structure. My harpies protect you and it from a swarm attack," he related. Then he walked out on the balcony and spread his wings. With a leap he was gone, as he disappeared into the morning mist.

Kari dressed, her mind occupied with Aron's words. Now, she understood why Shail wanted her with her father. There was a real danger that the whole planet could be lost. Her father would get her off Dora safely. As she went downstairs, the communicator began buzzing. John smiled at her, when she came into his den. He pressed the on button for the screen and the same police officer from yesterday, appeared.

"Mr. Turner, I have some information on your stolen hover craft," he began. "After we spoke yesterday, one of the officers remembered hearing about some men that dealt in the wild animal trade. They had an old warehouse south of town on the river. Anyway, I was in the area helping with this evacuation and I went by. Sure enough, there was your hover craft," he said.

"And my harpy?" John asked impatiently.

"Gone," the officer answered. "It looks to me they packed up right after they got him. The place was vacant except for a few empty cages. There were two dead harpies in there with their wings stripped from them but they had brown hair. Their bodies looked pretty abused. I hate to tell you but I wouldn't hold out much hope in getting your golden back. Apparently they ship these animals all over the galaxy to zoos and hunting ranges. He could be on any one of a number of star freighters right now if he even survives their care. We've had trouble with these men. They're a pretty rough group, who recently got out of prison for some vicious crimes. Anyway, what do you want me to do about your hover? Terrance is evacuating like I said. I'm leaving right now,"

"Just leave it at the warehouse. I'll get it when I can. Thank you, officer, you've been a big help." John disconnected the communicator and looked at Kari.

"I wish you hadn't heard all of that," he said to her.

She put her hand to her mouth, as she thought of Shail as a captive of these terrible men. Her father took her by the shoulders. "Kari, at least we know he's alive and they don't want him just for his wings. He's probably worth a lot. I'm sure they would take good care of him because of that. I'm going to call Hampton shipping right now. Maybe they know if he's left the planet." John said and punched in the numbers.

"Dora Shipping" the man said.

"Yes, this is Mr. Turner. I need some information on wild animal export. I'm looking for a golden harpy," he said to the man.

The man laughed. "Yea, isn't everyone?"

"This is serious," John growled at the man. "I had a golden harpy stolen from me and it's possible, he's being shipped off the planet at this time."

"Sorry, Mr. Turner, was it?" the man said more somberly. "Look, this place is a madhouse right now. Ships are taking off with out even logging their manifests.

I haven't seen any wild animal go through here in the last couple of days but then again, they could have loaded him outside. It's going take some time for me to check all these manifests. Even if I find this harpy, do you have documented proof that he belongs to you?" he asked.

"No, not documented." John answered.

"Well, I'm wasting my time if you can't prove ownership. Exotic animals are not required for registry like domestic animals. I'm afraid, even if I did locate him on a freighter or in this port, there's little you could do to get him back. Sorry," the man said.

"Look, I'll make it worth your time to look for him. I'll send you ten thousand credits if you notify me of his location," John snapped.

"Mister, for that kind of money, I'll do the paper work and keep an eye out for him," he smiled.

"You have my number?" John asked. The man said yes and they disconnected.

John sat down in his chair. "I wish there was some way, we could prove ownership but there isn't. Shail is considered a wild animal. Only if he were on my property would I have any rights to him. The only way to get him back is to buy him from these hunters. If that man in shipping calls, I'll have him contact those hunters with an offer," he told Kari. John sighed as he thought, "How much can a male golden harpy be worth?"

CHAPTER 7

▼

The two Turner employees walked down the beach towards the hovercraft. They had just left Mr. Turner with his daughter and the Indian. "I can't believe he's going to let those gold wings just lay on that cabin floor and rot when they're worth so much money," one man said.

"Yea, it seems pretty strange but what's money to Turner. Besides his daughter sure was rattled with that harpy's death. She'd freak if he cut off its wings," the other man responded.

"Hey, Jerry, do you realize, mounted gold wings are worth at least fifty thousand credits? That's a year's salary for the both of us. Besides, we may be out of job soon with these swarm attacks. The timber business is shut down. After Turner leaves with the girl, we could go over the mountains, grab the wings and no one would be the wiser."

Jerry stopped in his tracks. "Are you sure we could get that kind of money for them?"

"Hey, I catch the shuttle to Terrance all the time. There are plenty of shops that buy harpy wings. We'll just stash them where they can be cured and take them to Terrance this weekend. An easy twenty-five thousand credits for each of us. Turner will never know the difference."

Jerry thought for a moment. "It does sound easy. All right, let's do it. Can't hurt anything and I sure could use the credits right now."

They reached the hover and took off, heading over the mountains. After traveling for some time, they circled around and landed the hover a distance north of the cabin, walking quietly on foot to the cabin. They wanted to make sure that Mr. Turner had indeed left, going south toward his home. The two men arrived at the cabin and found the golden harpy still unconscious on the floor. Jerry reached for his knife, pulling up one of the wings. But, before he could cut, he noticed the harpy was still breathing. "Hey, this harpy is still alive" he said with surprise.

"Well, cut its throat and let's get the wings and get out of here. I want to be back before we're missed," said the other man named Sam.

Jerry pushed the harpy over to cut the harpy's throat and he stopped again. "He's not even wounded. Look, Turner just stunned him. No wonder he didn't take the wings. We'll put you out of your misery now, little fellow," he said, grabbing the sleeping harpy and put the knife to his jugular vein.

"Wait a minute," Sam yelled, "Turn him over all the way and make sure he's okay."

Jerry did it, looking at Sam in bewilderment. "What? I told you, there's nothing wrong with him Look, I want to kill it before it wakes up. I not big on slicing its throat, while staring into those big blue sad eyes. These harpies look way to human to suit me."

Sam examined the harpy and stood up. "We're not killing this one. We're taking him to Terrance right now. Listen, I was talking to a harpy hunter in a bar there. He found out that I worked on the Turner Estate. Said the Estate was thick with harpies but he was afraid to go there, because of Turner's ban on hunting. Said he had heard of Turner blasting the hovers right out from under some poachers a few years ago."

"So what the hell are we doing this for? I don't need to get killed for a lousy twenty-five thousand," Jerry said excitedly.

"No, my point is, that this hunter told me about an old warehouse on the river south of Terrance. Said, if I managed to catch a live undamaged harpy, I could take it there and they would give me triple the price of a pair of wings. Now we're talking about one hundred and fifty thousand."

Jerry smiled real wide. "For that kind of money, I can get out of this stinking jungle and go to a real planet. Grab his other arm, we'll drag him to the beach and bring the hover around. By the time Turner realizes what we've done, we'll be long gone. He's been so occupied with his daughter, I doubt he'll even miss us for a few days."

Sam grabbed Shail's other arm. "Now your talking my language, "he said as they dragged Shail to the beach. "Man, I thought this harpy would be heavy since he's taller than me but he's a lightweight. Bet he only weighs about eighty pounds. Never touched one of these things before."

They reached the beach and Jerry waited with the harpy while Sam went to fetch the hovercraft. Jerry noticed the harpy was beginning to stir when Sam returned with the transport. "Hurry up and get some ropes out so we can tie him. He's starting to come around. I heard, two stunnings so soon, can give one of these things a heart attack." They tied Shail's wrists together and had started with his ankles when Shail regained consciousness. He saw the men as they fumbled with the ropes. Shail immediately struck his tied fists hard against the closest man's face, sending him tumbling backwards. The other man lunged at Shail, while he lay on the sand. Shail kicked him with his half tied feet, throwing him flying towards the other man. Shail struggled with the ankle ropes to rise as both men leaped on him to restrain him. He flapped his wings frantically as the out-stretched wings battered the men as he still knelt. Again the men tried to seize him, seeing their fortune was going to fly off once the harpy made it to his feet. Shail hit them with his fists and wings as they tried to hold him down, sending the men soaring once again away from him. Shail coiled and hissed at the weary beat up men as a warning to stay away from him. The bloody men lay exhausted, gasping for air as they stared with dread at the quarrelsome slender harpy. Shail saw these men had enough and were not about to attack him again. He cautiously tried to rite him self, making a seething sound to intimidate them long enough to make his escape.

"Stun him, Jerry. My laser is in the hover." Sam yelled. Shail now saw the weapon hanging from the man's belt as the man blew the sand out of it. Shail feverishly fought the ropes to stand up since only then could he extend his wings fully to fly. He flapped and fluttered wildly until finally there was enough wind under his wings and he began to lift off. Then he heard the blast and felt the sting in his back. Shail fell a short distance to the ground and was still.

The men staggered to the unconscious harpy, wiping the sweat and blood from their faces. "Didn't think harpies could fight like that," Jerry puffed.

"Me neither," Sam agreed in bewilderment

"Wonder why he didn't attack Mr. Turner like that?" Jerry stammered.

"I don't know but let's tie him up good and tight including those stinking wings and then let's get out of here. It'll be dark before we reach Terrance," Sam said.

They tied Shail up and put him in the back of the hover. Sam flew the hover, while Jerry held his laser gun on the comatose harpy. They began the four-hour flight to Terrance. After an hour, Shail began to come to, as he heard the voices of the men. He wrestled fiercely with his bonds, tossing his body in a panic to be free. "Stun that vicious little fowl again if he keeps that up. I don't care if it ain't good for him." Sam yelled, still angry over his injuries.

Jerry pointed the weapon at Shail. The harpy immediately stopped grappling with the ropes and just stared intensely at the man. "I swear, I think he understood you. He sure as hell knows what a laser gun is."

"Fine, he's so smart, tell him we won't hurt him if behaves himself." Sam mumbled as piloted the hover.

Jerry began to laugh. "You tell him. He's glaring at me like he wants to chew me up and spit me out. I don't think you can threat this one. He's not a bit frightened. We'd be the ones in trouble if he got lose in here."

"It sure is strange, that Mr. Turner didn't kill him. Heck, that's all he's talked about for weeks, is killing this golden. Then he finally corners him and only stuns him. Maybe he really is a harpy lover, like some say," Jerry reflected.

"Well, lucky for us, he changed his mind. I'm making a list of things I want when we sell this harpy."

As the journey continued the men were cheerful despite their bruises with the money they would receive from their catch. Shail watched them through his long blond locks but did not move. It was impossible to break the strong rope. He sighed a little when he heard that Kari's father had spared his life. Shail had sensed all along that Turner had a good heart but was only confused. "By not killing me, his confusion has ended. He now knows, I am no threat to his daughter. I only love her as he does. He has accepted our bonding." Shail thought. Kari and her father could finally mend their relationship. He no longer stood between them. "With his hate of me gone, a harmony shall come to them," he realized and it pleased him. Shail turned his attention back to the men in the hover. He understood from their conversation that he would be sold. It was not only, the golden wings that they value but also his life. Shail swallowed a little hard. He knew of only one reason, men kept a harpy alive. It was to get greater pleasure from slowly torturing it to death. "I shall defy and challenge my captors and try to remain very brave, but in truth, I am only a lone harpy and I am very afraid," Shail worriedly thought.

They finally reached Terrance. Sam flew south along the river to the location of the warehouse. They reached it as the light faded to dark. "You wait here with the harpy. I'll go find that hunter," Sam said. Jerry agreed, keeping the laser gun pointed at Shail.

Soon Sam returned with three other men. He talked excitedly about the harpy, as he opened the back door. "Be careful. He's a mean little critter," Sam said with a grin.

"Well, let's see what you, boys caught," remarked a huge heavy man named Gus. Gus leaned in the hover door and looked at Shail. As this giant's face came close, Shail kicked him hard with his tied feet, knocking the big man to the ground.

"I warned you, he's a fighter. I don't even want to get near it," Sam said.

Gus leered at Shail as he got up, infuriated that a slender little harpy had managed to knock him off his feet. "Drag him out. I'll take the fight out of him." Two men grabbed Shail's feet and jerked him out, dropped him recklessly to the ground. "I need to see his wings before you get paid. Flip him over," Gus ordered. Shail fought and struggled in his bounds but he was helpless against five men. Gus stepped on the back of Shail's lean neck with his heavy foot, smashing his throat into the hard ground as the men cut the ropes off his wings. Shail tried to flap them but two men took hold of each wing and stretched them out. "Pull tighter," Gus ordered, "The more length, the more he's worth." With that encouragement, the four men unmercifully yanked Shail's wings with such force he thought they would be ripped from his back. Shail panted hard with racking pain as they measured the length of his wings. Finally they released their hold as the fanned out wings collapsed on the ground. His wings throbbed with such soreness he couldn't move them. "Sixteen feet almost fully grown. Too bad, this little buck would have made a fine trophy in a few years. Well, let see if he's sexually mature," Gus said as his foot continued to smashed Shail's throat in the dirt. Gus bent over and jerked Shail's sex organs out beneath his sash. Shail began to squirm with the abuse, making a low seething sound with his teeth but this only encouraged the man to grip and squeezed them hard till Shail could barely breathe and lay quiet to stop the stabbing pain. "Hurts like hell, don't it, little buck? I'll teach you not to kick me again," he chuckled. "He's good and hung and old enough to have probably been a stud animal. Now, those blond balls will make one expensive money wallet. I'll take him. Tie up his wings before he recovers," Gus said, finally released his harsh grasp and removed his foot. Shail immediately pulling up his legs to get some relief and breathed hard. He shuddered as he finally learned the purpose for the harpy castration. The soft blond furred skin, which made him a male, would be cut from him so it could hold the human money. Shail was too traumatized and in pain to fight back, as they retied his wings. Jerry allowed his laser gun to hang by his side and stared at the once rebellious slight winged male. Now the harpy pathetically trembled and panted while it tried to curl up in the dirt.

"Guess this poor harpy is in for a lot of torture before they finally kill him," Jerry said with a little pity to Sam as they both looked at the helpless wild creature and Gus came along side of them.

"Yea, he's a real beauty, all right. The lucky hunter, who gets this one, will want his money's worth. They say, these goldens should be live stretched before they're de-feathered. If their liver is poked with holes, the damaged liver and toxins turns the feathers a brighter shade of gold. Makes a nicer mount. Then he can be hung and castrated before they take the wings. This little fighter will suffer plenty for your bruises, I guarantee. But don't worry about that," Gus chuckled, "You, boys, have other things to worry about." In a flash, Gus grabbed Jerry's laser gun and ripped it from his belt. Now he aimed it at Sam and Jerry. "You have this laser set for stun. That's a mistake," Gus said, resetting the laser gun to blast. Shail glanced up from the ground. The large dark haired man had the weapon pointed toward his two former captors.

"Wait a minute, mister," Jerry cried, but before he could finish speaking, Gus fired at the two dumbfounded men. Their bodies dropped next to Shail and were still. Gus stood over them with a sick grin on his face as he kicked each corpse to make sure they were dead.

"Throw their bodies in the river and let the jungle take care of the evidence." Gus ordered his two men. "The freighter arrives in the morning and these fine gentlemen just gave us what we need."

Shail watched this vicious man in amazement. He had never seen a man kill another one before. The other two men returned after dumping the bodies of Sam and Jerry in the river. "Let's get this buck in the warehouse. I'm ready to celebrate with a drink." Gus said while reaching for Shail's neck. Shail had recovered enough from the throbbing pain and instinctively snapped at Gus's hand with the only defense he had left, his teeth barely missing the hand. Shail coiled like a snake on the ground and now hissed loudly and mockingly snapped at the men to keep their hands off him. "So this buck still has some fight," Gus said with surprise, "Time to teach it some fear and I'm going to enjoy this. Go get a cage for it. He'll be like a puppy by the time you get back."

Shail stared up at this huge man that weight almost four times as much as he did. Gus reeked of cruelty unlike his last two captors. Shail had sensed Sam and Jerry had no desire to hurt him. They only desired the money. But this Gus was very different. He could sense the great satisfaction this man felt as he inflicted pain and death on others. Shail managed to sit up, tossing his long blond hair and bravely sniffling at Gus while his eyes held a hostile stare. Shail decide, if this man planned to kill him, he would go down with a challenge rather than be submissive and accept his fate docilely like other harpies. Shail was a king among his kind and tried to behave like one, despite the consequences, he knew he faced by defying this monster. Gus took a short metal rod from his belt.

"A little shock therapy will knock all the fight out of you," Gus said and jabbed the rod against Shail's arm. Shail doubled over in agony, as an electric shock coursed through his body. He flipped wildly in the ropes with the stinging pain. No sooner had he recovered when the man did it again and again. Shail tried to cover himself with his feathers but each time the man found his flesh. Shail's heart raced out of control as he gasped for air. Never had he experienced this kind of pricking pain. His body shook violently and he was covered with dirt and sweat as his body thrashed uncontrollably. The two men returned with a long narrow metal cage.

"Hey, Gus, I thought you wanted this one undamaged," one of the men said seeing the harpy was battering itself on the ground.

Gus stood up and let the harpy calm down. Now Shail only laid still and shook, his eyes in a trance. "Yea, I suppose your right. He's had enough. Bet he never kicks or snaps at me again. Put him in. He won't bite now." Gus laughed.

Shail trembled so bad that the whole lightweight aluminum cage rattled slightly, when they placed him inside. He felt numb but at the same time like millions of thorns had stuck him. He swallowed hard and tasted his own blood, where he had bit his lip. The men removed the ropes from his wings and limbs but Shail could not fight or flee. His body could only quiver as he tried to catch his breath. Even breathing was difficult now.

The men replaced the ropes with shackles and chains that they attached to his wrists and ankles at the end of the cage. The men knew a harpy would chew through his rope restraints during the night. The cage was so narrow, Shail could only lay stretch out on his side and this would prevent him from opening and flailing his wings, which would damage the feathers. They carried him into a large damp building that reeked of animal waste. Shail closed his eyes and wondered if this stinging pain would ever leave him. After several hours, the trembling stopped and the throbbing eased. He glanced from side to side and noticed other animals in the cages around him. Then he saw two other caged harpies. He tried to call to them silently but they did not answer. Shail could not tell if they were dead or alive.

Gus came up alongside of him as he sipped from a whiskey bottle. "So, you've recovered. You're pretty strong for a harpy," he said. Shail gave a low soft hiss in defiance though he knew it would have been wiser to remain quiet. "Unbelievable, this thing still wants to fight with me."

One of the other men joined Gus by the cage. "Hey, Gus, this harpy gave you a shiner. In fact the whole side of your face in turning black and blue." he laughed. Gus frowned and Shail could sense his anger as the man adjusted his rod to a higher setting and then he held the rod close to Shail's exposed ribs. Shail frantically fought against the chains and pushed his body hard against the cage bars but he could not escape the striking distance of the rod in the narrow cage. He feverishly tried to flap his wings as the rod came closer. The intoxicated men laughed as they watched the frantic harpy try to escape the rod.

"Let's find out just how much this little buck can handle." Gus said, jabbing Shail's ribs with the cattle prod. Gus just held the rod against Shail's sweat-covered body for a long period of time. Shail thrashed for some time until his whole body seized up and went into uncontrollable convulsions, excreting all his bodily fluids as he lost all control. He went limp as his eyes closed and his body just twitched. The terrible affliction had caused him to lose consciousness.

Shail woke in the middle of the night. His body still racked with the burning pain and numbness. He tried to wipe the regurgitate food from his face as he glanced around timidly. Gus and the two other men slept on cots off to the side of the building and this made him relax slightly. Quietly, he tried to free himself from the chains around his wrists but it was of no use. The chains held him securely. Even if he could escape them and the cage, he wondered if he was even capable of walking or flight, his body had become so weak. He felt pathetic, filthy and afraid. Shail tried to pull his legs up to curl up but the chains would not allow this. It was a long night, as he wondered what the dawn would bring. "I must keep my strength and not be seduced by the peace of death. Too many depend on me now," he thought. But, he could feel his willpower slipping away. He laid his head against his outstretched arms and tried to control the trembling that still consumed his body. Shail knew his small-framed lightweight harpy body could not tolerate much more of this kind of torture. Either his heart would stop from the shocks or his mind would go into an irrevocable depression. In either case, he would be finished. Glancing at the two still harpies in the cages to the right of him, he knew now, what fate they had suffered. Their minds were gone, even if their bodies still lived.

Morning came, as the sleeping men stirred in their cots. Shail watched them skittishly as they finally rose. One of the men came to Shail's cage and looked in at him. "Hey, Gus," he called. "Your golden harpy is awake. He is pretty rugged to survive that shocking."

Gus sat on the edge of the cot and touched the side of his face. It was swollen and dark. It hurt as Gus felt his cheek. He angrily got up, grabbing the rod and approached Shail's cage. Shail felt panicky and jerked on the chains with what strength he had left. He cowered his blond head submissively and tucked his face into his wing and slid away from the man and the deadly rod.

"No more hissing? You're scared now, aren't you? I think you can handle a few more prods," Gus said, placing the rod against Shail's ribs and smiled as he put his thumb on the electric shock button. Shail grit his teeth and grabbed the chains as the excruciating pain entered his body. His frail body twisted sluggishly against the chains. Gus finally withdrew the rod as he stared at the harpy's dull half closed eyes. Only the harpy's breathing was rapid as its heart pounded out of control. The harpy shut its eyes as his trembling body rattled the cage.

"One more," Shail thought, "one more shocking like that and I shall die." Shail could vaguely hear the sound of a giant engine as it approached. After a few minutes, the men also heard it as it landed in front of the warehouse. This seemed to distract Gus and he looked out the half open sliding doors.

"The freighter's here. Get those cages ready to load," Gus ordered and walked past a cage holding a large grogin. He touched the animal with the rod as he passed it. The grogin let out a cry of pain and slunk to a corner of its cage. Shail wearily watched this as he tried to catch his breath. Apparently, this man relished in tormenting and hurting all animals, as well as killing his own kind. Gus was the worst of men, for Shail had never sensed such a dark evil heart and this sadistic man had become his master.

Shail could feel his body and mind shutting down. His nerves were raw, as he struggled to maintain control. He barely noticed Gus speaking to another person, until that person was leaning over his cage, staring at him. "Gus, you're a jackass. When are you going to learn that harpies are fragile? It's like shocking a bird. Knocks the life right out of them," said an angry woman's voice. She looked at Shail and shook her head. "Bet you were really beautiful before that moron got to you," she said while stroking Shail's trembling face. "This harpy is on the verge of going into irreversible shock," she yelled and took out a medical scanner. She went across Shail's body with it as Gus walked over to her. "On top of the shock, he's minutes away from having a heart attack. I can't believe you could do this to such an expensive animal. Your brother pays me to keep these harpies alive and you make it damned impossible when they're abused like this," she snapped.

"Look what it did to my face. Damned thing loves to fight with me," Gus hostilely replied.

"He's a golden, you idiot. It's his nature to be defiant. Besides his gold wings, that's what makes them so valuable. They're a more challenging game animal," she said as she began give Shail the drugs that would save his life. First she slowed his rapid heart rate, then treated him for the depression and pain and another drug to reverse the shock that had consumed his body while covering the trembling harpy with a blanket. She began to inspect the other cages. She looked at the two battered brown harpies and turned back toward Gus. "And what did these two poor things do to you that you had to beat them so badly?" she asked while looking at the lifeless brown winged harpies.

"Hell, their minds were going even with the depression drugs. They would have died in a few days any way. The boys and I were bored, might as well have a little fun with them before they croaked. I'll take care of them," he answered.

The woman returned to Shail's cage and stared sadly at the once handsome animal. Shail's sweaty pale body was cold and clammy and was smudged with dirt. His long blond hair lay caked with vomit and his body and wings were soaked with his own urine. "Let's clean you up, baby," she said softly. "I know you little guys like to be clean. Soon you'll feel better. I'm going to take care of you." She wiped the blood from Shail's full lips where he had bitten himself and began to clean his soiled body through the bars. Shail ignored her and stared in a trance through the cage bars. His eyes were fixed on Gus as this man dragged the limp brown winged harpies out of their cages. He tied their wrists together with a rope then tossed the end of the rope over a beam, hoisting their weak bodies off the floor. Grabbing each wing, he cut the vein under the feathers in the wing tip with a large knife. The blood began to flow out of them. Shail watched while he tightly applied a rope tourniquet at the base of the wings, near their backs. Gus then took the knife and castrated one of them, placing its furred organs in a clear plastic bag. The harpy barely moved. When he cut the second harpy, its wings began flailing wildly with the pain as its body twisted and tossed on the rope.

"Hey, Mollie" he laughed. "This one has some of its mind still working."

The woman shook her head and ignored him as she continued to work on Shail. Eventually, this harpy stopped thrashing and its body slowly squirmed as it dangled. Shail began to softly pant with anxiety and anguish while he watched this horrendous torture of these live harpies. The harpies' blood soon created a large pool on the floor. Next came the dreaded removal of the wings. Gus bent the wings back till he snapped the cartilage that held their wings to their backs from the hanging harpies. Then he hacked each wing from them, throwing the feathered limps in a pile. Shail could see that both harpies still twitched and breathed as this was done. Gus began loading their wings on the hover. Mollie finished washing Shail and she noticed he was panting much harder. He glanced up at her with distressed and pleading eyes but his gaze returned to his dying fellow harpies. She knew this terrible slaughter was stressing the pretty little golden male. "Gus, put those poor harpies out of their misery or do I have to do it? It's scaring the hell out of this golden," she yelled with aggravation.

Gus gave her a disgruntled look. "Let it scare him. Let him see what he has to look forward to. Besides I like to watch these harpies dangle, they'll die eventually after we leave." Mollie sighed with irritation and picked up her medical bag to destroy the hanging harpies. "Fine. I'll do it just for you," he said, seeing Mollie would use a euthanasia drug on the waning harpies if he did not kill them. Gus cut the ropes that held their bodies and they fell into the pool of blood. Gus kicked at them and they moved and squirmed slightly in the blood. He snatched up each of them by long brown hair and cut their throats, ending their pain. Shail's eyes stayed glued to the dead harpies while two men loaded his cage into the large hover.

"Are you happy now, Mollie? We need to get out of here before a swarm comes. It'll be two days before we're back in Hampton. This freight hover is not exactly fast," Gus said.

Shail's heart rate returned to normal but he was still flustered over the warehouse experience, he had suffered and witnessed. The woman grabbed his sex organs and began to insert a tube in them. The humiliation immediately snapped him out of his distress. Shail wiggled and frantically cover his body while hissing angrily at her. "You must be feeling better. You're getting some of that fight back. I'm glad." She smiled. "I can see now, how Gus got that black eye." Mollie took a harsh hold of the helpless harpy and forced the tube deep inside of him. "There, that wasn't so bad. You'll stay nice and clean now. Now I need to put a feed tube down your throat, since you must be hungry and I know you won't eat on your own," she explained gently while putting another tube towards Shail's mouth. He viciously lunged and snapped at it. Tossing his head so violently, she could not control him. Mollie sighed, "Guess, I'm going to have to keep you tranquilized to handle one like you." She gave Shail another drug in his arm. In minutes, Shail began to relax and feel dizzy. All his anxiety left his body and he could barely keep his eyes open. Mollie placed the blanket back on him as she talked softly and stroked his neck. She knew most harpies became calm when they were massaged around their necks.

"You talk to that animal, like he's a baby," Gus said sarcastically.

"He is a baby and should be treated like one. A calming voice can sooth a baby as well as a harpy even if they don't understand me. You have the poor little guy so shook up and aggravated, I can barely handle him. I'm trying to reverse all the damage and build some trust," she declared. She continued to faintly stoked Shail's soft hair, and rubbed his back and neck. Eventually the drugs and comforting touch, subdued him. He nuzzled the blanket and pushed it up with his nose as if it were a reassuring nest of moss, then he buried his boyish face in it. Closing his eyes, he drifted into a deep sleep

"Why don't you try and sooth me? I can show you a good time when we reach Hampton," Gus commented as the hover lifted off.

Mollie laughed. "I think I'd have a better time with this harpy."

Gus just sneered at her. Molly stayed by Shail's cage, since he was the most valuable of their cargo. Shail recovered from the abuse and was becoming even more defiant with his treatment. Mollie was forced to tranquilize him every time she tube fed him a soft mixture of pulpy liquid fruit. Shail was not aware of this treatment but always woke with his throat sore and his hunger gone. He lost all sense of time and didn't know if it was night or day as the large hover traveled towards Hampton. His only memory seemed to be of this strange woman, who stayed at his side. Her hands were on him constantly as she caressed his body. At first, he'd defiantly hiss at her to leave him alone but would never attempt to bite a female. By the second day, her persistence paid off and Shail gave up. He allowing her to groom and wash, and handle his body. This female human seemed to know a lot about harpies. When he'd become aggravated and struggle against the uncomfortable tubes or when he heard Gus's voice and he would hiss rapidly to threaten him. Mollie was there to calm and reassure him. At times, Shail would become too unruly even for her. He'd jerk savagely on the chains while throwing his body violently against the bars with his captivity. She would have no choice but to sedate him.

Gus walked over to Mollie and the caged harpy. "I've been watching you," he said to her. "I think you're getting too attached to this one. You just can't keep your hands off of him."

The thin coarse-featured woman looked up at him. "Just doing my job, Gus," she said with a grin. Mollie really was enjoying handling this wild sleek gorgeous harpy. She had never seen any thing as beautiful as Shail. Normally, she would keep caged harpies totally drugged and unaware during this long journey but Mollie allowed the drugs to wear off the golden. As the harpy's health improved so did his obstinate nature. She loved to see his fearless sparkling blue eyes that were filled with audacity. This plucky stunning harpy didn't cower with fear like other harpies. Instead he was totally arrogant, as he'd sniffle boldly and toss his blond hair to challenge the men of the freighter. Mollie smiled at Shail for he behaved like a little proud prince. "And maybe he truly was," she thought.

"There's a grogin over here that needs petting," Gus said, bringing her attention back to the man. "Care to stick you hand in that cage?" he chuckled.

She glanced at the angry feline like creature. "Harpies are gentle creatures that enjoy affection. They live longer if they are handled a lot and kept quiet. But you wouldn't understand any of that," she sneered at the large crude man.

Gus smirked. "Lady, I guarantee you that drugged golden you're petting is dangerous. You should have seen his former owners. Those boys were all beat up. Take away those drugs and turn him loose and he'd attack and rape you."

"I don't believe those stories about harpies. I've been around enough of them and they've always very sweet and timid. I'll admit this golden is a bit of a rebel and has attitude, but if he is patiently handled, he'll tame down. He so alert and intelligent, I've never seen a harpy quite like him and he has such a strong will to live, he seems immune to the harpy depression. I bet I could eventually hand feed this one and he'd make a good pet," she said while stroking the exquisite sleeping harpy. "I can't understand why you men want to kill such an elegant creature like this," she added sadly.

Gus shook his head. "One of these days, Mollie, you'll change your mind about these winged pests. A harpy is going to get a hold of you, when you don't control them. Then maybe you'll appreciate me".

She giggled. "Appreciate you. It'll never happen."

Gus grumbled. "You know, you're lucky I like you. I'd kill most people if they treated me this way." Molly just raised her eyebrows a little and fluffed her brown curls.

On the second night, the large hover set down outside the Hampton spaceport. They waited for the arrival of two spacious transports. Shail could smell the fresh cool night air. He opened his eyes to the star filled sky as he stirred in his bonds since the tranquilizers were wearing off. The men stood around talking to one another while they waited. An unfamiliar man looked into Shail's cage as he spoke with one of the men from the freighter. When the man moved away to move a cage, this new man said a word that caused Shail to focus on him. He said the word "Kari." "Are you Kari's gold harpy?" this new man asked him. Shail instantly started rattling his chains as he stared up at him with beseeching eyes. "I think, you are her harpy," the man said in amazement.

"Get away from that harpy," yelled an angry voice that was all too familiar to Shail. The man moved away as Gus stood over the cage. He had the rod in his hand and he tapped it against the cage bars. Shail froze with fear when he saw the rod. "Go ahead. Jerk those chains again so I can give you a good reason to jerk." Shail lowered his head and hid it under his wing. "Mollie's right, you do have a few brains." Gus chuckled.

"Don't hurt him, Gus," Mollie yelled as she hurried to the harpy cage.

Gus continued to tap on the bars. "Well, you better knock him out or I'll be happy to do it for you. He's getting a little too active here." Mollie promptly gave Shail a dose of the tranquilizer and he was once again asleep.

The day wore on as Kari and her father stayed around the house, waiting for the important call from the shipping clerk at the Hampton spaceport but it never came. Evening approached and John asked Kari when her harpy guardian would return.

"Aron may not come back tonight unless he finds Shail."

John only nodded his head. They were about to go to bed when the communicator began to buzz. John reached for the button and recognized the young man on the screen.

"Did Kari come back yet?" he asked.

"Yes, she's here." John answered. "Kari, this guy called before when you were gone."

"Kari! Hi, how are you?" Ted asked excited to see her again.

"Ted, you've called at a bad time. Things are not going well for me," she answered politely.

Ted's face became serious. "Kari, I need to talk to you alone if you father doesn't mind," Ted uttered. Kari glanced at her father and John left the room.

"What is it?" she asked.

"Are you still with your golden harpy? Your father told me you were a few weeks ago and he sure did not seem too happy about it."

"No, I'm not," she answered solemnly.

"Well, that's why I'm calling. Just a little while ago, a group of hunters came in here on a big freight hover. I'm working all hours now since some people are in a hurry to leave with the swarm threat in the west. All crafts are being prepared just in case the swarms come here. To get back to these guys, they landed outside the port and started unloading all these animals. I was curious, so I went over to see what they had. In one of the cages was a golden harpy. I didn't really think much of it until one of the men started telling me how rare he was. I began to realize, he might be your harpy. They had him chained so he could barely move and I think, he was drugged. He seemed pretty lifeless at first. But when the man moved away, I spoke your name to the harpy and he lifted his head and opened his eyes. Then he started yanking on his chains. He definitely responded to it."

"Chains! Oh, Ted, that is my harpy. I've been searching for him for days. Where did they take him? Do you know?" she asked frantically.

Ted nodded. "Some huge guy chased me out of there but I found out from another man that they had built a new hunting range in Hampton. They're putting the harpy up for auction. Figured, he would draw a big crowd since most people have never seen a gold one."

"When is this auction?" she asked, hardly able to contain herself.

"Sometime next week," he answered.

"Thank you, Ted. You have no idea how much you've helped me. I'll be coming to Hampton as soon as possible."

"Can I buy you that dinner, I owe you?" he joked.

"Ted, you need to get out of Hampton. It's not safe. The swarms are coming there. Catch the next flight to whatever planet is available. Do you hear me?" she vocalized.

"Kari, the swarms are a long ways off. They haven't even threatened the East yet," he said nonchalantly.

"Ted, I know about this. They are coming. Please believe me," she pleaded.

"Alright, I'll believe you but I'm not leaving till I see you. Listen, I have to get back to work now. See you in a few days then?" he asked.

She nodded to him and they disconnected.

Kari walked rapidly through the house and found her father in the living room. He was sitting in a large stuffed chair. He jumped up, as she walked in. He could see the distraught look on her face. "Shail is in Hampton. The harpy hunters are putting him up for auction and then he'll be killed in a hunting range there. I need to get to Terrance and catch the next flight to Hampton," she said frantically and went back to the den. John followed her and raised the communicator again from the desk.

"I'll call Terrance and see if there is any room on board that last flight," John said. He got his answer swiftly, as he talked to a woman at the port there. "The flight is full, as I feared it would be with this beetle scare. Kari, let's think this through before we make any decisions. Your mate, Shail and the brown one that comes here, both want you to stay here for your safety. I could go to Hampton and get the harpy back for you," he spoke quietly.

Kari reeled around and glared at him. "I'm going and don't even try and talk me out of it," she answered in a biting tone.

Her father's face was grim and he nodded to her. "I figured that there was no way to stop you but I had to try. The only way to get there now is in my small hover. If we fly day and night, it'll still take three days before we reach Hampton. When is the auction?" he asked.

"Next week. Apparently, they had not set a date yet," she answered slightly calmer.

"That's good. It'll give me time to go to the Hampton bank and see what kind of credits I'll need. These men are not stupid. An auction in Hampton is bound to draw some high bidders. Your golden male will not be cheap," he considered.

"How high do you think it will be?" she asked. Kari had never even contemplated this predicament.

"If it's just Dora's local hunters, it will be in my range. But, if these men put this auction on the universal web then we'll be up against hunters and zoos from across the galaxy. It could be very high, especially since he's probably the last golden male harpy. One of a kinds tend to get overly priced." he somberly mentioned.

Kari was visibly shaken and her father put his arm around her. "Let's not worry about that now. You go pack what you need and I'll get the hover ready. I know Charlie will want to come along. I think he's been in real torment over this even though he doesn't show it. I've tried to tell him that I am the only one to blame for this whole mess. But he still blames himself. Kari, be kind to him if you can. I deserve your anger but he does not." John expressed.

Kari pondered for a moment. "I'll go pack now," she said quietly.

When she came downstairs, Charlie stood in the foyer. His eyes were downcast as Kari stepped down the stairs. He glanced up at her with sad eyes and asked, "Can I take your bag for you?"

"Yes, Charlie," she said, handing the small sack to him. They went outside in the middle of the night. The rain had stopped and the stars filled the black sky. "There is something I must do before I go," Kari said. She walked across the meadow towards the jungle behind the house. John and Charlie could hardly see her slender figure at the edge of the jungle, lit by the outside lights.

Kari called silently into the dark trees. After a few minutes, a harpy flew down next to her and bowed. "You must find Aron and tell him that my mate is in the farthest human dwellings of the east. Hunters have him and I am going there to try and save him," she related to the brown winged harpy. He gazed at her perplexed.

"I am Reaf. I am Lea's mate. She has spoken to me of your bravery. But I must tell you this since, it was told to me by our golden ruler. He said I was to protect you and this human structure with my life from a swarm attack. It was not his wish that you leave this protection."

Kari communicated silently and firmly. "Reaf, I am as golden as Shail, heed my words. These are my wishes."

Reaf dropped to his knees, sensing this golden's displeasure. "I shall follow your wishes and find Aron."

She only nodded to him and the harpy jumped up and disappeared into the dark jungle. John and Charlie watched from a distance. They couldn't help notice the reverence the harpy had given to Kari. She walked back swiftly towards them and the hovercraft. "Let's go," she stated with authority, hoping inside. John and Charlie also climbed in and John started the engines. In minutes, they were in the air, flying east towards Hampton.

The jungle flew by as Aron's long brown powerful wings flapped towards the east. He would return to the river and the last gathering of his fellow harpies. He had never felt this much despair and worry in his life. All these seasons he had loved and protected is little brother, Shail. Now he was most likely dead. The harpies had searched frantically for him with no luck. It was as if he had disappeared off the face of the planet. And with Shail's loss, the harpies and the jungle may also be lost.

Reaching his destination, he fluttered for a moment to land among the massive clutch of more than a thousand harpies. Seth, the large male that had provoked a challenge with him yesterday, was there. He brazenly walked to Aron. "Is he found?" was all he asked. Aron lowered his head sadly and shook it. This male sensed Aron distress and heavy heart. He gently placed his hand on one of Aron's shoulders. "You grieve his death as if you were born of the same nest," Seth related to Aron.

Aron nodded. "We were of the same nest even if our feathers were of a different shade but I do not grieve his death only his loss. I still hope. Shail had a strength and a courage unlike all of us. He could survive his capture for many lights."

"It is unlike a hunter shall allow him to live for many lights. His gold wings made him very precious to these men," the large male said softly to Aron. He then turned to the other harpies. "This gathering is over. We came here, each with a golden feather, to honor our ruler and follow his words. But he has fallen to hunters. I return to the east and my family. It is they that need protection from the hunters and these swarms. My flock shall no longer hold the swarms west of the river to protect the fleeing humans. These humans made a destructive path through our jungle so they may travel from east to west. Now these swarms shall follow this same doomed path from west to east and kill the humans as they go. The human's destructive vicious nature has been their undoing. I fly to my home now."

"And what of the swarms, when these humans have died? Will you let the animals and trees die next? We must keep this gathering. Only with numbers, shall we defeat the swarms in the end. By the next rise of the round moons, these swarms shall be too many for your flocks of the east, too many for the river harpies and too many for my western harpies." Aron stated with anxiety to the large group.

"My eastern flocks shall destroy these swarms that threaten the northern mountains where our females and young dwell, just as the river harpies shall protect their young in the north and you, my brave little brother shall protect and defend your islands and the valued unborn golden fledgling. We, harpies, shall do, as we always have done, protect our own flocks," Seth stated. The large male moved closer to Aron. He tenderly nuzzled Aron's neck. "I shall continue to have my flock search for your lost golden brother and I shall hope as you hope, he is found," he quietly related to the distraught young male. Aron only nodded to him.

"It is my hope also, we shall all survive this," Aron said to this eastern harpy leader just before this male raised his wings to take flight, heading towards his home. Aron dismally watched the huge flocks depart until he was left standing alone with some of his own male flock. He knew it was impossible to stop them even if he challenged and defeated every harpy leader. Only a male with gold wings and hair would make them heed.

His harpies moved closer to him, distraught and confused as what to do next. Aron sighed, "We shall follow Shail's wishes as best we can with out the help of others. Pull all our harpies from the swarms. We can no longer hold them. We shall line our harpies along the Turner Estate borders. This is where we shall make our stand. Destroy any swarm that threatens this line. Shail had hoped to spare the innocent and human young but their fate is out of our hands now. The war of nature has begun. Pray my brothers, the harpies endure when this is over."

Aron slowly flew back in the dark towards Kari and the Turner estate. He would have to tell her the terrible news that her mate was still unfound and soon these swarms would be out of control. He would have to convince her that she needed to face the worst and possibly make plans to return to the safety of the stars. Aron's harpies had desperately risked searching every western human dwelling at night for Shail and he was not among them. His faith that Shail could survive the cruel hunters now wavered. A tear ran down his cheek as he thought of Shail and his wild carefree bold spirit. Late into the night he had reached the Turner Estate. Another harpy met him there. This harpy was so excited he almost flew into Aron.

"He is alive, Aron! Shail lives!" Reaf proclaimed. Aron fluttered and landed on a large dark tree limb and Reaf set down beside him.

"Tell me all." Aron asked.

"Our golden female told me to tell you, Shail is held by hunters in the furthest eastern structures. She leaves the Turner estate and journeys east to save him."

"You let her leave this protection? You let her risk her life and the life of our future male ruler?" Aron fumed with irritation.

Reaf lowered his head. "Forgive me for failing you but she is as strong and determine and as brave as her golden mate. No harpy could have stopped her."

Aron nodded. "I am happy to learn Shail lives but now it is not only he, I must worry for but also his mate and son. These fearless reckless goldens shall be the death of me when I die of distress," he muttered to himself. After a moment, Aron raised his head. "Reaf, fly the Turner estate border. Gather every male harpy that can be spared. Leave only the smallest sum to guard these lands and the islands. The golden harpies must be protected. Spread your words to the river harpies. We all fly east."

John followed the same narrow highway below but it was more difficult in the dark. He knew if they experienced engine trouble, the highway would be the only safe place to land the hover since the jungle covered the landscape. Unknown to him and all other humans, it was this so called safe highway that these swarms would follow, devouring the humans and their buildings along the way. It was these buildings of fresh cut wood that attracted the beetles and it was also the smell of human flesh.

"In a few more hours, it should start getting light and we'll be close to Terrance. We'll stop for food there," John said.

They flew on and as day broke, they approached Terrance. John took the hover to the airport. Kari recognized the colorful small town that sat along the banks of the mighty river but it seemed different now. There was no movement below. The vehicles sat idle and no people could be seen. John landed at the vacant port. All of the small hovercrafts were gone now. A man came running out of one of the buildings towards them, followed by a woman holding a child. They seemed frantic as they ran to John's hovercraft.

"Take us with you!" he pleaded when John opened the door.

"What's happened?" John asked.

"A swarm. A swarm is coming from northeast of the river," the man screamed.

"I can only take you a short distance. My hover cannot hold this many people."

The man climbed in and the woman sat on his lap. Kari reached for the child. "I'll hold him," she said and the woman placed the one year old in her lap.

"Can you fly a hovercraft?" John asked the man.

"Yes, I've flown some small ones," the man answered out of breath.

"Good. With any luck, I still have a hovercraft here that you can use. With this load, we can't out-fly a swarm," John said and veered his hover south along the river. After several miles, they came to the abandoned warehouse. John spotted his stolen hovercraft. It sat in a large lot a short distance from the warehouse. He set down along side of it and got out to inspect the craft. The man followed him as John pushed the start button and the engines fired up. John spoke to the man and Kari gave the baby back to its mother. She climbed out and went to the warehouse. The place smelled of death and fecal matter as Kari walked inside. She gasped hard and shook when she saw the two maimed dead harpies. Their wings sliced from their backs and they lay in a bloody mound on the floor. She cringed, realizing her beloved Shail could have been kept in such a terrible place. It was filthy with rags, feces and liquor bottles laying about the surface. She jumped with fright when Charlie touched her shoulder.

"You shouldn't be in here," he said quietly. She nodded and trailed him out of the depressing place. The family was now seated in John's stolen hovercraft. John talked to them.

"Okay, you think you can operate this one alright?"

"Yes," the man responded.

"Now don't forget, follow the highway west to Westend. When you get past the town, take the road to my estate and to the mill. Tell the men there, I sent you. The mill is secure from a swarm attack. You'll be safe there."

The man grabbed John's hand. "Thank you, Mr. Turner, thank you. You saved our lives," the man moaned.

John grinned slightly. "Just get going," he said returning to his hover that held Charlie and Kari. He jumped in and fired up the engines. Both hovers rose from the ground at the same time. One was headed west to safety while the other went east and the unknown.

John forced the hover to rise as high in the sky as it could go. From this distance, he could see the giant black mass that stretched northeast of the river. He moved the hover to the southeast of it. "If they swarm this way, it could be all over," he said nervously. Suddenly, he saw the beetles start to swarm, as they took to the air. But instead of going south, the swarm settled on the lovely little town of Terrance. The bright multi-colorful buildings were covered in black as the giant swarm landed. Kari watched in the distance as the hover traveled further and further away from the destruction.

"I wonder how many people didn't make it out," she said sadly.

"I think most of them evacuated in time. The man told me that the large flights had come early. That's why he had missed them. His vehicle had stalled. He and his wife had seen no other people as they ran for the port," John said.

They traveled the rest of the morning in silence. Every so often a barren area would appear, where a swarm had hit, destroying every living thing in their path. At noon they set down on the highway near a small bridge with a river flowing beneath. John filled up some containers with water and stretched from the long tiresome journey.

"Should have brought some food along, I guess," he said to Charlie as he glanced around. "Now, where did Kari go?"

"She went into the jungle that way," Charlie pointed.

In moments, Kari returned to the road and the hover. In her hands, she carried some large orange roots. She broke one open and handed a piece to Charlie and her father. "Try these," she said as she bit into the sweet root. The men ate a bite of the root and were pleasantly surprised by the agreeable flavor.

Charlie looked at Kari. "Your harpy mate taught you well in a short time."

Kari glowed a little. "Yes, he did, Charlie. Even you could have learned from him."

"We need to get going," John said as he climbed into the hover. His mind was on Kari's words. He realized that the golden harpy had indeed, also taught him. He had shown him, what real unselfish love was. John was ashamed that his half bird, half human indeed had more honor than himself. He vowed to save Shail, not only for his daughter's sake but for also his own. He felt a knot in the pit of his stomach. It was caused by the terrible remorse, he felt.

They journeyed east following the highway below. Stopping only briefly to take a break and trade drivers, as Kari and Charlie both took their turns operating the hovercraft. It was late afternoon while Charlie drove and John slept in the back seat. Kari looked at Charlie and realized she had hardly spoken to him since this whole horrible mess began. She spoke quietly and asked Charlie about his jungle encounter with Shail.

"You never told me the complete story, when you met Shail in the jungle," she said to him. Charlie glanced at her but did not answer. "Shail told me, that you spoke to him. That you told him, I was in the sky but I would return as an adult," she commented.

Charlie cleared his throat. "Yes, I did tell him those things a few years ago. It was very apparent that he sought me since he still longed for you. Why else would a young golden harpy seek out an old human man in the jungle," he smiled.

"But why did you tell him this, when you warned me to stay away from him?" she asked.

He took a deep breath. "It is hard to explain one's actions. I was conflicted on what was best for you. I had hoped, when you returned, the harpies and this male would be gone from mind and you could lead a normal life as a human. I also wanted the same for you, as your father. But," he shook his head sadly "I could also see the passion and commitment you had for the harpies when you were a child. And this young blond male had same passion and commitment for you. He had saved your life and risked death to bring you home and risked death again by bravely approaching a man with a weapon in the jungle, even if the man was an old one like me. I could tell from his begging eyes that he longed for you. I am not happy that in the end, you chose him. I have watched for a lifetime, the torment your father has gone through when he fell under a harpy's spell and bonded with her. You have no idea how it nearly destroyed him when he lost her. His commitment to her was as strong as yours is to your mate. And now, you may face the same life-long torment if your harpy mate should die. The odds of a long happy life with a harpy are not very good. And I wanted to see you happy, not just briefly but for as long as you live."

Kari was quiet for a while. "If Shail dies, the time I did spend with him is worth a lifetime of grief. Better to have loved and lost than to have never loved," she said, quoting her father. "Those are my father's words. He feels as I do, when it comes to being with our harpy mates."

John had been listening quietly in the back. He closed his eyes again and thought to himself, "Yes, the time with his wife, his harpy, had been worth all the torment. Knowing then what he knew now, he still would have bonded with her. That precious time together filled his soul like no other time in his life. He and his daughter were very much alike."

The little bright star of Duran had come and gone, as night came to the continent. Kari was in the back seat again and lay down to sleep. She still hoped that Shail would come to her in her dreams. She knew now, why he hadn't come for the past nights if he was drugged as Ted had mentioned. It would be impossible for him to focus the harpy telepathy on her with his senses. But still, she yearned for him. Perhaps the cruelties that he was experiencing were so terrible, he blocked her out so she would not know his pain. These things ran through her mind. She could only think of him. Even the jungle below had lost its beauty for her. She folded her arms to her chest, tucking her head down and pulled up her legs. Closing her eyes, she remembered how good it felt when Shail would wrap around her the same way. He would cover them both with his large fanned out wing as he held her and nuzzled the back of her neck. A tear rolled down her cheek with this memory.

John steered the hover along the road through the night. He spotted a distant light ahead. "We'll set down for a while at that light," he said to Charlie. They approached the light and saw it was a small inn. There were many terrain vehicles and two hovercrafts parked out front. He landed beyond the transports. When John opened the hover door, people's voices drifted out from the inn to fill the tranquil night air. Kari stirred from the back seat. They all got out of the hover. John walked to the inn door followed by Charlie and Kari. Once inside, a balding man behind the desk met them. He grinned wide and said, "Hello, I hope you're not looking for a room, since we're booked up."

"No, not a room but maybe some food if you have any," John answered.

The man smiled again. "I can help you with that if you don't mind Dora's finest native food. I just happen to have one table left that isn't filled." The man led them through a wide doorway that entered into a cozy dining room and a table in the back. All tables were filled with tired travelers. They ate and talked quietly amongst themselves. It was apparent these people had not traveled to this inn for pleasure. They were refugees fleeing the swarms in the west. The mood was somber, as the only topic of conversation amongst them, seemed to be the beetles and the hardship they all faced now. John overheard a man at the next table say, "Maybe we should go back. The swarms might have missed Terrance and our home there," he said, speaking in a low voice to the woman beside him.

John could not help but to intercede in this man's conversation. "A swarm destroyed Terrance this morning. We saw it, as it hit. There's nothing left to go back to." The woman at the table began to cry, as the man tried to comfort her.

Another man heard John and stood up in the dining room. "This man," as he acknowledged John, "said he saw Terrance destroyed this morning by a swarm." There was a hush and sighs coming from all around the small dining room.

An older man feebly walked over to John's table. His eyes were filled with tears. "Are you sure? Everything is gone?" his voice trembled. John just nodded. "I've lost everything then. A lifetime of work, my home, my store," the old man muttered and slowly returned to his table. He sat down next to an older woman and she put her arm around him as they both wept. John did not like to be the bearer of bad news to so many.

"This is just the beginning," John said in a low voice to Kari and Charlie. "It's going to get worse in time." They ordered their food and finished quickly. Soon, they were back in the hover and flying towards Hampton. John had ordered extra food for the journey ahead. Kari stared out the window into the darkness. She thought of the poor people at the inn. Most of them were just trying to live their lives in peace with their little stores and businesses. There was not a cruel harpy hunter among them. If Shail could be saved, she would have to convince him that the swarms must be destroyed before so many innocent people died. There had to be a way that a peace could be made between the humans and harpies before so many lives were in ruin. He was the key to all of this.

The night dragged on as they took their turn piloting the hover while the others slept. The next morning, John placed a call to Hampton on the hover communicator. It was Thursday and they still had some time before the auction took place the following week.

"Yes, I need to be connected to a new hunting range in Hampton." The woman acknowledged and put him through.

"This is Simpson's hunting range," said a well-dressed large man on the other end.

"I hear you have a golden harpy at auction next week. Could you give me more information on this auction and when it is?" John asked.

The man gleamed. "Yes, we do. The auction is Monday night at 7:00 P.M. but the viewing will take place Saturday and Sunday and is open to the general public for a price of ten credits." John glanced at Kari and turned back toward the screen.

"Can you tell me about this harpy and his condition?"

The man smiled broadly again. "Sir, he's exceptional. He has real attitude, which golden harpies are known to have. He's young but close to maturity with a sixteen-foot wingspan. The creamy gold wings are in perfect condition. His will is strong and he has remained in good health. He'll give any one a great challenge in our three acre range."

"Thanks for the information," John said.

"Sir, may I put you down on our list of bidders?" he asked.

"Yes. My name is John Turner. I'll be there Saturday morning to register in person."

"Thank you, Mr. Turner. I guarantee this harpy will not disappoint you. We're very pleased with him." John nodded and turned off the communicator.

John looked back at Kari. "It sounds like, he's okay. I doubt if they would hurt him, knowing his value." Kari motioned, she agreed. "Kari, we'll be in

Hampton by Friday night. We'll see him first thing Saturday morning but I must warn you. You can't act like you know him or make any kind of a scene. There are too many hunters that may guess you're a female harpy. If there's trouble, I'll be taken off the bidding list and we'll lose our chance to get him back. Do you understand this? It'd be almost better if you didn't go, since Shail may go nuts once he sees you."

She thought about this and her father could be right. She didn't know what Shail would do when he saw her. "I'll be calm and I'll tell Shail, he must be the same," she said.

"Alright then," her father agreed.

Thursday remained relatively quiet. They noticed more and more vehicles traveling east on the road to Hampton. The afternoon came and with it more rain. The rain seemed to last through half the night, making the hover rock against the sheets of wind and thundershowers. It finally let up, just before morning. They found another small store that was open and set down for a quick bite. Hampton was less than a day's travel and they were eager to end this long trip across the continent.

John finally saw the large buildings of Hampton in the distance. He felt a sigh of relief. His little hovercraft had made it without any trouble. It was not built to travel this far for such a long period of time. The hovercraft's solar system engine would take some regenerating, once they reached the spaceport.

The horizon filled with clouds blocking out the descent of Duran, as they landed outside the giant spaceport along side numerous other hovercrafts. A man was working on a small space ship when Kari approached him.

"Do you know a Ted that works here?" she asked while her father and Charlie unloaded the gear.

"He's over there. One lane over," the man pointed.

"Thanks," Kari responded. She walked over to the lane and called to the young man under one of the ships. Ted immediately came out and jogged over to meet her. They talked briefly about Kari's journey.

Ted asked her, "Are you going to see him tomorrow?" Kari just gestured, she was.

"Let me take you," he said. Kari glanced at her father, who stood a short distance away.

"Perhaps, I should go with Ted. If there's trouble, it'll appear I'm not with you and Charlie," Kari said to her father.

"Yes, and I'd feel better if you were accompanied by a man especially if your harpy makes a scene and tries to get to you," her father replied. Kari knew her father was more worried about the danger she could face if her true identity were revealed especially around so many hunters. John introduced himself to Ted and apologized for his rudeness on their first encounter. Ted shrugged and understood.

"Call me when you're settled. I'll pick you up first thing in the morning," Ted told her.

Kari agreed. She left with her father and Charlie. They took a shuttle to the same hotel that Kari had stayed in on her last visit to Hampton. Kari felt better after she had cleaned up and placed one of Doc's patches on her arm. She had an adjoining room with her father. Charlie had a room across the hall. They ate in the small dining room off the lobby and talked about the auction. John and Charlie were both eager to finally stretch out in a real bed for the night since the back seat of the small hover was very cramped for a full grown man. Both were very tired but Kari was excited. She finally would see her love and she was happy and worried at the same time. She went back to her room and lay down but sleep would not come to her. She rested in bed for hours thinking about Shail. Finally in the early hours, she drifted off to sleep.

Gus called on his communicator. He was angry, as another man picked up on the other end. "Bill, where the hell are the transports? We've been here at the port for a half an hour and I'm ready for a real drink," he yelled at the man on the other end.

"We'll be there in five. Just relax, brother. I have a good bottle with me. I figure you earned it with that golden. How's he doing?" Bill asked calmly.

"He's fine. You know, Mollie. She's about got him babied to death. Won't let me near him," Gus said annoyed.

"That's why I hired her. She knows how to keep these animals alive till we need them,"

"Well, she seems to be especially fond of this one," Gus remarked.

"Well, this golden harpy may pay for our investment on this lousy little planet. This beetle scare is not helping business but this golden is sparking a lot of interest. I'm almost at the port now," Bill said. Gus glanced down the road from the spaceport and could see the headlights of the large truck transports, making their way towards them.

"Alright men, the transports are almost here. Let's get ready to load these animals up," he shouted to the group of men who were relaxing against the cages.

The large transport drove on to the dark landing field and a few more men got out to help carry the cargo of wild animals. A large dark haired man came over to Gus and grinned at him. "Good job, brother. Now where is he? See if he's everything you told me he was," Bill asked.

"Over there," Gus pointed. "The cage by Mollie." The two brothers, who looked similar to one another, walked a short distance to thin middle-aged woman and the golden harpy. Bill looked in at the drugged harpy, as he slept.

"Is he alright?" Bill asked, trying to see the harpy in the dim light.

"He's fine," Mollie answered. "I had to dose him when we got here. Your brother loves to torment him. He'd even be in better shape if you kept Gus away from him."

Gus frowned. "Look at my face. That harpy did that. Did you really think I was going to let him get away with it?" Gus complained with anger.

Bill laughed at the black bruise that covered half his brother's face. "That little harpy did that to you?" He chuckled.

"Yes, and your brother almost shocked him to death because of that bruise. If I hadn't arrived when I did, you'd be bringing back a pair of yellow wings instead of a live harpy," Mollie said seriously.

Bill shook his head at Gus. "You need to control that temper of yours. We cannot afford to lose this one. Let's get him loaded and back to the range. I can barely see him in this light and I want a good look at him." Bill conveyed with enthusiasm.

Shail was loaded in a separate transport and taken back to the range that was a few miles on the outskirts of Hampton. They unloaded him and brought him into a room that was away from the other animals. Bill came over to the cage, as Mollie and Gus stood by it. He peered in at Shail, who had remained asleep during the move. Bill looked at the harpy and frowned as he shook his head with disgust.

"What's wrong? The shocks I gave him didn't even leave a mark. He's perfect," Gus said defensively when he saw his brother's displeasure. Bill didn't answer for some time as he grabbed the harpy's face between the bars and turned it. Then he lifted his wing and looked at Shail's long stunning sleek frame as he studied the harpy.

"Yes, he is perfect alright." Bill said with a sigh. "Maybe too perfect. Look at his face. He makes most men look like we're onions compared to him. He's got a gorgeous body and a face that will enchant any woman's heart. And on top of that, you say, he doesn't act like a normal harpy that hides and cowers in a cage. This could be trouble," Bill said slowly, as he continued to gaze at the harpy.

"Bill, you don't have to worry about the cowering part. He's scared of me. He trembles and hides every time I get near him," Gus said proudly.

"He's not afraid of you. It's that rod in your hand that frightens him. It would frighten anyone, if they were tortured nearly to death with it like he was." Mollie said sarcastically. "Besides there is a reason this harpy is different than most, besides the fact that he's a golden and they're known for their fearless combative nature," she said. Mollie reached in and pulled Shail's wing aside. "You see that?" she asked. "That little scar is a laser blast wound, that's healed on his side. Not only is it healed but also some one did laser surgery on it and not long ago. And look at these old scars on his wrists and ankles were he was bound tightly. His wing was also broken and healed. Look at the new feathering. There's no doubt, this harpy was wounded and captured. And then for that side wound to heal properly, he had to be in some ones care for some time. I think that probably explains, why he's so aggressive. He's been around hunters and survived it. He's lost his natural animal fear of humans," she said.

"Maybe the men you got him from treated him?" Bill asked Gus.

"Nay, those guys were scared to death of him. And if you could have seen the beating that this harpy gave them, I don't blame them. I know they didn't treat him."

"I have to agree with Gus," Mollie said. "This harpy's muscle tone is too good. If he were locked in a cage for that long, he wouldn't look like this. He'd have to be drugged and held down and force-fed. His skin would be pale and he'd be too weak to stand up much less put up a fight. No, he was either, treated by some one who was gentle or he managed to escape his captivity. In either case, he's been free for some time."

"Well, I can reacquaint this little buck with fear. That's not a problem. But, I don't understand why you're so worried about his looks. So he's a real good-looking harpy. What the hell difference is that going to make to the hunters. They're only interested in big well-feathered wings and whether he's hung good enough for a wallet," Gus complained.

Bill looked at Mollie. "You're a woman, Mollie. What do think of this handsome little devil? Are you going to care when he's hung and gutted?" Bill asked the woman.

Mollie reached in the cage and gently placed her hand against the beautiful sleeping harpy's face. "It'll make me sick, when they torture him. He is perfect, Bill," she said sadly. "I've handled some truly gorgeous brown harpies but this golden is very different. When I handle him, he doesn't even act like a normal scared harpy. He has a proud defiant attitude, like he's above us, humans. And he's just so terribly pretty and dreamy, he's the most perfect looking male, I've ever seen. He just makes you feel like hugging him. I really do like this one," she sighed. "This golden has a lot of spirit to go with his beautiful looks."

"This is what concerns me," Bill said with aggravation. "I'm not worried about the hunters. It's trouble from the public especially the women. We could end up with protesters and God knows what, after he's put on display. If I had seen him earlier, I would have never agreed to this public showing. But it's too late now. I've already advertised for the showing on Saturday and Sunday. And some reporters are coming Friday afternoon. Everyone in Hampton wants to see a golden harpy, the last golden harpy. I figured we could make a few extra credits off him but this could backfire on us," Bill said with disgust as he looked back at the harpy.

"Not everyone is going to fall for this harpy like Mollie here," Gus joked.

Bill just shook his head at his brother. "Mollie has handled more than one harpy. I'd say she's pretty immune to their effect on women. If she can fall for him, it will be worse for an average woman," Bill grumbled.

"Hell, Bill, you worry too much. Who cares what they think? If you want, I can beat those good looks right out of him and make him scared to death at the same time. That would solve all your problems. And I'd have a great time doing it." Gus chuckled.

Bill looked at Gus seriously. "Sometimes I wonder if you're really related to me. Tell me Gus, how many hunters are going to want to bid on an animal that's been beaten so badly, that it can't even flee? Huh? And it does matter what the public thinks. It's not good for business and it's not good for the hunters, if they're heckled." Bill stormed.

"I suppose," Gus said quietly.

"Well, there's nothing to be done about it now. Mollie, keep him sedated Wednesday and Thursday. And tube feed him good since I doubt if he'll eat on his own this weekend. Friday morning, we'll take him off the tranquilizers and put him in the display cage out front. He should get his balance back by the time the reporters show up in the afternoon. I've hired extra men for Saturday, Sunday and Monday for crowd control. Hopefully, we can get rid of him before the animal radicals get organized. If we make enough credits, it won't matter how many people are upset with us," Bill said worriedly.

Shail began to stir in the cage. "He's coming out of it. I only gave him a mild dose at the port. I wasn't sure what you had planned. I'll give him another." Mollie said.

"No, let's wait. I want to see this little defiant attitude of his," Bill said as he watched the harpy begin to regain consciousness in the narrow cage.

Shail slowly opened his eyes. He saw the woman first and then Gus, the huge dark haired man with the rod. And then he noticed another large man that stood next to Gus. Shail sniffed at them and could detect the same scent. It was obvious these large men were related. "Oh, great. The thing has blue eyes too, to top things off. I thought all harpies had green eyes," the man next to Gus spoke.

"Not this one," Mollie commented.

Shail began to focus and feel more like him self, then he saw the terrible rod in Gus's hand. Shail sunk low and cowered while pushing himself away from the bars and the rod. "I thought he was fearless?" Bill asked while staring at the frightened harpy.

"It's the rod. He's scared of it," Mollie voiced.

Suddenly, this other man yelled at Gus. "Get rid of that damn rod. I want to see how he's going to act when he's out front." To Shail's surprise, Gus did, as this man ordered. Gus returned and Shail sniffled boldly at him giving him an antagonistic stare now that he no longer had his shocking weapon. Bill laughed, "He is pretty bold now." Shail ignored these humans and looked around the small room to see if there was any escape from this place. He was in a cage, in a cage. Then this new man put his hand in the cage and poked Shail's ribs hard. Shail tossed his hair and hissed at him with contempt and did not show any fear. The man did it again and Shail breathed deeply with this provocation, shaking his head and mockingly snapped at him. He jerked on the chains to challenging this man, while making a low seething sound through his teeth to threaten him.

The man smirked at him, "He's definitely not afraid. You can tell he'd love to bite my finger right off. He's a nasty little sucker," Bill laughed. "You know, I think the hunters are going to enjoy a challenging animal like him. I can bill this hunt as dangerous. It'll be the difference between shooting a zel or a grogin. Most hunters would pay anything for a vicious harpy rather than a meek one. Yes, it may even bring more credits to the auction," Bill said and prodded Shail again. Shail breathed deeply while his piercing eyes seethed with irritation. He leaped at the bars and clung to them to frighten the man. Bill saw the more he tormented the harpy, the more aggressive it became. He smiled wide at the fierce beautiful male. "Yes, little guy, you'd love to get at me but I'm afraid if that happened, I'd have to beat you senseless," Bill teased the golden. "Change of plans. We're taking him off the drugs on Thursday. Gus, I have a job for you that you're going to love. I want you to start harassing him. I don't want him hurt, just tormented. See if you can get him as mean as possible. I want him hissing and lunging at those bars when he sees a man. Think you can handle that? Some more revenge for your bruised ego."

Gus smiled, "I can handle that."

"Do you think that's wise? Your brother can't tell the difference between torment and torture," Mollie said.

"Lighten up, Mollie. I won't do anything, he can't handle," Gus grinned.

"That's my point, you don't know what he can and can't handle. Bill, if you want to keep this harpy in good shape, you'll change your mind about this," she said.

"Oh, you really do have a crush on this pretty harpy. Can't stand to be away from him," Gus leered.

"Mollie, Gus knows he's valuable. He won't hurt him. Besides, just think of the credits he'll bring if he's in an out of control rage. He'll be crashing into those bars to get at the crowd. He'll bring a fortune," Bill said.

Mollie shook her head in disgust. "You guys really don't know anything about harpies. No amount of torture or torment is going to make him do that. If anything, you're just going to break his spirit. Then he'll be like all other harpies that just shivering in the corner of their cage. But, he's yours, just remember I told you so."

"I'll be here to keep an eye on things. It won't get out of hand. You can go ahead and drug him again. I'm ready to have that drink. How about you, Gus?" Bill asked. Gus agreed and they left the room, leaving Mollie with the harpy.

"It's better you sleep now and save your strength. I have a feeling you're going to need it," she said with sorrow and came near Shail with another plastic object. He was fully awake now and aggravated. He hissed loudly since he no longer wanted the drugs that forced him to sleep. The back of his throat hurt from the feeding tube and he always woke, feeling bloated and drowsy from this unnatural sleep. "Easy, my little prince. You know I don't like to do this to you." Shail stared at her and his instincts conveyed the deep remorse this woman was feeling that he would be destroyed. She was not enjoying keeping him alive so he could suffer such a terrible death. Shail relaxed a little and allowed her to give him the drugs. He nuzzled her caressing hand for the first time as he drifted off to sleep.

Shail did not remember anything the following day and night. But, when Thursday morning came, he awoke to the sick feeling of being over fed. He was still in the same cage and the same room that fit his last memory. His stomach ached as he squirmed in the bonds. He noticed the tube in his sex organs had been removed. Jerking on the chains, he found they still held him fast. The room was virtually empty except his cage as he looked around. Then he heard the door open behind him. Shail strained to see if it was his woman handler. Leaning over him was Gus. Shail hate filled eyes stared at this man as he quietly watched him. Gus smiled and reached through the bars to grab Shail's hair. Shail swiftly jerked his head to try and bite him. When this failed, he gave a loud warning sniffle.

"Why you little demon. Pretty darn brave, when I don't have my rod. I'm going to love giving it to you and your little girlfriend, Mollie, is not here to protect you."

He left the room and came back with the rod. Gus adjusted the rod to its lowest setting. Shail breathed hard and began to tremble. He gripped the chains and covered himself with his wing. Gus touched his chained arm and the rod stung him but this time it didn't have the searing overwhelming pain as before. "Doesn't hurt as bad." Gus smiled. Shail timidly blinked his long lashes and meekly lowered his head. "I guess it's just a matter of where I put this rod. I know where it would anger me the most," he chuckled. He reached in the cage and held Shail's wing back as he violently ripped the harpy sash off him, exposing the harpy's lean nude body. Still holding his wing back, Gus jammed the rod up between the harpy's legs and sent a mild shock against its sex organs. Gus released the wing and he watched the harpy go completely berserk in the cage. Shail threw his body hard against the bars and tossed vigorously. Gus tried to grab the wing again but the harpy bashed and flailed his wing frantically in the small cage, not caring if he damaged his valuable feathers. The creamy feathers began to litter the floor.

Hearing the racket, Bill walked into the room. "Gus, what the hell are you doing? You're terrifying him and he's destroying his wings!" he screamed. "Get rid of that damn rod. I want him mean, not battered and scared. You got that?" Bill yelled.

"Well, I'm trying to make him mean. If anyone shocked me below the belt, I'd kill them." Gus argued.

Bill shook his head with disgust. "Well, you're not a harpy and those feathers on the floor are like gold. Real gold. Think of something else. I want him to be a vicious killer not a terrified chicken. I've got a lot of work to do with this auction and there's a lot riding on this harpy. I hope you don't screw this up."

"Alright, Bill, don't have to lecture me like a kid," Gus grumbled.

When Gus finally left the room, Shail closed his eyes. He began to realize, there was no hope of escaping these abusive men. He was going to die and now he wished, this hunt would begin. When he was hunted, he would at least be free to attack and kill these men. Shail shook his head again. "I must control this hate and keep the hope of my escape," he thought. To lose the hope, would be an invitation for the depression to come. He tried to stay focused on the harpies and Kari. They needed him. Gus was causing a deadly hate to grow strong in him but at the same time Shail was losing his will to live.

An hour later, Gus returned. "You're going to like this new game," he said to the harpy. "In fact, it's completely painless. Bring it in, boys." The same two men from the warehouse walked in with a little fledgling harpy. Its hands were bound with rope as they dragged it into the room. Gus unlatched the locks and opened the top of Shail's cage. "Throw it in there. These animals are very social to one another. It won't take long for this male to adopt this orphan." The tiny harpy crawled over Shail's body and then slid along side. Shail immediately covered the fledgling with his wing to protect him from the men. "See. What did I tell you? These adult males would sacrifice their own lives to protect the young, let's leave them and let them get more acquainted," Gus said. The men left and the little harpy stuck his head out from under Shail's wing. Shail sighed deeply as he stared at the little guy.

"How did you come to be in this place?" he asked the little harpy.

"The metal bird flew faster than I and I fell to the ground with the sting of their weapons. My father flew down to lead them away and save me. But their weapons found him. They put me in a cage and I watched the hunters slowly kill my father," the little harpy said with a trembling silent voice as he buried his head into Shail's side. The fledgling appeared to be only four seasons of age. Shail rubbed his wing against him to comfort him, realizing the terrible trauma this young one had already live through. "Your wings are gold. My father told me pale winged harpies have much power and they protect us. Will you protect me with your power?" he asked Shail.

Shail sighed a little. "I am caged and helpless as you. This protection, I shall not promise. It is unlikely either of us shall survive this place." Shail answered truthfully as was the way with harpies. He covered him again with his wing as the fledgling clung to him. Shail was tormented he could not defend the helpless fledgling. He closed his eyes realizing what Gus's cruel motives were. If these men wanted to see rage, they get it if they hurt the little fledgling. Hours past and the tiny harpy curled up around Shail to sleep. Shail heard the dreaded sound of the door opening. The fledgling heard it too and ducked under the cover of Shail's wing.

Gus leaned over the cage with the same two warehouse men. Shail immediately began hissing violently at the men. He smashed his wings against the bars in defense of the baby harpy. Gus smiled. "I knew that parenting instinct is strong

in these males. This should really get him when we attack it. Let's get it out." Gus
ordered and opened the top of the cage. The two men held Shail's flailing wing
down as Gus snatched the little harpy out. Shail tried to beat them off but they
held the long cream wing down firmly and the slammed the cage door on him.
Gus held the fledgling by one of his little wings over Shail's cage as his other hand
held the shock rod. Shail's face filled with panic and anguish as he heard the
fledgling's subconscious pleas to save him. Shail went completely crazy bashing
both his wings recklessly against the bars as he yanking and twisted wildly in the
chains, hoping to distract the men. Gus just chuckled at him while holding the
struggling fledgling. The huge man placed the rod against its little ribs. The small
harpy shook for a minute and then went limp. It was over. The silent screeching
voice of baby no longer entered Shail's mind. Gus dropped it to the floor and
poked at it.

"It's dead, Gus," one of the men said as he examined tiny slender body.

"Well, hell that was no fun. I thought it would last longer than that. Remind
me next time to use a lower setting on these fledglings." Gus disappointedly said.
Gus leaned over Shail's cage, expecting the golden to attack or at least hiss at him.
But Shail lay quietly and only pathetically shook his head as if he were impaired.
"Is it hurt?" Gus asked with worry. He began to fear that the valuable animal had
badly injured its self.

One of the other men leaned closer to inspect the harpy. Just then Shail
lunged at him through the bars. The man jerked his head back but not quick
enough. Even with the short chains, Shail had managed to claw the side of his
face. "Damn thing almost scratched my eyes out," the man screeched as blood
ran down his face. Gus looked at the harpy while it seethed at him and its eyes
burned with anger. It was very apparent, the slight golden wanted to attack the
three huge men for killing the fledgling.

"That's a good little buck. Sapping that baby harpy did have the right effect
on you," he grinned and then looked at his pal's wound. "You'll live, go get your
self sealed up," he said unsympathetically as he turned to the other man. "Open
the cage and toss that dead fledging on him. Let him mourn. We need to get us a
bottle. We still have a long night ahead of us," Gus said. They threw the limp wee
body on top of Shail. It slowly slid to his side as Shail watched it. He moved his
wing against the small lifeless body but there was no doubt, the tiny harpy was
dead. Shail rattled his chains and breathed hard, feeling this hate grow stronger in
him. After some time he tried to calm himself, biting his bottom lip. Only the
thought of the swarms killing these men seemed to sooth him.

Time passed and Shail could see through a tiny high window, it was dark outside now. The door opened again and Gus and the two men were laughing as they walked back into the room. "Well, Gus what do you want to do to him next?" One of the men asked.

Gus mustered while gazing at Shail. "My brother told me not to hurt him but Bill's gone now. Besides, I know this harpy can tolerate a little pain. After we're done tonight, this winged beauty will be lunging at those bars to kill men. Grab its wing and pull it back," Gus said with a sadistic grin. Shail tried to flap it but the two men were able to get their hands on it and pull it away from his body. All three men now gawked and stared at Shail's long sleek naked body as the harpy twisted to lay on his belly to protect his ribs and sex organs from Gus's shocking stick. "Look at that little slender waist and rear and it does have a pretty little face. Imagine what would happen to this fine piece if it were locked in our prison. Us and every other inmate would get in a long line to ride it. What do you think boys? No line. And I'm long overdue after that prison and then being stuck in the lousy jungle. Besides," he chuckled, "I can't wait to see Mollie's face when she finds out what we did to her favorite little boy,"

"A harpy? It's not even human," questioned the man with the bandaged face.

Gus frowned. "He's close enough and since when have you gotten so picky? This harpy is better looking than most women I've seen you with. Besides, this proud little stud is a born fighter. Bet he'll wiggle for a good hour before he gives it up. Bill wants this harpy raging mean, this should do it."

"Well, it is tempting," one man muttered, "but I need to drink more whiskey before I can jump it."

"Let's get him out and put him over the cage while we're sober enough to handle him. We'll need some rope for those wings and rags for that snapping mouth also some oil. We'll lube him up. Don't want to tear up Mollie's baby," Gus laughed. The men threw the little dead harpy body to a corner of the room as they began to tether Shail's wings. Shail furiously flapped them but he was easily over powered in the small cage. After his mouth was gagged, they hoisted him out of his prison by his chains. Two men jerked each wrist, stretching him tightly over the cage top. After the wrists were secured, they fastened his ankles far apart to the bottom bars on the floor. Next they unfolded his wings and elongated them across the bars, retying them in the full fan out position so Shail's nude body was completely exposed. Stripped of all his defenses, Shail lay draped on his stomach, totally vulnerable. "Put some of those loading mats between him and those bars so he don't get bruised up when he starts bouncing around." Gus smirked.

Now the three large men sat back and watched the seductive lean frame squirm helplessly against the mats while they drank from the whiskey bottle. Shail breathed hard with fright as he tried to pull free of the wrenching shackles. He was unsure what persecution lie ahead from these black-hearted men. Gus staggered to his feet and approached Shail from behind. He poured the oil on him while fondling and tugged at the harpy's rear. Shail hissed low into the rags and nervously tried to move away from this touch. "I think I got a real virgin, boys," Gus mumbled and drooled. "This pretty stud has no idea what's coming." Gus was right. Shail had no idea that men could sadistically rape him.

The other men moved closer and unfastened their pants, exposing themselves. Shail became frantic, seeing these males were ready to breed and he was their target. He exploded, jerked on the shackles with all his strength to be free, causing his wrists and ankles to bleed.

"I believe, our little stud has figured it out," Gus said while his large hands groped and pulled at the slender body till he had forced himself in it. Shail thrashed and hissed rapidly to stop this invasion. This only stimulated the sexual appetite for the large heavy man. Gus lunged deeply, crushing the hysterical creature against the mats. Gus now allowed the terrified harpy's dancing body to stroke him as he remained firmly planted. Shail gasped for breath as he sweated with fear and panic. His wet struggling body massaged and entertained his huge attacker. The other men feverishly rubbed against the harpy as they waited for their turn while watching Gus cruelly ravage the frenzied animal. "Come on, keep moving, you almost got me there," Gus grunted. "Now you're gonna really feel it." Gus grabbed the harpy's hips, jerking him up and away from the cage. He began brutally ramming the horrified disabled winged male to inflict the demoralizing pain and achieve ejaculation.

"Hurry up, Gus, before you take all the fight out of him," one of the other men exclaimed with a panicky voice. Gus had no sooner finished, when another man leaped in his place and quickly penetrated Shail with quick rigid jabs. Shail went crazy as the burning stabbing pain gripped him. But, it was not just the pain. It was the absolute and total emasculation of his very soul. Shail's sleek muscles dripped their sweat and sperm as he was smothered by the smell of whiskey and their rank human odor. Soon the third man mounted him, wrapping his arms around Shail's waist and gripped the harpy in an uncompromising hold with his hands. "I'm going to ride and spur this baby on like a wild little mustang," he said with excitement. Squeezing tightly caused Shail to jump and contort his slim body as this performance stroked the man. Soon Shail felt sick and vomited into the rags that were tied in his mouth while softly hissing low in desperation. He could feel the men's warm fluids running down the back of his legs.

"Move I want to ride it. I'm just getting start on this animal," Gus slurred as weighty body thrust in and out until Shail thought he would be ripped apart. The other men laughed and tormented the harpy to keep it steadily lunging. Despite the fatigue and pain, Shail continued to toss his body in an effort to dislodge each rider. Unknowingly, it was Shail's resistance and unyielding spirit that excited and encouraged his assaulters. It was one of the longest nights of Shail's young life as the groping, molesting and rape never ended. A power struggle ensued between the unrelenting defiant little harpy and the large men, drunk with whiskey and lust. These men, who were there to anger the harpy, now were determined to break him.

As the dawn approached, the men won this battle against the spirited little harpy. Shail finally stopped struggling against the chains and against the men. He could feel his strong will to live slipping away as he lay totally exhausted and drained. He tried to cling to the things, he cherished but with this relentless onslaught, all things lost their value and he felt like an empty shell. His body's only purpose now was to satisfy these men. His emotions were gone as his mind began to sink into the deepest void of the harpy depression. The men had not only raped his body but they had also raped his mind and soul. Shail closed his eyes as a single tear ran down his cheek while the last man slowly and methodically humped against him. His mind was going quickly. Shail panted hard and tried to focus on his heart. Mollie's drugs were finally out of his system and they no longer hindered him "They may own this disgraced body but they do not own my mind. I must do this. I am worthless to all I love and soon, I shall be worthless to these men, as well," Shail thought.

With the morning light, the man toppled on top of Shail, releasing the last of his sperm. He glanced at the limp harpy body. "Hey, Gus, I think this harpy finally lost his fight. He's not moving. Maybe we did tame it," he said with a grin.

Gus rubbed his eyes as he wobbled to his feet. He walked to Shail and grabbed his hair and looked into the closed eyes of the harpy. Shail was barely breathing and his body lay motionless over the cage. "I'll make it jump again," he said and grabbed his shock rod. Gus set the rod to its highest setting and hit Shail in the ribs with it. Shail's heart had stopped but the high voltage of the electrical shock, jolted his body, forcing his heart to start beating again. Shail gasped for air as his body began quivering and shaking. But his eyes were fixed and dilated. "I told you I could make him jump," Gus slurred as he took another swig from the liquor bottle and soon passed out on the floor. Gus had unknowingly saved

Shail's live. Shail's mind was too far gone, to concentrate on attempting a second suicide. The disabling depression owned him now.

In the morning, Mollie went to the room to check on the golden harpy. She had been worried about him but there was nothing she could do. She opened the door and put her hand to her mouth as she saw Shail. He was fastened to the top of the cage his limbs were extended far apart and stretched tightly across the bars. Blood and fluid ran down his legs and pooled below him. Gus and the two men lay, exposed against the wall, past out. She dashed out and raced to Bill's office. He had just come in to get ready for the day. "I want you to see this," she said, fighting back the tears. Bill followed her to the room and found the harpy and his brother. Bill walked up to Gus and kicked him hard, waking the sleeping man.

"What have you done? You fool!" Bill screamed at him.

Gus scrambled to his feet. "What!" he snapped back. "Oh, the harpy. The boys and I were just having a little fun. We didn't hurt him. Well, not too bad. Hey, you wanted him angry. This is the best way to make a stud animal hate men. Besides I've been stuck in that lousy jungle. I wanted some," Gus mumbled.

"Just shut up!" Bill shouted. Mollie began to undo the shackles and ropes that held Shail's limbs.

"Hey, don't do that. He'll take off," Gus yelled.

"He's not going anywhere, I can assure you," Mollie seethed. As she unfastened the harpy, he slowly slid to the floor like an inanimate doll. His eyes were closed, as if in a deep sleep. Mollie opened one eye and shook her head.

"Is he going to be alright?" Bill fretted.

She breathed deeply. "I don't know. It looks like severe shock or depression. Take your pick. His whole body has shut down. Let's get him to that large display cage, where I can start treating him. It's going to take a lot of drugs to bring him back. I'll give him some anti-depressants and stimulants. We'll have to wait and see."

One of Bill's employees entered the room. Bill asked him to take the harpy to the display cage out front. The man gently picked up the lethargic fragile harpy in his arms. "Can you manage him alone?" Bill asked.

The man nodded. "He's an armful with his wings but his lean body doesn't weigh much, less than a hundred pounds," the man said. He carried Shail to the large cage and placed him in the straw. Mollie came in and administered the drugs. She gently tied Shail's little harpy sash around his hips, covering his nude body. As she did this, Mollie began to cry. She had never mourned for a harpy before. But this golden was different. He had not been some frightened animal that slunk in a cage. The lean young male had shown courage and intelligence. Mollie knew that even if he survived, all that would be gone.

Hours past and Shail did not move. Molly covered him with blankets to keep him warm and suggested they move the cage outside to enclosed hunting range. "The warm light and fresh air might help him," she said. She realized the harpy was very close to death.

"Mollie, can you wash and groom him? Make him look like we're at least taking proper care of him. The reporters are coming this afternoon," Bill said wearily.

The drugs began to work on Shail and he slowly opened his eyes to a blank stare. Every so often his body would tremble as if he were cold. The afternoon came and Bill escorted a man and woman out to the cage. Mollie sat nearby. "Yes, we have to keep him sedated for now. Of course, you've heard harpies are fragile. They just don't do well in captivity," Bill said to the couple. They looked at the golden harpy but Shail did not respond to their presence.

"Oh, he's so beautiful. Where did you find him?" the woman asked.

Bill answered. "Now, you know we can't disclose that information. I'd like you both to meet his handler. This is Mollie. She can answer more questions about the harpy's maintenance." Bill grimaced a little as he looked at Mollie. She knew not to discuss the events that had left Shail close to being dysfunctional.

"Hello," Mollie said quietly as she shook hands with the two reporters.

"What can you tell us about the harpy?" the woman reporter asked Mollie while they stood in front of his cage.

"Well, he is a rare golden harpy. It's said, these blond harpies protected the flocks of brown but since this is the last one, it's hard to say now what role they played in nature. Although this little fellow did display more courage than any average harpy."

The woman reporter smiled at Shail. "He's so adorable and seems very sweet."

"Well, he is sedated, as Bill said," Mollie remarked.

"So, he can be dangerous?" Is it true about the stories of harpies stealing and raping women?" she asked.

"I can't confirm or deny those stories. But, I find it hard to believe. I have found that male harpies are very gentle creatures when I handle them. This one is sedated more for his own safety. Wild adult harpies become severely depressed in captivity and they're hard to maintain. This why they make impossible pets."

Bill did not like the tone of the conversation and stepped in. "You can tell Mollie is very fond of harpies. But let me assure you, this golden is capable of rape and is dangerous. My brother was injured last week by this harpy when he tried to put it in a cage," Bill said hastily.

"I don't think I'd like being put in a cage either," said the man reporter.

The woman grinned as she stared at Shail. "I can see why you're so fond of them. He's absolutely gorgeous. I've never seen any man as stunning as him and those large deep blue eyes are to die for. Do all male harpies look like him?"

"All male harpies have tall lean handsome frames with almost a pixy-like face but this golden is the most striking harpy, I've ever seen."

The female reporter nodded. "Yes, if I could be enchanted in the night by a winged male fairy, this is the one I would chose. Can this harpy be handled or is he too wild?" she asked Mollie. Mollie just smiled and went into Shail's cage. She sat down beside Shail and coaxed him to rest his head on her lap as she began stroking his neck and back. Shail closed his eyes and cuddled closer to Mollie and the comforting touch. Unconsciously Shail nuzzled his nose and face against her side.

"I need to get some pictures of this. Look how friendly it is?" the man said and took his camera out. He began to photograph Mollie while she held the affectionate little harpy.

"Don't you want some photos of his wings? My men can hold him down and extend his wings out. That's what most people want to see. Did I tell you, he has a sixteen foot wing span?" Bill asked nervously.

The woman turned to him. "Yes, Mr. Simpson, you told us that already. Let me be very clear about our article. We're not game or sport writers. We're here to do more of a human-interest story. You have claimed you have captured the last golden harpy. This interests a lot of people that he will be destroyed in your hunting range."

"Well, most the people on this planet dislike harpies and are glad to be rid of them. Don't forget that when you write your story or you'll have some important people upset with your little rag. Harpies are nothing but a danger and a nuisance to the people of Dora," he snapped. This female reporter was beginning to irritate him and it was apparent she was instantly fond of the golden.

"Don't worry, Mr. Simpson, our story will be fair. I don't believe most of our readers have ever seen an adult harpy much less have an opinion of one. I plan on telling a complete story on this species." The woman looked at the hunting range. "Your range is very picturesque. It looks like a tropical garden except for the bars over the top."

This seemed to please Bill as he gleamed, "Yes, we went to great expense to make it look natural like the jungle. We wanted the animals and hunters to feel like they are in the wild."

"Well, not exactly in the wild. In the wild, the animals, like this harpy, have a chance of escaping their death. Here, they are eventually cornered against a wall or the bars. Doesn't seem very sporting," the woman reporter commented as she looked at the high log walls that surrounded the range and the bars overhead.

"Well, the animals had their chance to escape before they were captured and brought here. Some of these animals can injure a hunter when he goes after them," Bill growled.

"So, you'll just turn that pretty thing loose in here and the high bidder will hunt him down with his weapon?" the reporter asked and turned her attention back to the harpy.

"Yes, that's about it," Bill responded.

"I guess it's all about their wings. The sports hunters really enjoy hanging these feather trophies on their walls. It's unbelievable, they would want to kill such a beautiful creature that resembles a human being," she commented sadly.

"Is there anything else?" Bill said agitated.

"No, I think I have all the information I need. I'd like to have my photographer take a few more pictures of the harpy alone if that's alright," she asked.

"Fine," Bill stated with annoyance.

Mollie got up and left the cage as the woman began to instruct the man with the camera. "See if you can get a close up of his boy like face and eyes," she said. Shail lay quietly curled up on his side. He seemed to be in a trance and unaware of his surroundings. Suddenly he sniffed the air and his ears twitched under the blond hair as Shail heard and smelled a human that filled him with horror.

"Bill, you're wanted on the com," Gus called as he had entered the range and walked towards the display cage. Shail cautiously rose to a sitting position. His eyes became alert and his body shuddered with fright. The harpy breathed rapidly while his hands clutched the straw.

"There. Get that shot," the woman report yelled to her photographer as she saw the despondent harpy come to life. The man quickly took the pictures, just before Shail sprang to his feet and dove into the straw on the far corner of the cage. He burrowed frantically beneath the thick straw to hide. Now the yellow straw and his pale gold wings and blond hair blended together to create such an impressive camouflage, it appeared the harpy had vanished from the cage. The woman reporter looked at Gus when he came along side of the cage.

"This harpy is terrified of you."

Gus chuckled. "Yes, I'm the one who brought him in from the outback. See what that kicking little buck did to my face? It's still black and blue."

The woman reporter looked back at the covered harpy. She could see the petrified blue eyes peering out between the straw and his blond locks. The feathers on his wings quivered with fear, over the animals tightly curled up body. "I'd be more interested in what you did to him?" she asked.

Before Gus could answer, Bill interrupted. "This interview is over now," he grumbled. Mollie led the reporters out of the range and to the enormous front room, where the auction would take place.

Bill looked at Gus. "That reporter is going to crucify us with her story. She was taken with that harpy the minute that bleeding heart bitch set eyes on him," Bill said angrily.

"Hey, she saw my bruises," Gus said.

"Yes, and she also saw the harpy's reaction to you. It's apparent, you abused it."

Gus smiled at his brother. "Look at the bright side, Bill, at least the harpy reacted. Shows his mind is still working. Isn't it, fella?" Gus said to Shail. Shail desperately dug deeper, tossing the straw over him until he was completely hidden. Mollie came back after escorting the reporters out.

"What do you think, Mollie? This is the most movement we've seen from him all day," Bill asked her.

"Yes, the drugs are starting to work. Thankfully, I was able to treat him before his mind was completely gone. But the only emotion he has left is fear. He's a normal caged harpy now. When the auction comes, he'll just shiver and try to hide in the corner of his cage. And I'll have to keep him loaded with those drugs until the auction. There's only one thing that little harpy wants right now. And that is to die. Good job, Gus. You took the only harpy I've ever seen with backbone and turned him into a frightened bunch of feathers. And Bill, if you don't keep Gus away from him, it could all go south again. You could still lose him with one more bad experience. His state of mind is extremely fragile now. He could easily faint and slip into a coma from stress and shock. If it happens, no amount of drugs will bring him back."

"Gus, you and your buddies are to stay away from the harpy. You got that? There's too much at risk," Bill ordered angrily.

Gus just smiled as he watched the terrified harpy that finally feared him. "Sure, Bill. I think that harpy paid me back for the kick in the face." Gus then turned to Mollie with a fiendish smile. "Your beautiful little boy put out just fine. Didn't stop struggling till dawn. Just the way I like it."

Mollie shuddered as Gus got near her. She disliked him from the beginning and now, she loathed him. "Who knew what things he was capable of" she thought to herself.

Evening came and Mollie stayed with the harpy all night. She wasn't about to leave him alone with Gus still around. She gave Shail the anti depressants in his arm and he no longer fought back when she administered them. He had stopped shaking, after Gus left but it had taken a while. Mollie was surprised when she lifted Shail's head and poured some fruit juice down his throat and he did not resist any of this treatment. "They really did take all the fight out of you," she said sadly to the harpy. He would only curl up, burying his head in the straw and close his eyes. He definitely lacked any motivation and the will to live. Only her drugs were keeping him alive.

Saturday morning came and Shail's high twelve by twelve foot cage was wheeled into the large front room and then roped off. Bill came out of his office with the news media machine in his hand. "Well, they did it. It's nothing but a big sympathy story for the harpies. There's one small paragraph in there about the lack of proof of harpies attacking women," he said to Mollie with disgust. "Look, they didn't even use any of the pictures of you and the harpy, just one of his face. Hell, he doesn't even look like a harpy in this picture. He looks more like a movie star. Can't even see his wings." Bill rambled on angrily.

One of Bill's employees approached him. "There's a line of people forming around the building, Mr. Simpson. When do you want us to let them in?" the man asked.

"Not for another hour. The time is set for 10:00 A.M. I can't believe there's people here already."

Mollie looked at the article and remarked, "They're probably sick of reading about the destruction of Terrance and the swarms in the west. This harpy is something to take their minds off their fears."

Gus walked in. "Bill, have you seen all the people out front? It's unreal we'll make a killing. What do you want me to do around here? Act as a bouncer?" Gus gleamed happily.

Shail, who had been looking around a little, dove into the straw on seeing Gus. "Gus, look what you did now. You got the harpy hiding again. These people are going to be disappointed if they only see a few feathers and some of them are the bidders. I want you to take your two buddies and go to a bar for the day. And don't come back here until it's over. Is that clear?" Bill ordered.

"I think I can handle that," Gus said and headed for the back door.

At ten, the security guards opened the doors as the crowd began to file in after paying their ten credits to see the golden harpy. Mollie had given Shail a large dose of tranquilizers, along with the other drugs to control some of his trembling. Putting him in a room with hundreds of humans was not the best therapy he needed now but there was no other choice.

The people began to gather around his cage. Shail was so numb from the drugs that he just laid quietly on his side in the straw while gazing and listened to the humans talk. He didn't care about them or anything else. Only Gus and his two men would cause him to react with terror. Shail could only focus on the assault that left him devastated. In one night, he had lost himself. His human emotions of love, hate, joy and sadness had been all stripped away. Only the basic animal instinct of fear remained alive in him. And, it was only fear that held him to the present.

Mollie stood by his cage along with several security guards while the people milled around the harpy cage. She listened to the conversations about the harpy. Most of these people were seeing an adult harpy for the first time. When they looked into his cage, they became very quiet and sad. It seemed more like a funeral than an exotic animal exhibit. One little girl began to cry, as she pleaded with her mother for answers. "Why does he have to die, Mom? What did the pretty harpy do?" the child called loud enough for the whole room to hear her. Her mother could not answer the girls' questions.

And so, the tone was set. Apparently the crowd had come expecting to see a raping winged devil, a true monster from ancient Greek mythology but they were filled with sorrow when they saw, the harpy was no monster. "Bill was right," Mollie thought. "He knew this might happen the moment he saw the flawless golden." A sympathy rose in crowd for the exquisite young male with long flowing cream wings that resembled an angel, rather than any devil.

Kari and Ted pushed their way through the crowd until they finally were in front of Shail's cage. She smiled wide, when she saw him since he appeared to be unharmed. He was curled up and calmly glancing out at the crowd of people. She called to him silently, "Shail, I'm here. We're going to get you out of here soon," she communicated to him. But he did not answer her. Kari called in silence several more times, pleading with him to answer her but he acted as if he didn't hear her subconscious thoughts. Then she began to get a dark feeling from him. This was not the Shail she had known. Something was terribly wrong. She could not detect any of his feelings or emotions. It was as if he had none. Kari noticed a woman standing by the cage next to a security guard. "Is the harpy alright?" she asked the woman.

The woman smiled at Kari. "He's fine. We just have him a little sedated to keep him relaxed," Mollie answered.

"I don't believe you. Something terrible has happened to him." Kari said harshly.

The woman looked at her with surprise and then glanced back at the harpy but didn't notice anything different about him. Now Kari was becoming very upset. She cried out loud in a demanding voice. "Shail, answer me!" The whole room went quiet and stared at the strange pretty girl. But their attention soon went to the harpy's cage as the harpy uncurled his body and sat up. Then he slid closer to the bars and leaned toward the girl.

"Forget me Kari. I am lost to you," Shail related to her in silence.

"No, my father is going to take you out of here and we'll be together in two more lights," Kari answered with the harpy telepathy.

"No, though I breathe, I am dead. I wish no rescue. Leave this dangerous place and save your self and our son," he related and lowered his head and eyes. He then laid back down on the straw and curled up, covering himself with his wings.

"Oh, Shail," Kari spoke softly, "What have they done to you?" Shail would not respond to her further. Kari fought back the tears as she stared at her handsome harpy husband. Even the island hunters of Westend, who had nearly killed him, had not broken his spirit like this. She could only sense a deep dark terror within him.

A security guard came up to Ted. "I think it would be best if you both left now," he said after Kari's out burst. Ted nodded and led Kari outside. They sat on the edge of the sidewalk while Kari tried to get a grip on her emotions and the line of people passed them.

Soon her father and Charlie walked up. "Is it Shail? Is he alright?" John asked with concern when he saw his distressed daughter.

"He's not alright, Dad. Something awful has happened to him. He doesn't want to be saved. He doesn't want to come back to me. He only wants to die," she said with a sniffle.

"Ted, can you take her back to the hotel? I need to go in there and register for this auction." John asked.

"Sure, Mr. Turner. I won't leave her alone," Ted answered.

John put his arms around Kari. "We'll get him back and once he's free again, he'll be alright. He's suffered a lot in the last few months. Most harpies would not have survived a cage or the abuse he's been through. But, he's strong and even I know how much he cares about you. In two days this will all be over and then he can live on the estate in peace. I promise, I'll protect him from any more harm. You and Shail will have a long happy life even if I have to surround the estate with security guards. I promise, I'll get him back for you, Kari."

Kari looked helplessly up at her father. For the first time in years, she felt like a little girl again and her father was her hero. He was going to make everything okay. She hugged him and whispered, "Thank you, Dad."

Kari and Ted left, as John and Charlie went into the building. "They have a lot of security guards," Charlie mentioned.

John read the old man's mind. If they could not buy him back, perhaps he could be stolen. "Yes, too many," John said.

They walked up to the cage and looked at the harpy. Shail was curled up with his wings over him. They could barely see his sleeping face under the feathers. "It must be hard for her to see her wild spirited mate caged like this," Charlie commented.

John nodded his head. "I'll go find the office to register." John walked into the offices off the large room and found six other men waiting their turn.

"John Turner," said a man's voice.

John turned around and recognized the short stubby balding man seated to his left. "Senator, I'm surprised they're making you wait," John said to the man.

"Yes, well, I guess us senators don't get priority, when it comes to killing the last golden harpy. But I'm amazed you're here. I heard, you had become one of those harpy lover since you ban all the hunting on your property." the senator smirked.

John smiled smugly. "Maybe I put the ban on so I could do all the hunting myself. Why should I share with others?"

"Yes, I do remember that you killed a magnificent golden harpy some twenty something years ago," the senator said as he studied the tall blond man.

"Yes, I believe I still hold the golden record with that one. But, I've come here so I can have a matching pair of gold wings," John stated.

"I don't think that blond male will break any wing record, too young. It would have been better if he was at least in his thirties but it's hard to find one that old these days. Too many hunters but he certainly is a seductive handsome creature. Has all our women drooling over him. Of course, that has always been the magnetism of these animals. The sooner they're exterminated, the better. Wouldn't you agree, John?" the senator asked.

"Extermination is a pretty strong word. Are these harpies are some kind of threat to you?" John asked with a smile. The Senator Blackwell suddenly became very uncomfortable with the question and quickly fled with a sheepish smile, grateful, it was his turn.

John's turn came, as he walked into the office and was met by a large man. "I'm Bill Simpson, the owner. Nice of you to come, despite the negative publicity."

"Turner, John Turner."

"Say, are you the same Turner that has an estate on the west coast?" Bill asked.

"One and the same," John answered.

"I heard your place is loaded with harpies. What brings you all this way?"

"Well, I've been hunting that little gold male for some time. I'm not about to lose him now. But he doesn't look very lively and he acts awfully docile compared to last time I spotted him. Hate to spend a lot of credits if there is no challenge in the hunt."

"He's fine. We just have him tranquilized. When we take him off the drugs, he'll be wild and lively and give you a good hunt. Well, fill in these papers. You don't even have to verify your accounts. I know you're good for the credits. And I'll get you a bid number."

Bill returned with a number. "Two hundred and seventy six, I hope it brings you good luck."

"That's a high number. You have that many bidders already?" John asked.

"Yes, sir. They're pouring in across the galaxy. Well, thank you, Mr. Turner and I'll look forward to seeing you Monday night."

"Yes, well I may be back tomorrow to check on him. No sense in staying till Monday, if he takes a slide down hill," John said.

"Oh, we're taking good care of him. You don't have to worry about that. But if you do come back tomorrow, just show them your number and you won't have to pay the ten credits to get in," Bill said with a grin. John nodded and left his office.

Charlie was waiting by the harpy cage. "How is he?" John asked as he walked up.

Charlie sighed deeply. "Kari is right. This is not the same little bold golden we have seen. He is no longer proud or cocky. He shivers with fright but yet he does not fear the crowd. With them, he is indifferent. His mind is not right and don't think any drug would cause this. He acts like an unnerved wild animal that has suffered a terrible trauma and now is drugged," Charlie said as he studied the harpy. John stepped closer. Shail was awake now. He didn't even bother to look at John or the other people but gazed down at the straw. Every so often, his whole body would tremble and he would swallow deeply. It was as if he was trying to maintain control of himself. John approached the security guard that stood at one of the corners of the cage. He showed him his bid number.

"Would you mind if I take a closer look at this harpy?" John asked.

"Sure mister," the guard said and lifted the rope up that held the crowd back.

John looked directly in to Shail's eyes as he came close to the cage bars. "You know who I am?" John said quietly with a firm voice. "I have seen your courage. Don't let these men take it from you. You will survive this captivity. You and Kari will be together again, as it should have been. With the same honor you asked of me to protect her and your son, I now extend it to you. I will free you from this place. Stay strong, Shail."

The security guard moved closer and said, "Sorry, sir. Can't have you talking to the harpy. It may upset him."

"Sorry, I'm done inspecting him. He looks fine," John said and bent back down under the rope. Shail stared at Kari's father and breathed deeply. John nodded to him. Shail shut his eyes and tossed the long blond locks back. John could see the torment in the young harpy and knew, that Shail had listened to him. The harpy looked back at him and John could see the harpy's eyes water slightly as his face filled with remorse. Shail curled back up and laid his wings back over him. The feathers fluttered faintly. John shook his head sadly and wondered if the harpy could be saved, even if he was freed. The drugs were keeping him alive, just as they had kept Kari alive, when despair and hopelessness had filled her mind. "What had these men done to him to change him so?" he wondered, recalling his last encounter with this harpy. This gallant sleek golden, who boldly told him, he didn't care how he was killed, as he dropped to his knees without a fight and offered up his life for the sake of his mate and his unborn son. It was the bravest act, John had ever witnessed.

John and Charlie left to return to the hotel. Shail had listened to the man called Turner, Kari's father. As he dwelled on his words, he felt sick inside. He tried to swallow but there was a lump in his throat that he could not rid himself of. Yes, he wanted to be strong. Strong for his mate, for the son that would come, for his people, even for the jungle, that only he could save. But now, he couldn't even be strong for himself. He only felt weak and dishonored and terrified. He did not know how to rid himself of this doomed feeling. He trembled automatically when he heard the cage door open. He moved his wing slightly and saw Mollie coming towards him with another one of her drugs. She gently pulled his wing back and gave him a dose in his arm. He didn't even have the will power to rebel against it. "All the people are gone now. You did real good, my little prince," she said as she petted him. "We'll move your cage back outside again. I think you like it better out there. I know you don't understand me but those men will not hurt you again. I'll stay with you and protect you. Soon this will be all over and you'll get the peace, you want. You'll never have to shake with fear again," she spoke softly to him and massaged his shivering body. He rested his head against her and softly licked her hand. Shail understood her words, better than she knew. The peace she spoke of would come with his death. But oddly enough, this brought him comfort. Perhaps this strange woman did understand harpies better than most humans.

A couple of men moved the cage that sat on rollers, back to the hunting range and placed it under cover of an extended awning that came out from the doors. It was clouding up, as evening approached and could possibly rain. Mollie sat down on the straw next to Shail as she held a container of juice. She coaxed him to put his head in her lap and then forced small sips down his throat. It began to get dark so she stretched out on the straw. Shail curled up next to her. Her warm body consoled him while her kind hands stroked his neck under the long blond hair. She watched him close his eyes. Mollie realized that this wild unruly harpy had become totally domesticated. The men had broken his spirit completely. This harpy would be no challenging game animal when he was hunted. He had become as tame as a dog. The harpy would better serve as a human pet now. She prayed that possibly the harpy would be so docile and affectionate during the auction that perhaps a zoo would bid on him and spare his life. Shail nestled his head against her side and nuzzled her, encouraging her to pet him. She smiled at the sweet little harpy. "Yes, you just keep acting this way and maybe it will save you, even though I know, you don't want to live," she said softly. Mollie could not help but leaned over and kiss his cheek. They snuggled in the straw and soon were asleep.

In the middle of the night Shail heard a noise. It was the doors opening to the range. He then smelled a distinct odor. It was one he would never forget, the smell of whiskey. He sat up and saw Gus standing in the doorway. Shail immediately scrambled to the farthest corner of the cage. When he did this, it woke Mollie and she sat up. Gus walked in with the two other men. She could tell, that they had been drinking heavily.

"Gus, Bill told you to stay away from the harpy," she stated.

"He ain't my boss and I do what I feel like it," Gus slurred "Besides, me and the boys missed our little stud. Came to see if he missed us. But I see he has you. Why do you like that harpy more than me?"

"Gus, you're drunk. You need to go sleep it off," Mollie said and stood up in the cage. She walked to the cage door and unlocked it. As she pushed to open it, Gus slammed it hard shut again and grinned at her.

"Tell me Mollie, do you have as much fight in you as that harpy?" he slurred again.

"Gus, just leave the harpy and me alone," she ordered.

Gus glanced at the frightened harpy in the corner of the cage. "I'm not going to jump him again. We rode him till we broke him down the other night. But I gotta give that buck credit. He fought that riding longer than any tough inmate. Didn't you boy?" he said to Shail. "Besides, that harpy's gonna die making my brother and me rich. Don't wanna risk all that money but how about you, Mollie, care to be rode?" he laughed

"Gus, open this door," Mollie said a little nervously.

"Sure, I'll open it but the boys and I are comin in and you're not going any where," Gus said as he stepped inside the cage. "I've been thinking about all those women who are in love with this little stud. I wonder how they'd feel if he raped you. Bet that would change their minds." Gus had now moved in front of Mollie.

"That harpy won't hurt me or anyone else. He's as gentle as a little bird now, thanks to you." Mollie stammered and tried to move away from the vulgar man.

"Yea, he's pretty harmless now. But I, on the other hand really enjoy raping some thing that puts up a fight. It turns me on," He chuckled.

"Gus, don't do this. You don't want to go back to prison especially when you're about to be so rich," Mollie tried to reason with the huge drunken man.

Gus laughed out loud. "What makes you think I'd go back to prison? That only happens if there's a witness. The only witness is gonna be your scared little bird."

"Gus, please, you know I always liked you. I just like to tease you," she pleaded.

"Oh, Mollie, I like you too but this is business. When they find you dead and raped in this cage, they'll think the harpy did it. Everyone knows harpies rape women. This will solve all of Bill's problems. All those bleeding heart harpy lovers will change their tune and the hunters will bid higher to hunt a rapist killer animal," he said as he shoved her hard against the bars of the cage. "See, Mollie, I'm not that drunk. I'm smarter than you think," he leered and grabbed her shirt and ripped the front open, exposing her breasts. Molly went to hit him but he slugged her violently, sending her down on the straw. Then he savagely tore the rest of her cloths off. "Gag her mouth with this so the guards out front won't hear her," he ordered, handing her shirt to the other two men, who hastily jumped in the cage to feast on the naked female. Mollie was only knocked out temporarily and she struggled to get the many hands off of her that rubbed her body. "Hold her," Gus slurred as he frantically undid his pants.

"Gus, what about him?" one of the men asked, motioning to the scared harpy that hid in the cage corner.

Gus chuckled as he looked at Shail. "Don't worry about him. He can't hurt a fly now besides that little stud will see how a real breeding is done," Gus said and opened up a small container, popping a few pills in his mouth. He handed the contained to the other men. "Let's do another all nighter. This bitch deserves to feel what it's like be laid properly before she dies." He climbed on top of the nude, scared woman and forced himself in her. The pills Gus took, allowed him to stay stimulated throughout the night.

Shail watched as he hid under his wings. Each man took turns ravaging his gentle female handler. As one viciously copulated in her, the other two men would sinisterly fondle her body until it was their turn. Mollie only fought them briefly and soon she could only lay and moaned in pain, accepting her fate. They had done the same to him. The hours slipped by as Shail witnessed this brutal attack. Slowly his fear began to subside as it was replaced with other emotions he had lost. It was his rage and courage returning. He breathed deeply with anger, picturing himself beneath these men, as this endless cruel assault continued. His heart began to fill with the hate, the emotion that was not part of a harpy's true nature.

Gus was back on Mollie as he slammed her hard and cursed her. "Come on, bitch, move," he stammered with aggravation. Mollie's eyes were half closed and she lay limp. Gus copulated in her while the other men leaned against the out side of the cage, joking and sipping from the whiskey bottle. They were no longer needed to restrain the battered woman. Suddenly Mollie's half closed eyes opened wide and she stared past Gus. Behind him, stood the golden harpy.

In an instant Shail grabbed Gus by the neck and had him in a sleeper hold. The other men were so startled they could only watch the slender harpy quickly throttled and choked Gus into unconsciousness. Now they scrambled inside the cage door to save Gus. One of them pulled a knife from his belt. Shail released his hold of the large man and he collapsed on top of Mollie. Shail now faced the other two men as they backed him in a corner. "You grab him, I'll stick him," the man uttered holding the knife.

Mollie managed to slide out from under the huge stunned body of Gus and she crawled to the open cage door. She gathered her remaining strength and tumbled out on to the floor. Mollie limped toward the range doors but glanced back as the cornered harpy hissed at the two men. Then she staggered through the doors.

One of the men lunged at Shail but Shail grabbed his arm and swung him hard with force against the iron bars and he fell stunned into the straw. The other man tried to slash the harpy with his knife but Shail swiftly snatched his wrist. The harpy twisted the wrist harshly forcing the man to release the knife as he fought to be free. Shail jumped up and kicked him hard with both feet in the ribs, knocking him backwards. The man struggled to his knees, holding his broken wrist and ribs as he stared with shock at the quick powerful lean frame. Shail calmly picked up the knife and went to the petrified man. Shail clutched the man's hair and jerked his neck back, exposing his throat.

"Is this how it is done? Is this how you, hunters kill a harpy?" Shail asked the man using his soft human voice. The man screamed with horror as he tried to fight off the harpy's hold. Shail quickly cut the noisy man's throat and watched him, gag on his own blood. The other man, realizing he was next, feebly climbed to his feet and made a dash for the open cage door. Shail sprung at him and seized him by his hair, jerking him backwards off his feet. The terrified man crawled on his knees to escape while Shail casually walked in front of him blocking the exit. The terrified man stared up at the harpy as it flipping his long blond hair in annoyance and faced his kneeling victim. The harpy grabbed the struggling man's hair and jerked his neck back.

"No, please, no!" the man begged as he gazed at the harpy's face and saw the hate and vengeance that filled the royal blue eyes. Shail slit his throat and kicked the twitching dying body over, away from him.

Gus woke in time to witness Shail kill the last of his two criminal pals. The slender harpy boldly walked to him and stood holding the knife in his blood soaked hands. Gus slowly rose to his feet, astonished by the lethal little harpy. He cautiously watched the harpy toss its hair, while sniffling for a challenge. It leered at him with contempt and then amazingly, it spoke to him with calm quiet tone. "You stole my honor but some remains to give you a painless death as these others."

"You can speak!" Gus murmured with shock.

"Yes, I speak. I speak now so you shall know with this death, you taught me well to have this hate."

Gus suddenly lunged at the harpy, knocking Shail off his feet. They fought for control of the knife as they wrestled in the cage. The knife slipped from Shail's hand and it fell into the blood soaked straw. Gus tried to rest his huge body on top of the creature to pin the wild little harpy down but it was able to gather its legs beneath it, curling up and kicking Gus on the same side of his face that was bruised earlier. Then it slid out from under him. Shail sprung with lightening speed to his feet as Gus slowly got up and rubbed his sore cheek. He then laughed a little.

"When I get a hold of you, buck, you're gonna wish you were dead," Gus seethed in pain.

"This death, I already wish for," Shail said with his silky voice. They stalked each other. Gus weighed almost four times as much as the harpy but the harpy was much quicker. Gus hurdled himself at Shail. He knew, if he could knock the harpy to his back he could out muscle its limbs. Shail flapped his wings slightly and flew to the top of the cage over the man. Before Gus could turn, the harpy landed on his back and grabbed him by the neck. Gus struggled to throw off the wiry little harpy that rode his back. He jumped backwards, slamming Shail hard against the cage bars. But Shail continued to cling to this giant beast of a man. Gus became frantic as he realized that he was in the fight for his life. Though the harpy had a willowy lean body, it was all muscle, which made him strong and agile. Shail wrapped one arm around the big man's neck, while Gus continued to ram the harpy against the cage while pulling at its arm. Shail quickly managed to take his other hand and grab Gus's jaw. With several swift powerful twisted jerks, Shail finally heard the popping sound of Gus's thick neck breaking. The large man staggered for a moment before collapsing beneath Shail. The cruel man's whole body shook uncontrollably and he stared up at the defiant harpy that sniffled mockingly at his defeated enemy. With his last kick, Gus grinned. Shail shuddered as he sensed the sadistic man's last thoughts. He ruffled his feathers and stepped out of the open cage door.

Mollie stumbled through the building until she reached the outside. Finally she spotted a couple of security guards that were stationed out front. She screamed hysterical to them. "They're going to kill the harpy." They ran to the range while she followed them as best she could. The guards called on their radios for back up as they raced for the hunting range. None expected the gruesome sight that awaited them. The harpy's cage door was open. In the cage lay the three large dead men. The blood from their sliced throats dripped down the cage sides and pooled on the floor. One of the guards checked the bodies. "They're dead all right. Where to you suppose the harpy is?" one man said to the other as they peered nervously into the small dark forest of the hunting range. "I don't get paid enough to go in there after him," said the other.

By now, four other guards had joined Mollie by the doors. A security guard wrapped one of Shail's blankets around her as she cried out of control. Seeing the three dead men, the security guards stayed close to the entrance and called Bill. "The harpy has killed three men, one is your brother and it's loose in the range." a guard told him.

Stay by the doors and don't let it past you. It can't get out. I'll be right there," Bill said wearily. One of the guards saw Mollie's bruised face and the welts that covered her body.

"Did the harpy do this to you?" he asked gently.

"No!" she cried. "Gus and those men in the cage raped me and were going to kill me, the harpy saved me, do you understand, he saved my life? Please don't hurt him. Please," she begged.

Bill arrived at the same time as the authorities. Bill went to the harpy cage and saw his dead brother. He shook his head in grief.

"That woman claims, these men raped her and were going to kill her," a police sergeant told Bill.

"My brother would never do that. He probably was killed trying to save her. She was getting a little too close to that raping murderous creature. You've heard how these poor women lose their minds after they fall victim to a harpy molesting. Let me talk to her. She's only confused"

"Well, Mr. Simpson, at first light, we'll go in there and kill that creature. There's no doubt he's dangerous and needs to be destroyed," stated the officer.

"No, he's too valuable. He's going to be killed on Tuesday after my auction. My men and I can stun him and get him back into a cage. He can't escape my range. Have a little heart I just lost my brother. Besides that animal doesn't deserve a quick death. If you let me keep him till he's hunted, I can make it well worth your while." Bill enticed the officer in charge.

The officer grinned with the offer. "Fine. We'll assist you with the capture and if I'm satisfied the animal is secured properly, we may work something out but you need to talk with that female handler before she has others looking into this incident. They'll check the sperm's D.N.A. of this rape and see who really is guilty of assaulting her. It will drag out this investigation. In the meantime, your harpy will become property of the courts." Bill nodded, perceiving the inconvenience Mollie could cause. He went to her. "Come dear, there's a robe in my office we can put on you," he said and gently lead her away.

Once in the office, Bill put the robe on her and closed the door. "It must have been awful," Bill said.

Mollie began to weep again. "Gus was going to kill me. He and his men would not stop."

"Now, Mollie, you're just upset and confused. The harpy is the one who raped you and was going to kill you. Poor Gus gave his life to protect you," Bill said calmly.

She stared up at him in bewilderment. "But that's not what happened," she said slowly and uneasily.

"It is what happened and if you say different or cause me trouble, I may have to step in and finish what my brother started. And I'm a lot worse than he was. I just have more brains. I know the people that can make you disappear. Now, do we understand each other?" he asked coldly. Mollie only nodded with fear. "That's a good girl. I always knew you were smart. One of those nice officers will take you to a hospital so they can finish their report on how that nasty harpy attacked you" he said sweetly and opened the door. A policeman took her away.

CHAPTER 8

▼

Shail stepped out of the cage as he gazed back at the dead men. He breathed deeply, feeling this hate that burned within him. Spreading his wings, he flew the length of the hunting range. He soon learned he was still a prisoner in a larger cage. Shail found a small pond in the darkness and landed beside it. The men's blood covered his arms and legs and he wanted to be free of it. "They shall never soil me again," he thought as the cool water rinsed his body. With their deaths, Shail assumed his hate and scorn would wash away like their blood. But he was wrong. His mind could only dwell on how he had been cruelly molested and this had created a powerful hate that filled him with prejudice against all men. As the humans yearned to exterminate his race, he now only wished to exterminate them. He was consumed by this human emotion that ate at his soul. He did not fully understand the hate and it troubled him. Gone was his reasoning to see good from bad. He could only feel the tremendous desire for revenge. Shail wondered if he would ever be whole again. Shaking the water from him, he realized, his decision to rule wisely was lost. He would gladly sacrifice all of his male harpies to destroy these humans and satisfy his vengeance.

When the blood was gone, he flew to the highest tree near the bars of the cage. Shail tried to slow his heart rate and create his own death but the large drug doses remained in him and it was impossible. With the morning light, the men would begin their hunt and probably kill him. Shail was resolved and content with this fate knowing he could be a threat to his own race. The swarms would come and kill all these humans and cleanse the land. Hopefully, the harpies would survive somehow until his son was old enough to reign. Shail called out silently in the dark, hoping to contact one last harpy before he died. If any were close, they would sense him and come to this location. Shail noticed the first rays of dawn as it crept up into the dark cloud filled sky. It was then that a half grown harpy landed on the bars above him. Shail stood up from the tree limb as the young harpy stared down at him in awe. "Your wings are pale. You are our golden ruler, we search for!" the young harpy exclaimed and immediately bowed his head with respect.

"Yes, I am he. You must listen carefully to my words. Do you know if the beetles are near?" The young harpy nodded.

"Within five lights, they come to the east, my father says. They seek the flesh now and are drawn to this large human place. Do you wish my flock leader, Seth and others to come for you?" the harpy asked.

"No, I do not wish this. Many brave harpies would die with this attempt and I do not wish to be saved." Shail said while reaching back and jerked one of his largest feathers from his wing. "Take my feather to this Seth, so he and all other shall know, we have had these words. These are my wishes. All male harpies from all flocks must gather and kill the swarms after the humans have fled or died. The harpies must not flee to their families. Do you understand this?" The young harpy nodded.

"There is more. Somewhere among these human structures is my mate. She is accompanied by two men, if they can be found, they must be taken to a place of safety."

"You wish to save men?" the young harpy questioned Shail.

Shail could tell that this youngster did not have much experience in dealing with their golden ruler. "You do not question my words, you only follow them," he said firmly to the teenager. The young harpy nodded and lowered his head in shame.

"Heed these words now. These things I say, are very important. The jungle must be saved before the beetles grow too strong. And my mate carries your future golden ruler. These men protect her. Go now, before the light is upon you and you are discovered," Shail said. The young harpy grasped the long cream feather tightly in his hand and in a bound he disappeared into the gray sky.

In the distance, Shail could hear the sounds of many men's voices as it came from the doors. He breathed deeply. "I shall never flee or be hunted again." He stood up and flew toward the sound until he saw a large group of men that stood near the display cage and the doors. Shail landed twenty feet in front of them. They raised their weapons towards him with surprise.

"Don't kill him," cried out Bill.

Shail stared at this brother of Gus and could sense the strong motives to avenge his sibling's death. "This one longs to kill me himself. His weapon shall quickly end my suffering," Shail thought and he dauntlessly approached Bill.

"Mr. Simpson, be careful. It's set it's sights on you and is ready to attack," called a guard.

Shail stopped ten feet away from Bill. The silence was deafening as Shail calmly looked straight into Bill's eyes and waited for the deadly shot from his weapon. The guards and the police officers seemed to be in a trance while they watched the aggressive harpy begin to taunt the man. Shail paced ever closer, tossing and shaking his hair as he tousled and ruffled his feathers, extending and lowering his wings to challenge this adversary. He sniffled and hissed, to provoke his man to attack. All the time, the harpy gazed at the man with an antagonistic proud stare. Shail waited for Bill to grasp his laser gun that hung at his side and reap his revenge. Finally Shail was only at arms length from the man, he teased. instead of grabbing his weapon, Bill swung at the harpy. Shail instinctively fluttered backwards ducking the striking fist. Again, Bill charged at the harpy but Shail swiftly flapped his wings and leaped in the air, striking this man hard with feet. The large clumsy man fell to the ground. Shail stood over the slow stupid human, who had no chance of defeating him in physical combat. Shail sniffled again with aversion as he now sensed this man's true intentions.

"He wishes me alive. My life holds more value than his own brother's," Shail thought with disgust as he stared at the greedy man.

Bill lay stunned and glanced up at the nimble nervy harpy "Grab him," Bill yelled. Shail stood his ground determine not to flee. The guards leaped on Shail as he tried to fight them all off but with twenty men, he was quickly subdued on the ground. Shail struggled against the many hands that pinned him down. Soon the shackles and chains were once again on his wrists and ankles. As he finally lay quietly, Shail ignored these guards but keep a steady insolent stare towards Bill while the man climbed to his feet and stood over him. "Stand him up," Bill ordered his men. "I'll knock that fire right out of you," he threatened with confidence now. He stuck the helpless harpy hard in his stomach causing Shail to slump in the men's arms. "Get him up again," Bill yelled. His fist hit Shail again. Shail's knees buckled slightly and he coughed. "Come on, get him up again. I'm just getting started with this obnoxious little killer," Bill seethed. The men lifted him up. Shail raised his head and shook his hair incorrigibly from his icy cold blue eyes and hissed low and deadly at the man. Bill raised his hand to strike him again but this time a hand went to Bill's arm before it struck.

"That's enough. I'll not stand by and watch you beat this poor thing to death," threatened a young police officer that had joined the guards for the hunt with stun guns.

Bill looked at the officer and collected himself. "Yes, of course, he is nothing but a dumb animal after all. Put a shock collar on him so we have more control over this beast."

Shail snapped at them as they placed the tight leather collar on his neck but they clutched his hair and he couldn't move with so many men holding him. Bill injected him with one of Mollie's drugs. "That should be enough to stop him from shutting down his organs. Need to keep this killer alive for a few more days." The guards carried the harpy back to the display cage and tossed him roughly inside. The cage was now clean of the blood and filled with fresh straw.

The young officer, who stopped the beating, went to Shail's cage with another officer to have better look at this wild bold creature. The officer stared with great puzzlement at the harpy as it shook the straw and loose chains off it body and sat up. It also stared with curiosity at him. "Sure wasn't much of a hunt. Thing flew right to us." the other officer commented as the security guards secured the long chains to the outside bars of the cage.

"This is the first time I've seen one this close. He looks more like a man than an animal," said the young officer named Dale.

"Well, he has a human face and body but look at those wings and his intense wild eyes. You can see he's a savage, winged freak of nature and far from any thing human," said the other officer.

Dale turned annoyed. "How can you say that, no body really knows much about these harpies and look at him, he's as cool as a cucumber and acts pretty darn intelligent."

The other officer rubbed his chin as he studied Shail. "Well, I'll admit he is a handsome flashy little devil and does have guts. But he's still wild and dangerous. He killed those three men and raped and beat that poor woman. These harpies deserve to be hunted and killed."

Dale shook his head sadly. "I have a feeling this little harpy's been badly mistreated. That owner was ready to beat him senseless if I hadn't stopped him. And this is the first recorded case of a harpy killing a man and look how many have been killed by us. Maybe this one just learned to fight back plus there are conflicting statements with that handler's story. She initially told the guards it was the dead men who assaulted her and this harpy had saved her."

"Well, it doesn't matter, if he protected his female handler. He's now considered a man killer and will be destroyed. Wild animals can't claim self-defense like a human. I hear they're auctioning him off to a bunch of hunters Monday night. The sergeant said he's going to let the winning bidder destroy him. Those hunters love to slowly torture a harpy to death. It's odd the Dora senate has never passed a law to stop this kind of animal abuse with the harpies. You could be right about his intelligence. Maybe he flew right to us in hopes of a quick death. Well, I have to get back. I'll see you at the precinct."

Dale only gesture his farewell to the man as his eyes remained fixed on the captivating harpy. "I think, he's right. You really did just want it to be over. Why else would you fly to twenty armed men? Such a waste," he said quietly to Shail. He shook his head and was the last officer to leave the hunting range.

Shail lay down discouraged, longing for the comforting touch of his handler, Mollie. He learned she had lied and blamed him for the attack. Shail was not unsettled by her betrayal since he had found little honor in this race of humans. His own revenge and hate had motivated the killing of the men. She had treated him well and now he missed her caressing hands. Shail's instincts detected her devotion to him. She must have had her reasons for this falseness.

Shail's fear had left him with the death of Gus and the men but it had been replaced with hate. He sighed deeply. Fear he understood. It was a natural instinct that all animals exhibited. But this hate perplexed and scared him. Only men could create it within a harpy since harpies did not hate each other even in a male challenge. This hate was an evil emotion and it came from his human blood. It tormented him and he could not rid himself of it. "It shall destroy me for I lose the harpy in me and turns me into a black hearted human. I prefer the fear," he worried.

Bill walked up to the cage and looked at Shail. "If this damned harpy wasn't worth so many credits, I'd have him strung up on that pole right now and be skinning him alive." Bill said to one of the guards. Shail raised his head and could feel the hate rise in this man's presences. Shail sniffled and stared rebelliously at Bill as the man came closer to the cage bars. "I'd knock that hostile look right off that pretty little face of yours," he sneered at the harpy.

In the blink of an eye, Shail lunged his arms through the bars and jerked the man against the cage. Shail swiftly wrapped one of the chains that hung from his wrist around Bill's throat and began tugging with force as Bill choked. The guard frantically pulled on the chains, trying to free his boss. "His collar!" Bill sputtered as the chains sliced into his throat, cutting off his air. The man took a few steps to a remote that lay on a ledge beneath the cage. He pushed the buttons hectically as Bill's eyes bulge from their sockets. Suddenly Shail felt an electrical charge stun his neck. It was as painful as Gus's shock rod. The harpy dropped his grip on the chains and doubled over in anguish while he shook violently and clawed at the tight leather collar. The man released the button, seeing the harpy was subdued. Bill gasped for air and crawled away on the floor.

"That harpy is downright mean," the guard said and helped Bill to his feet. Shail also began to recover as the shock wore off. He pulled at the tortuous collar but it would not come off. Shail breathed rapidly and seethed angrily at Bill, his blue eyes filled with a loathing. Bill saw how terribly aggressive, the harpy had become as it crouched low, its wings slightly extended like a hawk waiting for another opportunity to attack its prey. Even an electric shock would not deter this fearless angry animal now. Bill, outraged, grabbed the remote from the guard and pointed it at Shail. The harpy sprung at the bars and clung to them while he mockingly snapped and hissed at the man. Bill lowered the remote and only smiled. "No, I'm not going to make you timid again by shocking you. You're exactly the way I want you. Gus was right. That abuse and assault did turn you into a man killer," Bill said to the harpy.

"Get the other guards in here. I want the chains on his wrists looped over the top of the cage. String him up, so he has to up stand. Secure those ankle chains to each side of the cage so he can't move. His days of being babied and curling up in the straw are over. The crowds should be arriving outside. This time, they'll see his full body and his wings and get that sash off him. Those hunters will want to see all the trophies he has to offer. Then wheel him out front."

Just then, one of the guards came in through the doors. "Bill, you're going to love this. Look at today's headlines. First article. The story even beat out the swarms."

Bill read the headlines, 'Harpy Kills Hunting Range Owner and Two Others' it said. Bill read the first line. "Gus Simpson, part owner in a hunting range, was killed along with two other employees, when they entered a harpy cage to rescue a woman handler who had been beaten and repeatedly raped by the harpy." Bill laughed out loud. "This is great. Even the harpy lovers are going to want him killed. Maybe I should sell tickets to it," Bill chuckled to his men.

The guards pulled Shail's arms up with the chains and secured each ankle on a side bar. Shail's limbs were stretched tightly so he could barely move in the center of the cage. Shail hissed and snapped at them as they removed his sash. Then they rolled his cage out to the front room, to await the large crowd that had gathered to see the killer harpy.

Kari had spent the afternoon with Ted at the hotel. She told him about her adventure with saving the golden harpy and the discovery of the ancient ship. She left out the fact that she, herself, was a harpy and the connection of the harpies and the swarms. Ted was supportive and concerned for her and the fate of the harpy since the creature meant so much to her.

John and Charlie returned from the hunting range. John convinced Kari that Shail would be fine once he had his freedom again. There was really nothing for them to do but wait and worry. Kari went to sleep Saturday night hoping that Shail would come to her in her dreams again but she did not hold out much hope of this after seeing him that morning. He could barely communicate with her, his mind was so terrified and full of drugs.

Kari woke eagerly Sunday morning to a knock on her hotel door and she opened it. Her father stood before her with gloom imprinted on his face. "Bad news," he said and handed her the Sunday news. Kari read the headlines as she slumped down on the bed.

"This can't be true!" she murmured, reading the story of the three men's deaths and the rape of the woman. "He would never hurt a woman. Male harpies only mate female harpies."

"Whether he raped her or not is unimportant. The fact is he did kill those three men."

"He must have had a good reason. You saw him yesterday. He was so afraid and full of anguish. Those men abused him terribly to break him down like that," she said.

Her father sat down next to her. "I'm sure, he had good reasons to kill them. I know I'd be fighting mad if I were exploited and caged. But, this story is very negative for harpies. The public now thinks all harpies are capable of rape and murder. It will take time to change their minds."

Kari frowned and glared angrily at her father. "It is the humans, who are the rapists and murderers. They kill us daily," she raged. John was quiet as he watched her pace. "And time to change their minds?" she said sarcastically. "They have had over hundred and fifty years to change their minds about us." Then Kari became calm. "It no longer matters what the humans think. Their time is up. And Dad, do you want to know something funny? The harpy, they want dead, is the only one able of giving them more time. Kind of ironic, isn't it?" she smiled with contempt.

John looked at her strangely. "Kari, I told you, I would do ever thing in my power to save Shail no matter what he's done."

"Dad, you don't understand. If you don't get him back, it will be the humans who need saving. It's too late now anyway. Shail's hate must be out of control if it pushed him to kill. He no longer feels like a harpy that protects all life. Even I could never convince him to save the humans on this planet," Kari said more to herself.

"What are you talking about, Kari?" he asked distraught over her words.

"The swarms, Dad. It doesn't matter if you know now. The harpies know how to destroy these swarms. But they will only follow their ruler. Shail is the ruler of all harpies. He has protected your estate from the swarm all this time since you protected the harpies from the hunters. This is the reason your estate has never been attacked by the beetles. The harpies still protect it and wait for my return."

John stood up from the bed, baffled by this revelation. "Shail asked me to protect his unborn son since he protected my lands," he murmured. "I didn't know what he meant till now. You should have told me sooner, Kari. If what you say is true, I could have gotten the Dora government to free Shail and stopped all this destruction."

"The Dora government? It is the senators who pass the laws and allow the hunting. They want us dead. Most of them are bidders at the auction and hope to be the one that kills the last golden ruler of the harpies. I doubt they would even believe you even if you did tell them. Not enough to free him," she stated.

"They would have to believe me. And to save their own necks, they would free him."

Kari nodded her head. "Alright. Suppose they did believe you and they freed Shail. Tell me, what guarantee does Shail have that the hunting would end. And why should he save a race that has persecuted and killed the harpies for generations?"

"But you know not all men are like that," he said.

"Dad, we can talk all day about who you would tell and who would believe you and who should be saved. But right now, there is only one to be saved. Without Shail, there is no hope. This whole planet may be doomed with out him."

John just nodded. "He was smart to create these swarms."

"Shail didn't create them," Kari said harshly. "For generations the harpies have always stopped these beetles from multiplying and turning into swarms. They learned it from their animal cousins, the loca eagles. When the loca eagles were hunted to near extinction, the harpies took their place and protected the jungle. With the harpies facing the same hunting extinction, Shail allowed the beetles to take their natural course. So you see, Dad, it is really the humans, who created the swarms by killing the loca eagles and the harpies. The swarms were inevitable. Shail only allowed it to happen sooner so he could save the harpies and the jungle. After the humans left, he and his harpies would attempt to rid the land of beetles. If the men knew the harpies and swarms were connected then the human ignorance would blame the harpies and more of us would die. This is why I could not tell you."

"Do you know how the harpies can destroy a swarm?" John asked.

"No. I only know that it is very dangerous and many harpies could die. Now, I just want to see him," Kari said quietly.

John nodded. "We'll go together. The more I know about your young mate, the more I'm impressed."

Kari smiled and they left for the lobby of the rustic little hotel. They found Charlie and Ted together while they drank some coffee.

"Kari, do you want to eat some breakfast?" Ted asked.

"No, I just want to get over there and see if he's alright." she answered. They took a rented terrain vehicle to the hunting range. A huge line of people wrapped around the building.

"It'll take some time to get in," Ted said when they parked the vehicle.

"Maybe not," John said.

They followed him as he approached one of the guards at the front doors. "Do I have to wait in line with the rest of the sightseers?" John asked, showing the guard his bid number.

"No sir, you and your party can go right on in. No charge," the security guard said and he allowed them to pass through the doors ahead of the line of people. The place was packed as they slowly made their way through the crowd towards the cage in the middle of the room. They finally saw Shail while he stood nude in the center of the cage. His wrists were in shackles with chains that rose to the top of the cage, forcing him to stand. He had a shackle on each ankle that were secured on both sides of the cage. Shail did not even look at the people. His head hung low, as his long blond hair floated across his face and his eyes were closed. The crowd of men yelled and taunted him hoping to frighten the harpy or make him respond but Shail ignored them. The guards were busy keeping the crowd from overrunning the ropes around the cage. Kari tried to get closer but there were too many people in this mad house. She could only stare with anguish at how the men had humiliated her beautiful mate. "He doesn't deserve this. These men have made him a killer," she spoke softly to Ted at her side.

Suddenly, a large man walked through the crowd with two security guards on each side of him. Bill had a big smile on his face when he went to the cage and unlocked the door. Stepping inside, he spoke in a microphone. "You've come to see the killer harpy? Let's make him perform for us," he yelled into it. There were cheers and clapping from the large audience of mostly men.

"He sure doesn't act like someone who just lost his brother," John commented to Charlie. Charlie nodded.

Shail had raised his head and stared at Bill. He saw that Bill now carried Gus's shock rod. Shail flung his hair while arching the ruffled feathered wings as he postured boldly to challenge him.

"Not a bit afraid of this stick any more, are you, boy?" he asked the harpy quietly. Shail made a deadly seething sound through his slightly open mouth and lunged towards Bill. Bill hit the restrained harpy in the ribs with an electric shock. Shail leaped with the sharp pain and desperately began pulling on the chains to attack the man. The crowd roared with delight like they were attending a bull fight and the matador had just driven a sharp spear into the ill-fated bull's shoulders to anger the doomed animal.

"Hit him again!" yelled a man in the crowd.

Bill nodded to the guards and they began pulling Shail's wrist chains on the out side of the cage. Shail was hoisted up from the cage floor and stretched tightly by the chains. He tossed his body wildly as his wings flapped frantically to relieve this hanging pain. Soon he realized that only by extending his wings, could he get some relief from this torture. Shail rebelliously folded in his wings but then he found, he could barely breathe. His own body weight was crushing his lungs in the agonizing position. Gasping for air, he relented and extended his wings. His heart began to race with the terror and panic from this excruciating pain and helplessness. Shail now comprehended, why the hunters hung harpies for the stripping of wings. It quickly disabled a harpy and zapped his strength while forcing the wings to stretch fully so no blood would get on the treasured feathers. Shail wiggled and squirmed like all harpies that faced this slaughter. Finally he tossed his head back in defeated and panted for breathe in a slight foreboding trance of harpy fatalism. Bill smiled, seeing Shail was nearly played out and ready to be easily handled. He calmly walked next to Shail prodding him with the rod and Shail only had the energy to jump slightly. Bill lifted the harpy's sex organs out from beneath the straight blond hair and smugly displayed them to the crowd. "Now, gentlemen, isn't this little stud the perfect trophy? He's aggressive and nicely hung with a fabulous set of cream wings," Bill stated. Shail docilely allowed the man to handle him while he dangled. His slinky muscular body dripped with sweat and all resistance seemed to vanish as he waited for the knife. "Extend those wings," Bill threatened as he hit a wing muscle with another mild shock. The wings fluttered and now fanned out completely beyond the cage bars over the crowd. Bill chuckled. "You're no different than any other harpy," he commented quietly.

This man's words seemed to snap Shail out of this despairing trance. "I am the harpy ruler and I shall not submit meekly to this death," Shail thought with conviction. He defiantly pulled in his wings and folded them against his back. The golden angrily hissed at Bill in between gulping breaths while it slowly suffocated itself. Bill outraged stung him again but the harpy won't relent and elongate its wings. Instead it went berserks, tossing in the chains. It was apparent the harpy was using all its remaining strength in his slender frame to break free its restraints to get at the man.

John was furious, shoving people out of his way to get to the cage. When he reached the ropes, he attempt to go over them but was stopped by several security guards. He yelled angrily at the hunting ranger owner, "Mr. Simpson. I'll be damn if I'll bid on a pair of wings at your auction! You're draining him of all his fight and it's killing him!"

Bill smiled and gestured for guards to lower the harpy so it could stand. "Sorry, gentlemen. Here's one of our lucky bidders. He's paying the big money and deserves all the fun." The crowd jeered and Bill stepped from the cage and came up to John by the ropes. "Don't worry, Mr. Turner. This one has plenty of fight left in him. So much so, you may wish I shocked him more, if you win him." Bill said as he pulled his collar down and showed John the cuts and bruises on his neck. "He did this to me this morning. Almost killed me when I got too close to his cage. Whoever wins him may be in for the hunt of their life. Never seen a harpy quite like him. Good day, Mr. Turner," Bill said and left the large crowded room.

John looked up at Shail. The harpy was panting hard through his teeth, creating a constant deadly seething sound as it tried to catch its breath. His eyes were savage and intense as he peered around the room, fiercely shaking and throwing the long blond hair from his face. Shail looked dangerous and edgy, as every muscle in his body was tense and poised to strike. Shail yanked on the chains as he shivered with nervousness causing his feathers to ruffle on his wings. Gone was his calm, cool mannerism that had impressed John when he first met this harpy. Shail no longer looked human but more like a menacing treacherous animal that even made John leery. The crowd loved taunting him, making him jerk wildly as he lunged and flapped against the chains to get at the humans. John shook his head and watched him. Shail had changed overnight from a timid creature that hid under his wings into a killer. His hate filled eyes continued to dart anxiously around the room.

Suddenly, Shail took several deep breaths and sniffled. He shook his hair and slowly his muscles and wings relaxed. It was as if he were trying hard to compose himself and calm his rage. He trembled slightly while wiping the sweat from his brow against his arm. When he lifted his head, the wild piercing stare had left his eyes. Shail glanced eagerly over John's head. John turned and saw the only thing in the room that could subdue the harpy's hate-filled nature. It was Kari.

She quietly gazed up at him and John knew, she was communicating silently to him. He lowered his head and closed his eyes and sniffled again. Pawing his foot in the straw, he took another deep breath. His looked back up at her. Now his face had the look of longing. Shail stared with anguish at his dauntless little female mate, who had risked coming among all these hunters to try and save him. John could see all of Shail's violent intense looks and mannerisms had vanished. Only sadness and worry filled the harpy's deep blue eyes. Security guards ushered the crowd forward so a new group could come in. The harpy show was over for this bunch of people. Shail's eyes followed Kari as she left the room with her father. He then put his head back down against his arms and ignored the shouts of the men.

Kari and her father walked to the vehicle. "Killing those three men totally changed him." John said quietly and Kari only nodded. John could see how distress she was. "Did he speak to you?" he asked with concern.

"Yes, we spoke. He's very upset with me for still being here and at you, for allowing it. He's worried since hunters surround me in there and he's worried about the swarms that will be here soon. Shail even threatened to break our bond just so I would leave him. Said, I should go with this man, who cares for me at my side. He was speaking of Ted. Shail still does not want to be saved. He only wants to die hopefully with some of his dignity," she said sadly.

"But why? He seems stronger and braver than ever."

"He's stronger and braver now. But it is driven by hate. The hate and rage has replaced his fear. But hate is not a normal harpy emotion. It scares him and he cannot control it or get rid of it. The harpy in him is gone and he feels horribly lost. He's being controlled by an emotion, he doesn't understand. He fears the hate will never leave him."

"But doesn't he understand that once I free him this hate will fade?" John asked.

Kari gazed somberly at her father. "Will it? I'm not so sure. I'm don't know what those men did to him but he has been badly scarred. I have never felt so much rage in his mind. You have to understand, harpies think differently than humans. They live in the present like most animals. They have a hard time seeing a future when it concerns their own state of mind. This is why a harpy dies when they are caged. They don't believe this doomed feeling will ever end. Right now,

Shail only wants two things, he wants me to return to the safety of the estate and he wants to die." John put his arm around his worried daughter.

"He'll be alright, Kari. It's understandable why the hate won't leave him when those men keep torturing and tormenting him. I believe Shail has the courage and willpower to over come any thing when he puts his mind to it. He overcame the harpy fear of being caged. Most harpies would be terrified, surrounded by hundreds of men. Don't worry, he'll overcome this hate, just as he has overcome his fears."

Kari smiled when she thought about it. "Yes, Shail is very brave for a harpy but he wasn't always like this. I wish you could have seen him when I first got him and made him go into the cabin. He was so cute and skittish. He'd jump at the cabin's threshold as if something would grab him every time he came in. He was determined to overcome all these harpy fears. Perhaps you are right. Maybe he has the strength to overcome this human emotion of hate as well."

"Why is he so concerned about the swarms? Doesn't he realize he's been taken to the east and the nearest swarm is at least a thousand miles away? How could he know if the swarms are coming soon when he's been caged and drugged for a week?" John asked.

"Shail knows where he is. And when it concerns nature or the jungle, I'll put my faith in his animal instincts. If he says the swarms will be here soon, it's the truth. Harpies value honor and truth above all else. It's the animal blood that makes them nobler than a man. But I don't care about the swarm or the risk of being exposed by the hunters in that building. I will not leave this city unless he's with me. I told him that I will never break our bond and I must at least try and free him." Kari said firmly.

Now John had become as worried as Kari's fierce little mate. "Kari, if you're in danger here then I don't blame Shail for being upset with me. He did ask me to protect you and your unborn fledgling. Can I convince you to leave with Charlie and I'll stay for the auction?"

"No, Dad. Unfortunately, I carry too much of your blood and I'm as stubborn as you."

Charlie and Ted came walking up to them, as they waited by the vehicle. "I can't believe all the people in there. It took us forever to get out. Your pet harpy must be rare to draw that kind of crowd. The whole city of Hampton wants to see him." Ted said.

"Yes, but it was a different crowd today compared to the women and children that were here on Saturday. This group was the kind that attends a bloody sports event. They wanted to see pain and torture and unfortunately Kari's little guy paid the price." John said with disgust.

"Well, Mr. Turner, I have to hand it to you. You stepped right up and ended their fun. That Mr. Simpson backed off in a hurry after you yelled at him," Ted said with a smile.

"He didn't back off because of me. I just reminded him of his priorities. Does he want to satisfy a blood thirsty crowd for a few credits or does he want to keep a valuable animal alive and in good health for an expensive auction? It was greed that stopped him."

They climbed back into the vehicle and drove to the hotel. John wanted to check the progress of the swarm in case Shail was right. At the hotel he discovered that the closest swarm was now eight hundred miles away, so he relaxed a little. He checked the estate and found it was still free of any swarm attacks. John was nervous about tomorrow's auction and the price of the harpy. If today's crowd was any indication on how popular Shail had become, he could be in trouble. He would know Monday morning the extent of his credit line.

The dark clouds rolled in over Hampton and it began to rain making for a dreary afternoon. Kari had suggested dinner on the coast at some small seafood shack where she and Ted had dined on their first night in Hampton. John watched Ted and in a short period of time had come to like the hard working, easy going young man. There was no doubt that Ted idolized Kari as he sought to please her every whim. But, Ted knew that Kari's only thought was to free her golden harpy. He was just happy to be with her and help her through this crisis and be her friend. It was apparent that she had not revealed to him her true heritage that she was also a harpy and Shail was her mate. They milled around the afternoon talking about the auction tomorrow night.

As evening approached, they decided to walk to the restaurant since the rain had stopped and a cool breeze swept through the streets. Kari and Ted walked ahead of John and Charlie. John watched them as they chatted ahead of him. "It's a shame things couldn't have been different," John said as he motioned to Charlie toward the couple a distance in front of them.

Charlie looked at Kari and Ted. "That boy could never make her happy. He's too tame for her. Her soul is as wild as the jungle. Always has been. Just like her spirited golden mate." Charlie stated.

"Oh, I know. It's just too bad. Things would have been so much easier for her. That's all," John said quietly.

They reached the restaurant and feasted on the homemade food. Afterward they walked down to the beach. The stars and moons had come out from under clouds, as they watched the waves roll in to the shoreline. "It's been a long time, since I've seen the east coast," Charlie commented.

Kari stopped looking at the water and began to stare toward the long dark beach.

"What is it?" John asked her.

"There is a harpy out there," Kari said, straining her eyes in the dark.

"I don't see anything," Ted remarked as he looked in the same direction.

Kari began to walk slowly down the beach alone. In minutes a tall brown harpy appeared out of the darkness and walked toward Kari. "My God, it is a harpy," Ted exclaimed and started to run toward Kari.

"Ted, wait here with us," John said calling him back.

"But he might hurt her," Ted said.

"No, he won't," Ted glanced at John and Charlie while they calmly watched the harpy approach Kari. It was apparent they knew something that he did not.

Aron walked up to Kari and lowered his head in respect. "I'm glad you are here, Aron"

"Yes, I am glad I found you, as well," he answered silently.

"I know where Shail is and tomorrow's darkness, we hope to free him from the men."

Aron did not seem pleased. "You have disobeyed him and put yourself in danger."

"Yes, I have ignored his wishes but I had to come here and at least try and save him."

"There is much reason for Shail's concern for you. This is why he wished you to stay in the west, which is guarded. These swarms shall be here soon. Sooner than these humans know. Perhaps as soon as two more lights. There shall be no escape for all who fall under them. I have come to take you and the two men away from here. That is his wish."

"We're not leaving until he is safe," she said firmly.

"But has he not told you, he does not wish to be saved. I, too, would want to go to that place which holds him. I would risk losing all my western male harpies, who follow me, in hopes of saving him but Shail has forbidden this,"

"You have spoken to him then?" Kari asked.

"No, I only came here the last darkness. But he spoke to another and gave up a flight feather to honor his words. When the humans have been driven from our lands, the harpies shall unite and destroy the swarms, as he had wished. Already they gather north of here. Also, with this feather, he commanded you be taken to a place of safety away from these human structures. These structures draw the swarms to them. You must not think of him now or your loss. All that is important is the future ruler of the harpies that you hold within you," Aron related.

"How can I not think of him? You talk as though he is already dead."

Aron lowered his head and kicked at the sand. "I think of him also, I would gladly give up my life for him. If he dies, I shall mourn his loss, like no other. But, he is our ruler and I must respect his wishes, as must you."

Kari looked up into Aron's watery eyes and could see the heartache he felt. He loved Shail, not as his ruler, but as his brother. The tall handsome harpy was in agony over the possible loss of his friend. She sighed deeply. "Alright, Aron, I will go with you but not tonight. If tomorrow night, I fail to get him out, I will go wherever, you ask for the sake of my son. But I took him from the hunters before and now you must trust me to try again."

Aron thought for a moment. "I shall respect your wishes and pray you succeed but by the next darkness, you must come with haste, whether Shail is free or not. There shall be little time to spare," he said.

Kari put her arms around his neck and embraced him as she whispered, "We will get him back."

Kari released Aron and he spread his wings. "I shall be in the darkness outside the human structure that holds Shail," Aron related to her. Then he flew off over the water and disappeared. Kari walked slowly back to the three men.

"Shail was right, Dad. The swarms will be here in two days. After the auction, we must go with the harpies, whether we have Shail or not. I have promised this," she said quietly.

"But, the swarms are a long ways off and they may never come to Hampton. Do you really believe in those harpy instincts?" Ted remarked with doubt.

"Then I guess we better find a place to land the hover near the auction," John said ignoring everything that Ted had stated.

"There is a small park a block away, where a hover can land," Charlie mentioned.

Kari glanced at Ted. It was obvious that he was very confused being surrounded by three people who believed in the harpy intuition over the modern satellite information. "Ted, I told you when you first called that the swarms were coming to Hampton. I even urged you to get on a ship, to take you off the planet."

"Because you believe in these harpies," he said smugly.

"It was a harpy that warned you to leave. We do know things about nature that humans do not," she said softly to him.

His eyes filled with a questioning as he gazed at her. Slowly he asked, "You're a harpy?"

Kari nodded to him. He now saw, how she did look very similar to the male golden harpy. Same hair, eyes, facial features, even the graceful long trim bodies were comparable. He knew why she had mystified him by her uniqueness. She was different than any girl he had ever met. Then it dawned on him. "You love him. You love that male golden harpy," he stammered.

"Shail is my husband," she answered quietly. "Now, you see why I must get him back. It is forbidden and dangerous for a female harpy to reveal herself to others. I'm sorry, Ted."

Ted rubbed his head and chuckled sarcastically. "And here, I thought harpies were only animals and Shail was your pet. But you sure fooled me."

John stepped to him. "She didn't fool you, Ted. Kari didn't know she was a harpy when you met her. I was the one that wanted to fool her and everyone else, including myself."

Ted looked at him astonished. "That's why you sent her to Earth, to be away from the harpies, away from him. They've been in loved with each other ever since he saved her at the lake."

"Yes, I'm guilty for trying to keep them apart and a lot more" John uttered with remorse. Kari took her father's hand and squeezed it to comfort him.

"Tomorrow night after the auction, you will come with us and the harpies. You'll be safe with them," Kari told Ted.

"No, I'll go to the auction with you if you still want me around but I must stick to my own kind, whether the swarms come or not." he said.

Kari smiled at him. "I would like you to go to the auction with me. All my life, it's been hard for me to make friends with humans. You're one of the truly good friends, I have. I hope it will remain that way even though you will see me differently now."

Ted grinned wide. "Kari, it was because you were so different that I liked you. I only understand you better now. I don't care what you are. I only hope, you'll keep me as a friend."

Kari hugged him. "Thank you, Ted. I don't ever want to lose you either."

It was getting late, as they wandered through the windy streets. It was a haunting feeling that in a few days all of this would be gone. It would be worse than any storm, for nothing would survive.

Sunday night came and Shail remained chained-up in the display cage. His whole body ached as he was forced to stand into the night. After Kari and her father had left in the morning, the harpy show had continued with the next crowd of people. Bill had entered the room with his men and made his way to the cage. But things did not go as well as before. The guards hoisted Shail up from the floor and he dangled quietly, waiting for the man's approach. When Bill went to handle him, Shail managed to twist his body and strike him hard with his powerful wing, a wing that had more punch than a human fist. Bill went crashing into a cage bar and sustained a bloody nose and lip. After that, Shail was never fondled again and Bill stung the harpy with the rod from a safe distance to make it flap its long wings for the pleasure of the crowd.

As the last group of people left, a guard asked if the harpy's chains should be loosened so it could lie down or if it should be given any food or water. "No. Let him suffer. He'll make it until tomorrow," Bill had said bitterly and he left for the night.

Two of the guards sat in chairs by the harpy's cage. Shail's cage was no longer rolled to the outside of the hunting range, as Mollie had recommended. The guards talked to themselves while they watched the harpy stand quietly with his lowered head resting against his half raised arms.

"How long do you think he can stand until he collapses?" one asked the other.

"I don't know but it's pretty darn cruel. I don't care what he's done. No animal should be treated the way these men have abused this little male. The poor thing has to be hurting from all those shocks and he's been sweating and panting all day. I bet he's dying of thirst. I'm giving him some water, I don't care, what Bill wants. I just can't sit here and watch an animal suffer."

"George, you better not go in that cage. He can still hurt you with those wings. Look what he did to Mr. Simpson. He's dangerous," the other man cautioned.

"You know what I think? I think he's dangerous to the men that abuse him. Gus and his two pals tortured every animal in this place. Their luck ran out. They abused the wrong animal and it came back and nailed them. They got what they deserved. And that female handler was begging us not to hurt this harpy last night when I got to the range. Said this little harpy had saved her life by killing those men. Anyway, he deserves a drink. I haven't hurt him and I don't believe he'll hurt me. I'll take the risk of getting struck by a wing," George said as the old robust guard got up with a plastic water bottle in his hand.

Shail raised his head when the man opened the cage door and walked in. "I'm not going to hurt you. I'm just giving you a drink," George said gently as he cautiously approached Shail. Shail tensed up and raised his wings in defense. He did not trust this man despite his kind words. The man put the bottle towards his face and Shail jerked on the chains and hissed as a warning to the man to get back.

"George, you'll get hurt messing with that thing," the other man warned again.

George took a drink from the bottle and tried to put it to Shail's lips. Shail tossed his long hair with agitation and his eyes filled with a loathing. But the man kept coming closer, speaking in a soft kind voice, coaxing Shail to take a drink. Shail bit his lower lip and swallowed as the enticing bottle came closer to his mouth. Finally, the water touched his parched lips and he took a quick nervous sip and jerked his head back and he stared curiously at the man. This was the first time in Shail's life that a human male had done a kind thing for him. Even the old doctor had held a knife over him when he examined his wounds. "See, boy, I just want to help you," the man said in a low voice. Shail's rage had clouded his natural instincts and he had difficult sensing this man's true nature. The man offered Shail another drink and he drank it apprehensively, still not quite trusting him. But Shail's thirst was great and he allowed the man to give him the entire bottle of water.

George smiled at the harpy. "It makes me feel good to see you drink. Shows you still have a little faith in humans, despite what you've been through," George said calmly. George put his hand on Shail's shoulder. Shail jumped, startled by the touch and instantly raised his wing to strike the man but hesitated when the man didn't cower. "Hit me, if it will make you feel better. I don't blame you," George said as he eyed the raised wing. Shail slowly lowered his wing and tilted his head, trying to understand this strange old man. George just chuckled at the confused harpy and turned and left the cage. He sat back down next to the other guard.

"Alright, George, so the harpy didn't hurt you. I still won't trust it," the guard said.

"You know, that harpy animal reminds me of a stray cat I took in. It was the meanest cat you ever laid eyes on. Tried to scratch or bite every time I came near it. Most people would have gotten rid of it. But, after I fed it and showed it some kindness, it turned out to be the best pet I ever owned. It followed me around like a dog. The poor thing had just been badly abused like that harpy. With enough abuse, anything will turn mean. That's the only thing wrong with that little guy. Being mistreated has turned him sour. He may be dangerous now but I doubt he was always this way. And if he were treated right he would probably revert back to being gentle. Just like my cat," George said.

"Well, a scratch or bite from a cat is one thing. But that harpy is as deadly as a pack of grogins. That skinny little winged thing took on three huge men at one time and killed all of them and they were pretty tough, especially that Gus. Snapped his neck like a twig. There's no amount of credits that would make me want to mess with that harpy," the other man said.

The guards talked through the night and George gave Shail several more bottles of water until he seemed to have his fill. With each bottle of water, George would give the harpy a gentle pat until Shail accepted this man's touch.

Morning came as Bill walked into the room. "Well, did he give you boys any trouble last night?" Bill asked as he looked up at the harpy.

"No, Mr. Simpson, but I have to tell you. He's been strung up like that for over twenty-four hours. I think by tonight, he's just going to be hanging from those chains. He'll be too weak to stand. It sure won't be a pretty sight, especially if you're trying to sell him," George said.

Bill studied the harpy, who had become provoked by Bill's presence. Shail hissed softly and arched his wings upon just seeing this man.

"He looks pretty lively to me. But perhaps you're right. I sure don't want to take any chances now. Here are the keys. Loosen the chains. I'll let him rest today. We'll hose him down this afternoon and string him back up before the auction. I want to have time to get him worked up again like he was yesterday," Bill smiled.

"Yes, sir, Mr. Simpson." George answered. George loosened the chains from outside the cage and Shail slowly lowered himself into the straw. He was exhausted as he curled up. George walked up to the side of the cage and put his hand through the bars. Shail watched this man's hand as it came close to his head. "It would be easy" Shail thought, "to hurt this man, even kill him now that the chains were loose." Instead, Shail could not bring himself to attack or even jerk away. He allowed George's hand to come to rest on his head as the man gently stroked his soft hair.

"Good, little fella. You just rest now. Don't let them get to you," George said quietly, while no one was around. "I'm going home but I'll be back tonight. Maybe I'll bring you some fruit"

Shail watched through the straw as the strange old man left the large room. He was still perplexed as to why this man had given him the water and was so kind to him. Kari had told him that not all men were bad but his experiences in their care had proven to him that they all were evil and should be destroyed. He thought about the hundreds in the large crowds that had gathered around him to watch Bill torture him with the rod. It had brought them pleasure as they witnessed his pain and rage. Shail closed his eyes. "Soon" he thought, "soon my suffering shall end and all these men shall be dead. My son shall not face a life with torture and death, as mine." This thought brought him some peace. He stretched out a little in the straw. His whole body slowly stopped aching from all the abuse it had been dealt. Only his stomach hurt him from the lack of food and the soreness from the rod's shocks. His weariness had finally caught up with him and he could no longer stay alert. Soon he was in a deep natural sleep, not induced by tranquilizers.

Shail woke in the afternoon to a tapping of metal above his head. He jumped to his feet, dragging the noisy rattling chains that were still attached to his wrists and ankles. He looked around startled and saw Bill standing a short distance from the bars. Bill laughed, "First time I was ever able to sneak up on a harpy. Damn thing must have been tired." Several of the other men joined him by the cage. "Go ahead and string him back up. He's had enough rest and tie those wings down. I don't want him hitting anyone with them, especially me. When you're done, wheel him outdoors to the range and give him a good bath and clean his cage. I want him looking good tonight."

The men followed Bill's instructions as they pulled the chains from the outside of the cage until they hoisted Shail up and secured the chains. The four guards entered the cage. Shail struggled but they had the chains as tight as possible and he could barely move. When they came near, he tried to beat them off with his wings. Two men grabbed each wing and folded them down close to his body and tied them with ropes. Shail wiggled and snapped at them but it did not deter them. He glared at the men with his mutinous eyes and seethed faintly while they worked on him. The display cage was moved to the warm outdoors of the enclosed hunting range. Shail breathed deeply with the fresh air. The guards hosed him down and began lathering him with soap. Their hands touched every part of his body. Shail became frantic with this, as his memory of his rape returned. For a moment, his rage left and it was replaced by fear as he squirmed and tried to bite their rubbing hands. But soon Shail realized that they had no intention of molesting him and his fear subsided. They took several instruments and ran them through his hair, removing the knots that had accumulated during his imprisonment. Washing his hair and wings, they finished by drying him off. This experience was painless for Shail, although it was humiliating as he was groomed like some pet show dog. When they were through, Shail tried to remove the strange perfumed soap scent from him. The men chuckled a little as the sleek harpy shook in his bonds. Shail's cage was wheeled back to the room after it had been filled with fresh dry straw.

Bill came out of his office and walked up to the cage. "Well, doesn't he look pretty?"

"He sure didn't like the bath. I wonder how those harpies stay so clean and don't smell," commented one of the guards.

"He's an animal. Most animals don't smell," answered another. Bill tapped the shock rod against the bars. "You men can start unloading the chairs and setting up the stage over there. I think I can handle him myself for now."

Shail took a deep breath and braced himself. He knew what would follow as the big man unlocked the cage door and stepped inside.

"You should be used to these shocks by now," he said to the harpy. Shail began hissing when the rod came near him. Shail clutched the chains as the shock stung him. The men watched from a distance while the harpy leaped in the chains and struggled. They could hear the chains rattle constantly and the harpy's distressed hissing as the huge man tortured it with continuous painful shocks. Finally Bill was satisfied that he reached the desirable affect on the harpy. It's clean body once again ran with sweat as the harpy gasped for air. His fiery piercing eyes once again betrayed the rage and pain this animal was feeling. "That's good. You're almost there. You're almost raving insane with this torture," Bill said with a smile as he held the rod against him again giving him one continuous electrical charge. Shail found he could hardly breathe as his heart raced out of control. Soon he collapsed and just hung by his wrists too weak to stand as his eyes started going dull and they were half closed. Shail no longer hissed or threatened. "Well, maybe you've had enough for now," Bill said while he watched the harpy slowly open his eyes and regain his balance. "I certainly don't want to make you afraid again," Bill gleamed and allowed the harpy to catch his breath. Shail tossed his wet hair back from his face as he gave Bill an ardent stare. He daringly leaned on the chains towards the man.

"Afraid? I shall never be afraid of you or your stick of pain. I shall take your life, just as I took your brother's." Shail seethed in a quiet stalking tone that was barely audible.

Bill staggered backwards unnerved by the talking animal that threatened him with its words. "You can speak?" Bill said horrified and bewildered.

"Your brother spoke those same words, just before I broke his neck," Shail whispered.

Now terrified, Bill moved even further away from Shail. The harpy's words sent a chill through his body. He stared at the harpy's smoldering blue eyes and could see the vengeance and loathing that had consumed the harpy. This creature vowed every word it spoke. He glanced quickly around to see if any other men had heard the harpy but they were too far away. Bill collected himself. "Take my life? You are the one who's going to die," Bill said defensively.

"We all shall die. This, I do not fear. But I promise you this; in two lights your own death shall be upon you. With your last breath, remember, it is I, who has killed you," Shail said with a low eerie voice.

Bill backed with fear against the cage door and yelled frantically to the men on the far side of the room. "Come over here! The harpy can talk!" Shail turned his head towards Bill as he shook the long silky hair to fall across his face.

"But, I only speak to dead men," Shail mockingly whispered in an un-human tone.

Now panicked, Bill leaped from the cage as the men came running towards him. "This harpy can talk!" he said excitedly. The men gathered around the cage and stared at the silent sultry harpy while it calmly stared back at them through the blond locks. "I swear, this harpy talked. It said, it would kill me in two days," Bill said a little hysterical. Bill turned toward Shail. "Tell them, tell them how you plan on taking my life in two days and how you broke my brother's neck," Bill pleaded with the animal. The men waited but the harpy remained silent. Bill chattered desperately about what the harpy had said to him. Now, all the security guards had gathered around Bill. But they no longer looked up at the harpy. They stared at their boss, who appeared to have gone insane.

Bill saw their questioning looks. "I'll prove it to you," he exclaimed and hastily took the shock rod, adjusting it too it's highest lethal setting. "I'll shock him until he speaks. I'm not crazy," he said irrational and began to step back into the cage.

"Mr. Simpson. Are you sure you want to do that? At that setting, you'll fry his brain or stop his heart. It sure is a lot of money to throw away just to get this animal to make sound," one of the guards reasoned with Bill. It was old George who had come back early to start his shift.

Bill stopped and looked down at the men. Bill chuckled a little embarrassed. "Yes, you're right. I don't want him damaged. I must have heard your voices and thought it was the harpy," he said and stepped down from the cage.

"Do you want him left strung up in those chains like that? You can hardly see his beautiful wings. That's what those bidders will want to see tonight. See the real animal in action, lunging at the bars rather than hanging like a side of beef." George said with a laugh.

"Yes, let's free him of the chains," Bill said nervously. "I'm finished with him but leave that shock collar on. We need some control over him. I'm going to my office now. I have a lot of paperwork to finish," Bill said with a slight panic in his voice. He glanced at the harpy one last time and breathed deeply. He felt like he had encountered a ghost. The harpy had revealed his true spirit to Bill. The harpy was not a dumb animal, only worthy of hunting but an intelligent deadly mortal, bent on revenge. The harpy had spoken but Bill couldn't prove it. Even if he shocked him to death, Bill knew now, this creature would not reveal himself to anyone else. Shail stared back at him and gave him a slight nod, confirming that his words to the man were valid. This gave Bill the willies and he quickly walked towards his office. "That harpy was deliberately enticing me to kill him and it almost worked if that guard hadn't brought me back to my senses," Bill thought. Bill realized if he had obliged the harpy, there would be no auction tonight. He would be in debt, his brother would have died for nothing and the harpy would be dead which is what the creature wanted. "That harpy is smart." Bill had left his office to torment the harpy but returned with the harpy tormenting him.

The ten men gathered around the harpy cage. "Okay, which of you men want to go in there and take the chains off. Mr. Simpson has made that harpy so violent he's bound to attack once those chains are loose. And there's not much space for all of us to get out of his way, especially if he starts flailing those wings around" one of the guards said.

"That harpy broke Gus's neck and he was bigger than any of us. Let's loosen the chains and drag him to one side of the cage and take them off that way and hope he can't get us between the bars," another said.

"You mean, like he almost choked Mr. Simpson the other morning?" said another.

"Just give me the keys to those shackles. I'll do it. If he attacks me, use the remote on the collar," George said.

"George, are you nuts? That harpy's going to tear you to pieces, when it's free. That shock collar might not work quick enough."

George smiled at the men. "Just give me the keys. He won't hurt me."

"Alright, if you're crazy enough to try it. None of us want to go near it," the guard said and handed George the set of keys.

George entered the cage as Shail looked at this same man who had given him water throughout the night. "I'm going to take these off your legs first," he said in same calm gentle voice. He bent over and removed one shackle and then the other off each ankle. The other men were amaze as the harpy stood calmly. It didn't hiss or threaten George in any way. "Good, little fella. Just stand still.

Now, let's get those ropes off your wings," George explained as he unwrapped the wings that had been tied fast to Shail's body. "Lower those chains," he told one of the men on the outside of the cage.

"Be careful, George. Don't turn your back on it," one man yelled.

George just frowned at the man and took hold of one of Shail's hands and undid the shackle. George cringed when he saw the deep bloody welts and cuts on the harpy's wrists from the creature fighting these shackles and chains for days. He just shook his head, "You poor little guy," he mumbled and unfastened the last shackle. "There now, you did real good, fella," he said as he gently patted the harpy's shoulder just as he done all night. Shail lowered his head submissively to show, he won't harm this man as he stood passively. George backed away slowly and came to the cage door. The other men let him out, slamming the door quickly shut as they looked at the subdued harpy.

"That harpy was like a gentle kitten with you. What, did you tame it last night?" one asked.

Shail slowly sat down in the straw as a confident younger guard approached his cage. The man boldly put his hand through the bars, thinking the harpy won't hurt him since it appeared gentle. "Here harpy," he called. Shail only docilely stared at him. "Look, he is tame," he said as he glanced and smiling at the men, proving he was just as brave as old George.

In a flash, Shail leaped at the young man, grabbing his arm and jerking it backwards. The man screamed to be free as Shail wrenched his whole body towards the bars. Before anyone could respond, Shail had him by the throat with his other arm. The harpy hoisted the heavy body off the floor and began to choke the man. The young man's feet dangled and kicked in the air wildly as he gasped for air. The guard with the remote hectically pushed the buttons that controlled Shail's collar. Shail jumped with the sharp pain and shook his head but refused to release his prey. The men saw the electric shock collar was stinging the harpy's neck but it seemed the animal would rather suffer than drop the man.

"Higher, push a higher setting! He's immune to those low shocks!" one man yelled while the other men grabbed the choking man's legs and tried to pull him free of the harpy. The young man's eyes were closed and he had stopped struggling. He was seconds away from death. Finally, with the highest setting, Shail could not longer endure this sting torture and freed his victim and fell into the straw. His body convulsed with the shocking pain. The harpy tossed wildly, pulling at the stabbing collar but the shock continued.

George saw the harpy could not endure much more and jerked the man's hand off the remote button. "He's had enough of those shocks," he yelled angrily.

Several of the men picked up the injured man as he slumped to the floor and carried him a safe distance from the cage. The young guard choked and gasped for air as he began to revive.

"His arm is broken. Man, that harpy is fast and strong. No wonder, it was able to kill Gus and those men so easily," a guard exclaimed while staring at the panting harpy lying on the straw.

"Better take him to the hospital," George told the others while he examined the twisted broken arm.

"George, you were lucky to get out of that cage alive. That harpy could have jumped you and broke your neck and we couldn't have stopped him in time," another guard declared.

Shail slowly rose from the straw and shook his head. His intense eyes had the look of triumph as he gazed with arrogance at the remaining wary men. George walked up to the cage but kept his distance and watched him. "You're no stray cat, are you, little harpy?" He said to the creature as he saw for the first time, how truly dangerous this harpy could be. The other guards were right. This deadly little harpy could have easily killed him if it wished to. George moved away from the cage with mixed feelings.

Shail curled back up in the straw in the middle of the cage. He peered out from under his wing at the distraught men. Rubbing his throat, he tried to relieve the ache the collar had given him. He watched while two men lead the injured man to the doors. When the doors opened, Shail could see the outside. He sniffed the fresh air, longing for anything that might lift his spirits. Mollie's anti depressant drugs had worn off and he was on his own to fight back the despair. The sting pain began to diminish around his neck and sides while Shail lay quietly on the straw. "Why had he attacked the young man, who had never harmed him," he wondered, though he knew, he would do it again if the opportunity arose. The hate and the rage had caused him to lose all reason. He only wanted to kill or inflict pain on these men. The gentle soul of a harpy had vanished in him. He had become as evil as his tormentors. He was powerless to change the way he had become. Every time one of the men came near him, the hate and rage would take over and he only wanted to strike out. But even choking the man had not alleviated the hate. It only made it grow stronger as he lusted for more of the brief satisfaction he felt. "Is this what drove Gus and the other men to perform such cruel acts? This brief satisfaction to quench the hate that filled them?" he wondered. Shail was plagued by these ominous and terrifying thoughts. Gone was his love of the jungle and harpies. Gone was the desire to protect all life. It just didn't seem important to him any more. Only the killing of these men mattered to him and this strong hatred over rode any desire to end his life. Shail now wanted to live so he could satisfy his revenge and this new mood puzzled and worried him.

After an hour, George came back to his cage and looked at him. Shail could sense this man was leery of him now and his trust had been shaken from Shail's attack. George sighed a little when he looked at the pathetic curled up male. The man could see the distress and confusion exposed on the harpy's face. It did not stare at him with hate filled eyes instead it had the look of persecution in its deep blue eyes. Even the harpy's threatened demeanor had vanished as it quietly rested its head on the straw.

"Come on," he sighed. "Come over to me, little fella," George beckoned to the attractive young harpy. Shail raised his head a little and after a moment, he obediently did as the man asked, by sliding across the straw, till he reached the cage bars. There, Shail meekly laid his head back down to display he would not harm this man. "You've just about reached your limit, haven't you, my poor little fella?" George said as his hand held several large berries. George reached in the cage and put one of the berries towards Shail's mouth. Shail opened his mouth, as he'd done last night and allowed this man to feed him. "You're not to blame, little harpy. You're just putting out what's been given to you," George said gently while the harpy swallowed the berries and gazed at George with mournful eyes. Shail had never known a man with such compassion and tenderness. George smiled. "I wish I was rich. I'd buy you at this auction tonight and then set you free. You would heal and lose this desire to kill," he said as he reached in the cage with the last berry. As Shail ate it, the man placed his hand on Shail's blond hair and stroked him like he was petting his old stray cat. Shail closed his eyes. The man's soothing touch and kind words, comforted him. Shail knew that even with his freedom, he would not be cured of the hate. In fact, it would allow him to kill more men. But Shail did not hate this man or want to hurt him and this perplexed him. This man who should have been his enemy, man who participated in his confinement. Shail nuzzled his nose up against the man's rough hand to encourage him to keep stroking him. He was so desperate for any form of comfort in this cruel place he would take it no matter who gave it to him. And so, in a brief span of time, the harpy accepted this man for his soothing words and simple acts of kindness and the man knew his kindness had paid off. The dangerous little harpy had spared his life and had become his friend.

Kari climbed out of the hotel bed and went into the bathroom. She splashed her face with cold water and stared with her deep blue eyes back at herself in the mirror. Her thoughts drifted to Shail, realizing he had also done his ritual with water, when upset. They were so similar in many ways. It was Monday morning the day of the auction. The long wrenching time of waiting to decide Shail's and her fate would be over tonight. She had remained positive her father would win the final bid. The anti-depressant patches that Doc had given her also helped. She doubted that she could have remained this calm without them. Kari smiled slightly with the thought that Shail would be in her arms tonight. She would not allow herself to think differently. Even when Shail told her he only wanted to die she had brushed it off and refused to think about it. Dwelling on his death might bring back the depression regardless of the drugs. The harpy depression had so disabled her; Kari refused to go down that road again. It had made her weak and useless. She could not afford to become those things now. She even refused to dwell on the terrible torture he must have endured to change him so radically from one day to the next. "I must be strong for him, for the harpies and for my fledgling son," she thought. To think the worst would make her curl up and wish for her own death. "Even if Shail dies, I must think of our son. I have to remain strong," she reasoned with determination. Ted had been a great distraction since he was optimistic and had no knowledge of her own life-threatening depression she would face her if she lost her husband. Her father and Charlie knew of a bonded harpy pair. Her life and Shail's life were so connected it would be like cutting a person in half. One half would have a hard time surviving without the other. For this reason, they had become very somber and worried. But, Ted did not know about these harpy behaviors. His ignorance, made his spirit lively and she was drawn to it. He helped her maintain. But now, he would be working at the spaceport all day, only to return this evening before the auction.

Kari splashed more sink water on her face to wash away the stress. "I will not think of Shail's suffering or death or Aron's doubts. Or the terrible worry, I see in my father's face or how somber and quiet Charlie has become," she told herself. "I will get him back. And Shail will be fine," she thought. Then her eyes welled up with tears, as for a fleeting moment, she realized that tonight he could be lost forever. More water was splashed on her face, hoping to squelch these doubts. There was a knock on the door and she opened it. "Hi, Dad," she said and cleared her throat. All the water on the planet could not wash away the worry exposed on her face, which Kari sought to hide.

"Kari, I'm going to do my best to get him back for you. I called the bank already. I'm taking a line of credit out on everything I have. Everything I own. No one will be able to bid that high, not for one harpy hunt. It will be all right. Tonight he'll be with you and he'll be okay," John said and tenderly took hold of her chin and he looked in her teary eyes. Kari only nodded. "Will you come have breakfast with Charlie and I before I go to the bank? I noticed you haven't eaten much since this whole mess started. I know, you're doing your best to hide the pain but I see it," he said quietly.

She nodded again, afraid to speak. If she started talking about it, she knew, she would break down and cry. She wanted to be in control on this last day. "I'll wait for you in the dining room then?"

"Yes," she managed to say. He closed the door behind him.

Charlie was waiting for him downstairs in the lobby. "How is she?" he asked.

John shook his head. "She's holding up but this waiting is getting to her. There is nothing to do but think how this could end. Charlie, I don't know what I'm going to do if I lose the final bid. She's so terrible in love with him. How could I have been so blind and stupid? I tell you, if I could trade my life for his, I would do it in a heartbeat. If her brave little mate dies, I'll never be able to live with myself."

Charlie nodded his understanding. "Don't be so hard on yourself. You only meant to separate them for a while. You made that decision when you only stunned him. You knew, they would end up together when you saw how deeply they loved each other. Your final choice is the one that counts and you chose to let him live. The rest has been bad luck for all."

"You can explain away all you want but her harpy mate wouldn't be trapped in that hunting range if I hadn't stunned him and made him helpless. My stubborn ignorant notion to protect her is to blame for all of this," John said.

The old Indian smiled a little. "You confuse blame with fate. It was the harpy's fate to be sought out by hunters because that is who he is and it was your fate to protect your daughter from danger and unhappiness. That is who you are. No one is to blame for these things. It is life and we travel through it, trying to make the best judgments we can. Some times there are missteps and hazards along this path. But if our hearts are good and true, we try to fix these missteps and overcome these hazards as you try now."

John just shook his head. "Blame, fate, call it what you want. All I know, I have to win that final bid tonight. It's not only Shail and Kari whose lives that are at stake here. If that golden harpy can really stop the swarms, then we're talking about many lives."

"Do not expect the golden male to save the humans of this planet. He has killed three and almost a fourth. Harpies are passive vegetarian creatures like sheep, it is not their nature to kill but the golden's mind has been twisted with hate from the torture. You must consider this, if you free him tonight. It may even be worse for the surviving human race on this planet. A leader with these vicious confused emotions can be deadly even if he is a leader of a gentle flock of harpies. Have you considered this? Shail is no longer the passive hunted creature that only sought to flee. The hunted has become the hunter with the hatred that burns within him. He could be deadlier than these swarms," Charlie stated.

Kari approached them, as they stood in the lobby. "What are you talking about?" she asked happily. She had masked her fears for now. John smiled reassuringly at her.

"Oh, just wondering where we should celebrate tonight. Think Shail will drink wine?"

Kari smiled back and they went into the dining room for breakfast.

After breakfast, John rose from the table. "I'm going now. This should not take long. When I get back, I'm going to the spaceport to make sure the hover is ready for travel. Who knows where those harpies will lead us tonight and how far. Do you want me to swing by here and pick you up? You may see Ted there," John asked.

"Yes," Kari answered. "He does take my mind off Shail but not the way you would like."

"Hey, I like Ted. He seems like a really nice guy. But I know where your love lies. I'm a slow learner but I do learn for an old guy," John gleamed a little.

John walked out of the hotel and went to his rented terrain vehicle. His mind was on the credit line he would receive. Although he had not told Kari, he was very worried. He was the largest landowner in the western outback but what was that land worth now, with these swarms. They could destroy the timber and make the land worthless in minutes. The swarms had demolished Westend's harbor and he couldn't even sell the timber he had right now. The harpies had protected the estate and it was undamaged but would the banks care. They would think he had just been lucky so far. Soon he would find out as he parked in front of the bank. This would be the first time in John's life he would have to ask for a loan. His father and he had worked hard to pay off the land. Every credit made, went to this, which had made him land wealthy. But actual credits saved, were minimal.

John met with the bank officer he had spoken to earlier in the morning. "Well, Mr. Turner, I've pulled your assets. You have quite a spread out west. Takes up most the coast line."

"I know what I have. I just need to know how many credits you're willing to lend on it," John said hastily.

"With all the equipment, transports and four hovers, plus the mill, out buildings, your home and the land, it'll come to about two million credits," the man said nonchalantly.

"Two million!" John yelled as he jumped out of his seat. "That's less than half a penny on a credit. Its value is worth at least two billion or more."

"Not in these times, it's not. You see those stacks of deeds over there. Those are just a few of the lands we've been forced to foreclose on. Honestly, Mr. Turner, the bank is short on credits ourselves right now. We're not loaning on any land in the west. We've made an exception with you on the two million since your one of our best customers. But if the swarms consume your property, it would be twenty years before the timber would come back. I'm sorry. We just can't take that kind of risk with any larger sum," the man explained.

John knew there was no sense in ranting on. Business was business. "Give me the credit voucher for the two million and pull the half, I have here. It will have to do," John said grimly.

"Are you buying some properties off Dora?" the man asked out of curiosity.

John shook his head wearily and smirked. "If I told you what I was buying, you'd think I lost my mind and you wouldn't give me any credits," he mumbled.

"Well, what you do with the credits is your business. I'm sure it's a wise investment, whatever it is," the man grinned.

John filled out the paperwork and soon was on his way back to the hotel to pick up Kari and Charlie. "Two and a half million" he thought to himself. "Could the harpy actually go higher?" It was inconceivable, but possible. The only other animal in that price range was a top racing horse and that was with the condition that the animal would earn it back with races and stud services. A harpy, who would be killed in minutes, his only value would be his trophy wings over some mantle piece. Would men pay that much to gloat? Yes, they may. A trophy is a trophy. Some men would pay anything for the right trophy, regardless how much it cost.

John arrived at the hotel, as Kari and Charlie stepped into the vehicle. "How much did they give you?" Kari asked.

John took a deep breath. "Two and a half million," he answered.

"Oh, Dad, that's plenty of credits. I heard, the value of gold harpy wings are fifty thousand," she said cheerfully.

"This is different, Kari. It's not only his wings, they want. It's the challenge of the hunt. And unfortunately your male harpy has become quite a challenge. The hunters will want him."

"How high could it go?" she asked more concerned.

"I don't know. But this is all I could get. With the beetle scare, they're not lending,"

"So, if you don't pay the loan back, you could lose the whole estate for only two and a half million?" she asked.

"Well, the half is mine but, yes. Don't worry. If I lost the estate and still won your harpy, it would be well worth it," he smiled. "Besides, your harpies are protecting my timber. I'm not worried about it."

They arrived at the port and met Ted. He helped John inspect his hovercraft and made sure that it was ready for any kind of long trip. They agreed to pick up the hover at six o'clock and arrive at the auction early. Ted suggested he'd drive to it since he had no intention of going with them. Kari tried to convince him but he had said, "No, you be with your harpy husband and be happy." She then sensed that it wasn't that Ted disliked the harpies, it was the fact that she would be with Shail and it would hurt too much to see her in the arms of another.

John drove back to the hotel, so they could pack their things and check out. Six o'clock approached as they returned to the port for the hover. It began to rain again when they loaded up the hover this time to an unknown destination, at the end of the auction. Charlie had been right about the small park that lay near the large hunting range. John landed the hover there and they walked a short block to the entrance. Kari was visibly nervous when she walked into the building and approached Shail's cage. She was happy that he was no longer chained. He sat calmly while his arms held his knees with his head resting on them. His long feathered wings lay draped around his slender frame. When he saw Kari, he immediately moved to the bars of the cage and held them as he knelt and stared out at her.

"Why are you here, when I have pleaded for you to leave this place and me," he silently related while his eyes were filled with anguish.

"Please, Shail, you know I could never desert you. Not if there's the slightest chance of getting you out," Kari communicated silently to him. "Aron waits outside somewhere and he will take me to safety whether you're with me or not. I have agreed to this."

"Aron is here? Then the young harpy spread my words with the feather I gave him." Shail questioned. Kari nodded ever so slightly. Shail relaxed a little. "This is very good for me to learn. I am pleased the harpies shall unite and destroy the swarms. And all the trees and animals shall survive." He gazed at her with a twinkle in his eyes now. "Though I prefer you elsewhere, I am happy to see you this last time," he confessed.

"Shail, I have missed you so much. I can't even imagine my life without you now."

Shail lowered his head. "Do not speak to me of these things. It only makes my heart ache more to know, you shall suffer much with my death."

"But my father is going to buy you and free you, don't you understand?" she said silently.

"I dare not hope for such things and even if I am free, I am not the same, Kari. The things I once loved and respected are lost to me. I am lost. Only the hate of these humans remains in me. My judgment to lead wisely is gone. My death would better serve the harpies and you."

"I do not believe this. All that is lost shall return. You must trust me on this. And your death would only serve these men you hate. Do not give up, my love," she tried to coax him.

The room began to fill up with men and Kari took a seat in front of Shail's cage, as John and Charlie joined her. Soon Ted came in and sat down next to Kari in an empty seat, that they had held for him. "How's he doing?" Ted asked.

"Who is this man, I have seen you with?" Shail silently asked while looking intensely at Ted through his long blond locks.

"A friend, new to this land, from the space ship I came on," she communicated to Shail. Then she turned to Ted, "He wants to know who you are?" she said quietly to Ted.

"Just a friend." Ted said in a low sarcastic tone.

"Tell him, he lies, he does not look on you with the eyes of a friend. He longs and desires for you to be his mate. It is plain to see," Shail related to Kari and jerked his head back with agitation.

Kari smiled a little at Shail. "Shail, is this jealousy I feel coming from you? I didn't think harpies had this emotion since harpies can have several mates," she teased him.

Shail now stood up and paced the cage a little. The chatter in the room ceased as the hunters stared at his beautiful long cream wings that slightly dragged across the straw and his lean muscled six-foot frame. He tossed the long blond hair back to his shoulders and glared at Ted. "It is true that some harpy males have several female mates. It is necessary since the males are scarce from the hunting. But no male harpy would allow another male to plant his seeds in a female mate. If this human word is called jealousy, then it is also a male harpy feeling. I would fight any man or harpy to the death for breaking such a sacred bond," he raged silently in her mind.

"But yesterday, you told me to go with him that you wanted to break our bond. Do you remember?" Kari related to Shail.

Shail paced the straw and she could see the fire in her elegant little mate. He sniffled with frustration and she longed to hold him, when he was like this. He stopped and looked down at her with weariness. "I did say these things to make you go and stop this human stubbornness. I worried so. It was your safety I only considered. But in truth, I do not wish you with any man if I die and prefer you take a male harpy. The only men I wish near you and my son is your father and this Charlie," he related as eyes held a deadly gaze towards Ted.

Kari smiled a little. "Shail, you are the only mate, I will ever want and you're not going to die. But I do adore you when you're frustrated. You need not worry about Ted. He knows you are my mate and I only love you. He is no threat. Only a good friend, who has helped me fight the despair during my loss of you."

Ted leaned over to Kari and said, "He looks a little agitated."

"Yes, he is. He is jealous," she said to Ted.

"Of me?" Ted questioned.

"He said you are a liar. That you want to be more than just a friend." Kari said as she kept her eyes fixed on Shail.

Ted was quiet and watched the exquisite lean male light-footedly and gracefully pace in the straw, tossing his long blond hair with antagonism as his alert large blue eyes dart at him. "Not only is he very good looking, he's also very perceptive." Ted stated sadly, understanding why this wild handsome winged male owned her heart.

Kari turned to Ted. "I'm sorry, Ted. I didn't mean to hurt you," she spoke softly.

Ted nodded. "You're right." Ted called in a low voice to Shail. "I'd like her to be more than just my friend but we both know she only loves you."

Suddenly, Mr. Simpson entered the room. Shail no longer even looked at Ted. Kari could see and feel Shail's rage and hate rise in him as his eyes flash with a deadly malice toward this man. "Welcome gentlemen and ladies," he added when he noticed Kari in the front row of seats. The crowd of hunters quieted down as he spoke in the microphone. "We're here tonight to auction off the rarest and most spectacular game animal in the galaxy a golden harpy, the last golden harpy. For the sake of the new bidders, who just arrived on the planet, I would like to give you some information that you may or may not be aware of. Three days ago, this harpy brutally killed my brother and two other men, as they entered its cage to save its female handler. The woman had been severely beaten and raped. Despite its delicate looks and slender build, this light animal was capable of attacking and murdering three huge men all at once. Luckily, the woman managed to escape as the creature snapped my brother's neck. Yesterday morning, this is what it did to me when I got too close to his cage." Bill said as he pulled a bandage from his neck, exposing his wounds. "Only the shock collar he's wearing now, saved my life. The harpy attacked one of my security guards this afternoon. The man sustained a broken arm. I bring these facts to light, so you fully understand and have been warned that this slight blond is unlike any other harpy, you have ever seen or hunted. He viciously attacks without any provocation. He's as lethal and challenging as he is beautiful. His wings are sixteen feet in length from tip to tip, which is pretty close to maturity. The feathers are the typical powder puff creamy yellow of a young harpy. We're guessing his age is in the mid twenties. He's sexually full developed and we are hoping this aggressive little stud has impregnated one or two females in the wild so there will be future golden males to hunt." John's hand immediately clutched Kari's to comfort her. Bill moved close to Shail's cage and Shail hissed loudly and lunged at the bars. Immediately one of the guards pressed the remote buttons on the shock collar. Shail fell to his knees as the powerful shocks hit his neck. He tossed and flipped his body wildly in the straw until Bill nodded to the guard and he released the button. Shail lay subdued on the straw and could only pant and shake. Bill and three other guards quickly entered the cage. They lifted Shail up and unfolded his wings and fanned them out so the crowd could see them. "The wings are flawless. No feather loss." Bill said as reached down and exposed Shail's genitals from under the blond hair. "As you see, he's the perfect trophy. The lucky bidder will get a rare golden furred wallet or pouch out of this one." Shail shook his head and hissed softly and the men knew he would recover quickly so they fled his cage. "That little demonstration also shows his vicious nature. This harpy is very fast, smart, extremely handsome, and also very deadly. You'll never find a more game animal with prized trophies." Bill said with a grin. "I hope the winning bidder, will enjoy using our new hunting range. You will have back up hunters for protection and will be in no danger, if you hunt him here. Also there's no risk of missing your target and having that money fly away. We suggest he's hunted with stun guns since his trophies are so valuable. You and all your friends can take turns hunting him for days with no risk of damaging the feathers or genitals. We have a pole for hanging, stripping and gutting him. We hung this one several times on Sunday. Instead of him tossing and tiring quickly as well as becoming meek like most harpies, this little devil actually became more aggressive. I won't be surprise if he fights that hanging right up to his last breath and after he's been defeathered." Bill chuckled. "We also will treat his wings and tan the skin and ship them to any place in the galaxy. All this is included in your auction bid at no extra charge. So, without any thing further, let's start this auction."

Shail stood back up in the cage, recovered from the high voltage shock. He flung his head back, tossing the hair out of his eyes and he shook the straw off him. He looked fierce and rebellious as he ruffled his feathers, hissing quietly at Bill. Ted took Kari's hand and looked into her eyes. "Do they really do those things to male harpies?" he questioned quietly. Kari could only nod. "It's barbaric," he said with dismay and disbelief.

"We are treated and slaughtered like other game animals," Kari said quietly. They could hear some experienced harpy hunters talking behind them as they watched Shail.

"I can't believe that harpy is back up after that shocking. And look at him, not a bit frightened or intimidated. He wants to attack that range owner again. The thing really is a man killer," one man said to the other.

"We'll start the bidding at one hundred thousand credits. Do I have a first bid?" the auctioneer said to start the auction. "Thank you," he said to a man in the back. "Do I hear two hundred thousand? Thank you. How about three? Thank you." the numbers began to rise as Kari glanced worriedly at her father.

"Do I hear one million?" he said. John raised his hand. "One million thank you, sir." John knew that most of the local hunters and zoos were out of the auction at these prices and only the truly rich remained. "One million one. Do I have a bid for one million one? Gentlemen, you'll never get another chance at owning an extraordinary animal like this. He's one of a kind. Thank you, sir, one million one, do I have a bid at two, one million two?" John nodded. "Thank you, sir." John turned to see, who was bidding against him and saw the stubby senator, he spoke with when he registered on Saturday.

The Senator Blackwell noticed that John had turned to look at him. He gave John a mocking grin and a nod as he flashed his bid card to the auctioneer. The price was now at one million three. The price kept going higher as John bid against the senator. Kari's heart would jump with each new raised price. She had come fairly confident, her father would win but as it reached two million, her hopes began to waiver. It was at two million two when the senator backed off and by putting his number down, he motioned that the price was beyond his limit.

"Two million two! Do I have a bid of two million three?" the auctioneer asked. Kari held her breath, as she glanced around the large room of faces. The auctioneer announced it again then a third. It seemed, that her father had won the final bid.

Suddenly, Bill announced, "Two million three. I have a bidder on the com. with an off planet bid. The bid is now at two million three, sir. Do you wish to go four?" the auctioneer asked John. John took a deep breath and nodded. "Two million four. Will he go five?" the auctioneer asked. Bill related the quote to the bidder on the communicator. Bill nodded and with that, Kari's heart sunk. She knew, her father could go no higher as her eyes began to water. The auctioneer asked John for the next bid and John shook his head in defeat and sorrow. "Two million six, anyone?" the auctioneer asked. "Wait, another bidder has come on line," Bill stated excitedly. "The new bidder has just made an offer of three million."

"Three million! Will your last bidder go three, one?" the auctioneer asked. The crowd watched as Bill communicated the last bid of three million one. Bill shook his head. "Anyone here willing to go three million one?" the auctioneer asked the crowd. The whole room was silent. "Sold, for three million," the auctioneer exclaimed, striking the small mallet on the podium.

Kari could not longer control herself. She jumped to her feet and shouted to the auctioneer and Bill as they shook hands on the small raised stage. "You can't sell him. He's not an animal. He's just as human as anyone in this room!" she screamed as she stood before the large crowd of hunters. The room went dead silent. All eyes were fixed on Kari. "He's my husband," Kari said with a sob and quickly ducked under the ropes. She grabbed the cage bars while Shail dropped to his knees. Their arms went through the bars and wrapped around each other. With this embrace, they kissed passionately. One of the guards stepped forward but John stood up between the guard and the golden harpy pair. "Let her say goodbye to him," he ordered and the guard backed off. Everyone in the room was stunned as they watched the two apparent lovers kiss and nuzzle each other. With the tenderness and affection they showed to one another, it was obvious, these two had some sort of relationship. The girl was crying between the kisses and the male harpy was very distressed as he frantically nuzzled her face and wiped her tears.

"I love you, Shail," Kari muttered between the kisses. The tears flowed down her cheeks while she held her mate for the last time. The male harpy's eyes were also teary which displayed his sadness. Gone was his rage and hate as he tried desperately to comfort the gorgeous slender girl. Bill could see the effect these two were having on the audience of hunters. The male harpy no longer behaved like a wild dangerous animal. He looked like a compassionate handsome man with wings. A questioning filled the room among some of the off planet hunters. Was this harpy really just an animal?

"Get her away from him before he hurts her," Bill yelled at his security guards. Two of the guards walked towards Kari but they could see the harpy would never hurt the girl.

"I'll take her," John told them. "Kari, we must go now," he said quietly and gently pulled her arms from Shail's neck and held his daughter tenderly in his arms. "I'll take care of her and protect her as well as her baby," he sadly and quietly told Shail. Shail motioned with a slight nod. Shail leaned his head against the bars and watched John usher his trembling mate toward the front doors. John walked slowly through the crowd as all eyes were fixed on them. Kari leaned against her father for support while she wept softly.

The Senator Blackwell was standing by the exit when they approached. He leaned over to Kari and gently petted her head and said in a low voice, "Poor, baby. She could die now with the loss of her mate. Now I know why you wanted that little stud so badly, John. You wanted to own the last golden breeding pair. I'll buy that pretty little female alone for two million and take the risk of losing her. The golden harpies could be saved if you let me have her. I'm sure, I could convince Mr. Simpson to sell that stud's sperm to me before the animal is hunted. She could be artificially bred." The senator tried to entice John. John stopped and leered at the man.

"Get your damned hands off of her," he growled as his temper rose and he fought to control his anger. He wanted to strike the man but instead he walked past quietly, ignoring the senator's offer. John had to concern himself with what was best for Kari. She had fearlessly announced to the worst harpy hunters in the galaxy that the harpy was her husband. Many of these men, like the senator, now knew that she was also a golden harpy with no more rights than an animal. Kari could be more valuable than her mate especially since she was pregnant. The hunters like this senator would want her now.

Bill Simpson's voice echoed over the microphone as they left the doors. "Gentlemen, please" he said to the crowd. "You all know how these male harpies effect our women. That's why we need to increase the hunting on them. In the future, I plan on making this range exclusive for harpy hunting. To support your demands and wipe out this threat." There were a few cheers from the crowd but most were watching the male harpy. He still stood, holding the bars and watched Kari leave. The creature had become very docile and seemed very distressed. Finally he lay down in the straw and covered himself with his wings and appeared to be mourning. Bill immediately went to his cage and tapped on the bars with the rod while of the room of hunters watched.

"Get up!" he yelled. But the harpy ignored him and everyone else in the room. "He'll be alright. He's just upset, he couldn't rape that girl," Bill said to the audience. But every one had seen the harpy was gentle and affectionate towards the girl. Bill was desperate to make the harpy respond. He had promised the crowd that this golden was vicious and he didn't want to appear like a liar. Most of these men were his future customers. Bill leaned towards the harpy and said in a quiet voice. "It's obvious that girl is really a harpy and your mate. My monitor will check her blood and hair and prove, I'm right." Shail removed his wing as he sat up and stared incensed at the man. "Yes, that's right. Get your back up. I know you understand me now. Yes, it would be worth a trip to the Turner Estate to snatch that little beauty. She may even be pregnant. Bet she and your fledgling would fetch more than you." Shail leaped from the sitting position and flew at the bars, crashing into them to get at Bill. Bill jumped backwards, barely escaping the harpy's grasp. Bill smiled. "That's better. I can't wait to really hang you and cut you up. You won't be so handsome when I'm done. Then, I'm going after your female. She'll pay dearly for my brother's death. I'll breed her, just like my brother bred you," he sneered quietly at Shail. Shail glared at the man while he clung to the bars with his hands and feet. Slowly he dropped to the cage floor.

"As I promised, you shall be dead before you ever touch her." Shail whispered to him. Bill glanced around and again there was no one close enough to hear the quiet speaking harpy. Bill just shook his head and walked away from the creature. Shail lowered himself back into the straw as the room cleared and the crowd wandered out into the night. "If they free me in the range, many shall die this time. I shall satisfy this revenge before my death," Shail bitterly thought.

George came up to the cage and stood in front of Shail. The other guards were busy tearing down the stage and chairs. "I wish I could help you and give you back to that poor girl. It's apparent you were her pet." George said with sadness.

Shail moved closer to the bars and lowered his head to the man. George reached in and once again petted his silky hair. The harpy then raised his head and stared at George with indecision. Shail sighed deeply and said with his soft voice. "You have been very kind to me. This treatment, I have never felt from a man. I shall return this kindness with a warning."

George's eyes widened with the harpy's words. "Bill was right. You can speak and you have understood all my words," George said with surprise.

Shail only nodded. "Hear my words now and heed their warning. Soon the swarms shall cover these human structures and all here shall die. I do not wish you among them. Take your family and travel this darkness to the mountains."

Shail plucked out one of his small feathers and handed it to George. "My feather shall save you. Show it to other harpies and they shall help you. Tell them you fall under my protection."

George took the feather and glanced up at Shail. "You told Bill, he would die in a few days. This is what you meant?" George asked.

Shail nodded. "We harpies know the movement and lust of these swarms. Trust me on this. The swarms shall come and come soon. Do not linger, with this knowledge and warning I give you."

George nodded. He did not question the noble winged mortal, who had spared his life. "Thank you. I still wish I could help you some how." George reached through the bars and patted him.

"Knowing I have saved one worthy man is thanks enough. It heals this tormented soul." Shail rubbed his head against the man's arm to show his devotion to this unlikely friend.

"George, are you making friends with that harpy?" one guard said with surprise as he saw George petting the tranquil harpy.

George glanced at the man and removed his arm from the cage. "Yes, I believe I am. That girl was right. He's no animal. I'd trust this harpy with my life." George said to the man. He held the small cream feather up to Shail and nodded. "Thank you, again." he said quietly to the harpy. "Tell Simpson, I quit," George announced to the guard and he walked towards the front doors.

A well-dressed middle-aged man came in just as George started to pass him. "Can you tell me which of these men is Mr. Simpson?" the man asked.

"He's the big guy with the shock rod in his hand, who loves torturing innocent harpies." George said gruffly with disgust and left the building. Upset he could not save the harpy.

The man seemed a little puzzled by this temperamental security guard but continued on through the building towards Bill. "Mr. Simpson, I represent the com. high bidder of the auction. I believe you received the credit voucher but some paperwork has to be filled out," he said to Bill.

Bill smiled. "I didn't expect you until the hunt. They're eager to get a look at him, I bet."

"Yes, my client is anxious to obtain ownership. The harpy will leave tonight. We will not be needing your services or the use of your range for the hunt."

"Now, wait a minute. I was looking forward to this hunt. Plus this animal is very dangerous. He has to be handled with extreme caution and I know how to do that here."

The man smirked. "According to your claims, it appears your handling is very inadequate. Isn't it true, he's managed to killed three men, and injured you and another?"

Bill was getting upset, realizing he would miss the harpy's torturous death. "That's true but we have learned to handle him safely now. No one would have guessed that a harpy could actually turn deadly. I'm offering use of my range. We'll strip and treat the wings and genitals plus include shipping, all free with your client's bid," Bill beckoned, hoping to convince the agent to hunt the harpy here.

"I'm sorry, Mr. Simpson but my client has his own private range. He wants to enjoy this expensive game animal for some time. There will be no quick slitting of the throat or death for this one, I can assure you. And we are perfectly capable of handling any killer animal."

"Well, I still insist he use my range. The death of this harpy has gotten very personal with me. My dear brother was one of the men, this harpy killed," Bill said with determination.

"I'm sorry for your loss but if it was that personal, you should have never sold him. Then you could hunt him yourself. I thoroughly read your agreement on the purchase of this creature. There are no clauses claiming the harpy must be hunted in your range. Furthermore, at the price my client is paying, he should be able to hunt him wherever he wishes," the man stated.

Bill realized there was no way he could keep the harpy here and watch it die. "Do you think I could travel to this private range and just witness the hunt?" he asked.

"Sorry, but my client is very private. Now, can we take care of the paperwork and ownership transfer, I'm anxious to move him," the man stated.

They finished the paperwork in Bill's office and went to the harpy cage. Two other men came in, carrying a lightweight cage covered with padding. "You're going to need to shackle him inside that cage. The shock collar is set to a high voltage. I'll knock him down long enough to make him helpless," Bill said, holding the remote that controlled Shail's collar.

"No. That's not necessary. I brought a small stun gun for him. It's virtually painless and less traumatic compared to an electric shock. After he's down, I'll tranquilize him. At three million credits, I can't afford to have him injured or stressed before he goes to my client."

Shail listened to this new adversary with a loathing while he nervously paced the cage. He saw the narrow cage they planned to place him in. It was similar to the cage that confined him earlier as Gus tortured and assaulted him. His new caretaker stared up at Shail and could see the aggressive nature of this winged creature. It tossed its long blond hair wildly with aggravation as it almost light-footedly pranced back and forth, constantly extending and ruffling its wings to threaten and challenge its new handler. The animal's large blue eyes flashed with a temperamental moodiness as it made a low seething sound through its slightly open mouth. "So this is a golden harpy. My God, he is exquisite with such an elegant frame and long creamy wings. He's rather flamboyant and doesn't seem to have one cowardly bone in him. Yes, my client will be very pleased with this one." the man said calmly as he admired the harpy. He retrieved a small stun gun out of one of his pockets and pointed it toward Shail. Shail froze for a moment as he stared at the weapon. Kari had taught Shail, how this weapon worked. As the man press the firing trigger, Shail plunged into the straw. The stunner hit one of the bars behind him.

Bill laughed. "You're going to need better aim than that, if you want to stun this one. Good thing he's in a little cage or you'd never hit him." Shail sprung to his feet while he eyed the man with the weapon. He hissed at him with animosity for trying to hurt him.

"He is pretty fast. I've never had this problem before with an animal," the man acknowledged. He took careful aim again and Shail jumped sideward. The stun missed the harpy again. "He knows when I'm going to fire the laser. He's not only quick but smart," the man said in amazement and moved closer to the cage. He had moved close enough. Shail dove at the bars, grabbing the weapon and the man's hand, jerking his victim hard against the cage. Shail twisted his wrist to retrieve the weapon as his other arm went swift around the startled man's neck. Suddenly, Shail felt the electrical shock hit his neck as Bill pressed the remote. His whole body convulsed with pain and he was forced to release the small weapon and his hold on the man. Shail dropped to the straw, tossed frantically as he pulled at the collar but the pain would not stop. The powerful shocks continued to ravage his body, draining all fight from him. Finally he curled up in a ball and could barely breath as tears ran down his cheeks and he could feel this was the end of his tortured life. Then he went limp, slipping into unconsciousness.

"Stop," screamed the man at Bill. Bill smiled finally released his hold of the remote button.

"Thought you could handle him? You don't need to tranquilize him now. That long of a shocking will knock him out for some time," Bill gloated with a chuckle.

"Open his cage," the man yelled with panic and jumped into the cage. Knelling over the comatose harpy, he checked the harpy with small medical monitor.

"You fool! You almost killed him." the man raged while examining the valuable game animal.

"Mister, I just saved your life. That harpy had you in a death grip and another minute, he would have snapped your neck," Bill beamed.

Shail's eyes were close but his body trembled as he labored unconsciously for air.

"Let's get him out of this retched place and in the transport, where I can start treating the poor creature," the man ordered his two men. Shail was placed in the small cage and then quickly loaded into a transport out side. Bill watched as the vehicle rose and disappeared around the corner of the street. Bill grinned a little. Content he had inflicted one last blow to the mutinous deadly harpy.

John led Kari down the street to the small park, where the hover sat. Ted and Charlie followed in silence. There was nothing to say at this point. When they reached the hover, a dark shadow stepped out from a cluster of trees. Aron walked toward Kari and her father. Kari threw her arms around the brown harpy and began crying openly. Aron knew Shail was lost to her and the harpies. Aron was distressed that Shail had forbidden any attempt of his rescue. It was one of the first times he truly questioned Shail's leadership and judgment. The harpies desperately needed a golden ruler in this time of turmoil. With the swarms attacking and the fledglings and females divided between the islands and the far northern mountains, the harpies required a pair of the gold wings to follow and give them courage in the many lights ahead. But Aron would follow Shail's wishes and hope the land and the harpies would survive with no one to steer them.

Right now, he had been given the honor of protecting Shail's mate and the harpy's future golden ruler. It was her safety that was the most important thing on his mind. "Kari, you must leave now. You have promised me this. We can no longer dwell on Shail at this time. His fate is out of your hands," Aron related to her. Kari gazed up at Aron and nodded sadly. "We must go now," she said softly to her father.

Aron motioned as he raised his head slightly. Two brown harpies stepped out of the darkness and came alongside Aron while he stood before Kari and the three human men. "These harpies shall escort you to sanctuary. Have the metal bird follow them north to a place in the mountains. Others have gathered there, to wait out the rampage of the swarms." Aron communicated to Kari.

Kari told her father Aron's words. John stepped in front of Aron. "She will be safe there?" he asked the harpy. Aron nodded. John now focused on Kari. "Charlie and you will go in the hover with the harpies. I must stay here and try one last attempt to save him."

"But how?" Kari asked. John took a deep breath. "If there weren't so many guards I would steal him but I'm afraid, it would fail. No, I have another plan. The governor of this planet is Henry Blake. We used to be friends many years ago. Perhaps I can persuade him to step in and save Shail. I'm sure the high bidder will not hunt him or ship him off the planet till tomorrow. I still have tonight to stop either from happening."

Charlie stepped forward. "John, you should tell her all of this governor."

"Yes, don't get your hopes up too high. We were friends twenty years ago. He is a descendant of the Dorial explorers and was an avid harpy hunter. When I banned hunting on the estate, he called me and voiced his disapproval. I have not spoken to him in over ten years and our last conversation was heated," John said. He could see the disappointment in Kari's eyes. "But, Kari, if I can convince him that only your golden harpy can stop the swarms then he may listen. He knows me and knows I am a man of my word. He will believe me."

"But Dad, what about the swarms that are coming? I could not bare losing both you and Shail," Kari said somberly.

"Have a little faith in your old man. Those swarms will not get me and they won't get Shail and neither will any hunter. Kari, I promised you, I would do everything in my power to save him. Now I must stay here and try this. You know me. I would feel like a coward if I ran to the mountains leaving Shail and all these people behind. I could never do that."

Kari hugged her father and whispered, "Oh, Dad be careful. I love you. I don't blame you any more for what has happened. I know you chose not to hurt Shail."

John sighed. "I still blame myself. I have to get him out for the sake of my own sanity. I love you too and I want you to be with him. I want you to have the same happiness I had with your mother." They pulled apart after a long moment. Kari climbed into her father's hovercraft with Charlie. The rain had let up and the stars dotted the sky. A cool wind whipped around them as they stood in the dark silent park. As Charlie forced the small hover to rise in the air, the two harpies spread their long brown wings and leaped in front of the metal bird. They flapped their wings hard toward the north as the hover followed a short distance behind them. The hover lights lit up their brown wings in the black night. Soon, only the distant lights of the hovercraft flying over the doomed city could be seen.

John, Ted and Aron watched as the lights slowly disappeared. John turned to the tall brown winged harpy and Ted. "If I and Shail should die, I am asking both of you to raise her son. He should know of the human in him, as well as the harpy. This man," he told Aron as he motioned to Ted, "is good and will be a friend to your harpies." He then turned to Ted, "And this harpy has loyally guarded and protected Kari. You should know this about one another if all fails. Shail gave me the honor of protecting his fledgling. If I die, I pass it on to you both. Do you accept this commitment?"

Aron sensed the meaning of Turner's words. He did not have to be asked by a man to protect Kari or Shail's baby. He would die protecting them. But he understood that this new man would be included in the golden's protection. Shail had said if all failed, Kari's father could return her to the stars and away from the fated land. This other man named Ted would take Turner's place if, he were lost by the swarms. Aron lowered his head to John in agreement.

"Sure, Mr. Turner," Ted stated. "You know I would do anything Kari and her baby. I'd take care of them if any thing happened to you."

John walked to Ted's old terrain vehicle, which sat on the street near the park. "Does your com work in this thing?" he asked as he looked at the late model.

"It works," Ted answered.

John got into the vehicle and turned it on. "The governor's mansion," he said to the operator. A man soon appeared on the screen. "My name is John Turner. It's imperative I speak with the governor tonight."

"What does this concern?" the man asked.

"I have information that the swarms are coming to Hampton soon but they may be stopped by a harpy. I need the governor's cooperation and it must be done tonight."

"Hold on, I'll see if he's available to take your call regarding this," the man said. After five minutes, the man returned. "You are the John Turner which owns an estate in the western outback?" he asked.

"Yes," John answered.

"He has given you an appointment for ten o'clock tomorrow morning," the man corresponded.

"It may be too late by then. This harpy may be dead by tomorrow. He's the only one that could save the town," John said with urgency in his voice. The man looked at John skeptically.

"I'm sorry. This is the only time he is willing to see you, Mr. Turner," he said politely.

"Don't you understand this is an emergency?" John yelled with frustration.

"I have relayed your message to him. It will have to wait till tomorrow. Good night, Mr. Turner."

The communication shut down. John got out of the vehicle and looked around. "Where is Aron?" John asked Ted.

"He flew off," Ted answered.

John thought for a moment and sat back down in the vehicle. "Let's go back to the space port. It's the only building in Hampton that's made of metal and the beetles can't eat through it. We could begin to secure it and prepare for the worst. And it's large enough to hold the population of Hampton if all the cargo, ships and equipment is cleared out."

"You really trust these harpies? The swarms are still a long way off," Ted asked.

"I have come to know that harpies value honor and they are far more truthful than us. If they say the swarms may destroy this town as soon as tomorrow, I don't doubt them. Now, let's get going. There isn't much time," John said. Ted started the terrain vehicle and it rose from the ground. It sped through the dark quiet streets towards the spaceport.

Once they arrived, Ted found a small group of men still working the grave-yard shift. He convinced them that Mr. Turner had absolute proof, the swarms were coming tomorrow or the next day. The men reluctantly went along with the preparation of the port as they helped remove all the large crates and stacks of lumber to the outside of the large domed port.

"Ted, you better be sure of this or we could lose our jobs," one man said.

"I'll take all the responsibility if nothing happens. It's better to be safe than sorry," Ted answered them.

Soon one of the supervisors came back from a late dinner. He was livid, when he entered the half empty port and saw the men moving the heavy equipment out side. John approached him as he screamed at Ted. He could see the man was a skeptic and definitely would not believe the truth. And he was no pushover like the other employees.

"May I speak with you alone?" John asked the supervisor, cutting in on the tongue-lashing he had unleashed on Ted. The man walked to John with a huff. "Now, I have reliable information that the swarms will be here tomorrow or the next day. I'm not ready to disclose, how I got this information but I assure you, it's true," John said as he pulled out a piece of paper from his pant's pocket. "This is a credit voucher for two and a half million credits. If I'm wrong and the swarms don't come, the money is yours for all your trouble. If I'm right, we may save a lot of lives with the work we do here tonight." John said with authority and firm-ness to the man.

The man took the bank voucher and examined it. Then he studied John's face. "Alright, mister, your proof must be pretty reliable to gamble with this kind of money. I'm not a greedy man. But I hope you're wrong, for the sake of all the people who could die if a swarm hits Hampton. We'll get the port ready for an attack. I'll call in all my shifts and notify the other supervisors. By dawn, this port should be secure," the man said. John agreed.

The men worked throughout the night, protecting the ventilation systems and water flow to the port, placing metal strips on any thing made of wood. As Duran surfaced on the ocean's horizon, all was prepared for a swarm attack. The supervisor rushed out of one of the offices towards John. "Mr. Turner, you may be right. The satellites detected the swarms covered a lot of ground in the night. They're only a hundred and fifty miles away and heading toward us. The word on the news is people should start getting prepared. I notified them that the port is secure. It'll be announced soon. I don't know how you knew or who told you, but they sure did save a lot of lives today."

"I'll tell you who told me. It was the harpies," John said. The man looked at John with suspicion and disbelief. John chuckled a little. "I know it's hard to believe. Thank God, you had more faith in my money than the winged hosts of this planet. They did warn me and I hope you will spread the word to the people of this city, it is the harpies that have saved their lives."

"Hey, I'll tell them but they'll think I'm as crazy as you," the man said and John only smiled and nodded.

The town people began arriving at the port in droves as they went into the giant domed building. If the swarms flew straight through to Hampton, they could be here by mid morning. But no one knew what the beetles would do. They could arrive tomorrow or the next day, if they stopped in the jungle before town. John watched the monitors on the walls as they reported the swarms' distances. The first swarm was only fifty miles away. People were panicking, as they raced inside to the huge empty spaceport.

Suddenly the monitors went dead and the lights went out. People began to scream in the dark, eerie building. A voice could be heard over the crowd. "The generators will kick in shortly. Relax everyone," called a man's voice. After a few minutes, the lights came on and the people quieted down. Ted came up to John.

"The swarms must have hit the power station. That's only twenty-five miles south of here on the coast," Ted said.

"Ted, do you know of a hovercraft I can use? Your terrain vehicle is blocked in with all these others. They're jammed up and down the streets," John said quickly.

"Yes, I was working on one out back. The ventilation is out in it but the engine works fine," Ted said with a questioning in his eyes.

"I need it," John said and he reached in a tote bag that he had brought with him. John held in his hand his laser gun.

"Mr. Turner, where are you going? The swarms will be here soon," Ted exclaimed.

"It's too late for the governor to save Kari's harpy. I'm going to the range and get him out. With all this confusion, most those security guards are only going to be interested in saving their own necks. I can't let that harpy die. He's too important," John said and walked toward the door.

Ted stopped him at the doorway. "I know you love your daughter and she loves him but to risk your life for a harpy?" Ted asked.

"Ted, Shail is the key to everything on this planet. It's not just for Kari. The harpies predicted the movement of the swarm but they can also destroy them. But they will only do this, if their ruler tells them. Shail is the ruler of all the harpies. If he dies, the beetles will turn this planet into a desert devouring every living thing. Now do you understand how important he is?" John said as he brushed past Ted to the outside.

"The hover is over here." Ted motioned as they jogged around the building towards it. "I'll go with you."

"No. I must go alone. I want you alive to care for my daughter. If all should fail, even the harpies, Aron will bring Kari to you. I want you to get her on a ship somehow and get her off this planet."

Ted nodded and watched John fire up the small hovercraft. Soon it was airborne and flying over the buildings of Hampton. In a short period of time, he set the hover down in the park near the range. He ran to the range doors with the laser gun held in his hand. John pushed the unlocked doors open and ran into the large room where the auction had been held. John stared dismally at the empty display cage.

"Sorry, we're closed," came a voice from a nearby doorway. "Why, Mr. Turner, have you come to use my hunting range? You look like you're ready for it," said Bill as he saw the laser gun in John's hand. He casually walked in the room, holding a small bag.

"Where is he? Where's the harpy?" John asserted.

Bill grinned. "Gone. His new owners took him last night. But I'll have others, if you're interested, just as mean and deadly as him now that I know what it takes."

John was angry and pointed the weapon towards Bill. "What does it take to turn a gentle little harpy into a man killer?" John asked and put his finger on the firing mechanism.

"It was my twisted brother that discovered the way to turn a harpy into a killer." Bill said cynically. "I shouldn't talk about Gus that way, after all, he did make me rich and died in the process. But the truth is, my brother was a very sick warped man. Always in trouble with the law."

"What did he do to him?" John stormed.

Bill smiled widely. "Probably one of the worst things any proud little stud could imagine. My brother and his buddies tied him to the top of a cage and took turns raping that pretty thing. Gus told me the harpy wiggled and struggled constantly. Apparently, once their mounted, they're inexhaustible and they stroke you all night. Gus claimed that harpy was the best piece he ever had. Of course, with three men riding him so hard and forcing an eight-hour performance out of him, it broke the harpy's spirit temporarily. But as you saw, the animal recovered with a bit of an attitude. It is kind of ironic that my brother's best piece of ass ended up killing him. Guess that little harpy didn't enjoy it as much as my brother," Bill remarked with a sinister grin.

John felt sick inside, upon hearing how Shail had been violated and he lowered the gun. He understood completely why Shail had killed those men and wanted to kill all others. "Well, the harpy is gone. I assure you. You can check the place if you wish. There are some leftover little fledglings in the back room if you want some target practice. I won't need them. Help yourself, my compliments," Bill said.

Suddenly, the whole building became dark, as if a great shadow had passed over it. "The swarms!" Bill yelled and raced for the door. John thought about stopping him but instead ran toward the back room. In a small cage, he found two tiny fledglings crouching on the straw. They were so small they still had down on their wings. John knew they could not fly yet. John blasted the lock on the cage and opened it.

"Come to me. I'm going to free you," he said to the little harpies. Overcome by fright, they could not move. John reached in and gently took one in his arms. The little cherub looking harpy wrapped its arms around John's neck. John smiled at it as he thought of Kari's baby. This is how it would be when he became a grandfather. The other fledgling crawled from the cage and into John's other arm. John raced from the building, holding the little harpies. He ran towards the park. The swarms of beetles blackened the sky overhead as they flew on to the heart of the city. John glanced ahead to the meager park but the hover was gone.

John was desperate and angry by the stolen hover. He had to get out of there fast before the swarms settled upon him and the harpies he held.

John saw a terrain vehicle nearby, probably belonging to Simpson. He opened one of the doors with his free hand while the harpies clung to him. Climbing into the vehicle, John placed the harpies in the passenger seat. He started the vehicle and it floated above the ground. It was then that the first beetle landed on the windshield. Then another. John pushed the vehicle forward to its top speed but the further he traveled the more the beetles began to hit the top of the vehicle. He only went two miles when they invaded the engines. The vehicle fell a short distance to the ground as the engines were clogged and solar panels were covered. Now, the vehicle was cloaked with the large man-eating bugs. John peered through a crack in the windows and saw everything outside, was blanketed with this black deadly mass. There was no place to escape to. The little harpies trembled and tried to cover themselves with their little brown wings in defense. The crunching and buzzing sound was deafening. John sighed as he glanced at the two pint-sized harpies. "Come to me," he said and opened his arms, motioning to them. They crept into his arms and he held them. "It would soon be over," he thought.

CHAPTER 9

▼

Shail slowly opened his eyes and felt sluggish and groggy. He was familiar with this dizzy feeling. It was the effect of the tranquilizer drugs in his body that forced the unwanted sleep. He lay still for a long time, only shaking his head as he tried to clear his mind. The first thing he noticed, was his body resting on something very soft that consumed and comforted his resting body. He touched it with his hand and the material was smoother than any flower's petal he had ever felt. As his eyes began to focus, he peered up at a great white ceiling with flower designs embedded into it. Shail shook his head again slightly, trying to rid himself of this lethargic feeling. He raised his head a little and discovered he was in a large room. Plants in large pots sat on the floor mixed with beautiful colorful furniture. Shail breathed deeply and could smell the fresh air and the jungle that was near. The room did not hold the filtered air that stank of men and their toxins. He moved his hand to rub his forehead and discovered that his wrists were free of chains and shackles. Reaching for his neck, the electric shock collar was also gone.

Shail forced himself to elevate his head above the pillows and noticed a clean harpy sash draped around his hips. He sniffed the wonderful free air again and his attention was focused on an open balcony door. The gray sky and trees could be seen beyond this opening and no cage bars stood between him and the outdoors. Only his weak drugged body was keeping him back from the open sky and freedom. He struggled desperately to sit up but his mind reeled with dizziness and he was shaky. He knew, he could not walk or fly from this human structure. It would take more time to recover before he could flee. He glanced down as he felt a patch on his arm. It was the same tranquilizing patch the old doctor had put on him. Shail ripped it off, knowing it would stop these drugs from coming into his body. Lying back down, he waited and hoped to regain his balance and strength before the hunters would come and hinder his escape.

Shail heard the distressing sound of a door opening. He saw this new handler enter, who had fired the small weapon at him while he was caged. Shail timidly curled up and cowered to the man as he came along side his bed. "Easy, little fellow. I'm not going to hurt you. I just want to see if you've recovered," the man said gently to the frightened harpy as he pulled out a small monitor.

Shail breathed deeply and could feel the rage building inside of him as he purposely acted leer of this man. "Yes, come closer to me," Shail thought. "I may look scared and weak but I still have enough strength to reach up and rip your throat from your cruel neck." Shail tensed up, pulling his limbs close as he mustered his resilience. The man leaned over the terrified curled up harpy with a monitor. Shail was nearly ready to pounce on the oblivious man when a voice came from the doorway.

"Step away from him, Doctor, before he hurts you." Shail turned his head and saw a blond middle-aged woman standing in the doorway.

"He's still very weak and drugged and too frightened from that shocking to be dangerous," the man smiled.

"He's not frightened and he has enough strength to reach up and rip your throat from your neck," she said and walked into the room. The man cautiously moved away from the harpy and the bed. Shail stared curiously at her. This female had spoken the exact words that dwelled in his mind. "Could she be harpy?" Shail wondered. He watched this lovely slender woman glided across the floor in a long white gown. Soon she was standing at the side of his bed.

"Leave us now. And thank you, Dr. Watkins," she said to the man. She gazed into Shail's questioning large blue eyes. "Yes, I am a harpy," she said. Shail sniffed her and she had the scent of a harpy. Her eyes were as blue as his and her long blond hair hung over him as she sat down on the bed. There was no doubt this female was a golden harpy. Shail looked up at her with confusion. He had assumed that he and Kari were the last of the golden harpy line. She smiled as reached for his brow and gently pushed aside his soft blond hair from his puzzled face. "I have longed for twenty years to do this again to my son. And you have grown into such a handsome and beautiful golden, just like your father."

Shail swallowed hard as he stared in disbelief. His mother was dead. How could this female harpy claim to be her, "I am your mother, Shail. I am not dead, only secluded from the harpies all these years. But now is the time I expose myself so I can help you and the harpies. You are consumed by the human hate and must be rid of it. The harpies depend on your guidance now. But this hate has blocked all reason and animal instincts from your mind. So much so, that you would eagerly rip the throat from a man instead of sensing his good heart first. He has only come to our land to help you and the harpies. You must release this hate that clouds your judgment. It is not part of a harpy's mind but the only a terrible imprint placed on you, by evil men."

"I know no way to rid myself of it or if I should. It has given me the strength to live through any hardship and kill with little remorse. I must still slay the remaining men, who escape the swarms," he related to her silently.

"You would willingly throw truth and honor to the wind, to gratify this revenge?"

Shail lowered his head with guilt. "I no longer know the right answers or what is true and honorable. I only know, these men should die."

"Perhaps they should, but it is a judgment you should make with a clear mind, not a wounded heart." she answered.

"But how? How can I rid this hate from me? It grows deep inside of me," he pleaded.

"Yes, it is there. And you have protected it since it protected you. It saved you from the harpy depression and supplied you with purpose. But now, it is no longer needed. You must let it go, for it has become a curse that shall only destroy you and those who live under your rule. It distances you from good and all the things you love," she stated.

Shail nuzzled his head against her leg. "How can I do it then?" he asked sadly.

"You must expose the hate. You have sheltered it, by not facing the horrors that created it. Your mind has concealed these horrors since they were too painful to dwell upon. Only by bringing these painful hidden memories forth, shall the hate and rage no longer hold you captive."

Shail breathed deeply and gazed up at his mother. "I do not wish to dwell upon or remember these things the men did to me," he pleaded like a terrified fledgling.

She gently stroked him to ease his stress. "It shall be very painful but it shall free you, Shail. The harpies need a wise ruler not only a brave one. I know you would prefer to keep this hate until all men were gone but as a golden ruler, you must do what is best for your flock, not what you desire. Do this for your harpies so you shall have a clear mind, not a clouded one." Shail sighed and finally nodded. "I want you to remember and relive all the terrible things that created this hate that holds you hostage. Remember, Shail."

Shail clutched her leg and he closed his eyes. He began to focus on all the incidents that had created his hate. He began at the beginning when he first felt these agonizing emotions. It was several seasons ago when he and Aron had heard of two slain harpies. They flew to this place and discovered the two dead harpies hanging from a tree. Their wings gone and unspeakable torturous acts had been inflicted on them. Shail recollected the sick knotted feeling in the pit of his stomach as he gazed at the maimed bodies of these once beautiful harpies, he had known and loved. Yes, it was the beginning of the hate. Soon after, he released the swarms upon the humans to drive them off the land. Then he moved to the time when he was gravely wounded by lasers guns and captured. These island hunters kicked and beat him as he lay bound and dying. He relived the unbearable pain and fear. His hate had grown personal now against the men. Shail next recalled the night he was sold to Gus and how he almost didn't survived his deadly shock rod. His hate grew strong and the killing instinct crept into his gentle harpy soul.

Now Shail began to shiver as his thoughts drifted to the most dreadful night of his young life. The night he was completely stripped of his love and emotions. He recollected how Gus and the two men viciously raped him. How he struggled desperately against the chains as each man penetrated him over and over again. Plunging deep, as he squirmed beneath them. If he slowed or tired, one man violently clutch his genitals, squeezing them unmercifully, prompting Shail to wiggle frantically despite his fatigue. This movement stimulated and stroked another man mounted on him. They cruelly tortured and ravaged his body until he was worn down and drained of all fight, pride and honor, finally becoming submissive to his masters.

Shail began to tremble and breathe hard with these vivid memories. Suddenly, another remembrance was evoked from his subconscious. It so horrified him it had been erased from his mind. Removing the rags from his mouth, Gus had shoved something down his throat. Soon Shail's own body became aroused. Gus continued to assault him, as another man grasped his firm aroused male organ and began harshly massaged it until Shail's mind was wild from the sex drugs. He began copulating hard against the cage until this man forced the flow of his sperm. After it was done, Shail went completely insane, snapping and hissing violently as he fought against any future caressing. These men laughed with pleasure and new incentive, seeing how this revitalized and angered the nearly broken down harpy. Many more drugs were forced in him until his body and mind became inflamed with the itchy feverish sexual lust that he could not control or stop. Each man continued to mate him like he was female while another would fondle and stoke him. With the sexual drug over dose and the stimulation, it caused his slender body to frantically fornicate instinctively as he desperately strained to release his own seeds over and over again into his cage.

This had been the ultimate rape, this sacred right that a male harpy reserved for only his female mate. As the drugs faded, they were replaced with tremendous shame, grief and revulsion, which caused Shail to lose his will to live and eventually nearly destroyed his mind with the despair. The attack on Mollie awakened the deadly hate that saved him but also owned him now.

Shail raised his head and looked into his mother's eyes. Tears were streaming down her cheeks as her son's gruesome memories were revealed to her. He placed his head in her lap and shuddered as he curled up in a tight ball. Shail began to cry. "Let it go, son. Let all your grief flow out of you. You have done nothing wrong. This disgrace and mortification you feel, only shows the decency and honor that lies within you. And this grievous shame and regret has created a powerful hate in you." Shail continued to sob. He could not stop the flood of tears. His insides ached and he felt physical pain as he wept. His once silent vocal cords whimpered softly. Never before, had he done this. When he would try to stop and gain some control, his mother would encourage him to shed more tears. "Release it all. Release all this suffering, Shail," she whispered as she held and caressed him.

The early morning passed with his mother consoling him with her wise and comforting words. After some time, he pulled from her side and managed to collect himself. His blond locks were wet from his tears. "The anger and rage leave me," he managed to say, "but I feel weak and empty inside. My body is numb. The hate gave me a goal and a strength, now, I have none and life holds no joy for me."

His mother smiled at him and pushed the wet hair from his face. "The joy shall come again but it shall take time and this hollow feeling will be filled. When you fly from here, you shall appreciate the freedom you nearly lost. Soaring over the trees, you shall eventually see their beauty. Holding your mate in your arms again, the love that binds you to her shall awaken and when you finally look upon your son, you shall be healed. Do not lose faith, Shail. You have experienced the worst of evils. No harpy has suffered as long or as terrible as you and survived it. That shows you have great strength and your wisdom has freed your harpies. You shall continue to be a great harpy ruler. Only if you allow the hate to return, shall you fail."

"How is it, you know all of this?" he asked her.

"You are my son, though many seasons have separated us. I know your heart and I sense your soul. You have the willpower to overcome all and be whole again. This torment and loss, I also have felt, for it nearly ended my life. I once was nearly destroyed by a man as you."

"Tell me of this and how it is, you still live when a trusted one, told me you had died."

She reached into a bowl that sat on an end table and produced a piece of fruit. "I shall tell you all, as you eat and rest. Soon you shall need your strength to do what lies ahead." Shail took the fruit and leaned back on the soft pillows.

"I must start at the beginning for you should know of your parents. When I was nearly an adult, my father brought me to the gathering, to search for my future mate. All the harpies across the land and islands united at the base of the sacred mountain. It was a time to pick a new ruler. The old one had broken a wing and could no longer fly and his health was failing. He had willingly relinquished his leadership. It was a wonderful time for the harpies. All the golden males had come to compete against each other for three lights. Back then there were many beautiful golden males. It makes me sad to think, they are all dead now. Killed by the hunters. I watched these brave handsome blond males defy death and each other in the treacherous harpy games but it was your father that stole my heart. In the end, he was the most daring, fierce and wisest. Before the gathering ended, he sought me out and asked if I would become his mate. I willingly accepted. He was then chosen, as the new ruler.

"The old leader chose him?" Shail asked as he stretched out on the pillow and ate another piece of fruit.

His mother looked at Shail with surprise. "No, Shail, the brown harpies have always had the power to chose who would lead them. But these times have changed, since you are all that remains of the golden line. I hope, someday, you shall produce many sons and there shall be another gathering of harpies. And the browns shall chose one of your sons as the next ruler."

Shail's eyes brightened at this as she continued. "Your father and I bonded soon after this. As the new ruler, he did not wish me to be near the humans, so we lived near the base of the mountains in the jungle below. Over the coming seasons, many harpy hunters left the east and came to the western outback. Gold wings had become greatly valued and they relentlessly slaughtered most of the fearless golden males, who defended their flocks. Your father was helpless to prevent this and it tormented him, as it does you. When you were born and grew to the age of five, he worried you would be the last one. He had heard of a golden female, who chose to bond with a powerful man to the south. When she gave birth to a female fledgling, he went to her. Your father did not fear this man named Turner since it was known he was sympathetic to the harpies. Your father told the golden female that he had a son and he wished a future bond between her baby and you. She told Turner their daughter would be the mate of the next golden ruler. Turner rejected this harpy bonding, as you know. Your father was very proud and stubborn but so was this Turner. A conflict in sued over your mate's future, would she be raised human or harpy? Your father wanted the golden female to leave this unyielding man. I told him this decision was not his or Turner's. It would be the decision of the female fledgling. When she matured, she would choose her mate and whether he was a harpy or a man. But I knew once this Kari saw you she would love you just as I loved your father. Finally, your father agreed. He went to tell the golden female that she could remain with the man and raise their fledgling together. It was then that this man accidentally killed his own mate and then mine with his anger.

When I learned of your father's death, the hate and grief consumed me and I lost the desire to live. Rue, was your father's best friend. His son, Aron and you played together. Aron, being older, always watched out for you. I called Rue to me and told him to take you and raise you on the furthest island, where no hunter would come. He sensed I had lost all will to live and the harpy depression would soon kill me. And he was powerless to help me. After you were gone, I went to the jungle to die. I walked for many lights in a trance and finally I lay down under some ferns and waited for the despair to take me."

"It was then that the most unlikely thing happened. A harpy hunter found me close to death. This man took me to a cabin and tried to save my life. In his desperate and feeble attempt to revive me, he distracted my mind from the powerful depression as I fought him. He forced the food and water down my throat and kept me alive. When I gained a little strength, I tried to escape but he tied me up. I watched his man light after light as he stayed by my side and worried while he nursed me back to health. He was so kind and gentle I gave in to him. He promised me, when my body and mind had healed, I would be set free. This hunter knew much of us harpies and knew I was no woman. The time finally came and with tears in his eyes, he released me. I left for one light but then returned. This gentle man had cured my hate and grief and healed my despairing soul. He was older and I did not love him like I loved your father but I began to care for him. You were safer with Rue and Aron on the islands. With Rue's guidance, you would become a strong and wise ruler. I discovered also that this man was very powerful among the humans. I realized if I remained with him, perhaps I could help our people somehow. He no longer hunted harpies but always feared a male harpy may come for me, so he did nothing to stop the harpy hunting. After many seasons, our trust for one another grew. Him realizing I would never leave him and I telling him of you. You were the last golden male and much sought after. As you grew, so did my fears. My human mate knew your death could destroy me. With his wealth and power, he toiled to become the ruler to save you and the harpies. But it was the senators, who decided the human laws. Though he became governor, he still hid his desire to end the harpy hunting since he needed hard evidence that we were more than just animals. So, we plotted to expose the true nature of the harpies by hiring Dr. Watkins. If there was proof, the harpies carried the human blood then the hunting would end since most humans of this land had little knowledge of harpies and held no malice against us."

"My mate, Kari, has said these words to me. And she discovered such proof in the sacred mountain and was going to give it to a man, called Watkins," Shail injected.

"Dr. Watkins has this proof but the land is in turmoil as the swarms approach. There is no time to use this disc, I have seen."

"And your human mate, what does he say of these swarms, we control?" Shail asked.

His mother's eyes filled with sadness. "Time is fleeting for all. He is dead and never learned of this swarm control. His heart was weak and it had plagued him for many seasons. When we learned of your capture, the stress was great for both of us. I feared your death and he feared mine if you were lost. His heart, which had shown me so much love, gave out on him. I hid his death, until I could free you. I did not wish these senators to know that it was the governor's wife, who had bought you and your freedom. It would only arouse their suspicions."

Shail's mind and body were finally free from the tranquilizer and he sat up from the bed and wrapped his arms around her. "I am sorry for your loss and grateful to your man mate for trying to help the harpies. I must now ask, if you have knowledge of these swarms. My mate is heavy on my mind, for she refused to leave the city many times when I asked her. She is stubborn like her father as you have said of him."

"Ease your mind, Kari is safe and taken to the northern mountains. The swarms approach the city as we speak."

Shail stood up from the bed and stared at her with perplexity while she remained sitting on it. "How is it, you have all this knowledge when you have hidden yourself away from the harpies all these seasons?"

"I have spoken with Aron throughout the night. He was faithfully here, curled up at the end of your bed while you slept," she said and she could still see a questioning in his eyes. "After he sent Kari to the mountains, he heard this man, Turner say that this would be the last night to save you. He remained at the hunting range and watched. When he saw Dr. Watkins take you from it with only two other men, he called his western harpies to him as they flew in darkness above the traveling vehicle. He said you had forbidden any attempt of your rescue. But he could no longer obey your wishes. As the vehicle came here, he and the harpies descended upon it. If I had not revealed myself to them, they would have harmed Doctor Watkins and the two other men, who work for me. Aron did not know that you had already been saved. The harpies gather here now since you are within these walls. They await their ruler."

Shail walked to the balcony doors. He could see many harpies as they amassed beneath the trees on the lawn. "Aron is among them then?" Shail asked.

"No, he has gone to fulfill your last wishes. You had told him to protect your mate and her father, Turner. It is this man, he now seeks to rescue before the swarms kill him. Why Shail? Why do you protect a man, who has caused us, both so much grief?"

"Yes, the grief is great but there are many things, I had to consider. Turner thought my father had come to take his mate and daughter from him. I could understand his anger of this if it were done to me. He is the fiercest of protectors. He protected the harpies on his lands from the hunters for many seasons. And though he killed my father, I believe his protection did spare me during my reckless youth. When he thought I was a threat and a danger to Kari's welfare he was relentless in his pursuit of us even risking his own life. And as your human mate changed from a harpy hunter to a friend of the harpies, so has this Turner changed. When he realized I was no threat to Kari, he sought to save me from the hunting range. I thought my life was over and it was he I choose to raise and protect my son. I wanted my fledgling to have this same strength and honor I have seen in this man's heart."

She went to Shail, placing her hands around his head and gazed into his eyes. "You should never question your leadership again. You are wise and just. You can forgive when I could not. Despite all that has been done to you, you still can see the truth of such things."

"I do not feel, as you say. It was my decision to allow the beetles to flourish and now they kill the innocent, as well as the evil. I shall never rest easy with the deaths of so many, now that my hate towards them leaves me," he said quietly.

"But, is it not true that you only sought to save our people? You only wished to drive the humans from the land, not kill them. It is the beetles that have changed matters, not you. The blame lies with the humans, for if they had not killed the harpies and loca eagles, these swarms would not be upon them. By not choosing to release these swarms now, all living things on this land would have eventually perished with the death of the last harpy. Rest easy, my son, your honor and judgment is not misplaced. You have saved your harpy flock and the jungle with your decision."

"These words, you speak, are true, but it still does not ease my mind. There was a time at the hunting range I dwell upon, now that my full memory returns and I relinquished the dark days. It was after the worst had happened to me. I was in great pain of body and soul. They had given me many drugs to save me but I still can remember when all these innocent humans came to see me. I heard the words of the children and women. These humans were actually mourning my coming death. I did not know these humans could hold such compassion for a harpy. My hate had blocked this memory from me but now it returns to haunt me. The harpies shall now live in peace but I am not proud of the way this has come about," he said somberly. Shail stretched his wings in the large room as he watched the harpies from a distance. "I must go and be among my harpies now so they see with their own eyes that I live and I am capable to lead them. There is nothing to be done for the humans most have perished. I must think of my male harpies and the many lights ahead. It shall be difficult to eradicate these swarms from this land. They have grown to vast numbers and I fear the loss of many brave harpies when this must be done."

Shail stepped onto the balcony and spread his wings. The morning light fell upon them and the cream feathers turned to a bright gold with rays of Duran. From the trees, the harpies saw him and bowed their heads. Shail leaped from the railing and soared down among them as all the harpies dropped to their knees with respect. Shail told them to rise and walked among them. He then noticed a teenage harpy. This young one still held Shail's valued flight feather in his hands. Shail went to him. "You did well to spread my words."

The youngster nodded the praise.

"But now, a time of great danger draws near as we adults must fly into the swarms. I do not wish you should risk your young life here." Shail could see the disappointment in the youngster's eyes.

"But, I can fly very fast, as fast as any here," the young harpy argued.

Immediately an adult harpy at his side grabbed his son's shoulder in disapproval and bowed to Shail. "Forgive my son's rudeness. He has been raised in the east, away from our rulers. He has not learned his place or the respect he should show you," the brown harpy apologized.

Shail nodded. "Yes, I am aware of his nature but you should still be proud. He has done a great service to me by delivering my words and saving my mate with them. It is now, I shall ask of his services again." Shail turned and faced the teenager. "You claim to fly fast and you are capable of delivering my words. I shall send you on a great errand for me." The young harpy's face lit up. "Do you know the way to the sanctuary of the northern mountains, where my mate and the others wait?" Shail asked. The teenager nodded. "Go there now swiftly and tell my mate that I am alive and free. She shall welcome this important news. I do not wish her to be troubled any longer. And tell her I shall join her when this land is safe again." The young harpy raised his wings to fly and Shail stopped him as he placed his hand on one of his wings. "Also, tell her, I love her."

John held the frightened little fledglings and saw the first beetles burrowing through a hole, they had made in the plastic floorboards of the terrain vehicle. He tried to stop them by plugging up the hole with his shoe but the beetles found ten more places to enter. It was hopeless. Then John heard a slight bump on the roof of the vehicle, and then another. Into the darkened vehicle, light began to filter in through one of the windows as the beetles scurried from the glass. The beetles were crawling off the demolished terrain vehicle. John saw the flash of a brown wing go past the roof of the transport. Then a brown harpy gazed in through the windows at him and the fledglings. The harpy beckoned with his hand, for him to come out. John slowly opened the door. It was Aron and two other adult male harpies. John stepped from the vehicle still holding the little harpies. In an instant, the harpies grabbed his arms and pulled him to the roof of the transport as the beetles quickly consumed the place he had stood. One of the adult males opened his arms and the fledglings leaped to him. This harpy spread his wings and flew rapidly away. Aron held up a green gluey sap in his hands and pointed to his own feet. The sap was on both harpies' feet. He nodded to John and put some on his shoes.

"This will keep the beetles off?" John asked. Aron nodded again. Aron gestured his head towards the sky. "Yes," John replied. With that, Aron took a tight hold of one of John's arms while the other harpy grabbed the other. With a leap, they flapped their wings hard with the heavy load and John was lifted into the air. The swarms were beneath them as they flew over the tall buildings. These buildings were covered in black as the giant swarms covered the entire city. The harpies flew north and John wondered how long could Aron and this other harpy possibly carry him. Surely they would not take him all the way to the mountains. Suddenly John saw the colorful trees again. In the distance he recognized the governor's mansion. It seemed it was the only building that had been spared by the swarm. Aron and the other harpy flew towards this building as John glanced back at Hampton. The capital of Dora would soon be gone.

At the governor's mansion more and more flocks of harpies began arriving as word spread that this was the gathering place for the assault on the beetles. Shail sent harpies out to recruit others for this time of need. One harpy flew in carrying two small fledglings. He rushed to Shail after he set the little ones down. Bowing he said, "Aron and my flock leader, Seth follow, carrying a man. It is the man whom you call Turner. We saved him from the swarms as he saved these fledglings, I have brought."

Shail glanced at the tiny twin male fledglings as they cuddled under the wings of an adult, who was obviously their father. The harpy frantically nuzzled and licked his little sons, overjoyed they had been found. "Turner saved them?" Shail questioned.

"Yes, he took them from the hunting range." Shail only nodded. He knew why Turner had returned to the range and it was not for the fledglings. Shail was right about this man. He was a great protector. And now, it was he that this man sought to protect.

Shail watched over the jungle trees as Aron and Seth appeared. They were carrying a man under his arms. They flew to the great house and set him down upon the steps by the front doors. The surprised man looked upon the hundreds of harpies and then went inside.

John was bewildered that Aron had brought him to the governor's mansion. He was even more astonished to see the massive group of harpies under the trees. Knocking at the door, he was let in by a man. "I must speak with the governor immediately. There isn't much time."

"Time for what, John Turner?" said a beautiful woman in a long white gown as she walked into the large room. "Where is the governor? Henry must listen to me. There is a golden harpy that must be saved. He is probably on a space ship now. The governor can order the return of the ship. This harpy knows how to destroy the swarms." John exclaimed excitedly.

"Is this the reason, you want this harpy? Or do you wish to mount another pair of gold wings on your walls?" she scornfully asked.

This woman, who addressed him in a bitter tone, perplexed John. "Who are you?"

"I am Henry's wife and it is too late for you to save this golden," she stated hostilely.

John slowly asked, "Where is Henry?"

"He is dead. He died almost a week ago," she answered coldly.

"Then, who is running the planet?"

She smiled widely. "Why, the harpies are or haven't you noticed them. They rule Dora again as it should be. You shall never harm or kill another golden harpy, John Turner."

"I have only killed one harpy and it brought me no pleasure," he said quietly.

"You lie! You have killed two and nearly destroyed three others. All, goldens," she sneered.

John stared at her in disbelief. "Who are you?" he asked again. Very few knew that John's wife was a harpy and he had accidentally killed her. His stubbornness and anger had nearly killed his own daughter with the depression and it caused Shail's capture where he still faced a cruel death but how did this woman know all this and who was the third golden, he harmed?

"She is my mother," came a soft male voice from behind him. John wheeled around and saw Shail standing in the doorway with Aron at his side.

John breathed a sigh of relief. "Thank God, you're alive," John exclaimed. He lowered his head. "I am so sorry, Shail for all the pain I have caused. Surely you must hate me and wish me dead and I deserve it. I have learned, how badly those men hurt you."

With a light step, Shail approached John. "You are wrong. I have never hated you or wished your death. And all the men who have hurt me are dead, except one and even he shall soon die under the swarms. I seek now, to only rid myself of this human hate." John looked in amazement at the lofty handsome golden male.

Shail was calm and reserved. The anger and rage had left the harpy as he stared at John once again with his intelligent keen eyes. Shail's mother came up along side of her son.

"He is more forgiving, than most. Would you not say this?" she asked.

"You're the fifth golden I harmed and the anonymous high bidder of the auction."

"Yes. When you killed Shail's father, it nearly ended my life. Henry saved me. And yes, I am the high bidder. Do you really think I would allow my only son to suffer the same fate as my harpy mate?" she answered spitefully.

"I know I have caused great pain to your family and even to myself. When my wife died, it was only my daughter that kept me from going insane," he said sadly.

Shail shook his head. "Let us not dwell in the regrets of the past. Your misjudgments are far less than my own. By not stopping these swarms sooner, I am responsible for the deaths of many female humans and their young who perished to the south. This is a far greater burden, I shall carry."

John glanced up at Shail. "But they are not dead yet. The people of the city are hiding in the metal spaceport. It will protect them from the swarms for a while, but if the swarms stay, they will die from lack of food. And if they leave, the swarms will attack them."

Shail breathed deeply and turned to look out at the gathering of male harpies. He was deep in thought with this unexpected news. He knew he would be forced to make the decision whether or not to save their lives. John walked up along side of the streamlined harpy.

"You and your harpies have suffered much in the hands of the humans. I honestly, don't know if I would lift a finger to help them if I were you. But, unfortunately, you male harpies have only experienced the sadistic harpy hunters. Most the humans, who hide in the port, are good people, who have never harmed a harpy. I can assure you," John said somberly.

"So I have been told," Shail spoke very quietly. "If only the good hid there, my decision to save them may be easier. But as it is, these hunters dwell among the good. If I let all die in this port, only I shall carry this heavy burden of remorse and I would gladly suffer a life of sorrow if it would spare just one harpy."

Dr. Watkins had entered the room and heard Shail and John speaking. "I do have the proof that the harpies are another race of beings, related to the humans. These hunters can not kill you as animals any longer," Watkins said.

Shail stared at him. "Can you truthfully vow this? Do not think me the fool, Watkins. I am more aware than your mind judges me. I know it is these men called Senators, who rule the humans and they have known for some time, we carry the same blood. Yet it is these senators, who have always sought to spill our blood just as their fathers did as well as their father's fathers before them. These cruel men, whom humans honor, are the ones who first came to our jungles and began this lying and killing of harpies," Shail said with annoyance. Watkins only lowered his head realizing the golden harpy was very well informed about the scandalous senators and their Dorial ancestors.

"Shail, the humans are governed by laws. With Dr. Watkins proof that the harpies are not animals, it would be easy to pass a law to protect the harpies. The men, who broke the law would be punished and your harpies would be safe," John explained.

"I know it is these senators, who make your laws. Tell me why would they now wish to change these laws and protect us?" Shail asked cynically.

"They would not. But the senators only hold this power of laws since the people give it to them. When all the people find out the truth that these senators have promoted the killing of an innocent race only to protect their own selfish agenda, the senators will lose their power. This truth is what they have feared all along. It is because of this truth, they want you dead," John stated.

Shail paced a little with his head down as he considered all of this. "Your laws are made with human words. The humans have proven to me, they hold very little honor in their words. These laws are no guarantee for the safety of my harpies. This much I know. Our wings hold much valued to the hunters and I have seen hunters kill one another for them. I have sensed this greed in the minds of men and it is very strong. I do not believe a law would stop them. All these things, I must consider. To rid this land of swarms is no easy task and some of my harpies shall die. I shall not waste one harpy life, only to find we are still the hunted in the end," Shail said with a slight defiant low voice.

John and Watkins were silent as they watched Shail continue to nervously pace, shaking his hair in frustration as he wrestled with his decision. Dr. Watkins leaned over and said in a low voice to John, "He truly is no animal. I never dreamed that these male harpies were so intelligent."

John only nodded as he stared at Kari's wise young mate. Initially John had admired Shail for his courage and loyalty but now a new recognition grew for the harpy. Shail's knowledge of the past and the perception of the humans were surprising for a wild male harpy who had only dwelled in the jungle. "I see why my daughter loves him," John thought to himself. He slowly walked up alongside of Shail.

"Every thing you have said, Shail, is true. Even with this law, there still may be men, who would kill a harpy for his wings, just as they break our laws and kill other humans. But believe me when I tell you, these men are few. Right now, you rule the fate of every one on the planet. It is a powerful tool. By saving the humans, the harpies would get their respect and devotion. The people will want a law that protects you. With this tool, you could demand your own lands and it may be easier to keep the bad humans out. If they came on your land and harmed harpies, it is they that would face a cage. At worse, Shail, if the humans broke their word, you could release swarms again. Only the harpies know the secret to destroying the beetles," John said.

"Your words are valid and hold honor. You have given me some choices with these words," Shail said quietly while glanced down at the deep cuts on his wrists. Then he looked up at John and John could see the distress in this young male. "Though I seek to end this hate in me it is still lies in wait. It waits for me to call it back. I hope it is not called and I chose wisely. I have known the worst of your kind but I also have seen your good. It is a hard decision to save them all. And if I chose to save them, I could be killing my own flock. I shall go and consider all these things. I must also think about my son, who is coming. I shall not have him suffer, as I have." Shail turned to leave.

"Shall I go with you?" Aron related as he approached his troubled younger brother. Aron sensed Shail agony over this decision that could affect all their lives. Shail leaned over and buried his face in Aron's dark locks and nuzzled his friend's neck.

"I must decide this alone, Aron," Shail communicated silently to him.

Shail spread his wings and flew off to the jungle. John watched him disappeared beyond the treed horizon. "If he decides to saves them he's more humane and compassionate than any of us," John commented to Dr. Watkins and Watkins agreed.

Shail soared over the jungle and reached the city of Hampton. The buildings were black as the swarm covered everything. Soon the buildings would not exist. Just as Seth, the eastern flock ruler, had predicted, the swarms had followed the highway east all the way to Hampton at a rapid pace. The numerous stores, inns, small towns and farms had been like breadcrumbs for the beetles. The smell of human flesh and cut wood of the buildings had gathered many swarms along this path to the sea. Now, like bees draw to honey, the large sum of humans that hid in the dome port, kept these swarms from leaving.

Shail fluttered in one place for a moment as he watched the destruction. If he had not been captured and sent to the range, he would have been at the harpy river gathering. It had been his plan to slow the pace of these swarms and allowed the humans to flee across the land and hopefully beyond into the sky. But now, these humans had no time to flee to the stars and they were trapped with the ocean at their back. Shail knew that he alone remained as their only hope for salvation. "Can I release this revenge? Can I truly be a harpy again?" he wondered, "Can I be a protector of all life even a protector of these humans?" His thoughts drifted to all those innocent women and children, who in a brief time had seen him. And how they had cherished him and were truly sadden by his captivity and coming death. He thought of old George, Doc, Mollie and Charlie and even the young police officer, which stopped Bill from hitting him. It was all of these who made this decision hard. "Can I save them and still protect my flock?" he wrestled with this dilemma.

The muscles in Shail's wings felt stiff and ached slightly from the lack of use but he knew these pains would fade as he used them more. He turned his head and went to the jungle on the outskirts of the city. Below him was a small stream that winded its way through the giant brightly colored trees and ferns, Shail flew down to it and settled along its bank. Wading knee deep into the stream of pebbles and rock, he began to splash the water on his face and wings as if to wash away his worries. He stepped from the stream and beheld the splendor and magnificence of the towering trees surrounding him. His mother was right. This hollow empty feeling began to fill as he realized how much he loved the jungle and had missed it and his freedom. Shail jumped when he heard the snap of a small twig. He whirled around nervously to see what had caused it. Hidden under a large fern, two small human children peering out at him.

"Look, Tom. It's the gold winged harpy that Mom took us to see on Saturday. I'm so glad he's not in that awful cage anymore," whispered the little girl to her brother. The little girl then crept from the fern closer to Shail.

"Anna," her brother called worriedly, "Dad said that harpy was dangerous. Come back here."

The girl child ignored her brother and bravely inched closer to Shail. "I want to give you something, harpy," she said and produced a tiny wilted flower she had crushed with her little hand. She offered it to Shail. Shail crouched down, so he was eye level with her and took the small pink flower from her hand. Now, the boy had joined her, seeing the harpy was harmless.

"Isn't he beautiful, Tom? I knew he wouldn't hurt us. Mom cried all day after we saw him. She said she was sad because he was too wild and pretty to be locked in that small cage."

Shail realized, their mother had not cried because of his cage. Her tears were shed since she knew of his coming death. A torturous death, she had concealed from her virtuous children.

"Wait till I tell Mom, he is free. She will be so happy," she said with the enthusiasm of a child as she reached for Shail and he allowed her to pet him and stroke his feathers. "He's just like us except for those big soft wings."

Shail heard the sound of swift moving footsteps as they came near. He stood up from the children. A man suddenly appeared, his face filled with horror as he saw his children standing next to the golden harpy. "Come to me quickly, children," he said with panic and fear.

The boy came but the little girl looked at her father. "He won't hurt me, Dad. He likes me cause I gave him my flower."

"Anna, come to me now!" he ordered more forcibly and urgent. The little girl obeyed as her father grabbed his children in his arms and stared at the tall dangerous harpy.

"She is right," Shail spoke softly to the man. "I would not hurt you or your children."

The man was dumbfounded. "I didn't know that harpies could talk."

"Perhaps there is a lot we do not know of one another," Shail said quietly. The man seemed to relax a little.

"We just moved to this planet. There is a lot I don't know but what I heard about harpies doesn't seem to be true. I was told that you were wild treacherous animals but you seem like us."

"Yes, we are similar. We seek only freedom and peace and to raise our young ones." Shail said as he glanced down at the children.

Now a woman crept up and stood next to her husband. "Maybe you could help us. I've never been in the jungle. We were going to the port and got cut off when the swarms came. I took my family in the jungle and now we're lost. Do you know the way to the city?" he asked.

"Look mom, it's the harpy that was in the cage," the little girl said.

"Your city is gone and belongs to the swarms. It is safer now to remain in the jungle. Follow this stream. It shall take you west and away from the danger."

"But we have no food. How will we survive?" the man asked.

Shail saw the same vine that Kari and he had eaten from while they traveled to the mountains. Shail reached down and dug up one of its large orange roots. "This can be eaten, as well as those fruits in that tree," Shail said as he pointed to a tree nearby. "The jungle shall provide for you."

The man stepped forward and took the root from Shail's hand. "May I shake your hand? It is something we do, when we meet a friend."

Shail offered his hand slowly as the man grasped it and shook their hands.

"Perhaps we'll meet again some day," the man said with a smile.

"Perhaps we shall."

The man gathered his family and started to head up the stream but the little girl pulled away and raced back to the harpy. She threw her arms around one of Shail's legs. "Good bye, harpy," she said and squeezed his leg affectionately.

"My name is Shail."

"Good bye, Shail" she said as she looked up at him.

Shail rested his hand on her small head, "Good bye, Anna." The child grinned and then ran back to her parents.

"Thank you, Shail," the man called. Shail only nodded to him.

Shail watched as the human family disappeared into the trees along the stream. "Maybe that is all that separates us, just fear and ignorance of each other," he thought to himself. "Did so many have to die because we do not know one another? I shall offer this peace to the humans. It shall be up to them, to prove their honor to me." There was something else that plagued his mind. It was a conversation he had with Kari within the mountain. She had told him that even if all the humans died on the planet, more would eventually come from the stars. Even the swarms would not hold them back forever. And he or his son would be faced with the same threat again. He did not trust the humans but if there would ever be peace, this was the time for it while the humans needed the harpies and he had this powerful tool to make them yield. He spread his wings and flew back towards the governor's mansion.

It was late afternoon when he returned. John and Dr. Watkins jumped to their feet when he entered through the front doors. Aron saw Shail arrive and also flew to the mansion. Shail motioned to Aron to come in with him. They stood silently waiting for the golden harpy to speak. Shail sighed slightly.

"I have decided to give this peace a chance though I am uneasy with it. If the humans can prove to me they hold honor and truly shall let my harpies dwell in the security and safety of our trees, I shall save them."

Aron took Shail's shoulder and gazed at him with worry. "You trust these humans after what they have done to you and the rest of our people?" he asked perplexed.

Shail could sense how unhappy Aron was with his decision. "No, my brother. I do not yet trust them but if we do not make a truce now, I fear more humans shall come from the stars after we have rid the lands of the swarms. They shall blame us for the deaths of so many since the swarms and us are related. They shall take their knowledge and weapons and kill us all. Aron, this must be done now while we are needed and they see our value. To kill them all shall not end this threat but only increase it in the future. We must take this chance now. Though I would prefer to seek the revenge for all we suffered, I do this for my son and all fledglings so they never face this danger again."

Aron nodded his understanding but he was still leery of Shail's offer. He had far too many doubts, to trust a truce and he feared this truce and the harpy's safety and freedom would be short lived. Once the swarms were gone, the humans would continue to hunt and slaughter the harpies. But he would obey his rule's wishes and hope Shail was wiser than himself. That Shail's decision was the right one.

John smiled at Shail. "This will work, Shail. I'll go to the port with your demands. The harpies will be protected and have the same rights as humans and also your own land."

"I trust you, John Turner. Though at times, we have been enemies. But it is our values we respect and cherish which bind us."

John nodded to the harpy ruler. "I promise I won't let you down."

"I will also go. I have the disc and all the people should see it. Plus the DNA blood evidence that shows harpies and humans are very close to the same species," Watkins added.

Shail wheeled around to face Dr. Watkins. "The same species?" Shail questioned in a raised voice. "We are not the same. The blood of the loca eagle also dwells within us, making us very different. As the birds in the sky, we are gentle and do not have this cruelty that dwells in humans. But even a bird can turn deadly cruel, when she defends her chicks. Do not fail with this attempt at peace, for I shall become that mother bird, if I must," Shail declared. His voice was strong and defiant. For a brief moment, John and Watkins could see the fire in his eyes, like a smoldering rage that could be easily ignited again, if he was provoked.

John and Dr. Watkins took one of the hovers from the mansion. Aron provided them with the sap that repelled the beetles temporarily. They all agreed that Shail would follow a few hours later after they had explained the harpy's demands. If there were any doubts Shail would be the living proof that harpies were more than just animals. And Shail wished to see these men face to face and sense if their hearts held any honor.

John took the hover close to the spaceport doors while Dr. Watkins dropped the sap in the area they would set down. "I sure hope these beetles stay put. If they start to fly while we're over them, it's all over," John remarked.

The men inside could hear a hovercraft through the doors and cracked them slightly open to peer out. John set the craft down and he and Watkins made a dash for the doors. The men opened them long enough to let the two men inside.

"Who's in charge right now?" John asked.

"The lieutenant governor over there seems to be running things. Him and a few of the senators," the man answered.

John walked in the direction of the offices as he pushed through the crowds of people. "It's urgent I speak with the lieutenant governor." John said to an officer by the doors. An officer stuck his head inside and conveyed John's message.

"I'm Sam Waters, the lieutenant governor. I'm in charge since we have been unable to contact the governor and I'm not even sure if he escaped the swarms. The officer said you had urgent information," said a tall lean black haired man.

"You are in charge. The governor is dead," John said.

"I feared as much. Is this the urgent news?" Waters asked.

"My name is John Turner and this is Dr. Watkins. I know a way of destroying these swarms but it comes at a price."

Waters looked at John. "If this is true, I'd say, you could name your price. All these people are going to die. The beetles have penetrated the water system we thought was protected. And they're burrowing through the wooden sliders on the doors. We've called for help but the nearest ship is weeks away and will not hold all these people. How much do you want, Mr. Turner?"

"It's not money and it's not me that you have to satisfy, it's the harpies," John said.

"The harpies?" Waters questioned with surprise. "I heard a rumor in here that it was the harpies that warned us of these coming swarms."

"It was no rumor. They did warn you," John stated. "The harpies can destroy these swarms but they want a guarantee that the hunting will end and they will be treated with equality and have their own land, the entire western outback and the islands. They're own country, so to speak so they can live in peace away from humans."

"The harpies but aren't these winged creatures just animals?" Waters asked.

"They're part human, part animal but they're just as intelligent as any man. I would categorize them as another mortal rather than animal. I have the scientific proof of their genetic make up that backs my findings and a disc which shows the harpies ancestry." Watkins stated

Waters thought for a moment. "I really don't care what they are. If they can wipe out these swarms, I don't think we have a choice but to accept their offer. Tell them we agree."

"No, not just like that. There must be a law passed and documents signed, guaranteeing their demands. These harpies have been on the losing end since Dora was colonized. I'm here to make sure they get a fair shake out of this deal and every thing is legal," John stated.

"But that takes time and we don't have that kind of time." Waters said worriedly.

"Well, I guess you'd better get busy. The harpies have plenty of time. They could easily wait until every human is dead and claim the whole planet again. They're only making this offer since harpies have more compassion than we do. Now that the tables have turned, it proves we truly are the inferior race. Their blond ruler will be here shortly. And despite his compassion, he's in no mood to be toyed with after years of harpy abuse and don't even try to manipulated him. He's animal enough that his instincts can sense deception," John stated.

"I need the approval of the senate," Waters said.

"Not these senators. They are the ones who want to keep the harpies as game animals and would not pass any law to give the harpies protection, rights or land.

I suggest you take this vote right to the people. Let them decide on this law and treaty with the harpies," John said.

Waters grabbed a microphone and went before the crowd of thousands of people. He explained the harpy's proposal. Some yelled, "Give them what they want," others snickered at the harpies' demands not believing the harpies were mortal or that they could destroy the swarms. The senators, as expected, were livid at the idea.

"Harpies are only winged beasts and they can't kill these swarm," one senator voiced. The place was in total chaos. Two hours had slipped by with nothing being resolved. Waters was at his wits end. John pulled him aside. "There is one that may resolve all the doubts and convince the people that the harpies are not just creatures of the jungle and they are sincere with this offer. Come with me."

John walked with Waters to the doors. John slid them open slightly and peered out. A brown harpy sat on the hovercraft. "Bring your ruler here," John told the harpy. The harpy flew away and in a short period of time Shail returned. He fluttered by the doors before he set down and John slid the doors open and let him in. The large crowd went completely silent as Shail with poise entered the enormous port. "Look, it's a trained harpy," a heckler yelled but he was quickly silenced by the people near by. The people seemed mystified by the graceful long cream winged creature with the slender handsome human male frame and face. It flung its long blond hair from its wild piercing blue animal eyes as it gazed with defiance back at them. All questioned, "Could this mythical mysterious harpy creature really save them?"

John whispered to Shail. "This is the human leader and he wishes a truce. But the senators are against you, as you said. The people are confused and don't know what to believe."

Shail's alert blue eyes stared around the massive port filled with humans. He had never realized there were so many. "You rule all of these?" Shail asked Waters quietly. Waters could only nod, shocked by the soft low voice of the handsome talking harpy and it's incredible elegant mannerism.

"It is a simple question you need ask. Do they wish to live or die?" Shail said.

Waters regained his composure. "The answer is simple, of course they want to live."

Shail nodded. "We, harpies wish to live as well. It comes down to trust. I shall save your humans, if you shall save my harpies. Perhaps these doubting humans must hear my words to believe I am more than a hunted animal and can destroy the swarms." He glanced up at a large crate that stood ten feet above the crowd. Shail extended his large wings and leaped into the air as the several in the crowd gasped. He lightly landed upon the crate and folded in his wings as he curiously gazed down at the humans below him. The giant port was dead quiet as the people watched Shail with fascination.

"I have come to offer you life, an offer you denied us. We can destroy these swarms and shall. But it is your decision, if we do it before or after your deaths. We only ask to live in peace on this land, as you do. If you cannot agree, then it is your own fate that you seal. By next light, you must decide." He floated down and landed near John and the new governor, who stood by the doors.

Waters smiled at him. "I do believe you got their attention."

"I shall return with the early light. Do not fail. I see many innocent females and young here and do not wish their deaths. But if there is no law or treaty for my harpies, then this innocent blood shall be on your hands as well as it is on mine." Shail stated to him. Shail then pushed open the doors and stepped outside. In a flash, he was gone.

"My God, he's pretty charismatic and direct, isn't he?" Waters commented.

"Yes, he is. But as I warned you before, he's not one to toy with. He means every word he says," John stated.

A man's voice could be heard on the P.A. as he stood on a small loading platform before the crowd. The people quieted down to hear, what he had to say. John recognized the short stubby man as Senator Blackwell, who had bid against him at the auction. "Ladies and gentlemen, please, do not listen to this freak talking harpy animal. This is the same golden harpy that raped that poor woman and murdered those three men at the hunting range. You've heard how harpies abduct and assault our women and he's living proof of it. It's a trick. He wants us men dead so he can have our women. If he can really destroy the swarms, that means he controls them. He has set this plague upon us. Harpies are evil creatures we should not trust them. The swarms will move on, when there's nothing left to eat. Just give it some time," he pleaded.

John and Waters went to him and walked up the platform till they were along side of the senator. The crowd burst into chatter. Now, Waters spoke to the people.

"Senator, I think these people should be allowed to hear both sides of this debate. I confess, I know nothing about harpies but I do know they warned us that the swarms were coming. This gave us the time to prepare this port. Right now the ventilation systems would be clogged and we would all be dead, if not for their warning. This man next to me seems to know quite a bit about the harpies and the swarms. I think we should allow him to speak before we make any rash decisions."

The senator glowed. "Of course, I know Mr. Turner. He's a well-known harpy hunter. Holds the record for the largest pair of gold wings. Yes, let him speak." He told the crowd and handed the microphone to John. John took a nervous deep breath. He knew his words would mean the difference, if these people lived or died.

"My name is John Turner," he began. "It's true, I did kill a harpy one time as the senator stated. But it was a mistake. Since then, I've discovered the truth about the harpies. Something I hope, you will also discover. I want you to know, I was married to a harpy and my daughter is half harpy." The congregation of people's voices rumbled through the giant room. John continued. "Many of you wonder how this could be possible. The harpy females look human. They have no wings. They have walked among us for years. Their disguise has allowed the harpies to survive. But, with the extreme hunting pressure, their males are on the verge of extinction. Then this race will be lost. Yes, they are a race. Not animals, as the senator claims. You all saw and heard the golden harpy ruler speak, surely there's not one among that could call him an animal. He and the other harpies are part human. Dr. Watkins, down there, has the DNA blood to prove this and an ancient ship's log that was discovered in the western mountains that explains how this happened. It's something I think, everyone in this port should see. The harpies have never stolen or raped any of our women. The Dorial explorers who came here a hundred and seventy-five years ago started this lie. They are ancestors of our senators. These explorers started these lies because, in truth, they were the ones guilty of stealing and violating the female harpies. Then they slaughtered the males for trying to rescue their own female mates. Our senators have known all along, the harpies are intelligent beings, capable of exposing the true history of their cruel ancestors. Our senators still promote the slaughter of innocent harpies to hide this shameful truth and retain their political power."

The senator screamed from the raised platform. "That's a lie! What about the poor woman that was raped this weekend by your precious golden ruler, she was no female harpy!"

A woman was pushing her way through the crowd and approached the raised platform. "I was that woman." she called to the men that stood above her.

"Here she is" the senator yelled. "Now the truth will come out how vicious and deadly these harpies are," he gloated as he gently helped the woman up to the platform.

Mollie was visibly shaken as she took the microphone from John. With a trembling voice, she said, "It's true. I was raped and nearly killed this weekend." The audience listened quietly while the scared nervous woman talked into the

microphone and the senator beamed next to her. "But it was not by the harpy. Gus Simpson and his two men raped me and were going to kill me. They thought that if the harpy were blamed, it would increase his value, which it did. That harpy saved my life. He killed those men when they attacked him. He's only guilty of defending himself and me. I lied because Simpson's brother threatened my life if I told the truth. I've worked with caged harpies for several years. They are the sweetest and gentlest of creatures, not capable of rape or harm. I hope you will listen to this Mr. Turner. The harpies don't deserve the horrible treatment they've received. They deserve to live in peace." Mollie lowered her head and handed the microphone back to John.

"Thank you," John quietly said and Mollie left the platform to disappear into the crowd.

Senator Blackwell still tying to convince the crowd grabbed the microphone. "All this proves is the harpies want revenge for the hunting. If the harpies can really destroy the swarms, why didn't they do it sooner? I'm telling you they set this swarm plague upon us. They only want a truce to get us out of this protected port so they can kill us. We cannot trust them. We should wait until the swarms leave before we sell ourselves to these devils."

John took hold of the microphone and eyed the senator. The senator released it, for he could see the anger forming in the tall blond man's eyes. John took another deep breath to calm him. "Look, I know, everyone here is scared and confused right now. The swarms are not leaving. They smell us and are going to stay until they manage to dig their way in. We do not have the food to wait them out. It's true, there is a connection between the harpies and the swarms but it is not as this senator would have you think. For decades, the harpies have prevented the beetles from multiplying and turning into swarms. The harpies did this to protect their jungle. But when faced with extinction, this protection was stopped. It was stopped if only to make us realize, we are the true plague on this planet. By allowing the hunters to annihilate these winged guardians, we have allowed the annihilation of ourselves as well as every other living thing on the entire planet. We truly are the ones guilty of creating these swarms by killing so many harpies. Now if the harpies wanted us dead, as the senator suggests, they wouldn't need to make a truce with us. They would only have to wait and let the swarms kill us. And truly we deserve it for what we have done to them. But harpies consider themselves guardians and protectors of all living things including us. These beautiful gentle beings are willing save us if only to be allowed to live in peace in their jungle and be treated with equal respect. This seems like a small price to pay for our lives. Many harpies will die, when they attempt to destroy these swarms.

What kind of people are we to deny the harpies some land, some rights, and some tranquility when they are willing to forgive and protect us."

The assembly of people broke into noise as they spoke to each other. "Give the harpies their demands!" several yelled.

Waters took the microphone and spoke. "As governor, I'm issuing a state of emergency with this vote. I assume I have the senate's approval. The senator nodded. He could see, the people were against him and there was nothing else he could say.

"By a show of hands, we will vote this new law into effect. It will outlaw the hunting of harpies and give them the same rights as a human. It will also return the western outback and the islands to them. How many here are for this new law and treaty with the harpies? Please raise your hands." The massive domed room became a sea of raised hands high above their heads. "Those that are against this new law and treaty?" A few scattered hands were raised. "Then it is unanimous. We will give the harpies, their demands," he said and a roar rose from the crowd. Waters turned to John. "I'll draw this up. I used to be a lawyer before I went into politics. When I'm done, you can look it over before I sign it into effect. I guess we just better hope your friend, the harpy, doesn't change his mind. It'll be up to him now, to fulfill his part of the agreement and rid us of the beetles."

John smiled. "He'll return and do as he says. The harpies regard honor, above all else. They really are remarkable, once you get to know them."

Waters motioned to Dr. Watkins to come to the platform. "Now would be a good time to play that disc on the monitors. I'm anxious to see it myself and it will reinforce the crowd's decision, if all you say is true."

"Yes, it truly is an extraordinary ship's log, the creation of a new race. I'm sure these people will be touched by it and the harpies," Watkins said.

Waters raised his hands to the crowd of people, to quiet them down, so he could speak. "This is Dr. Watkins. He is a genetic scientist hired by our late governor to do research on the harpies. He will play the disc that was found in the old space ship for you now. If you have any questions, please address him after the disc is over. And thank you, ladies and gentlemen. We can come together as a people and do the right thing, when we must."

Dr. Watkins played the old disc of Captain James and the freighter, Princess, on all the monitors throughout the giant domed port. The story of the first men to set foot on Dora was revealed and how, they created the harpy hybrids which were part human, part loca eagle. The last log of the elderly Captain's compassion and love of his children and grandchildren caused many women to weep and the men to be ashamed as they listened to the old man speak. All knew that the harpies had been wronged all these years. And a new admiration rose in the crowd for the harpies, which had been named after Jack Harper.

Dr. Watkins asked if there were any questions at the end of the disc but none were sought. Governor Waters shook his head. "How could just a few evil lying men, cause this much pain and suffering to an entire race?"

John nodded. "I believe, that history has proven time and time again that this is all it takes, just a few evil powerful men."

"When this is over, there's no doubt the senators will be replaced, if they even choose to remain in office. I doubt they'll have the nerve after this scandal." Waters commented. "Well, let's go into one of these spare offices and draw up this new law and treaties with the harpies. I am going to make sure that they get their rights and their land, whether they succeed in destroying the beetles or not. This should have been done regardless of this crisis."

"You're a fair man and I think once the harpy leader gets to know you, you both will get along fine," John said with a smile.

"I'm anxious to get to know him. He has such a graceful lofty mannerism with a witty mystique that captivates you. I couldn't take my eyes off of him," he said to John.

John laughed, "Yes that describes him. He is rather handsome and unique but he's more than that. That slender harpy has a heart of gold, more golden than his wings. He's dauntless with his devotion and courage. I don't believe I've ever met a more striking individual."

Night came. John and the new governor worked on the laws and treaty, making sure there were no loopholes in the agreement that could hurt the harpy's future. The people in the port tried to sleep in the cramped quarters. Most of the water was gone now and the crowd was anxious. Talk of the gruesome harpy abuse and their wings hanging in the store windows were discussed in whispered voices as fear grew among the people. Could this race of winged men be that forgiving after all the atrocities the humans had done to them? In the late hours all was finally quiet except the dreadful humming and buzzing of beetles on the outside. The children slept soundly during the night but the adults knew their destiny if the harpies abandoned them. It was a long night of fear and worry.

Shail had returned to the mansion as evening approached. He went among the harpies again since their numbers had doubled in his absence. Most of these eastern and river harpies had never seen him before but were willing to follow him because of his gold wings and hair. There were several thousand and the number surprised Shail. He was astonished by how many had survived all these years.

Many had lived just outside the large city, oblivious to the harpy hunters, who would journey to the western jungles in search of their prey. The eastern harpies had become creatures of the night. Daring not to show their wings during the day. As darkness came, Shail returned to the large structure called the governor's mansion. His mother met him when he entered. She tenderly wrapped her arms around him.

"I am very proud of you," she communicated. He embraced her.

"Do you think it wise, I have chosen to save the humans?" he asked.

"I know many good humans that hide in that port. I would mourn their passing if you chose different. But it is the harpies that are my concern. Only do this, if it will benefit them."

"I have already given the honor of my word to save them, if they agree to a truce."

His mother gave him some human food of nut bread. After he had eaten it, Shail curled up on a soft rug in front of a fireplace in the main room near the front doors, a small fire burning within as he glanced around the enormous room. This fear, of sleeping in a human dwelling, had long past. There was little which could frighten him now. A man came in and bowed low to Shail. He then asked, if he could get him anything. Shail looked up at this man, who had showed him the same reverence as a harpy. The man could see the puzzlement on the golden ruler's face.

"My wife is a harpy. You are her king and so, you are mine, for I honor the harpy's ways," he explained.

"I need nothing," Shail responded and curled back up as the man left the room. His mother stayed and watched Shail slowly drifted off to sleep with his cream wings, folded over him. She sensed his dreams and smiled. He had merged them with his mate again. She could feel the anxiety and tension leave him. It was replaced with contentment when he embraced his mate in this illusionary state. She left him, knowing that he was slowly becoming whole again and the scars of abuse were fleeting.

Shail woke with the first rays of dawn filtering in through the windows. He went to the outside while the massive group of harpies stirred beneath and in the trees. Aron approached him and Shail put his hand on one of Aron's shoulders as he spoke. "Have them rest and eat. These lights ahead shall be hard on all. I must go and see if the humans have chosen life and our demands. I shall return before this light is high in the sky."

Aron nodded and gave Shail some of the repellant sap wrapped in a large leaf. Shail spread his wings and flew south to the spaceport. He reached the doors and hovered over them long enough to drop some of the sap in front of the doors. The beetles scurried away from it and Shail landed in the empty space. He tapped lightly against the doors. A man soon peeked out and saw him. He yelled loudly into the room of people. "He's here!" Shail walked in slowly as the people stirred and came to their feet. All watched him in silence. He stopped a short distance inside when he saw John and Waters approach him.

"They have agreed to the truce and the new laws," Waters said happily. Shail looked at John for validation.

"It's true, Shail. The harpies are now protected by law and have the same rights as a human, the western outback and islands belongs to the harpies now even my estate."

"We'll remove the surviving people off your land," Waters added.

"I am not familiar with this owning of land. I do not wish to remove any living thing from its home. If these humans cause no harm to the harpies or our jungle, they may stay."

"That's very generous of you. Now, will you uphold your side of the agreement?" Waters asked. Shail only nodded. Waters smiled. "He has agreed to save us!" Waters yelled with joy to the crowd. The room erupted with the sounds of cheers and clapping. Shail jumped slightly and shook a little from loud response, unfamiliar with how much noise these humans could make. After some time, the cheering subsided. Shail looked at Waters.

"They have heard all the truths of us then?"

"You friend, Mr. Turner here, is responsible for convincing them. It would not have happened without him," Waters answered the harpy.

Shail stepped before John. "I was told, if you take your hand in mine, it would mean, we are friends. Is this true?" Shail asked John.

John grinned and took Shail's hand. "I am honored, you consider me a friend. But, you are more than a friend, Shail. You are called a son-in-law. Which in human customs means you are like my son since you bonded with my daughter." John took hold of Shail's shoulders, the harpy way of greeting a friend. "And I couldn't be prouder, if you were my own son."

"I am glad this harmony has finally come to us. I have respected your honor longer than you know. When you protected my harpies on your land all these seasons, I sensed the goodness in your heart," Shail responded in his low voice.

"Shail, I think you will see the goodness in this new governor as well. He will be a great friend to you and the harpies. Even if the harpies fail to save these humans, he has made sure, the truce will still last," John said.

Shail nodded slightly to Waters to show his appreciation. He then turned to leave. "Don't you want to say something to all these people?" Waters asked Shail.

Shail stared out at the thousands of humans. It was obvious, from their smiling faces, they were happy to see him. Shail reluctantly walked toward them slowly as the people cleared a path for him. Finally he reached the center of the room and was surrounded by the crowd. John had remained at his side. Shail confidently gazed at them. He had quelled all his trepidation and anxiety when he stood before so many humans. Shail raised his head with composure and forced his soft harpy voice to be heard.

"For many seasons, I have awaited this light. When the harpies fly freely without fear. You have learned, the same blood flows in us and so we are related. But the blood makes no difference. I have learned it was the fear and ignorance of one another that truly divided us. I hope this shall be in our past. We shall save you from the swarms or die trying. With our lives and yours, we have made this peace and may it last amongst our offspring and the future of both our races."

The crowd roared until the rafters shook. The sound was so deafening it caused Shail to flinch again. He began to sense a true admiration coming from the minds of these people. It was not only that he would save them from the swarms but he also sensed a reverence towards him, just as he felt from his own harpies. Shail glanced at John a little puzzled.

"They know you don't have to save them and they honor you for doing this. And they see, you are very noble and worthy of their respect," John remarked with a smile as the crowd kept the noise up.

Shail stared at the cheering people. He was not so easily exploitable to completely trust these humans despite their enthusiastic response. After all, some of these men wanted to see him slaughtered only days early. He knew he needed to remain leery and cautious. Shail began to make his way out through the crowd, when suddenly he sensed strong hatred coming from the mind of someone near. Without the drugs and the hate, his animal instincts and telepathy were becoming keener. Shail froze as his piercing eyes nervously scanned the crowded room and he sniffled low with agitation, his wings slightly raised from his back.

"What is it?" John asked when he saw the harpy's tensed menaced demeanor and his large eyes darted anxiously towards the people.

"A threat," Shail responded quietly.

Suddenly a man's face leered out at him behind several other people. Shail recognized him immediately. Bill sneered at Shail. He was angry that these idiot people had elevated this killer animal, to the status of a hero, a creature that had killed his brother and had nearly killed him. He pulled from his small bag a laser gun and pointed it towards the harpy as he stepped out in front of the crowd.

"This harpy murdered my brother and if you fools don't know how to deal with it, I will," he shouted. The people saw the weapon and fled in fear. A large space separated between Shail and this man. The crowd became quiet as they watched this drama unfold. Shail stood his ground and only John stayed with him.

"You're going to die now, harpy," Bill yelled with scorn. As he pulled the firing trigger, John jumped in front of Shail. The laser blast hit John in the back and he fell to the floor. With lightening speed, Shail leaped a crossed John's body and flew at Bill with force, hurling his light body against the large man. The hard blow knocked Bill down as he lost his grip on his laser gun and it slid across the floor. The slender harpy rolled and sprang to his feet and was in the air while Bill staggered to rise and retrieve his weapon. Shail fluttered over Bill and began kicking the man hard in the face till the big man fell to his knees. Bill vainly swung at the harpy as he got up but the harpy flew like a bat out of hell and relentlessly attacked him with his fists and feet from the air. Shail continued to dive-bomb him until a final hard blow, sent Bill collapsing in pain. Shail landed next to him and paced with agitation, waiting for his battered prey to rise and so he could strike it again. Bill wiped his blood and sweat from his face as he glanced up at the fierce little harpy that was as tenacious as a mocking bird after a cat. The man realized he was no physical match for the swift flying animal. Bill spotted a long iron-suturing rod that lay at his hand's reach. He grabbed the six-foot rod and swung it at Shail. Shail jumped backwards as the rod barely missed slicing into his stomach. Bill stood up and charged at the harpy, swinging the rod wildly. Shail fled to the air then dove straight down, descending behind the man before he could swing the rod at him. Shail lunged at the rod, grabbing a hold of it in the middle. Both Bill and Shail clung for control of the rod as they tried to out muscle one another. They pushed against the rod and each other's bodies, forcing the rod down on the other. The rod began to move towards Bill as the lean harpy and its flapping wings seemed to be out-powering the big man. Bill in desperation kneed Shail hard in his ribs. The harpy lost his grip as Bill flung Shail to the floor. Bill slammed the rod hard on top of the downed harpy but Shail rolled and ducked the assault. Bill frantically struck at the crawling harpy before it could get to its feet and take flight. Shail scrambled side wards eluding his attacker.

"Shail, take this!" came a voice from the crowd as Ted tossed Shail another rod. Shail caught it just in time to deflect several more blows and fluttered to his feet, holding his rod. He nodded and sniffled bravely towards the man acknowledging, he did not need wings or flight to defeat this human beast. Bill and the harpy now stalked each other in a large circle of people. Bill swung again and his rod clashed against Shail's. Shail swung back and the rods crashed against each other. With each swing, the rods collided as these enemies fought like ancient knights with swords. The rods continued to clang as Shail warded off each of Bill's thrusts. The crowd realized this was a fight to the death between these two adversaries. Bill swung again and this time Shail dropped down, dodging Bill's swinging rod. He spun around and rose, crashing his rod against the unsuspecting large man's back. The devastating hard blow sent Bill flying. He lay sprawled out on the hard surface. Shail paced nearby, panting slightly. He tossed his shiny blond hair incensed and gave a low fatal hiss, encouraging his foe to rise and fight him again. As Bill lay on his belly, he stared up with defeat and exhaustion at the taunting deadly slight harpy. Bill now spotted his laser gun a few feet away. He lunged for it, grabbing it tightly in his hand. Bill pointed it towards Shail and the harpy backed away. A hideous grin covered Bill's face as he clambered to his feet. "I have you now. You're going to die just as I promised." Bill puffed breathing heavy with all the exertion and pain. Shail penetrating eyes gazed rebelliously at him. Before Bill could fire the weapon, Shail swiftly threw his rod hard towards the man. The rod acted like a spear and bayoneted Bill in the chest, causing him once again to drop his gun. Bill staggered for a moment as he looked down at the rod, stuck in his chest. He glanced up at Shail, his eyes filled with horror and shock. Soon the huge man dropped to his knees and watched the harpy calmly approach him.

"Remember my promise." Shail's soft voice seethed quietly to him. Bill gasped his last breath, his mind only focused on the harpy's prediction that it would kill him in two days. Bill crumbled to the ground and was still.

Shail looked quickly over to John and saw Ted and Waters leaning over him. Shail rushed across the floor to John. He slid to his knees and carefully lifted John's head into his lap. John looked up at him as blood trickled from the side of his mouth. "Did you get him?" John asked. Shail only nodded to him. "Good." John gasped. He then gripped Shail's arm as he struggled to speak. "You'll take good care of my daughter?"

"I shall," Shail said softly.

"I do love her so much. I'm glad she chose you. You deserve her more than any man. I'm sorry I misjudged you, Shail," he said weakly as he fought back the pain. Suddenly, he gasped and was still as his breathing ceased. Shail swallowed hard and felt John go limp in his arms. The man released his hold on the harpy's arm.

"He's dead, Shail," Waters said to him.

Shail held him for a long moment as he stared down at John's lifeless body. "You were a great protector. You even protected me," he said quietly to John. Shail breathed deeply and gently removed the body from him. He rose to his feet, his arms dripping with John's blood. Shail could feel the rage and hate returning within him. He stared at the many faces in the utterly still port. "Step forth, any amongst you, who also wish to shed my blood. Let us end this hate this light," he stated in a loud and threatening voice. The place remained silent and no one moved. Shail's body quivered slightly, shaking his head as he tried to collect himself and control the anger. "Then honor this man, for he has saved you. He sought peace between us and has paid for this peace with his life," Shail said to the crowd. Shail walked quietly to the doors as the sea of people parted and Waters ran after him.

"Shail, does this change things? Are you still going to destroy the swarms?" the man worriedly asked.

Shail flipped his long blond hair back from his eyes and glared at the man. Waters could see the harpy's eyes were slightly moist but burned with fire. "I shall keep my word. But you had better keep yours. We harpies are not killers but as you have seen, we can be if we must." He shoved the doors wide open. The black deadly swarm lay in front of him as he stared out at it. Shail stepped towards it but before any beetle could latch on to him, he sprung into the air. Waters closed the doors quickly but left them open a crack, to watch the stunning golden winged harpy fly against the black deadly landscape, until he disappeared.

CHAPTER 10

▼

Charlie flew the hover all night as they followed the two brown winged harpies in darkness. He could hear Kari weeping quietly. Her golden harpy mate lost to her, she now felt lost herself. Eventually, she drifted to sleep exhausted with worry and grief. Charlie also wondered if John would succeed in his quest to rescue Kari's harpy. Right now, he was more concerned about John and it wasn't the coming swarms that had him worried. He knew John was a stubborn and hardheaded man and once he was committed to something, he could not let it go. It was that same determination that had driven him to find Kari, when she had left with the golden harpy. Despite all reason and advice, he would do things his way regardless of the outcome.

Charlie realized if the governor did not help him, John would go to that hunting range and free the harpy by himself, regardless of how many guards, he had to overcome. There was no way, he would let Kari's mate die. So this had Charlie plenty worried, although he kept it to himself. The old Indian was convinced of this after one of their last discussions in the hotel lobby when he and John waited for Kari to come down to breakfast. John had said something that revealed his motives and upset Charlie terribly. John had said, he would gladly trade his life for the harpy's. Charlie reflected on this and knew it was not idle talk from a man who was just sorry. John never said anything unless he meant it. So, Charlie worried and feared for this man, he cherished as a son. He just hoped the governor would step in and save the harpy before anyone got hurt or killed.

Charlie stopped the hover several times in the night to allow the harpies that they followed to rest. But these harpies seemed impatient with this and continued to motion him on. Their energy was relentless as they pushed through the night.

But by daybreak, they appeared weary and so was Charlie after traveling all night. He set the hover down in a small clearing surrounded by the jungle.

Kari sat with the two harpies while they ate crackers and fruit that Charlie had packed. Charlie ate some beef jerky and watched the three of them communicate in silence. Kari returned to Charlie, after they had finished the food. "Before the light fades, we arrive, the harpies say," she said to him. Charlie could see she was at ease with these winged men and even her speech would change to their broken tongue, after she talked with them. Eventually, she would revert back to normal language.

Soon they were on there way again. At noon, Kari began to use the communicator to reach someone in Hampton but all communication was down. Kari looked at Charlie with even more worry in her eyes. It had to mean, the swarms had struck the city.

"Don't worry, Kari. They're not going to let a three million credit harpy get consumed by the swarms."

She looked at the old man. "Yes, but I'm also worried about Dad."

Charlie grinned slightly at her. "No beetle will get your father. I'm sure of that and I seriously doubt anyone would want to go on a harpy hunt with the swarms coming. Your father and Shail are someplace safe for now," Charlie said trying to ease her mind. She just shook her head and kept playing with the communicator, hoping to reach someone, anyone with some kind of news.

By late afternoon, they could see the northern mountains looming in the distance. They stopped one more time to give the harpies a break. Charlie was amazed that these beings could keep up their speed and endurance this long. He realized at top speed, these harpies could easily out fly the hovercraft and were faster than any migrating bird in the land. Sweat now covered their tan bodies and they consumed plenty of water from a nearby mountain stream. Charlie gave them food and they took it hesitantly from him. They were not defiant or as bold as Kari's golden harpy. They eyed this human old man with mistrust, never turning their backs to him. Charlie watched them with amazement. He had never been around harpies this long. "They are beautiful creatures," he thought. Their sleek thin muscular bodies glistened in the afternoon light. Charlie thought, they looked more like well-conditioned race horses, than like birds. Their dark brown hair rested shoulder length upon their shoulders. They were not men with wings at all but something more. Their wild nature and mannerism made them very different, as they were alert to every sight, sound and smell around them. And then, he looked at Kari she too, was gorgeous with the same thin body and lovely face. She moved gracefully among them and she was taking on the same nature as they. There was a big difference from watching an animal in a zoo and watching the same type of animal in the wild. The zoo animal relaxed and didn't care about its surroundings as long as it was well fed and comfortable but the same type of animal in the wild, was always watching and nervous and never took anything for granted. And so, that was the difference that Charlie saw in the harpies and men. He began to pack up for the last leg of their journey and looked at the harpies again. "It would be a shame, if they were ever tamed," he thought to himself. He could see Kari was like a zoo animal set free. Slowly she was beginning to go wild again and embrace this uncivilized side of herself. Even if her mate died, she would never return to the zoo, the human world. She would rather be free, than comfortable.

The light began to diminish, as they set down on a small plateau in the mountains. Charlie and Kari grabbed their gear and began to follow the harpies up a steep path. The harpies could sense how weary the old man was. One took Kari's and Charlie's bags as he flung them over his strong shoulder across the wing, while the other stood before Charlie as if it wanted some thing from him. "This harpy wishes to fly you to this place we are going," Kari told Charlie. Charlie laughed.

"He thinks I'm too old and tired to make it on my own? You tell him, I'll let him know when I reach the point that a harpy has to carry me." The tall winged male sniffled at the shorter old man then the harpy turned and continued the climb up the narrow rocky path. Kari didn't have to translate the Indian's words. Darkness came, when they finally reached the opening of a cave. It was windy and cold high up in the mountains, just as it had been in the western side. Kari entered a large expansive cave and found many female harpies gathered around a fire. Others tended little fledgling females and males. They all stopped what they were doing as soon as they saw Kari. They dropped to their knees and bowed when she approached the fire.

"Rise, please rise," Kari related to them. She could not get used to this honor that was bestowed on her, simply because she had blond hair and was the mate of their ruler. Kari sat down near the fire and Charlie joined her. He was definitely feeling out of place, being the only human and the only adult male. After he warmed himself, he wandered to the cave entrance. He was delighted to find the male harpy that had carried his bag. It was apparent this harpy was guarding the entrance now that Kari was inside. The harpy nervously jumped away from Charlie. "Easy, boy, I won't hurt you. And I doubt, if I could even if I wanted to," Charlie said with disgust of his weary old body. The harpy stared at him and settled down slightly. Charlie began to ramble on to the harpy as if he were talking to an old friend. He was more comfortable with this mute male, than all those talking females in the cave. The harpy listened to him with interest and after a while, they formed some kind of communication as the harpy nodded and shook his head with Charlie's questions. Charlie found if he talked very direct without a lot of adjectives, the harpy sensed the meaning of his words. Soon it became very cold. The harpy pulled his wings around him and curled up against the side of the cliff, out of the wind. Charlie was very tired and said good night and returned to the inside of the cave.

Kari smiled at him. "You have found a friend?" she asked.

Charlie nodded. "Yes, one that speaks, even less than me," he smiled back at her.

"They have prepared a sleeping place for you," Kari said, showing him a large bedding of soft mosses against a wall.

"That actually looks comfortable to me right now," he said while climbed on top of it. "I feel like a bird in a nest," he joked and closed his eyes. Soon he was asleep.

Kari talked some more with the other female harpies. Some had lived their entire lives in the jungle and had gone unnoticed. While others lived in Hampton, like Lea, on the outskirts of town and there were two who had bonded with men. She was surprised, when she found out that their mates had worked for the governor but they were reluctant to discuss it. Their only response was that they were not allowed to talk about anything there, until they were told differently. Kari was curious about their secret. She thought it odd that they refused to disclose their life to her especially since she was considered a golden harpy and ruled over them. Only Shail supposedly, had more power than herself. "Who else could possibly demand their silence?" she wondered.

Kari was tired now. She was grateful these females distracted her mind from Shail. The very thought of his captivity and possible death filled her with anguish and distress. And she was stuck in these mountains, helpless to aid him. She had left that chore up to her father and now, it plagued her. Curling up on the soft moss bed, she soon fell asleep. She was not physically tired but mentally she was a wreck.

As her dreams came to her, she found herself in the jungle again. She pushed away many ferns, since the path was unclear. She called silently to Shail, wishing he would appear through the massive blue ferns and red trees. Kari continued to call and walk, until she was lost. Lying down under a giant white barked tree, she began to weep in this dream. All hope was gone. He was as lost to her as she was lost in the deep woods.

"Do not cry, Kari," came a soft gentle male voice. Jumping to her feet, she saw Shail as he pushed away the giant foliage. Kari leaped into his arms and hugged him tightly as he embraced her. "I return to you now that I am free of the men and my mind is calm," he said and tenderly kissed her. Then he wearily lowered his head, hiding his face in the comfort and solace of her familiar long blond hair and breathed deeply.

After a long moment, Kari pulled from him and looked up. "Shail, is this just a dream I am having because I miss you so much or are you truly well and alive?" she asked him in the illusionary world.

"It is I and no mere wishing dream. I am not completely well, for I still fight these demons of hate, created by the hunters which caged me but I slowly heal and there is a golden female harpy that aids me in this fight against darkness." They held each other for a long time. "I leave you now with this morning light. But, I shall return, when darkness covers the land we dwell in and our bodies are deep with sleep, once more." He pulled from her and disappeared into the jungle.

Kari's eyes opened and she looked toward the cave opening. The dim morning dawn could be seen from the entrance. She rubbed her eyes and climbed to her feet. All in the cave still slept as she made her way to Charlie. The smoldering fire gave off just enough light for her to see in the darkness. "Charlie," she whispered and knelt down beside him. "Charlie" she spoke again shaking the old man from his sleep. His eyes opened and he leaned forward quickly.

"What is it? What's wrong?" he asked startled. He then could see her broad smile in the faint light.

"He is alive. Shail is alive and free," she said happily. "He came to me in my dreams again. Everything is going to be alright now," she said in an enthusiastic low voice. Charlie looked upon her angel like face. He had not seen her this blissful and joyous since she was a small child. Charlie wondered if her dream could be true or just a dream of longing that had brought it on. It didn't matter. He was delighted her sorrows and despair had faded. Kari returned to her nest and thought about the dream. She wondered, who this golden female harpy was, that was helping Shail to heal. She had, like Shail, presumed that she and Shail were the last of the golden harpies.

Daylight came and brightened the cave and it also brightened Kari's spirit. She happily played with the fledglings in the cave now. The little males practiced their flying skills as they fluttered to the high ceilings of the large cave. The small females chased them with this game. Kari discovered there were other caves in this mountain range each of them holding the females and young. Charlie had wrapped himself in blankets and went outside to be near the male harpy, who continued to guard the entrance. A few other males would appear occasionally, bringing food and firewood to their females and young. Kari became like Lea, who treasured the dark. She could hardly wait until she was united again with Shail in their dreams. Charlie would come inside on occasion to check on Kari. He continued to have his doubts about her dreams but he dare not relate this to her.

As evening approached, they gathered around the fire, to eat the fruits and nuts brought by the male harpies. It was then, that an adolescent male harpy entered the cave. His body was covered with sweat, despite the cold weather and he panted out of breath. It was apparent that he had traveled a great distance. Kari rose to her feet when she saw him. Her eyes were intently fixed towards him. But, it was not he that caused this spell to come upon her. It was, what he held in his hand a three foot long pale yellow flight feather. The feather was battered and broken in many places as the quills had separated. It was so dirty the color was barely visible. Kari walked to him and touched the feather. Then she leaned over and smelled it. It was Shail's. She had come to know his scent.

"Our ruler has sent me to tell you, he lives and is free. He shall join you soon when the land is safe," the young harpy related to her. Kari tossed her head back toward the ceiling and closed her eyes. A tear of joy ran down her cheek. Now she had the proof, she sought. She also had not completely trusted the dream. "There is more," the teenager continued. Kari brought her attention back to him. "The master says he loves you." Kari only nodded. After a long savored moment, she told Charlie the good news.

Shail flew towards the ocean and cliffs. He was not ready to rejoin his harpies and have them sense his terrible distress. The wind from the cliffs caught his wings and he soared upon the updrafts. He had never mourned for a man but his heart was heavy with grief. Shail reflected on this man's words, when Turner had come to the hunting range for the first time and Shail was at the lowest point in his life. He had lost his pride, his courage and even his will to live. Turner had told him, he would survive this and be strong and then this man swore on his honor, he would protect him. Turner had made good on that promise. Shail closed his eyes as he drifted on the cool ocean air as he thought of this honest brave man that was totally devoted and committed to the things he loved. And Shail wondered if he would ever meet another man like him, a rare man that deserved the harpy's admiration and respect.

After some time, Shail flew back to the huge harpy gathering. He set down among them and Aron went to him. Aron had been raised with this blond male and could always tell, when Shail was very upset even when he sought to hide his emotions.

"What trouble has come, Shail?"

Shail glanced at Aron. "John Turner is dead. He died saving my life."

Aron breathed deeply and nodded. "As I dwelled near him, I could sense, as you, how worthy he was. You were right to protect him these last two seasons."

"Perhaps we protected each other since we both loved Kari," Shail answered.

Shail could see the other harpies were waiting for him to guide them. He flew to a large tree stump that had been cut down long ago. He observed his harpies from this view while he stood over them. "This light is like no other. This light we are free of the hunters. Peace has come between the harpies and humans. It is a peace that had to be made. Many of you may think these deadly swarms would free us by killing all humans. This would be true but it would be a short-lived freedom. When the swarms are gone, new trees shall spring from the ground just as new humans shall come from the sky. And things would return as before. We would still be the hunted. I want our fledglings to have a safe future so I have made this truce with them. By sparing their lives, they shall finally see our worth and honor and it is a needed friendship we shall reap. It shall be the same friendship that binds the bird and zel. The calling bird warns the zel of approaching danger, while the moving zel chase the insects from the thick brush so the bird can feed. This is how we shall dwell, apart yet together and no longer as the prey and predator. We fly now amongst the beetles and destroy these swarms. I have given the honor of my word on this. The harpies have always been the guardians of the jungle. We cherish and protect all life. We shall save the jungle trees, the animals and these humans. To do not, would make us less. Fly swiftly now, my brothers. The swarms are perilous." Shail spread his gold wings and leaped into the air. Immediately the sky erupted with brown feathers as the large flock of harpies followed him to the city.

As they neared the giant black void, Shail could see that the dome building was the only thing that remained. All the other human structures were gone. Shail motioned to a younger male as he flew. "We shall pair. I, the taker, you, the follower. Fly down and retrieve the wood which is needed," Shail said to him. The young harpy nodded, elated that their golden ruler had chosen him. Shail slowed so he could catch up with him. In minutes Shail's harpy apprentice returned with a stick of wood. Other harpies were also gathering small pieces of wood from the jungle below that stood at the edge of the swarms.

Shail flew to the port. He first wanted to remove these swarms that were threatening this structure and its doors. He stared down at the massive bugs that covered the ground and hovered over them. His giant extended wings worked rapidly to hold him in one place without touching the beetles. This was difficult for a harpy, since they came from the loca eagles that soared through the sky and were not built to hover in one spot like smaller birds. Soon Shail saw that which he sought. It was a beetle that was slightly larger than the others, though a human would have a hard time recognizing this. Shail fluttered over it, hoping the wind from his large wings would not blow others on top of this particular beetle. He carefully swooped down and seized the larger female beetle, holding her in his hands so she could not bite him. The beetle instantly started making a clicking sound. Shail watched, as the frantic insects below him, began to expose their wings, preparing to fly. Shail now darted fast into the sky and joined the young male.

The swarm rose up and began to chase the harpies, who had stolen their queen. The queen's distressed clicking was calling to the swarm's drones and workers to rescue her. Shail flew only twenty feet from the ground, so not to lose any of the beetles from this swarm. He reached the ocean and continued out over it for several miles, the swarm in hot pursuit. He nodded and the young harpy dropped the wooden stick in the water and then flew straight up. Shail hovered over the stick, gently laying the unharmed queen on it. He then flapped his wings furiously upward, narrowly escaping the angry swarm. The beetles gathered around their queen, landing on this watery grave. With their wings wet, they could no longer fly. The helpless swarm floundered on top of the water, until they and their desperate queen eventually drown. Shail stared across the ocean as countless other harpies performed the same feat each racing against the speed of a deadly swarm. Soon the dark green ocean's waves were turned to black, as they held millions of beetle corpses.

Shail flew back to what remained of the city, as the young harpy joined him with another stick in his hand. Shail hovered again and looked for another queen.

In the past, the harpies had destroyed all these new queens of a beetle mound and kept the beetle population down. The harpies discovered they could easily move a swarm by moving its queen. This is how Shail had protected the Turner estate from any swarm invasion.

Shail finally spotted another queen among the masses of beetles. He descended upon her and picked her up carefully. This queen started clicking and he again raced to the sea with his catch as the insects flew hastily to save their queen. The harpies performed the same ritual as before with Shail darted toward the sky to join the other harpy and escape the path of the ferocious swarm. Shail watched their demise in the secure elevation, high above them. Then he noticed something floating upon the water among the black waves of beetle corpses. From a distance, it appeared like several logs, clustered with scrambling beetles but when Shail flew into range, his heart sank, discovering it was two dead harpies. Their beautiful majestic wings and sleek bodies floated limply on the water as the tormented beetles bit into them. They had been over-flown and had not escaped the swarm's wrath. Shail agonized over the risk of carrying their bodies from the water so they could be honored and mourned for their brave deaths but to do so would mean the aggravated beetles would easily merge on him. He hovered over them for some time with a grief-filled heart. "Before this light fades, how many of my handsome devoted males shall meet this same fate? A fate I chose as their ruler by allowing the beetles to over-populate and swarm," he wondered with worry and sadness.

Shail reluctantly left them to the sea and slowly flew towards the dome building once again. He and the other harpies continued their quest of search and destroy until evening approached. On his last visit to the demolished city, he could see that he and his flock were making progress. This domed building, which held the humans, was vacant of beetles for now. But many still lay a few miles away.

Duran was setting and Shail gave the order, that the harpies should stop their crusade against the swarms on this day. They could have continued but Shail did not want any weary harpies performing this task in dim light. Aron joined him as he flew along side. "Take the flock back to my mother's home and have them rest. I shall join you soon," he said to Aron.

"You should rest as well."

Shail nodded. Aron again was always so concerned for him, just like when they were fledglings. "I shall but I must speak with this new leader of the humans before this darkness comes."

Aron veered away motioning the flock to followed him north to the mansion. Shail watched and then swung south toward the human building. He landed again by the doors and tapped them lightly. The same man smiled when he opened the doors wide for Shail. The harpy walked in and was met by Waters. Waters saw Shail's slender frame was soaking wet with sweat. His blond hair was drenched with it and the man could see, the harpy ruler had toiled hard throughout the day. "I'm happy to see you again," he said to Shail.

Shail only lowered his head slightly. "The swarms, which threaten your doors, are gone but it is still not safe. The beetles lay near and would return swiftly if you left this shelter. As some small bugs are drawn to the scent of flowers, these beetles are now drawn to the scent of your flesh. So, do not be fooled by their absence."

Waters sighed, "We do have a problem. The water has been gone since this morning and our children are thirsty. We noticed the beetles were gone and I was just getting ready to send some men out to the far wells, so they could fix the breakers that were damaged."

"Can one do as you say? If more go, the swarms shall fly swiftly to this place and feast upon them before they return. Your humans shall die for this water," Shail told him.

"I can fix the breakers," stated Ted as he walked towards Shail and the governor.

Shail looked at Ted. "Yes, he shall do. He is not so large, I cannot lift him if I must and there is a trust in this man. As my mate calls him a friend, so shall I."

"Alright then" Waters said. Ted ran and got the tools and new connector for the breaker he would need and returned quickly. He and Shail stepped from the back spaceport doors and walked across the giant vacant lot of the outside landing strip. Ted talked to Shail while walking in the dark.

"Do you know if Kari is alright?"

Shail looked at this man, who had deep feelings for his mate. "She is well or I would have heard of it" Shail answered him. Ted wondered how the harpy would know, if Kari were in the mountains. Surely the harpies were not capable of using a communicator.

Shail could feel this question from the man's mind. "Our senses and dreams relate such things."

"She certainly does love you," Ted remarked as they continued to walk.

"And I, her."

Ted suddenly remembered Kari's mate harbored emotions of jealousy towards him and now he was a little worried and scared of this harpy. Ted had developed a healthy respect for the slight winged male after watching him bombard and assault Bill Simpson and finally kill the huge man. Shail was extremely swift and deadly when provoked. This willowy slender harpy could easily whip and bring down most large men in hand-to-hand combat. They had reached the well as Ted turned on a light and began to fix the damaged connections. Shail sensed this man's fear of him. He leaned against a large water tank and watched Ted work.

"You need not be afraid of me. My mate cares for you and it would displease her if I harmed you. And I am grateful, you helped her, when I could not."

Ted stopped working long enough to stare up at the harpy in bewilderment. "Man, it's so spooky the way you can read my thoughts," Ted remarked jokingly.

He now noticed that Shail was ignoring him and was peering out into the darkness.

"We must go. There is no more time," Shail said hurriedly.

Ted looked in the same direction. "I don't see anything. And I'm almost done. Just another minute" he said as he replaced the broken connector with a new one.

"It is not my sight that warns me. It is the sound of a swarm that comes."

Ted listened while he tightened the new part. "I don't hear anything either," he mumbled.

Shail could waste no more time arguing with this doubting stupid man. He reached over and grabbed Ted under his arms, jerking him to his feet. "Drop these metal things now," he ordered while flapping his wings and lifting Ted into the air. Ted released his hold of his tools as the harpy and him lifted into the evening sky. Ted glanced down and saw his solar light below. In an instant, it was quickly covered with a huge shadow of black. Shail flew hard with his heavy load that weighed twice as much as he did.

He flapped his wings frantically across the expanse of the large lot only stopping to drop Ted in front of spaceport doors. Ted threw the doors open and jumped inside while Shail folded his wings down far enough to glide side ways over the threshold. Ted slammed the sliders shut, just in time, to hear the swarm hit the doors and the outside of the building. The sound of thousands of popping noises as if heavy raindrops fell on a tin roof, were heard inside the building.

"Wow, that was close! Too close, I'm sure glad you have good ears," he exclaimed excitedly to the harpy which fluttered and landed beside him.

Shail tossed his silky hair away from his forehead. It had been close, even for the harpy. The extra weight had almost cost Shail and this man their lives. Shail wearily leaned against the doors. He truly was exhausted now and only wished the comfort of a cool stream to bath and a soft nest to sleep. But he could not seek either, until the swarm had settled and stopped its pursuit.

Waters came racing towards them. "You did it! The water is working," he said happily. Then the governor could hear the beetles smashing into the doors and the port.

"It was really close. A swarm almost got us. Shail, here saved my life," Ted told him while good-naturedly placing his hand against his harpy companion's arm.

The sullen harpy sniffled a little at the hand and Ted removed it quickly seeing harpies were not fond of men touching them. Shail gazed at Waters and told him, "I must remain, until all of this swarm lands." The governor could tell the harpy was not happy being forced to stay among the humans.

A woman walked through the crowd, holding a bottle of newly poured water. She walked up to Shail while he leaned against the doors. "May I give you this and thank you for saving my life, twice now?" she asked.

Shail took the bottle from Mollie and drank some of it. "You kept me alive, as well," he said to her. Then he slid down and sat holding his knees and rested his chin on them. His huge wings floated in front and around him as the feathers joined and wrapped around his feet. Mollie sat down next to him and watched him. This breath taking golden harpy had become more than an animal to her, more than a harpy, even more than a man. Mollie's insides ached with the desire to hold and caress him as she once had, when he was caged and helpless. Now Shail was beyond his need of her. She sighed, realizing she had fallen deeply in love with him. "Can you forgive me for betraying you?" she asked sadly.

Shail took her hand and put it to his mouth, nuzzling and kissing it since he sensed her yearning and desire to touch him again. "There is nothing to forgive. I long to forget this misery and memory, we share," he said softly. Mollie only nodded her understanding.

The popping sound came to an end. But right after, came a tap from the outside. Shail rose to his feet and went to the doors, his instincts detecting other harpies. "Is it safe to open them now?" asked the man who stood by the doors.

"It is safe," Shail said to him. The man opened them as Shail looked out. The beetles were no longer near the doors. Instead, he saw several harpies in front of the threshold. "I am well, Aron," Shail related to him and stepped to the outside.

Aron breathed deeply with displeasure and frustration aimed at his rash young ruler. "I had a harpy watch over you. He has told me of this reckless crazy attempt to flee a swarm while caring the weight of a man. It is not your place to take these risks and be so careless with your life." Aron related with irritation. "Do you have a death wish?"

"This disrespect you show me in front of others, is it a challenge?" Shail asked firmly, boldly confronting Aron eye to eye. But Aron noticed the twinkle in Shail's eyes.

Aron backed away submissively and bowed low. "Forgive me, Master, I dare not challenge you. It is my worry for you, which causes me to lose my place," he conveyed. Aron knew Shail was not displeased and his cocky display was only an act for others. Shail was actually glad Aron had come since it allowed him to leave the port.

Waters stepped beyond the doors and into the ring of harpies. He could see the beetles were only ten feet away and covered the steps of the building. He nervously approached Shail. "I just wanted to thank you again, Shail, for restoring the water," he said as he offered Shail his hand. Shail took it reluctantly. "I hope some day to be your friend and you will trust me as you did Mr. Turner."

"Honor our truce and the trust shall come," Shail said. Shail noticed a small girl inside. "You have water but what of food?"

Waters raised his eyebrows. "We don't have much but we will survive, until the swarms are gone."

"Your young should not suffer this hunger. This harpy is called Aron. His behavior is bold enough to face your large human crowd. At dawn he and others shall bring you food of the jungle. I can spare him for your needs," Shail said while glancing slyly at Aron. The other harpies knew Aron was being punished with this task for his irreverence toward their ruler. Any harpy would gladly risk his life and face the swarms, than deal with humans. "It shall be good you learn of one another," Shail added.

The harpies left and rejoined the gathering at the mansion. Shail stayed with them this night instead of returning to the mansion. He curled up at the base of a large moss-covered tree limb and closed his eyes. He knew, he must seek Kari in his dreams but it was the first time, he was reluctant about it. The dream overtook him and he searched for her. Their minds finally merged as he found her waiting for him in the jungle again. As Shail approached, she ran and jumped with joy into his arms. But slowly she pulled away, feeling his sorrow. "What has happened, Shail?" she asked him in the dream. He could not answer but only wished to hold and comfort her. She stared up at him. "I feel great sadness coming from you."

Shail swallowed hard and sighed. "Your father is dead," he finally related gently. Kari's face filled with panic. This dream had become a nightmare for her. And in a puff, she was gone. Shail wandered back into the trees. He knew that this tragic news had broken the harpy telepathy and woke her.

Kari found herself sitting up on the moss bed. She could barely catch her breath as she stared blankly ahead at the dark cave wall. Then she began to cry softly. Charlie awoke, upon hearing her and went to her nest.

"What is it, Kari?" he asked with concern.

"Dad is dead, Charlie," she cried to him. Charlie no longer doubted her dreams. He sat down beside her and held her. Tears fell from his old wrinkled cheeks. His worst fears had come true.

Shail slowly stirred in the tree branch as the dawn broke through a golden sky. He stretched his wings and they were stiff from the muscles that had lay dormant for so long and had been used quite extensively the previous day. Other harpies began to wake near him and they watched their sovereign ruler drop to the ground. Their eyes were fixed on this assertive young blond whose aggressive nature dominated the flocks of thousands. Shail confidently strolled among them as they meekly lowered their heads and moved out of his way. It was known now that this golden was so fearless he had even attacked and killed men, something unheard of by the gentle timid harpies. Shail casually ate some nuts while the warm light climb over the trees. Aron came along side of him and began grooming and pruning Shail's hair and feathers with his hands. This tender behavior to another male proved to the other flock leaders that Aron, the young western flock leader, truly was a nest brother to the golden. "You still wish me to gather this food for these humans?" Aron asked.

Shail only nodded to him. Aron sighed slightly as he untangled a blond knot.

Shail turned his head towards him. "Aron, I chose you to do this, not because you challenge me with your words. It is because you may learn from the humans. I seek your advice often and it is better to know ones enemy as well as one's friend. With the knowledge you gather, you shall gather for me, as well." Aron nodded. "Take each of your fingers the number of all for the harpies you shall need. Pick the very young and old in this task. I wish only the very fastest to remain with me when we seek the beetles on this light." Shail instructed him. Aron would pick one hundred from the over two thousand harpies that had finally gathered. He sent out several harpies to collect the material, which these fruits could be placed in and taken to the humans. Aron waited for their return with Shail.

"I would ask one other thing of you," Shail related. "That as my council, you learn their words and muster your voice that has always lay dormant in the harpy males."

Aron looked at him with surprise and disbelief. "You wish for me to make the humans sound? It is a human thing you ask of me. Only the females do this and only to blend. It is not the harpy way," he communicated with distress.

Shail raised his head. "Do you see me as less, since I have made this sound?" Shail asked him. Aron barely shook his head. "This lack of noise has protected us from discovery in the jungle but as things have changed, so must we. The silent talk shall remain with the harpies but with these humans, they must learn to know us and our hearts, these shall make the peace last."

"I shall obey you with these tasks, you ask of me, since you are the golden and my ruler. But as a brother, I must tell you that it brings me no pleasure to gather food or speak the human words."

Shail placed his hands on Aron's shoulder. "I ask more of you than most but trust me on this. You shall see the good of it soon."

They parted with Shail taking most of the harpies with him as they faced the swarms of beetles once again and Aron taking a hundred harpies to the jungle to accumulate the food for the stranded people in the dome port.

Aron went to the doors of the port and could see Shail's group had removed the beetles that had come in the night. He tapped the doors lightly while he and several other harpies held the bags of fruit, roots and nuts. A man opened the doors wide, when he saw the harpies. "Come in, come in" he beckoned to them. Aron hesitated for a long moment and then mustered his courage to step over the threshold. He stared at the thousands of humans in the building. They were smiling at him but as this crowd came closer, his fear overwhelmed him and he dropped the fruit and fled to the safety of the doors. A man's voice rang out over the crowd.

"Let's give these harpies a little space, shall we?" said Waters to the people when he saw how frightened Aron was of this large crowd. "Thank you for the food. Our children were getting very hungry. The harpies can just place the food near this door," this man said and smiled at Aron. Aron only nodded. He could understand some of the man's meaning through his senses but did not understand all of the words. Aron glanced at the harpies outside the doors.

"Place this food here," he told them. Each harpy brought their bag inside and gently dumped out the contents. All of them eagerly scrambled to leave this large cage that held the humans. They quickly fled to the sky, after they had performed this task. Aron stood with his back to the door, realizing how truly brave Shail was to go here alone and face this huge mass of people.

Governor Waters continued to talk to Aron but Aron was too distracted to concentrate on his words or sense their meaning. He fidgeted with apprehension as his green eyes darted with suspicion towards the men in this port. "How many of them had hunted harpies" he wondered. He was not as forgiving as Shail for these past crimes. He timidly forced himself to stay, until all the harpies were finished with this first load of food. Glancing at Waters, Aron knew, he should at least try to learn this man's words, but his mind would not focus on this impossible task. "Shail's mate had taught him the human language thus making the learning easy and pleasurable." Aron thought to himself.

"Maybe I can help you, as well," came a voice into his mind. He slowly turned and saw a lovely female, who stood at his side. Her green eyes sparkled in the dim light of the port as her long flowing dark brown hair hung across her shoulders. He sniffed her and could detect the harpy scent.

"You are harpy." Aron said silently with surprise.

She nodded. "How is it you are among these humans?" Aron asked her.

"Both my parents are dead and few male harpies need a mate here. So, I sought out my human side and looked among men. But I must confess, only a male harpy do I desire. When the swarms came, I sought shelter here." she related as she lowered her head. Suddenly Aron's mind was no longer on Waters or the giant room of people. He stared down at her.

"The search for a mate should be short, for one as lovely as you," he said to her.

She smiled at the tall good-looking male. "Shall I teach you these human words, you must learn?"

"Yes, if it pleases you. I too, have no mate but I have never sought one either. I feared her death could come with mine, or the loss of one of my fledglings by hunters. So, I have chosen the pain of loneliness, rather than face these fears." Aron related.

She took his hand. "But times have changed. And these fears shall fade with this peace that comes to the harpies." With her hand wrapped around Aron's she spoke to Waters.

"Governor, I am a female harpy and would gladly translate your words, for our males only can sense some of their meaning."

"That would be great. I realize that most male harpies do not understand our language completely. Aron, is this acceptable to you?" Waters asked.

Aron gazed at the pretty female that held his hand and translated the human words. "Yes." Aron said in a quiet whisper of a voice, similar to Shail's. It was the first time he had ever spoken.

Shail and the other harpies attacked the swarms as they had done on the previous day. Many swarms had merged on Hampton, making it easy for the harpies to locate them and their queens. By the end of the day, Shail halted this assault against the beetles. He and the harpies were worn out from the constant neck-breaking speed and agility that was required to do this mission without losing their lives. He was content that most of the swarms, which covered this city, were gone now. But as the beetles were removed, the death and destruction was revealed. Many skeletal remains were seen in vehicles and the rubble of the devastated structures. Not all the humans had made it safely to the port.

Shail wandered through the ruins of the once mighty human civilization. He had sent his flock back to the mansion to rest and recover. He wished to be alone with his conflicting thoughts. Gone was the rage that had consumed him. He only felt sick as he looked upon the bones of a small human skeleton. He knew in many ways, he could have prevented this. The harpies could have stopped the swarms two seasons ago, though it would have been a difficult and toiling chore, since their numbers had been depleted to cover all the land. So, he chose to save this people and allow the swarms to drive out the humans that had shown no mercy to his harpies. He bent over and touched the bones of this little child. He had killed it, as surely as if he had snapped its neck by failing stop this threat sooner. A great remorse settled over him as he took from his sash, a small wilted pink flower, he had kept. It was from the tiny girl child named Anna, who had bravely approached him by the stream. Shail kept walking down the street that once had tall buildings on either side of it. There was no joy in this victory he accomplished. Shail had become a true harpy once again a lover and protector of all life. The light faded into dusk, when he finally spread his wings and flew slowly to the domed port.

Governor Waters greeted him at the doors and explained that they were grateful for the food that Aron and the other harpies had brought to the people. Shail only nodded as he looked beyond the doors at the thousands of humans. "I only come to tell you, the swarms no longer dwell here. You may leave this shelter, if you wish."

"You've killed all of them?" Waters asked in amazement.

"No, only the ones, that threaten this place. Many still lay across the land. It shall take us many lights to lower their numbers but we do not seek to destroy all. These beetles served the land, as we do. Many animals eat of them and when a mound creates a bare spot in the jungle, new life comes from it. The zel and large lizards eat the new shoots of the young trees and so the cycle of life continues. In the future, we shall work hard to guard their numbers, as we also are creatures of the forest and play this role with nature. And with this peace, my harpies shall flourish and the beetles shall no longer swarm."

Waters gazed at the intriguing harpy as he looked out over the wasteland. "Shail, I know you could have killed these swarms after we perished. I talked to your woman handler named Mollie. She told me how terribly you were mistreated and tortured by those hunters. Why in the world did you bother to save us after what you've been through?" Waters asked.

Shail turned toward him. "It is a harpy's nature to value and protect all life but it is true at that time, I valued none. But as the guardian of my flock, I must do what is best for all and put away my pain and bitterness. There are different types of jungle animals that live and dwell together in friendship because there is a need. This need came to the humans and harpies. The humans are many and my harpies are few. Even with your deaths, more humans would come from the stars and eventually destroy us. We both needed to be saved."

Waters looked in to his deep blue eyes that seemed to reflect the harpy's very soul. "You are wise beyond your years. And your intelligence and shrewdness make you a worthy adversary, as well as a friend. I hope we will always be friends. You could teach me many things."

"Perhaps we may teach each other. I sense, your heart is good. This eases my doubts. I long to know more men of your kind."

Waters nodded. "Yes, unfortunately you and the male harpies have had to deal with some truly heartless and abusive men. Most harpy hunters are a pretty cruel bunch. When things have settled, I plan on seeking them out and making life pretty uncomfortable for them. They had to know all along that the harpies were more than just animals and they slaughtered your race anyway. It's unforgivable."

Shail began to relax the more he talked to this man, this ruler of the humans. He trusted his senses and instincts more than any law of written down words. As evening came, Shail returned to the gathering of male harpies. Shail found Aron with a group under a large tree. "I have told the human leader they may leave this structure called a port. You shall be glad to learn, your gathering of food is no longer needed."

Aron hid his disappointment. "I learned this killing of swarms goes well. We have lost three to the number of fingers, plus six of the harpies with this battle against the beetles. Far less than we expected."

Shail realized, thirty-six harpies had been killed by the swarms although he was pleased that the number had not been higher as he and Aron had initially thought, one was too many for him and he was saddened by their loss. "Yes, it is far less than we planned but it is not over. One more light in this place and then we move across the land and search for the scattered swarms."

"Perhaps I should gather food for the humans another light if I am not needed for those few swarms, which remain here?"

Shail looked up at him with surprise. "You wish to gather the food and face the humans?" Shail asked. Aron only nodded. "There are many harpies. Your absence shall not be missed. I am pleased you are no longer apprehensive. This man, Waters, seems like a good man and you have spoken to him?"

"I have used my voice and are learning his words," Aron related.

Shail again looked at him with a questioning. Something was drawing Aron back to the port and it was not the humans or because he feared destroying the swarms. Since Aron did not relay to Shail what it was, he decided to leave well enough alone.

Shail went to his mother at the mansion and they talked into the night since their time together would come to an end. When it was very late, Shail curled back up on the same rug, once again as his mother bid him good night. In his dreams, he found Kari. They did not speak. They only embraced and nuzzled one another passionately until the dawn was upon them. And they were returned to their realistic world of awakening.

Shail woke and went out among the harpies. "We shall seek out the swarms that are half a light's travel from the sea. The ones beyond this, only the queens shall be destroyed. With these new queens gone, the beetles shall no longer swarm and shall go their own way into the jungle, and do, as beetles must. This shall be the hardest of feats, since the travel to the sea shall be long and treacherous. I only wish harpies that can endure this task. Others may go with Aron to help where needed with the humans. I value all your lives so choose wisely in this decision. Your bravery shall be wasted when you perish if your wings can not out fly these swarms over this long distance of land."

Aron and Shail watched as all of the harpies choose to go with Shail and risk their lives. Aron sighed deeply. "They would follow you with broken wings, such is their love and devotion to you. Your bravery and wisdom overshadows all here and all other goldens before you. They no longer call you the ruler of the harpies but have named you, "the Prince of Dawn."

Shail was stunned as he stared out at the vast number of harpies. "Why?" he asked slowly. Aron touched his shoulder affectionately. "You are as golden as the dawn and like the dawn that chases the darkness from the land, you have delivered your people from the darkness, the darkness of fear and death. They now fly freely in the sky without worry. They have seen that your light has not only saved them but also the land and all that dwell on it. Even these humans revere you, even their leader. He has spoken your praises to us as we brought forth the food. His words and the words of other humans have spread throughout the harpies. No harpy has ever held such high praise from humans and harpies. Do not question this honor, little brother. For all that is spoke is true. You are like the precious rare stone covered with clay. When the men sought to crush you, they could only crush the clay and in doing so, exposed the bright shining stone from which you are made. Your strength and wisdom outshines all."

Shail breathed deeply as he looked out at his fellow harpies. This was high praise to bestow this honor upon him and only days before he had distrusted his own capacity and insight to lead the race of harpies. "Perhaps there is truth in the old saying, 'that which does not destroy one, makes him stronger,' he thought to himself. He certainly was living proof of it. He feared nothing now. "And without fear, maybe better judgment comes."

Shail raised his wings into the dawn light. "Those that would follow me, come forth. We finish what we start," he communicated to the harpies. He flew high into the pale golden sky as all the harpies heeded his call and rose to follow him. Aron glided along side of him as they soared towards the western jungle. Shail glanced at him. "What of the food?" he asked Aron.

"There is enough for the humans. I wish to pair with you on this last main attack if you shall have me?" Aron asked.

Shail nodded. Though Aron was not needed, Shail was happy to have his harpy friend by his side once again. The large flock of harpies scattered over the colorful jungle. All were searching for the dispersed swarms. "We shall fly further than the others," Shail related to him.

Aron was displeased with this, knowing he and Shail would be taking the greatest risk. And again he was always concerned for Shail's safety but he only nodded in agreement. Shail was no longer his little adopted brother, who needed protection. They flew four hours, traveling west. All of the other harpies had since disappeared and were gathering swarms closer to the ocean. Shail spotted in the distance a huge black void in the jungle. As he and Aron approached it, Aron hesitated.

"Shail, it is too big. There must be many queens in this swarm."

Shail's eyes sparkled. "Then it shall take us both to gather them all. Tear half of the cloth used to gather food. I shall take half and place my queens within as you take the other. We shall meet in the center and carry this swarm to the sea." Aron looked at the massive swarm. It was nearly as big as the swarms that had destroyed Hampton. Shail could sense his doubts.

"Aron, there are too many beetles to just kill their queens. All of these must be destroyed," Aron glanced at him.

"Again, this death wish, is upon you," he related grouchily to Shail.

"I do not wish to die. I look forward to seeing my mate and next season my son."

"I too wish these things," Aron said.

Shail stared at him perplexed then he understood. "It was not the gathering of food that drew you back to the port. You have found someone?"

"Yes, a single female harpy among all the humans. She was like finding a lone flower in a meadow of grass," Aron reflected as they soared high above the swarms.

"So, you both have chosen to bond then?" Shail asked.

"Yes, if I am not killed this light with this foolishness," Aron snapped at him.

Shail was amused by Aron's aggravation. "We are the swiftest of the harpies. No swarm, no matter the size, shall out fly us. Let us finish this. The sooner the swarms are gone, the sooner I return to Kari. It is her I seek, not death," Shail said sincerely.

Aron sighed. "Let us do this thing. I feel there is more of the crazy loca eagle in your veins, for this is loco."

"When you see the beetles begin to swarm on the other side, you shall know I have captured my first queen." Shail said to him. Aron nodded his understanding. He watched Shail fly a great distance across the swarm till Aron's keen eyes could barely see the cream wings. Aron flew down to his side of the great mass. He spotted a queen and waited till the beetles began to fly on Shail's side. He watched as the black cloud lifted up from the ground in the distance. Shail had a queen.

Aron now dove down and grabbed his queen and threw her in the cloth bag. He did not wait for her to start clicking but flew towards the center. He saw another and grabbed it quickly. There was no time to hover as he glanced back and saw his swarm following him. Flying on, he snatched another. The beetles were actually flying into one another as they desperately sought their endangered queens. By then Aron had moved on till another was spotted. Suddenly the whole swarm rose up in the confusion of clicking queens. Aron flew straight upward out of their reach. The air was black and boiling below him as he searched frantically for the gold wings. Sweat dripped from his brow while he stared at the agitated, chaotic beetles below him. He knew in seconds, they would hear his bag of calling queens and fly up to him. His heart raced, for he still could not see Shail in this madness. A fear and doubt began to creep over him. It seemed impossible for anything to survive below. Then he saw the flash of a gold wing in the thick black cloud of beetles. The creamy wings darted upwards towards him as the swarm followed only a few feet on Shail's heels. Aron soared lower to draw the swarm off of Shail. But now, he was in danger as the beetles heard his clicking bag. Shail pointed east towards the ocean. And Aron frantically began flying swiftly in this direction. The swarms were only a stone's toss away from catching him. He reached the untouched edge of the jungle as Shail met him there and they traveled together, the massive swarm close behind. They had to keep this steady fast pace up, for to go slower, they would be devoured and to go faster, they would lose these swarms.

Aron glanced at Shail. He became infuriated when he sensed, Shail was actually enjoying this taunting with danger. "This pleases you?" he fumed with annoyance. "The swarms were upon you and you should be dead."

Shail smiled slightly at him. "Yes, there was one more queen I wished to gather when they came on me but there were so many alarmed queens, it must have baffled the beetles and they failed to bite. Aron, do not be displeased or angry with me. Soon we shall be at peace. We shall lay lazily around with our mates and surrounded by our fledglings. We shall look back on this memory as a time when we were young and fast and fearless."

Aron glanced back at the enormous black swarm that trailed them. "I hope that is true. That it shall be a memory," he related unhappily.

They flew on for hours until the ocean appeared in the distance. "The port lays to the north, we must not get too close to it," Aron said.

"These swarms shall stay with us, even if we flew over it."

Aron stared at him bewildered and trouble, questioning this ridiculous decision, which may endanger these humans they had chosen to save. Shail's eyes brightened, tossing his hair happily against the wind. "We fly south of the port away from the humans. It is this insincerity, which creates worry that Kari calls humor. I must practice it, since I shall be with her soon," Shail related lightly.

"Practice it elsewhere. This is not the time for such humor. I worry enough without you adding needlessly." Aron growled.

"Aron, shall you ever give me the respect of a golden harpy ruler?" Shail asked his tired and distressed companion.

Aron shook his head. "Perhaps not, since it is you that does not always act as a ruler but more like an unruly careless fledgling with no common sense."

Shail's lips curled slightly with a smile, an expression, he was learning from his mate. "That does sound like humor to me, since I sense, you are not sincere."

The people of Hampton had come out of the domed port and were trying to salvage the remains of items, not eaten by the beetles. They looked to the western sky and saw the giant mass of swarms moving to the south. A panic took hold as they raced back toward the shelter of the port. But for many, it was too late to reach it in time as this mammoth swarm moved across the sky. They crouched in fear, for they knew there was no escape as they watched this cloud of death move towards them.

Aron's female harpy stood alongside of Governor Waters. "We better make a run for it" he yelled with terror. He began to flee when the female harpy tugged at his arm and calmly pointing in front of the swarms.

"No, Governor my harpy eyes can see, it is the prince of dawn, my golden ruler and Aron that controls these swarms. The beetles do not seek us. Our master and Aron shall take them to the ocean and destroy them." The governor watched in disbelief that only two male harpies could control such numbers of beetles.

"Shail and Aron certainly are brave," Waters stated while his eyes stayed focused on the immense swarm.

"Yes. No other harpies would risk this," she said with great pride.

The giant mass continued on out over the water as the female harpy had predicted. The people breathed a sign of relief and watched the black cloud move on till it was far away.

"We have no wood for the queens but this material shall float long enough to bring the beetles upon them," Shail said and loosened the bag, so the queens would not drown too quickly. Aron did the same. They increased their speed, so they would be far enough ahead of the swarms to make their own escape. Shail and Aron gently opened their bags and set them lightly on the water. Aron noticed that Shail had collected twice as many queens as he had.

"I did not know this was a harpy game!" Aron related while they both madly flapped their wings in a frenzy racing upwards out of the path of the swarms. After they were high above the beetles, they looked down to see the black mass settle upon the water.

"If it was a harpy game, I have won," Shail declared like a giddy fledgling.

"I can see why only you goldens are foolish enough to play these deadly harpy games for leadership. You are welcome to this victory. I am only glad to still live," Aron related with relief. They slowly flew across the ocean towards land.

When they reached the shoreline, Shail landed on the beach. "Are you as tired as I?" Shail asked as he waded knee deep in the cool water.

"More," Aron answered and joined him.

They were completely covered with sweat and the muscles in their wings were exhausted. Shail finally lay down in the water as he allowed it to float over his body. Aron just sat down and splashed the water over the top of him with his arms and wings.

"My mother told me, I would heal and feel the joys of life again," Shail reflected. "This moment I do feel the joys of this cool water, being here with you, my brother, as we savor our defeat of the giant swarm. I have not felt this peace since I was a fledgling and we dwelled on that far off island, so many seasons ago."

"I can see this frisky playfulness and joy that has returned to your nature. I am glad of it for you have been long without it. But I also feel this joy and peace that has come. It has come to all harpies again because of you. And Shail, I do respect you as the golden ruler, even if your daring nature is not what I would choose, but then, this is why you lead." Aron said somberly.

Shail climbed from the water and went to the beach and ruffled the water from his feathers. "Perhaps since I lead, we should seek out another giant swarm?" he said as he eyed Aron.

Again, Aron knew his words lacked sincerity. "Tell me, did you learn this falseness and jest from your mate, who dwelled among these strange humans too long?" Aron asked as he too stood up.

"Yes, it is a human thing but she has said it causes no harm to make this fun. Let us return to the port. I wish to meet this female harpy, who has swayed you to bond with her. She must be very special, since you always considered it a burden, you did not wish to have."

Aron flung back his brown shoulder length hair and shook the water from it. "Times have changed. And I wish for a family. It was the burden of the loss I always feared. With this new hope of peace, I am ready. Besides, my son shall be needed to look after yours, if he is anything like you."

Shail glanced at him. "This humor, I think you begin to grow fond of it."

They flew towards the port, which lay north of the beach. Darkness had come and as Shail neared, he could see many campfires outside the port. He and Aron landed on the steps by the doors. Shail's mother stood there with Governor Waters. Shail stared out at all the people and he could see his two thousand harpies that skirted this human crowd. He looked at his mother with a questioning.

"I told the harpies it would please you if they went among the humans." she said to him. Shail watched his harpies. He could tell they were anxious and shy as they forced themselves to remain near these outgoing humans. Many glanced wearily up at Shail and he nodded his approval. This made them bolder as they skittishly came closer to the humans, who were beckoning to the wild little harpies. Many humans were coaxing them to come with the offer of food. The timid harpies slinked close enough to snatch a piece of fruit from their human hands and then fluttered a safe distance away to eat it.

"It shall take a long time for my male harpies to overcome their fear of humans and perhaps there are many, who never will. They shall stay wild and remain hidden in the trees all of their lives," Shail said to Waters.

Suddenly, a small space ship appeared overhead and set down inside the domed port. Waters smiled on seeing the ship. "Your gift has arrived, Shail. Ted and all the mechanics in the port worked all day to repair that fast little ship. They wanted to bring you some cargo, to show their gratitude." Shail wondered what could possibly be on this ship that he would want. Soon Ted came through the doors with a man, who Shail recognized as one who worked for his mother at the mansion. Ted had a huge smile on his face as he called out to Shail.

"I have something for you, I think, you'll want." He held open the doors and waited. Kari walked through the doors followed by Charlie. Her face lit up when she saw Shail and walked toward him in a harpy robe. Shail swallowed hard and could not move for a moment he was so stunned by the sight of her. She reached him and gently put her arms around his neck as he leaned down and gave her a kiss. As his surprise wore off, he lifted her up into his arms and hugged her tightly passionately kissing his mate. Being united once again, they were delirious with jubilation.

The little female harpy from the port edged near Aron. He nodded to her, placing his arm around her shoulders. She leaned against him and rested her head on his chest. They watched Kari and Shail hungrily try and quench their long craving of one another, as they continued to nuzzle and kiss each other.

Only when Waters noisily cleared his throat, did the exquisite golden harpy pair pull apart and take notice of the others around them. In a loud voice, Governor Waters spoke. "Ladies, Gentlemen, Harpies. I give you the true hero of Dora, whose wisdom, courage and honor has saved us all."

The harpies that surrounded the human crowd instantly fell to their knees and bowed their heads with love and respect for their ruler. The human population, upon observing this harpy custom dropped to their knees, as well, to pay tribute to Shail with the same regard. The great crowd knelt with their heads bowed in silence. Kari stared out with astonishment and disbelief as this massive crowd of humans and harpies knelt with overwhelming idolization and reverence towards her mate. Even the Governor went down on one knee and lowered his head to the golden harpy ruler.

"Please rise," Shail said softly. But when they rose, the humans showed their acknowledgment and devotion as a great roar of voices and clapping hands escalated and intensified from the humans sending the flock of spooked harpies into the air. The loud sound and brown wings filled the night sky. Shail put his arm around Kari's waist as he watched the human crowd and his flock, which soared above them. She gazed up at him with great love and pride. Shail's deep blue eyes sparkled in the starlight. And Kari reflected how at one time, she had only seen him as a beautiful persecuted wild creature of the jungle. How he had changed in her eyes and in the eyes of all, who inhabited the planet. But, perhaps the change was not in him. Maybe it was, that his true undaunted spirit had finally been revealed to everyone.

Kari's only regret was that her father was not here tonight to see both races pay homage to her mate. But possibly, John Turner had known in the end, how extraordinary and admirable Shail was. Shail truly was a great ruler and hero of Dora. She smiled wide as she watched her handsome golden male, quietly gaze out at all his people.

THE END

0-595-31690-5